P9-DWG-691

VOLUME
SEVEN

IMAGE COMICS, INC.

Robert Kirkman
CHIEF OPERATING OFFICER

Erik Larsen
CHIEF FINANCIAL OFFICER

Todd McFarlane
PRESIDENT

Marc Silvestri
CHIEF EXECUTIVE OFFICER

Jim Valentino
VICE-PRESIDENT

Eric Stephenson
PUBLISHER

Corey Murphy
DIRECTOR OF SALES

Jeff Boison
DIRECTOR OF PUBLISHING
PLANNING & BOOK TRADE SALES

Chris Ross
DIRECTOR OF DIGITAL SALES

Kat Salazar
DIRECTOR OF PR & MARKETING

Branwyn Bigglestone
CONTROLLER

Susan Korpela
ACCOUNTS MANAGER

Drew Gill
ART DIRECTOR

Brett Warnock
PRODUCTION MANAGER

Meredith Wallace
PRINT MANAGER

Briah Skelly
PUBLICIST

Aly Hoffman
CONVENTIONS & EVENTS
COORDINATOR

Sasha Head
SALES & MARKETING
PRODUCTION DESIGNER

David Brothers
BRANDING MANAGER

Melissa Gifford
CONTENT MANAGER

Erika Schnatz
PRODUCTION ARTIST

Ryan Brewer
PRODUCTION ARTIST

Shanna Matuszak
PRODUCTION ARTIST

Tricia Ramos
PRODUCTION ARTIST

Vincent Kukua
PRODUCTION ARTIST

Jeff Stang
DIRECT MARKET SALES
REPRESENTATIVE

Emilio Bautista
DIGITAL SALES ASSOCIATE

Leanna Caunter
ACCOUNTING ASSISTANT

Chloe Ramos-Peterson
ADMINISTRATIVE ASSISTANT

www.imagecomics.com

SAGA, VOLUME SEVEN. First printing. March 2017. Published by Image Comics, Inc. Office of publication: 2701 NW Vaughn St, Suite 780, Portland, OR 97210. Copyright © 2017 Brian K. Vaughan & Fiona Staples. Originally published in single magazine form as SAGA #37–42. All rights reserved. SAGA, its logos, and all character likenesses herein are trademarks of Brian K. Vaughan & Fiona Staples unless otherwise noted. "Image" and the Image Comics logos are registered trademarks of Image Comics, Inc. No part of this publication may be reproduced or transmitted, in any form or by any means (except for short excerpts for journalistic or review purposes), without the express written permission of Brian K. Vaughan, Fiona Staples, or Image Comics, Inc. All names, characters, events, and locales in this publication are entirely fictional. Any resemblance to actual persons (living or dead), events or places, without satiric intent, is coincidental. Printed in the USA. For information regarding the CPSIA on this printed material call: 203-595-3636 and provide reference # RICH–719204. ISBN 978-1-5343-0060-6

FOR INTERNATIONAL RIGHTS, CONTACT: foreignlicensing@imagecomics.com

FIONA STAPLES
ARTIST

BRIAN K. VAUGHAN
WRITER

FONOGRAFIKS
LETTERING+DESIGN

ERIC STEPHENSON
COORDINATOR

CHAPTER
THIRTY-SEVEN

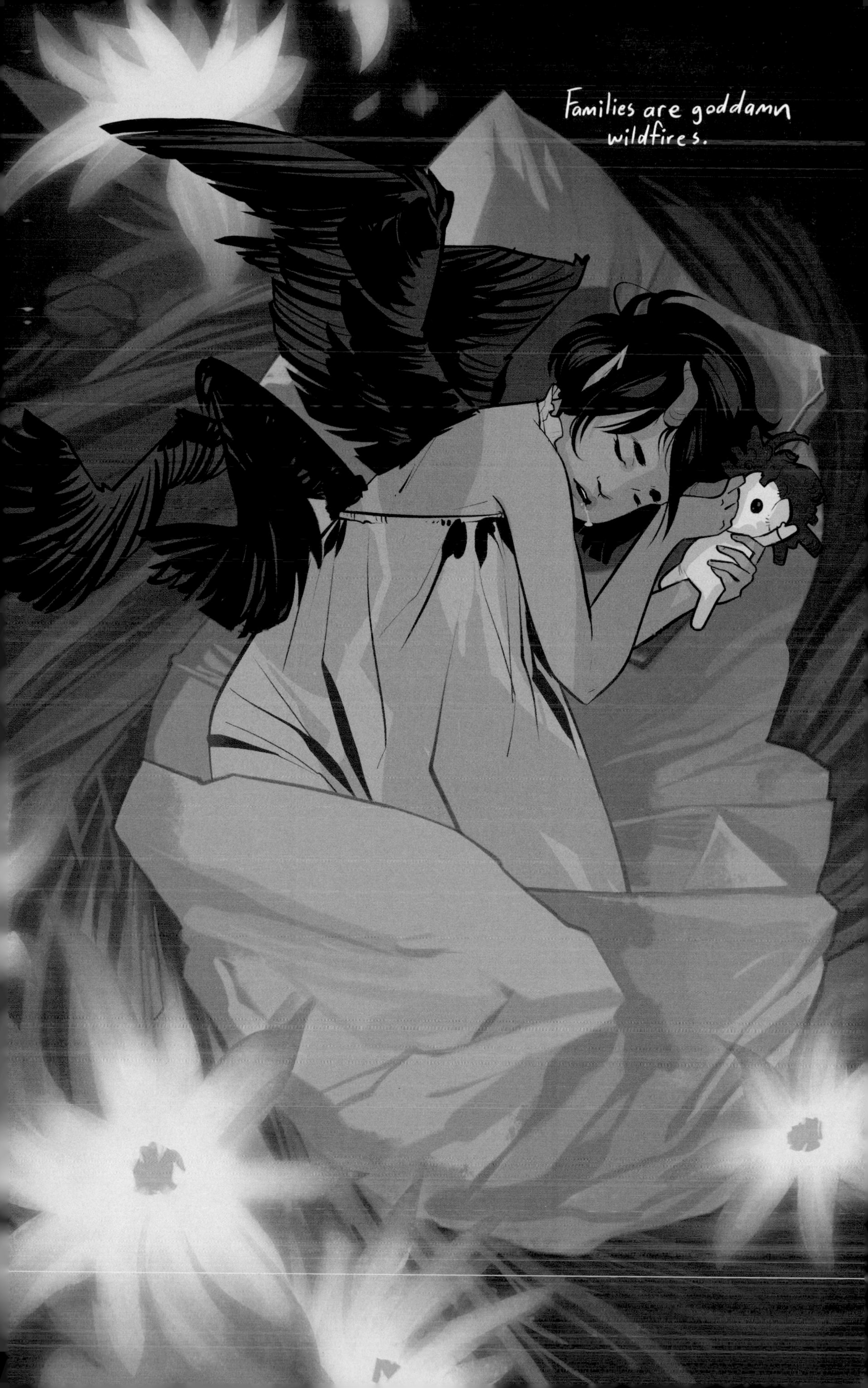
Families are goddamn wildfires.

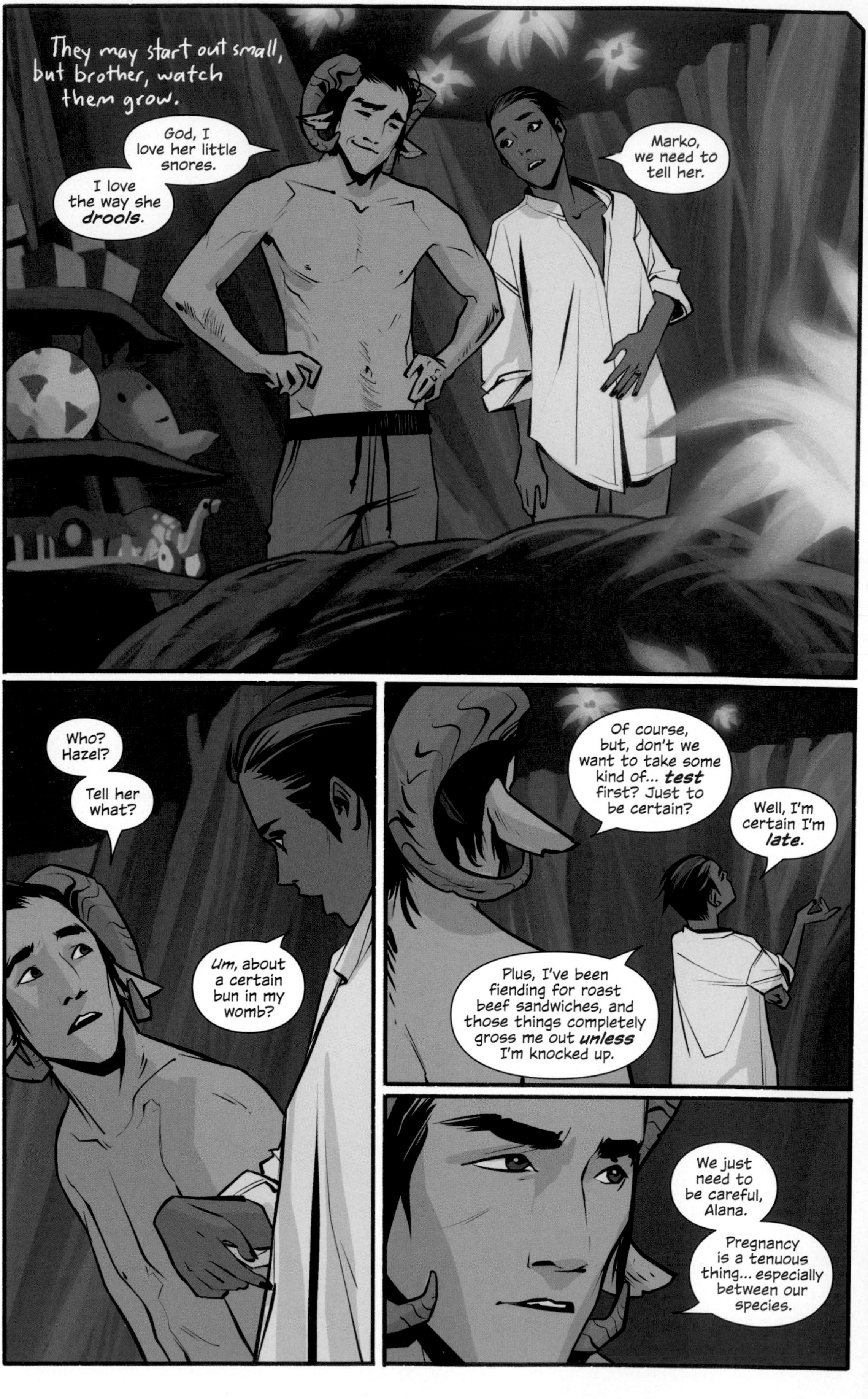
They may start out small, but brother, watch them grow.
God, I love her little snores.
I love the way she *drools*.
Marko, we need to tell her.
Who? Hazel?
Tell her what?
Um, about a certain bun in my womb?
Of course, but, don't we want to take some kind of... *test* first? Just to be certain?
Well, I'm certain I'm *late*.
Plus, I've been fiending for roast beef sandwiches, and those things completely gross me out *unless* I'm knocked up.
We just need to be careful, Alana.
Pregnancy is a tenuous thing... especially between our species.

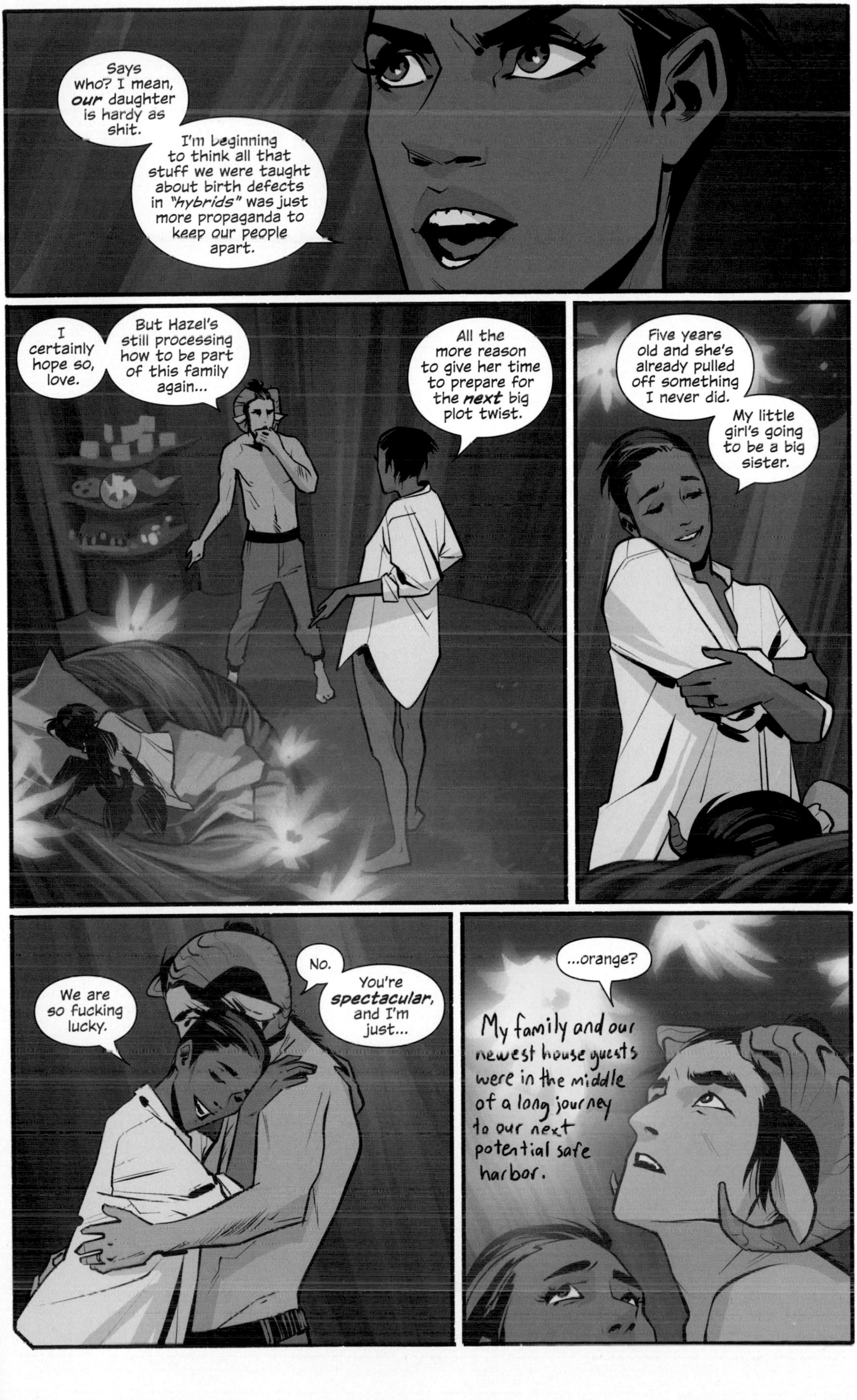
Says who? I mean, ***our*** daughter is hardy as shit.
I'm beginning to think all that stuff we were taught about birth defects in *"hybrids"* was just more propaganda to keep our people apart.
I certainly hope so, love.
But Hazel's still processing how to be part of this family again...
All the more reason to give her time to prepare for the ***next*** big plot twist.
Five years old and she's already pulled off something I never did.
My little girl's going to be a big sister.
We are so fucking lucky.
No.
You're ***spectacular,*** and I'm just...
...orange?
My family and our newest house guests were in the middle of a long journey to our next potential safe harbor.

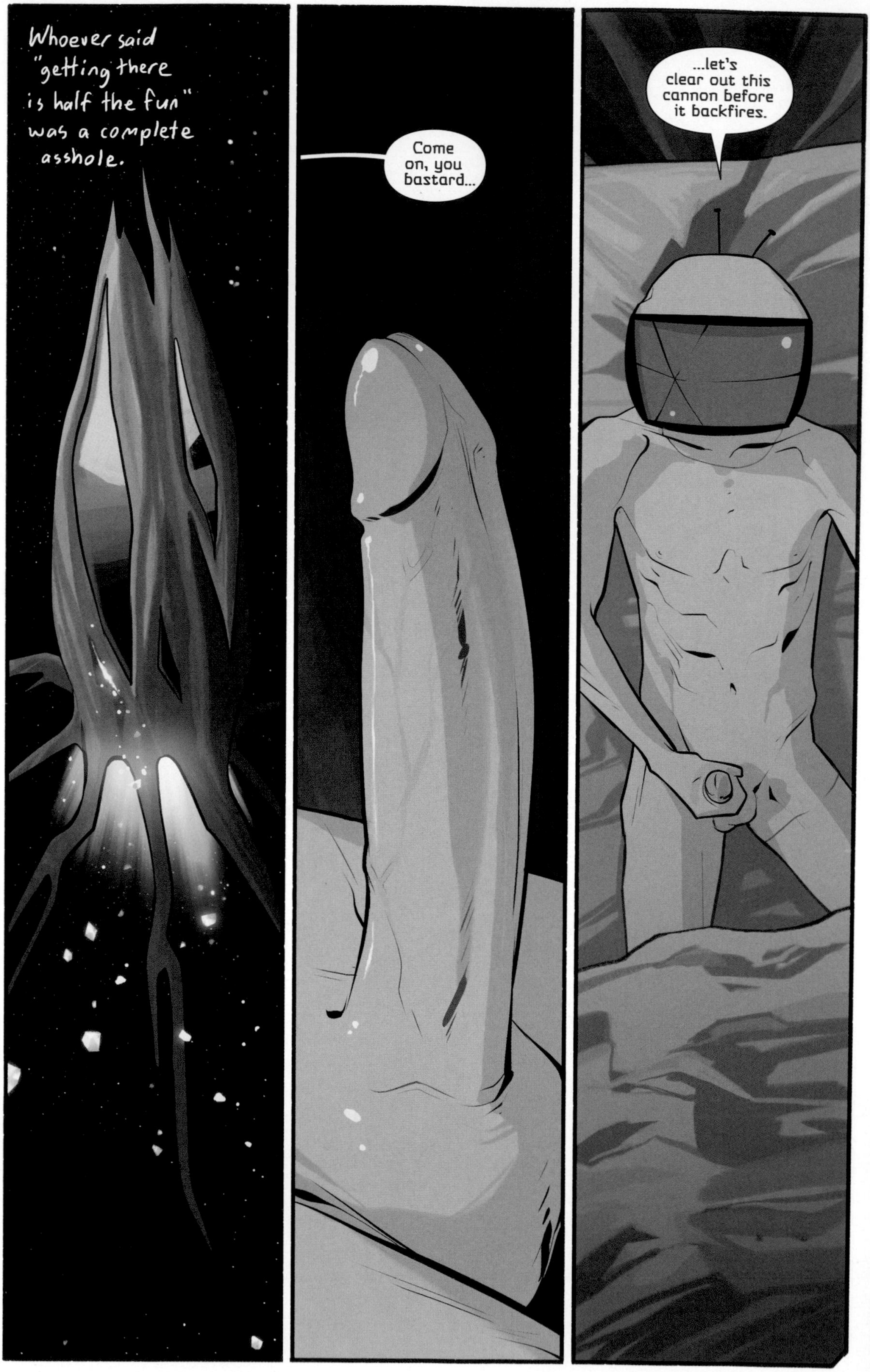
Whoever said "getting there is half the fun" was a complete asshole.
Come on, you bastard...
...let's clear out this cannon before it backfires.

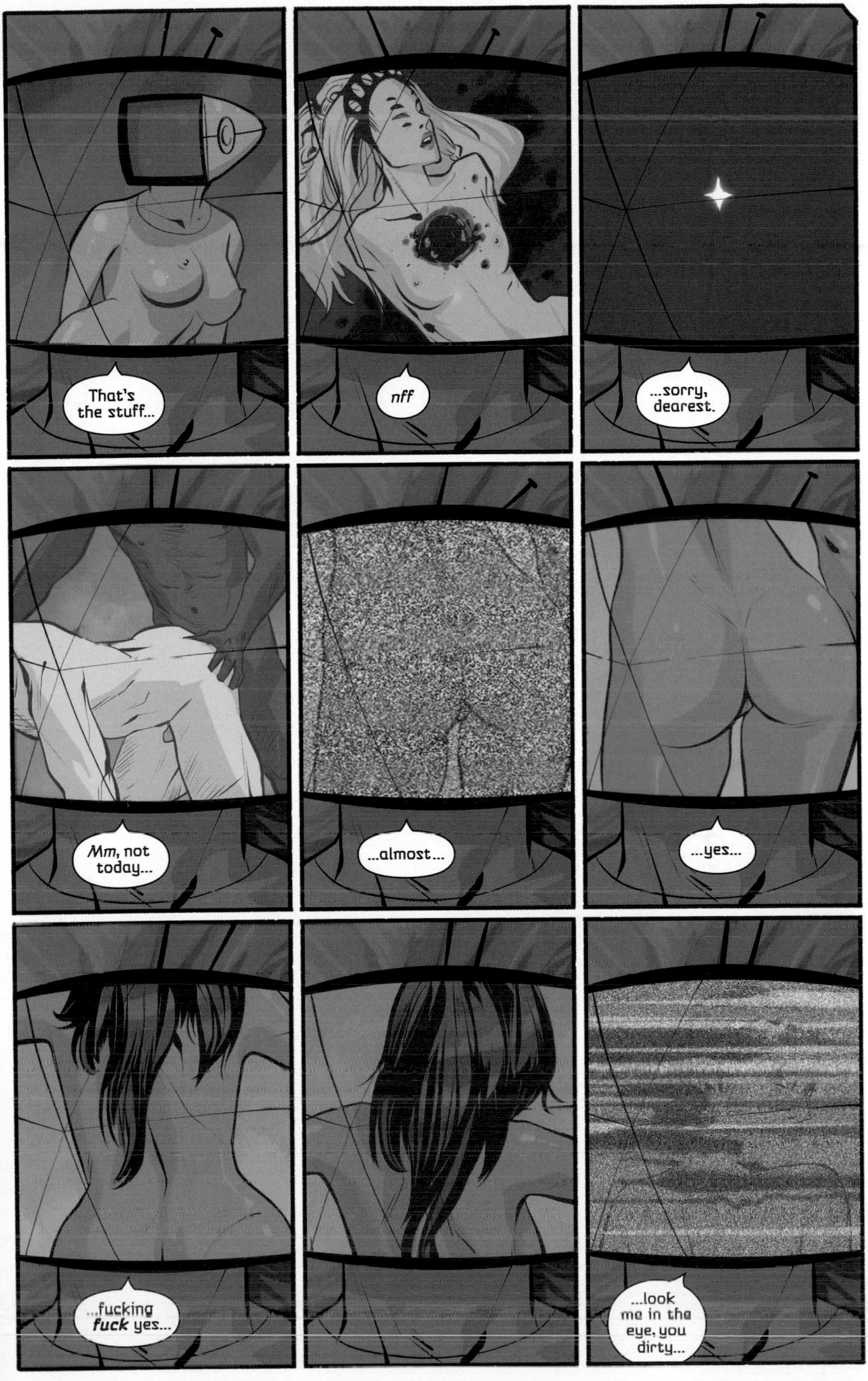

That's the stuff...
nff
...sorry, dearest.
Mm, not today...
...almost...
...yes...
...fucking ***fuck*** yes...
...look me in the eye, you dirty...

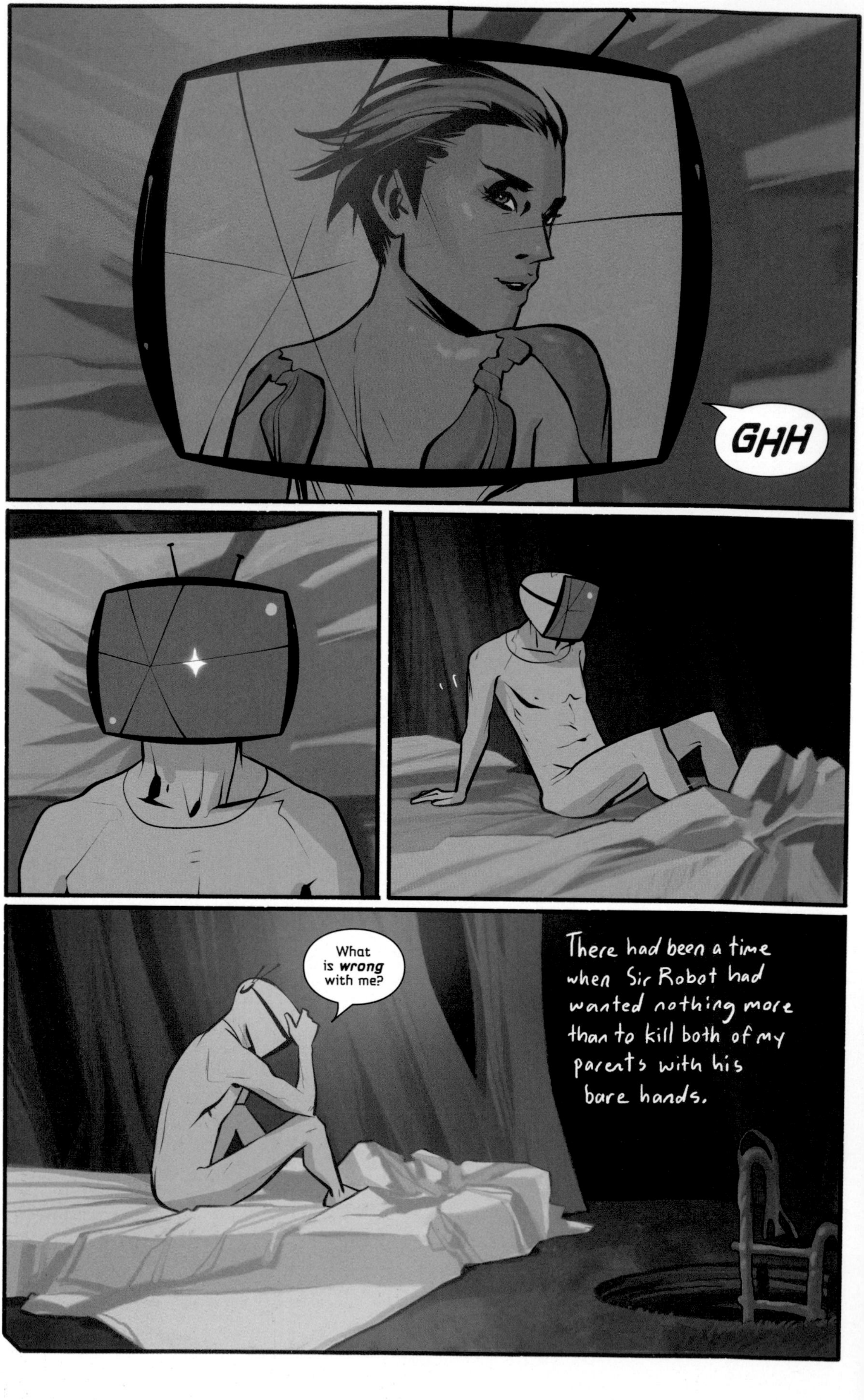
GHH
What is **wrong** with me?
There had been a time when Sir Robot had wanted nothing more than to kill both of my parents with his bare hands.

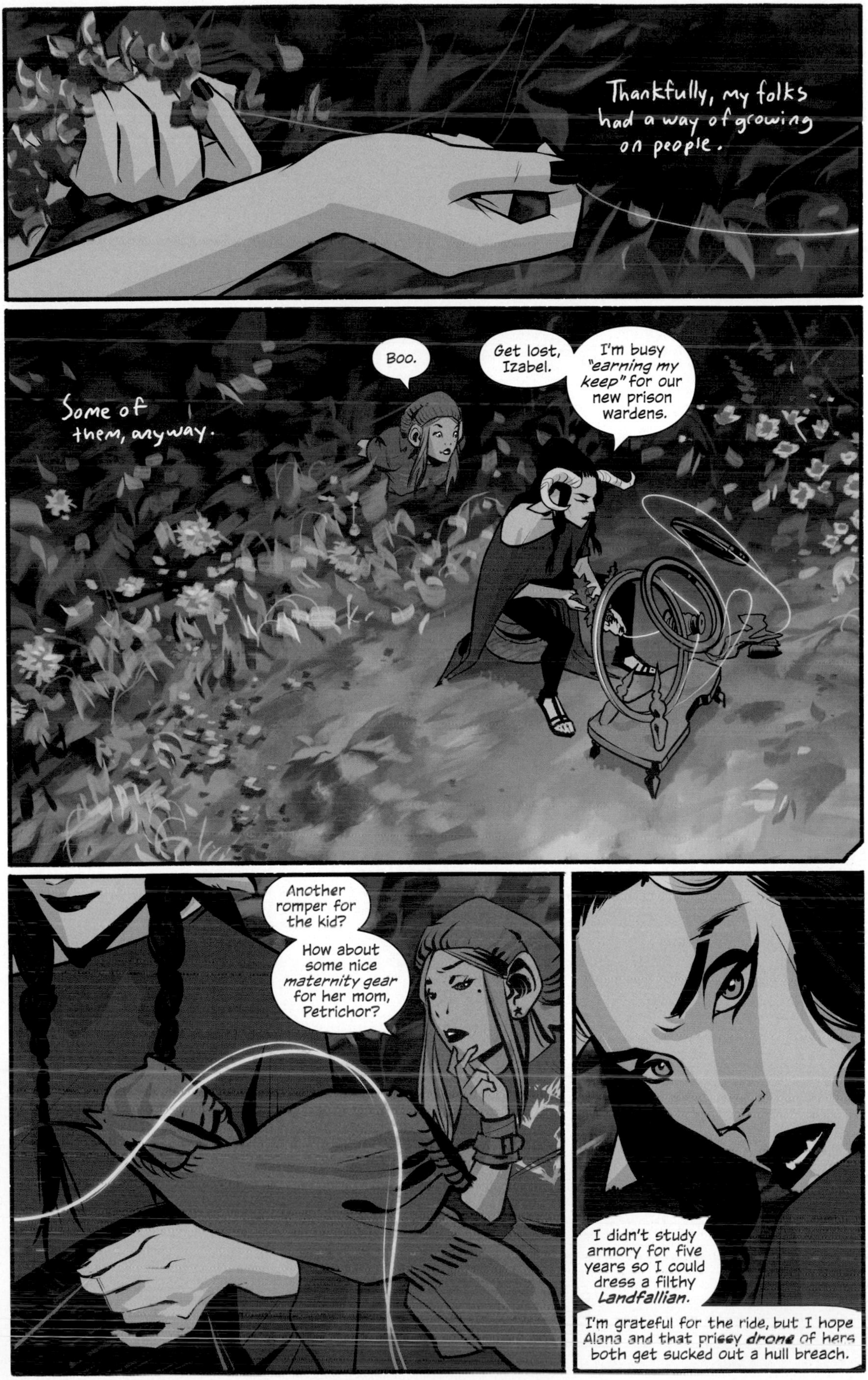

Thankfully, my folks had a way of growing on people.
Some of them, anyway.
Boo.
Get lost, Izabel.
I'm busy "earning my keep" for our new prison wardens.
Another romper for the kid?
How about some nice maternity gear for her mom, Petrichor?
I didn't study armory for five years so I could dress a filthy Landfallian.
I'm grateful for the ride, but I hope Alana and that prissy drone of hers both get sucked out a hull breach.

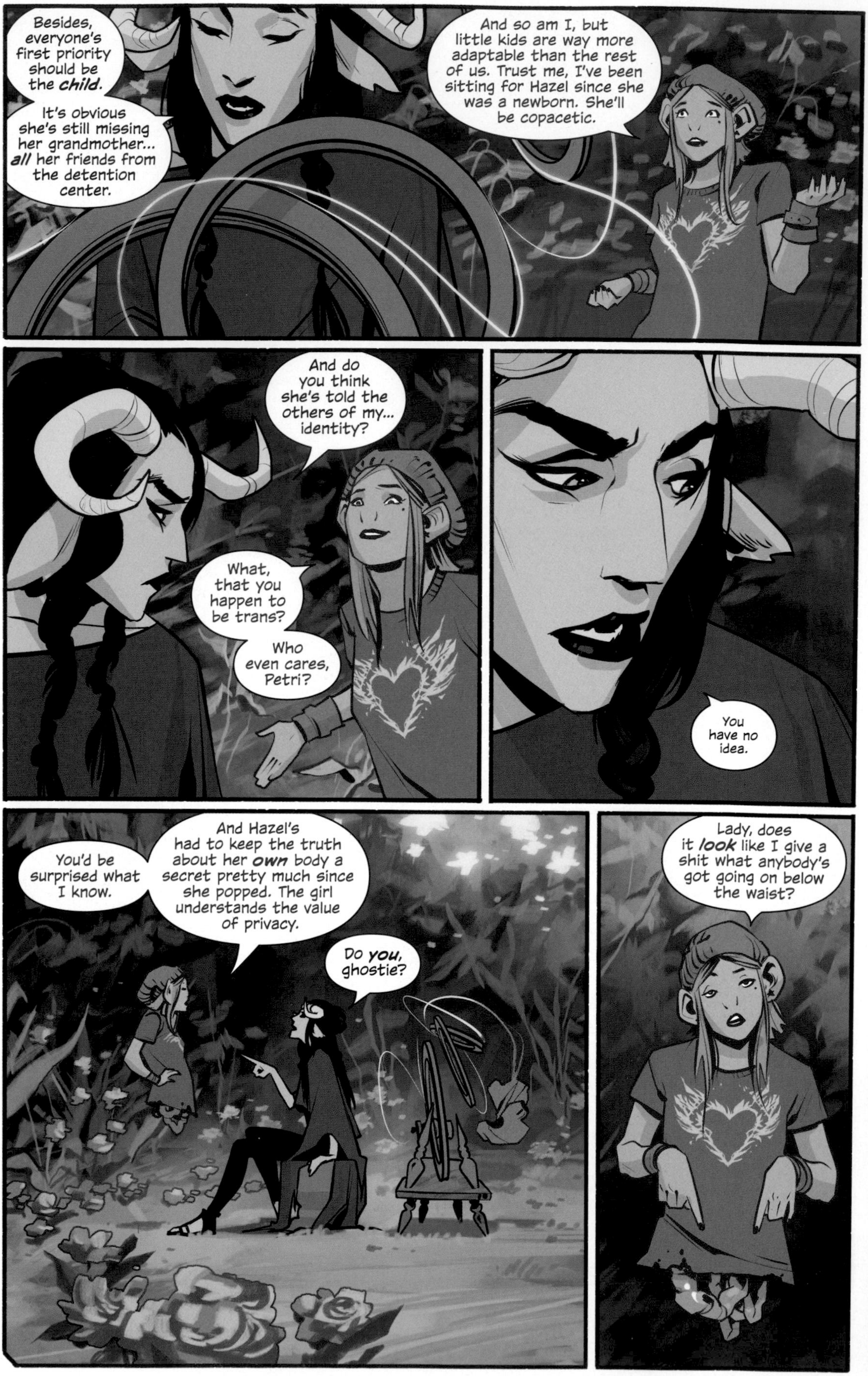
Besides, everyone's first priority should be the *child*.
It's obvious she's still missing her grandmother... *all* her friends from the detention center.
And so am I, but little kids are way more adaptable than the rest of us. Trust me, I've been sitting for Hazel since she was a newborn. She'll be copacetic.
And do you think she's told the others of my... identity?
What, that you happen to be trans?
Who even cares, Petri?
You have no idea.
You'd be surprised what I know.
And Hazel's had to keep the truth about her *own* body a secret pretty much since she popped. The girl understands the value of privacy.
Do *you*, ghostie?
Lady, does it *look* like I give a shit what anybody's got going on below the waist?

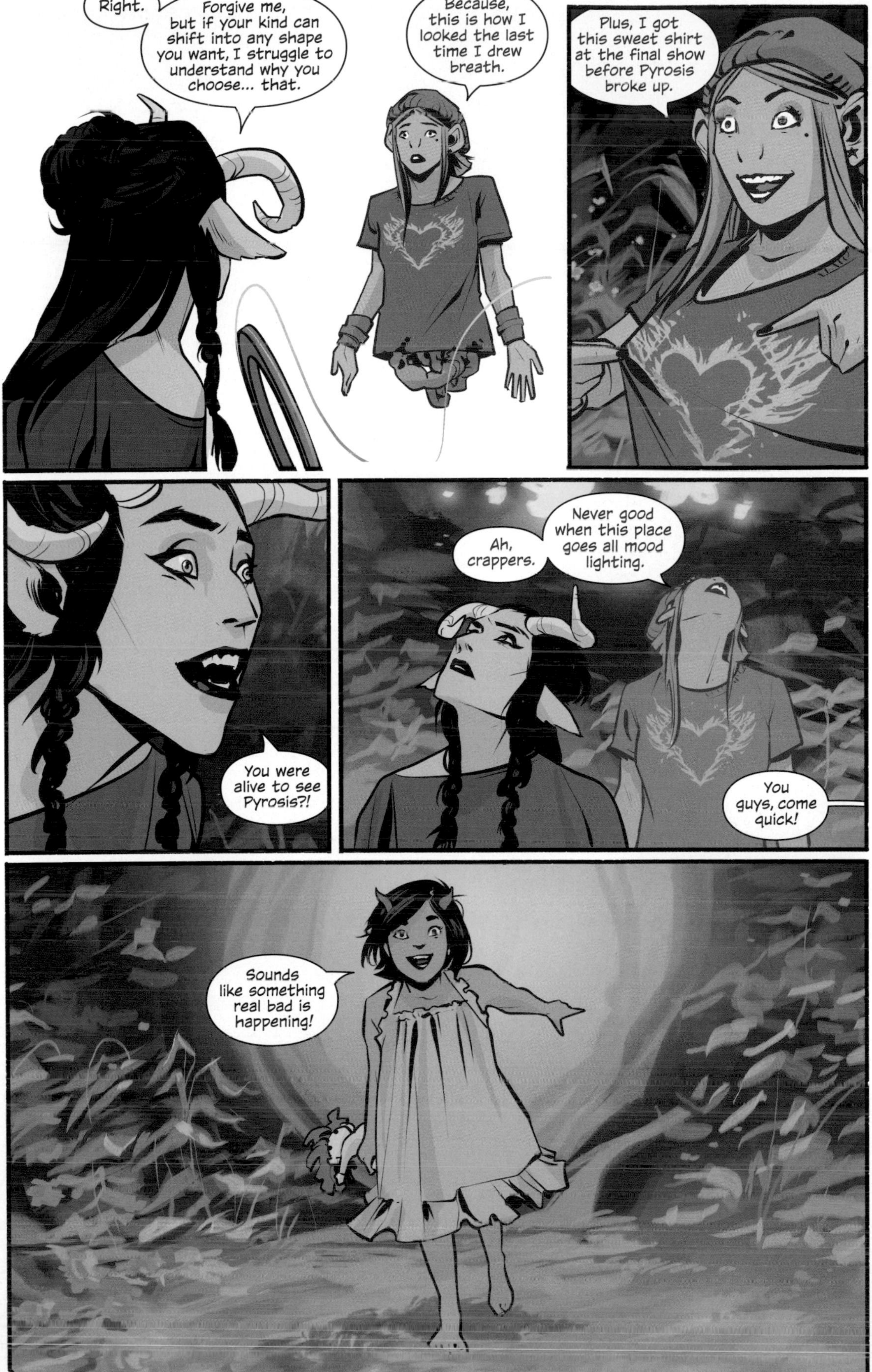
Right.
Forgive me, but if your kind can shift into any shape you want, I struggle to understand why you choose... that.
Because, this is how I looked the last time I drew breath.
Plus, I got this sweet shirt at the final show before Pyrosis broke up.
You were alive to see Pyrosis?!
Ah, crappers.
Never good when this place goes all mood lighting.
You guys, come quick!
Sounds like something real bad is happening!

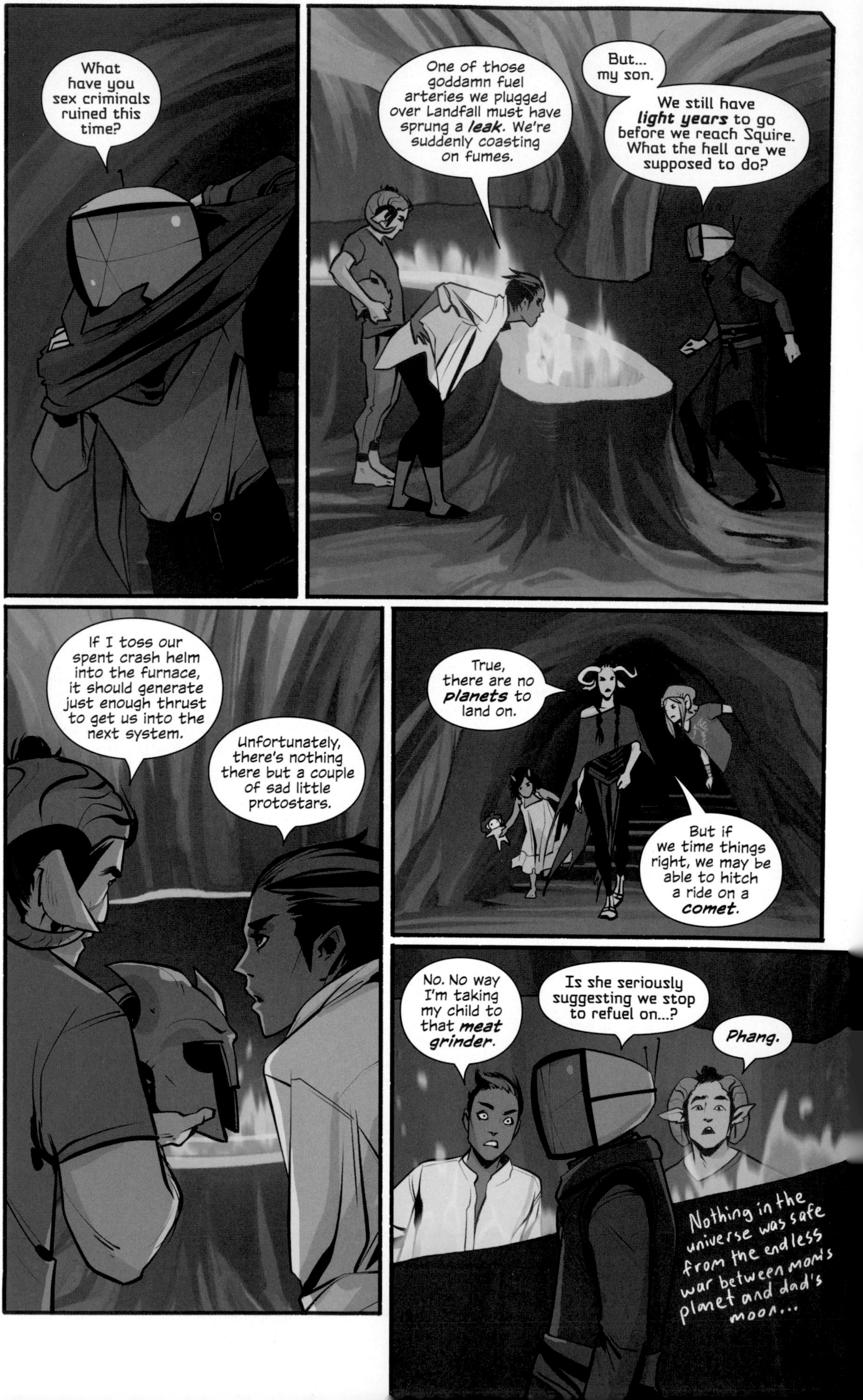
What have you sex criminals ruined this time?
One of those goddamn fuel arteries we plugged over Landfall must have sprung a *leak*. We're suddenly coasting on fumes.
But... my son.
We still have **light years** to go before we reach Squire. What the hell are we supposed to do?
If I toss our spent crash helm into the furnace, it should generate just enough thrust to get us into the next system.
Unfortunately, there's nothing there but a couple of sad little protostars.
True, there are no ***planets*** to land on.
But if we time things right, we may be able to hitch a ride on a ***comet***.
No. No way I'm taking my child to that ***meat grinder***.
Is she seriously suggesting we stop to refuel on...?
Phang.
Nothing in the universe was safe from the endless war between mom's planet and dad's moon...

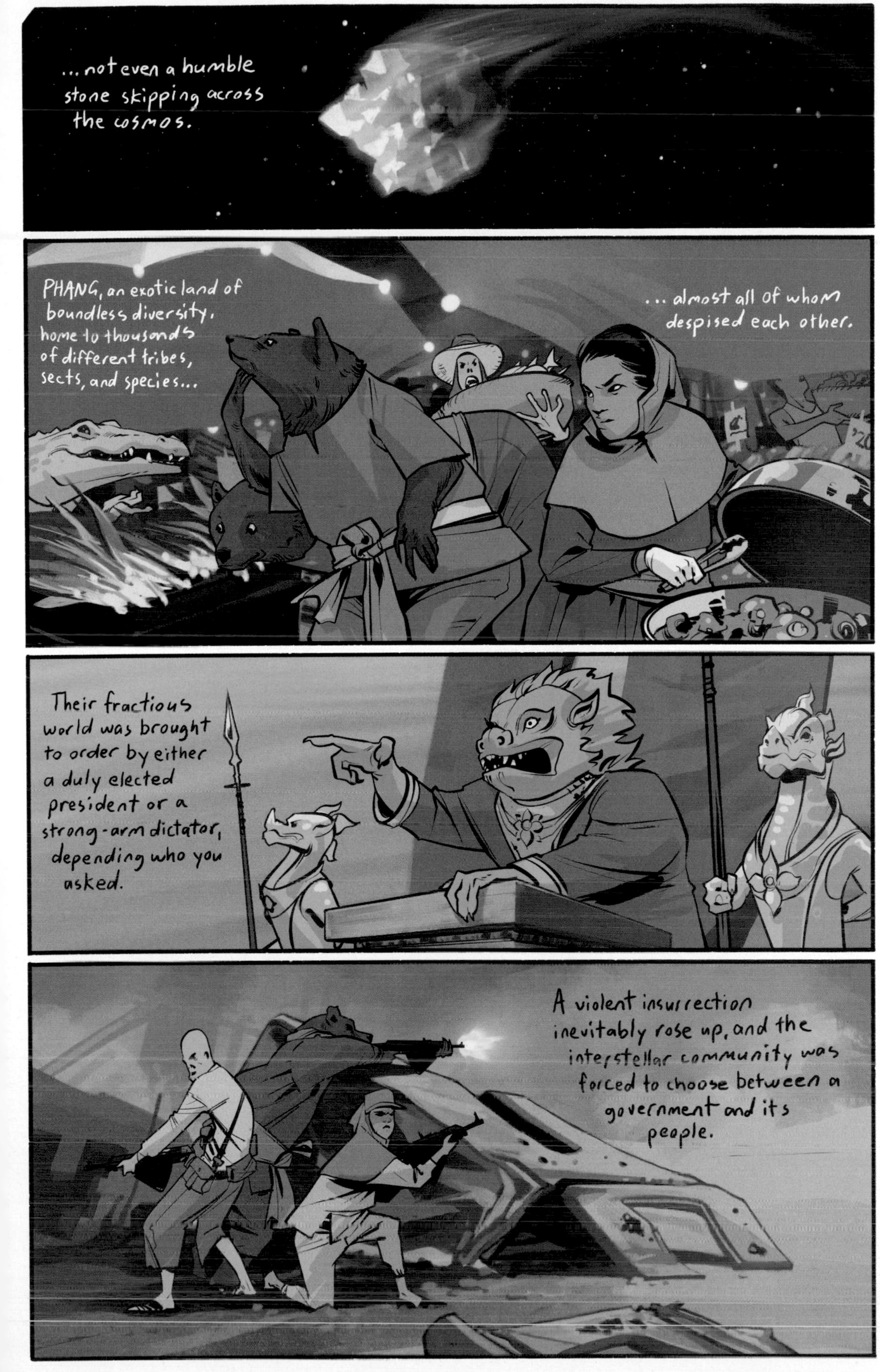
...not even a humble stone skipping across the cosmos.
PHANG, an exotic land of boundless diversity, home to thousands of different tribes, sects, and species...
...almost all of whom despised each other.
Their fractious world was brought to order by either a duly elected president or a strong-arm dictator, depending who you asked.
A violent insurrection inevitably rose up, and the interstellar community was forced to choose between a government and its people.

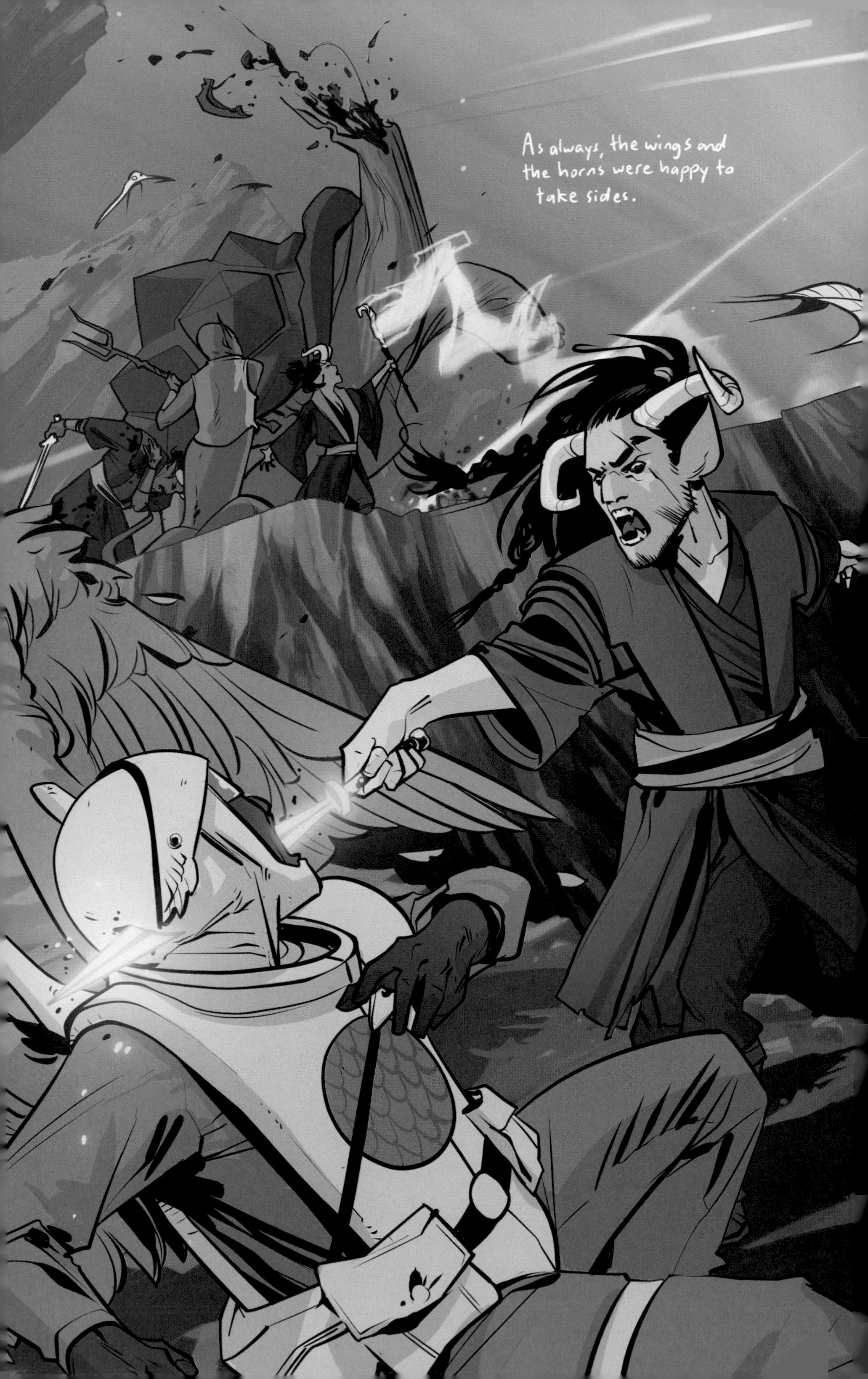
As always, the wings and the horns were happy to take sides.

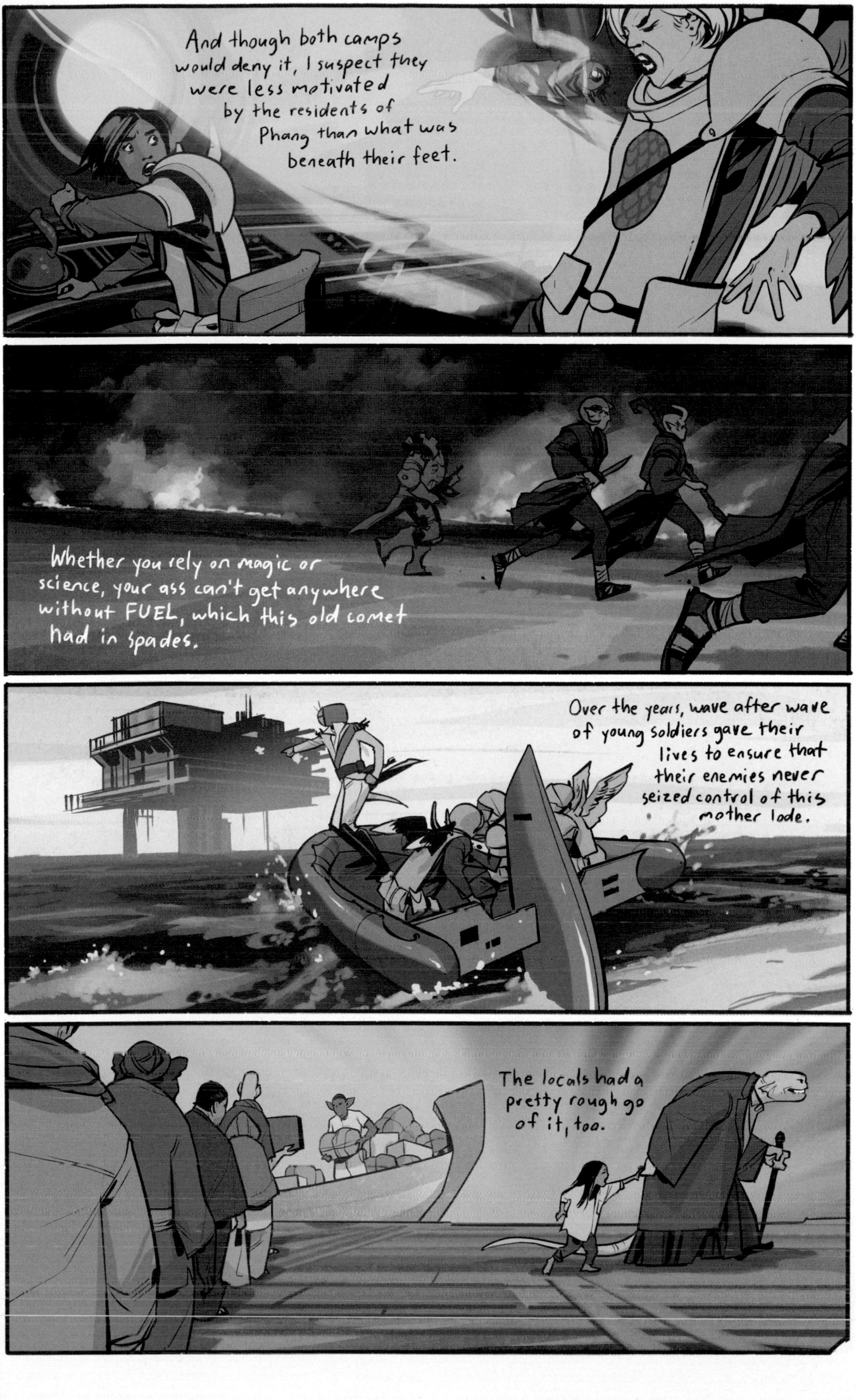
And though both camps would deny it, I suspect they were less motivated by the residents of Phang than what was beneath their feet.
Whether you rely on magic or science, your ass can't get anywhere without FUEL, which this old comet had in spades.
Over the years, wave after wave of young soldiers gave their lives to ensure that their enemies never seized control of this mother lode.
The locals had a pretty rough go of it, too.

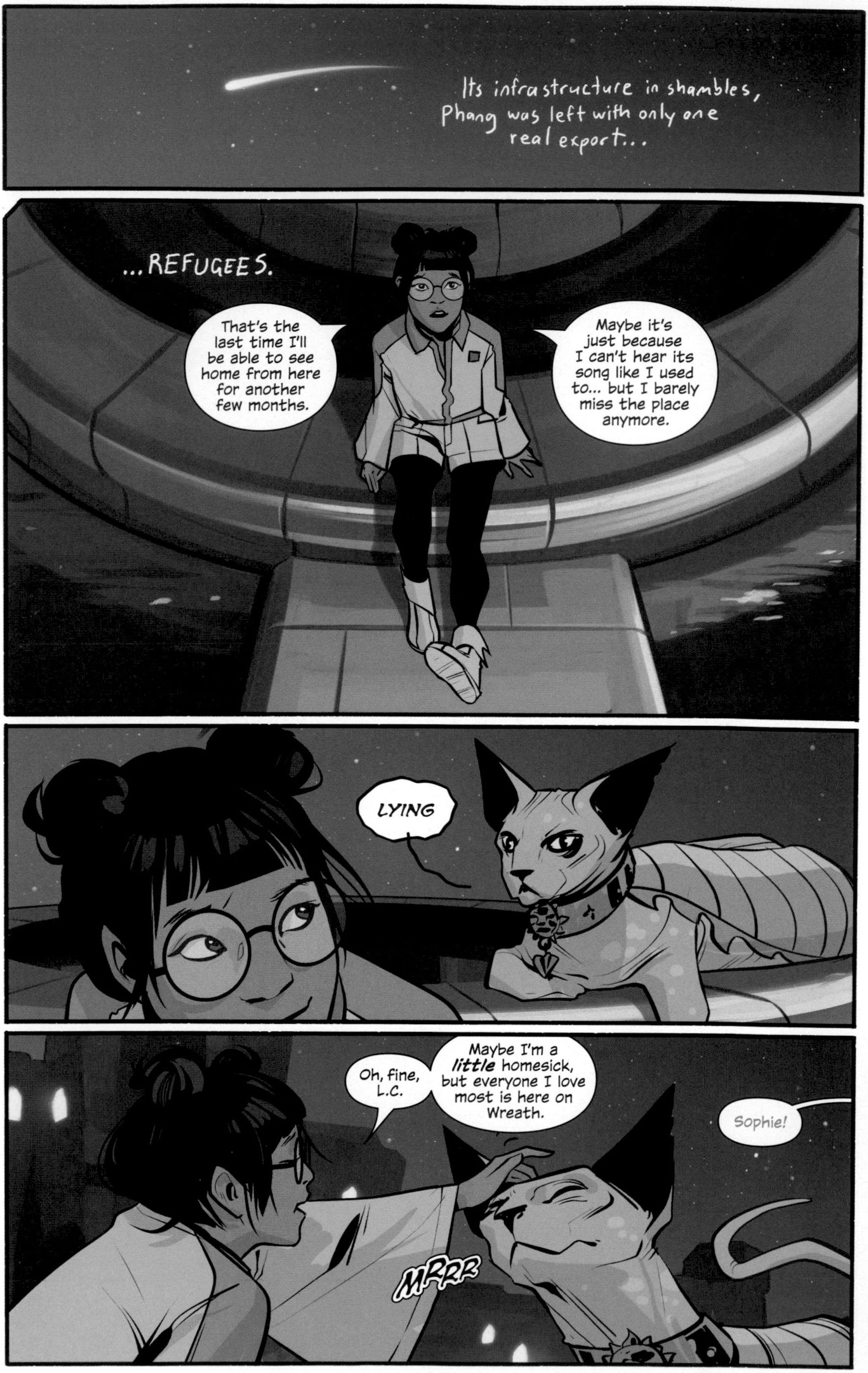
Its infrastructure in shambles, Phang was left with only one real export...
...REFUGEES.
That's the last time I'll be able to see home from here for another few months.
Maybe it's just because I can't hear its song like I used to... but I barely miss the place anymore.
LYING
Oh, fine, L.C.
Maybe I'm a *little* homesick, but everyone I love most is here on Wreath.
Sophie!
MRRR

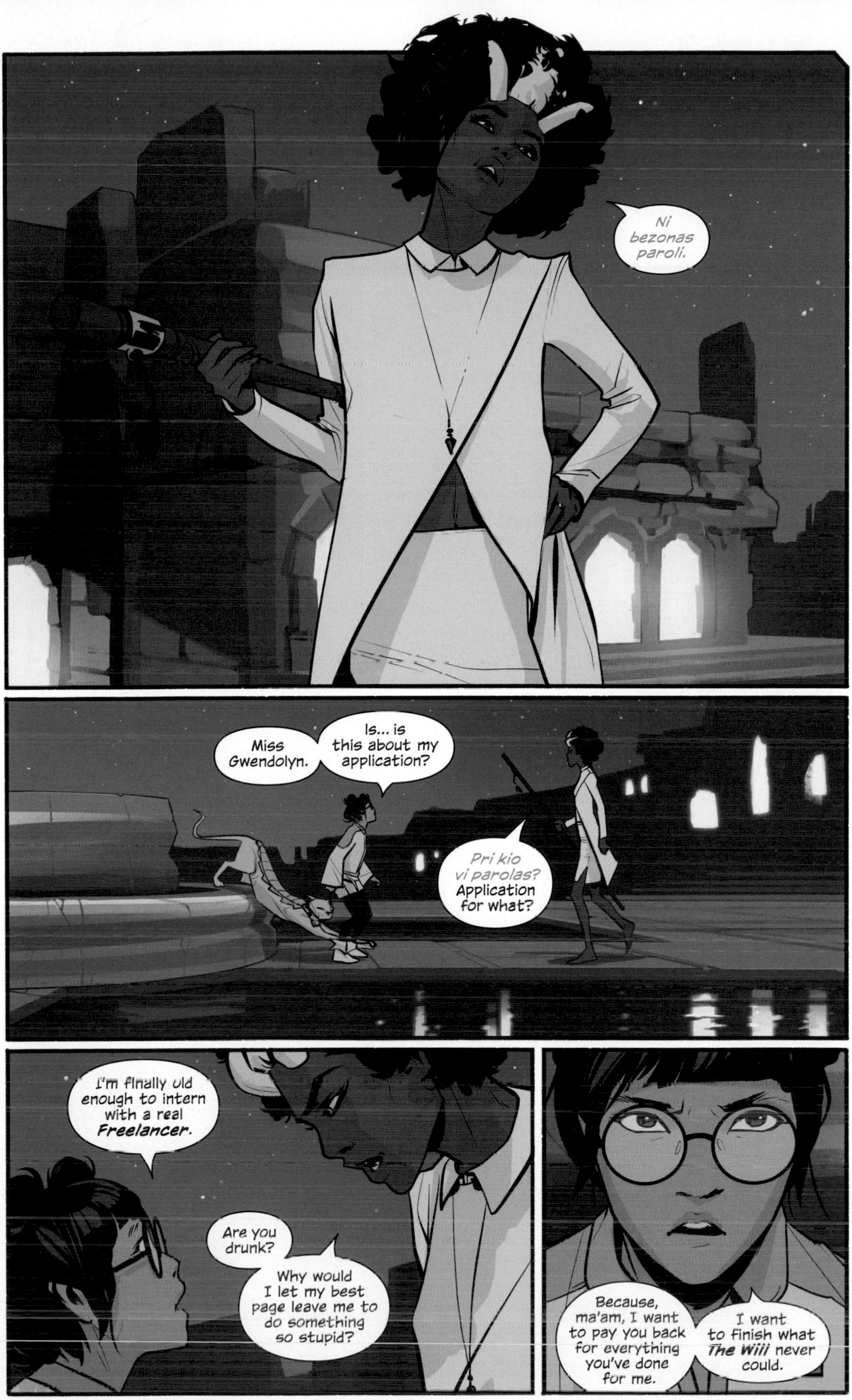
Ni bezonas paroli.
Miss Gwendolyn.
Is... is this about my application?
Pri kio vi parolas? Application for what?
I'm finally old enough to intern with a real Freelancer.
Are you drunk?
Why would I let my best page leave me to do something so stupid?
Because, ma'am, I want to pay you back for everything you've done for me.
I want to finish what The Will never could.

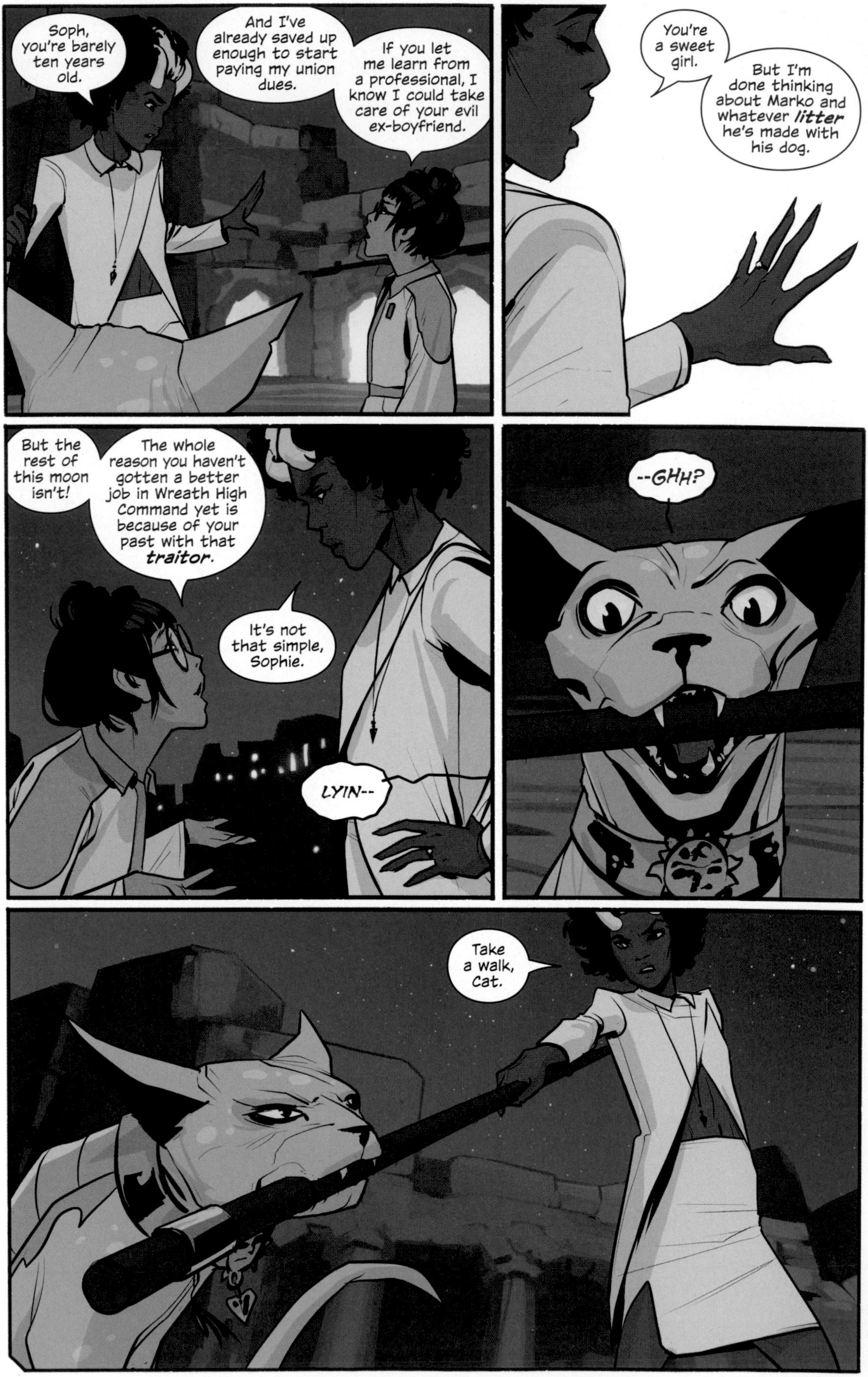
Soph, you're barely ten years old.
And I've already saved up enough to start paying my union dues.
If you let me learn from a professional, I know I could take care of your evil ex-boyfriend.
You're a sweet girl.
But I'm done thinking about Marko and whatever litter he's made with his dog.
But the rest of this moon isn't!
The whole reason you haven't gotten a better job in Wreath High Command yet is because of your past with that traitor.
It's not that simple, Sophie.
LYIN--
--GHH?
Take a walk, Cat.

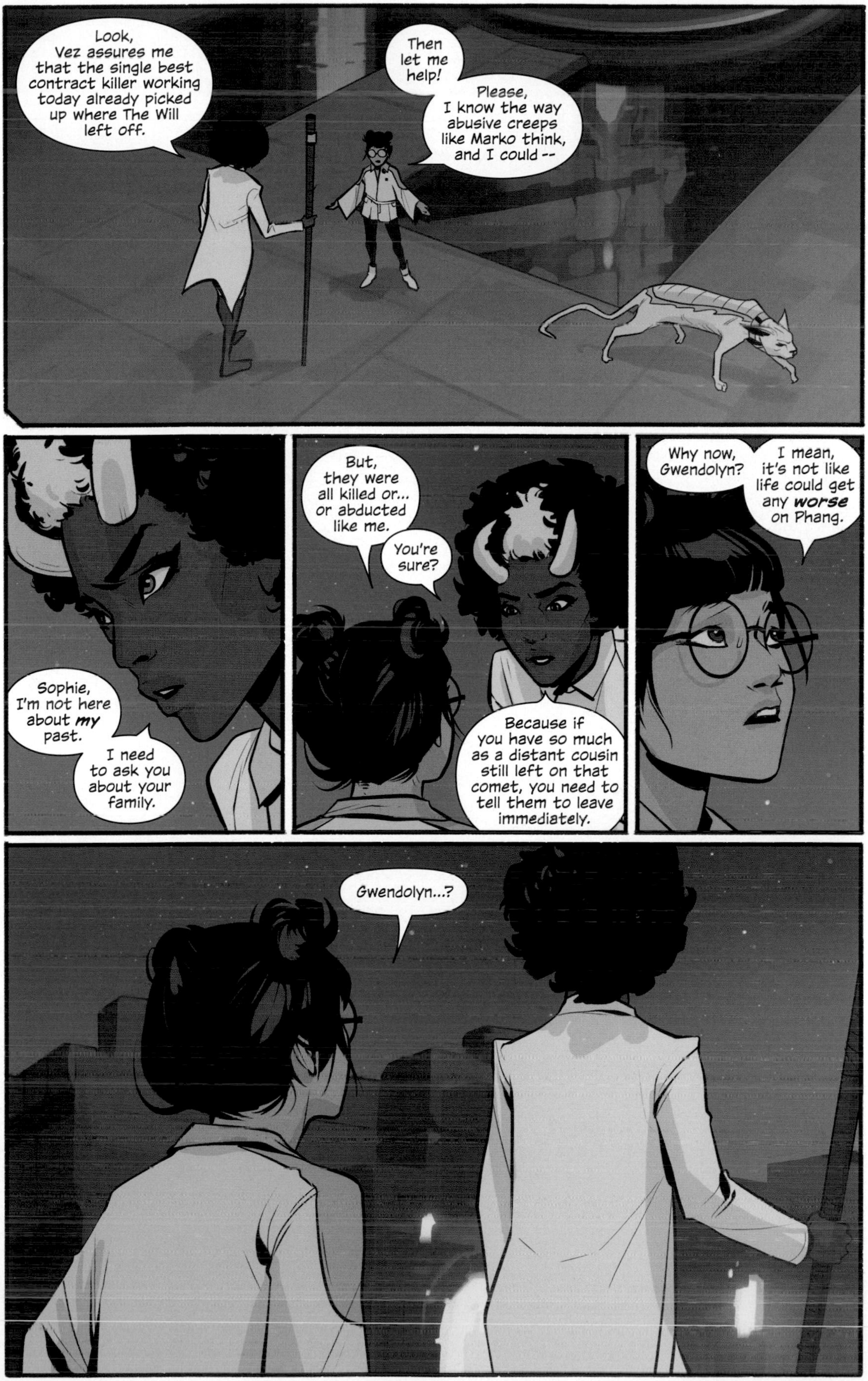
Look, Vez assures me that the single best contract killer working today already picked up where The Will left off.
Then let me help!
Please, I know the way abusive creeps like Marko think, and I could --
Sophie, I'm not here about *my* past.
I need to ask you about your family.
But, they were all killed or... or abducted like me.
You're sure?
Because if you have so much as a distant cousin still left on that comet, you need to tell them to leave immediately.
Why now, Gwendolyn?
I mean, it's not like life could get any *worse* on Phang.
Gwendolyn...?

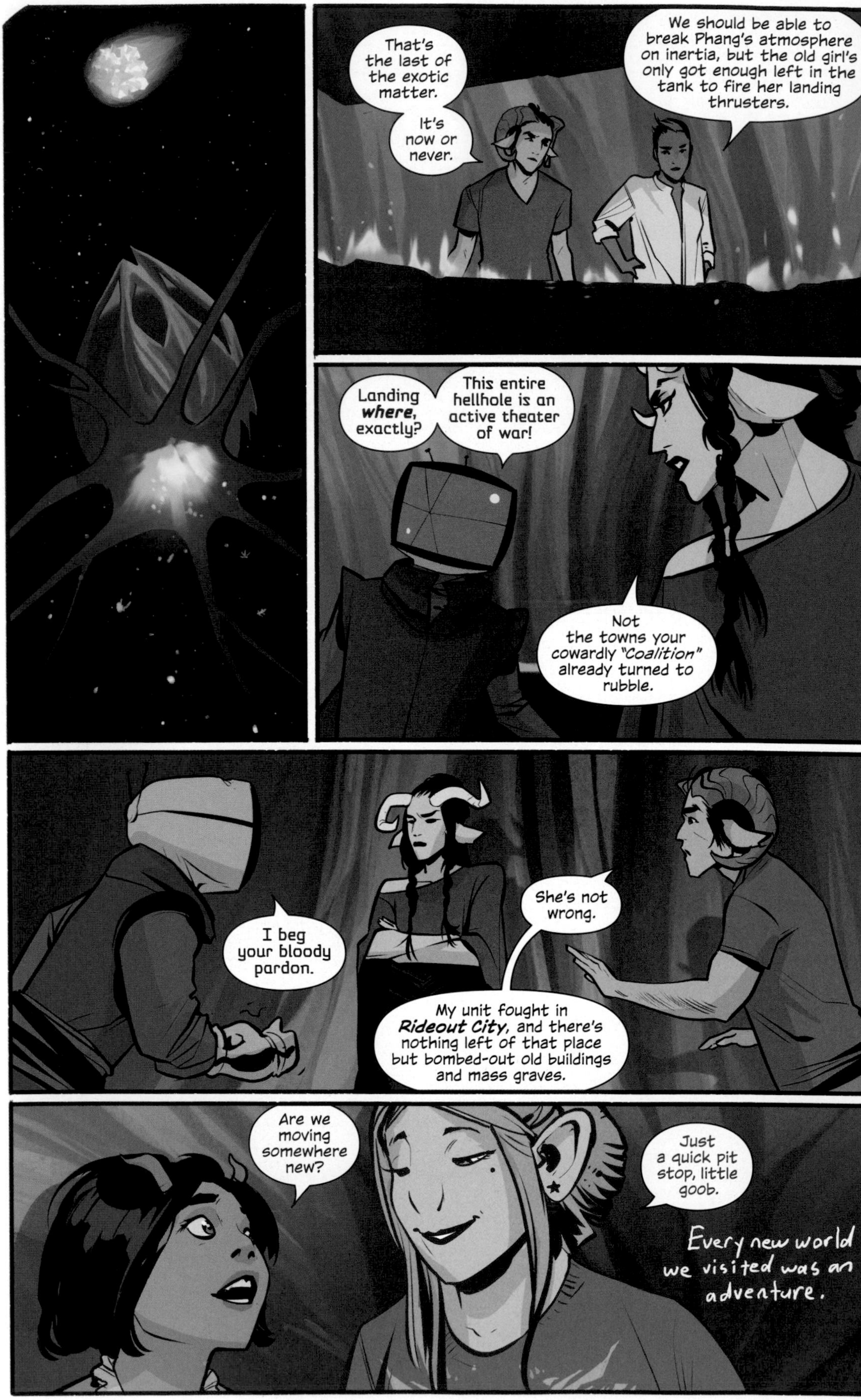
That's the last of the exotic matter.
It's now or never.
We should be able to break Phang's atmosphere on inertia, but the old girl's only got enough left in the tank to fire her landing thrusters.
Landing *where*, exactly?
This entire hellhole is an active theater of war!
Not the towns your cowardly *"Coalition"* already turned to rubble.
I beg your bloody pardon.
She's not wrong.
My unit fought in *Rideout City*, and there's nothing left of that place but bombed-out old buildings and mass graves.
Are we moving somewhere new?
Just a quick pit stop, little goob.
Every new world we visited was an adventure.

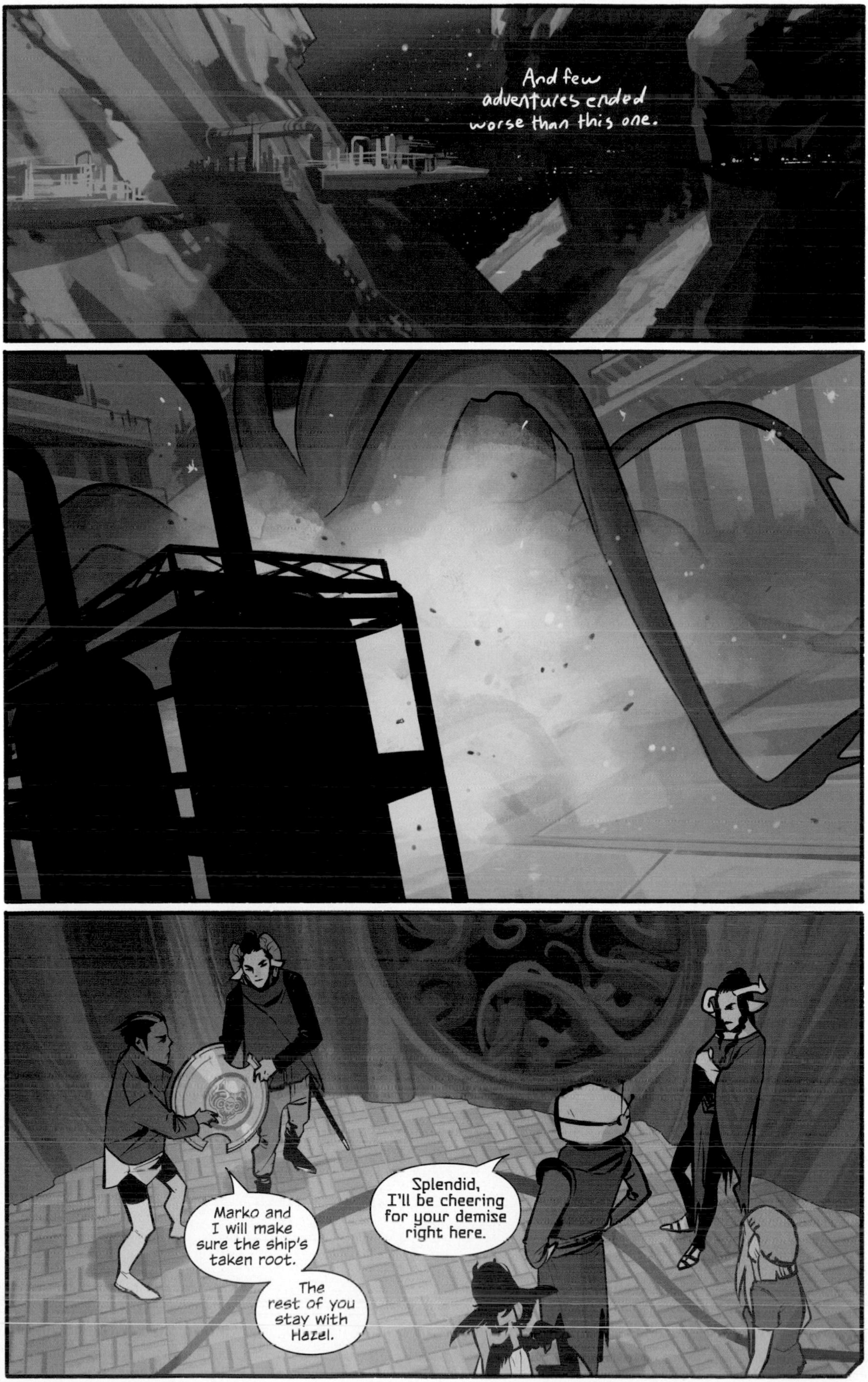

And few adventures ended worse than this one.
Marko and I will make sure the ship's taken root.
The rest of you stay with Hazel.
Splendid, I'll be cheering for your demise right here.

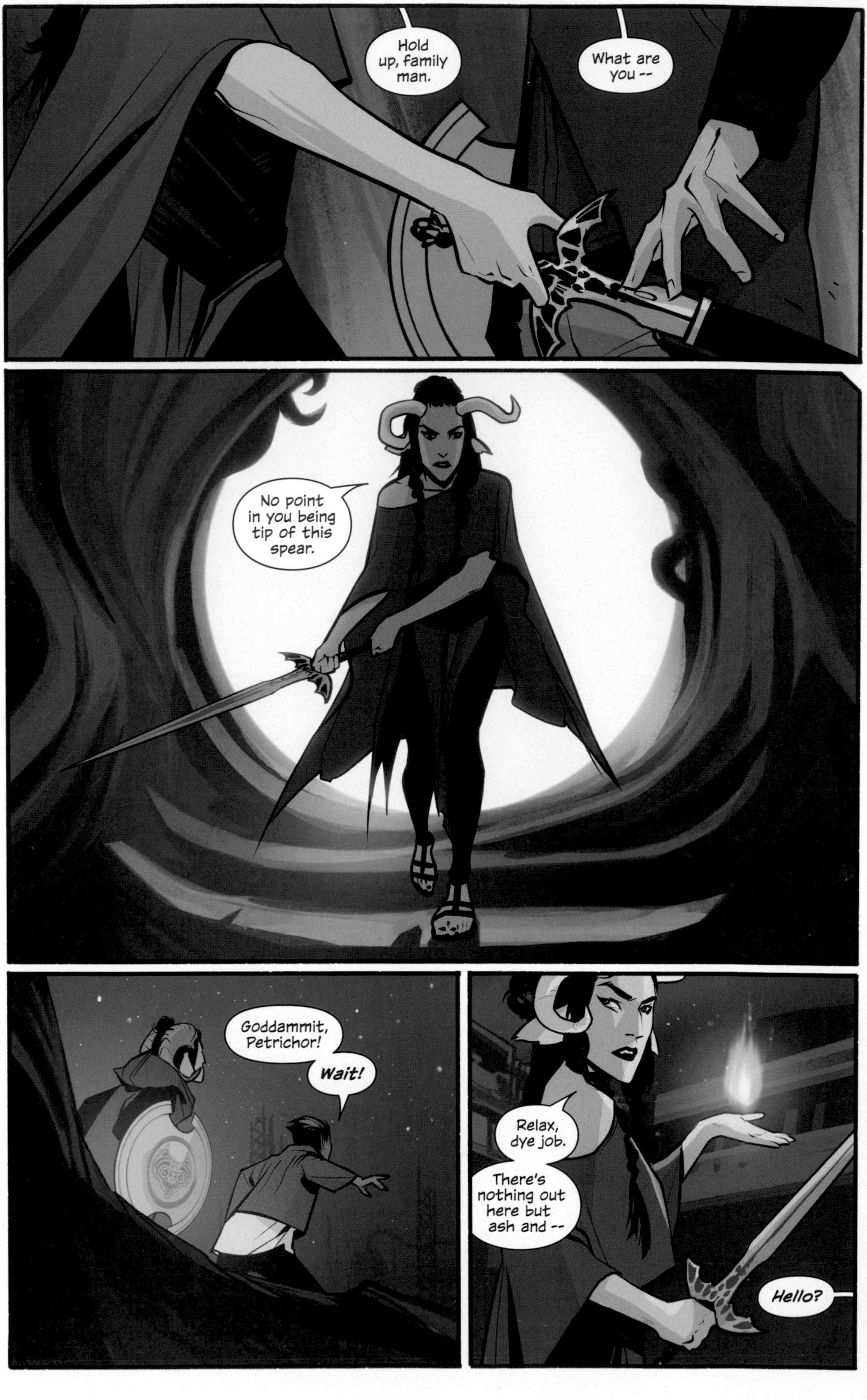
Hold up, family man.
What are you --
No point in you being tip of this spear.
Goddammit, Petrichor!
Wait!
Relax, dye job.
There's nothing out here but ash and --
Hello?

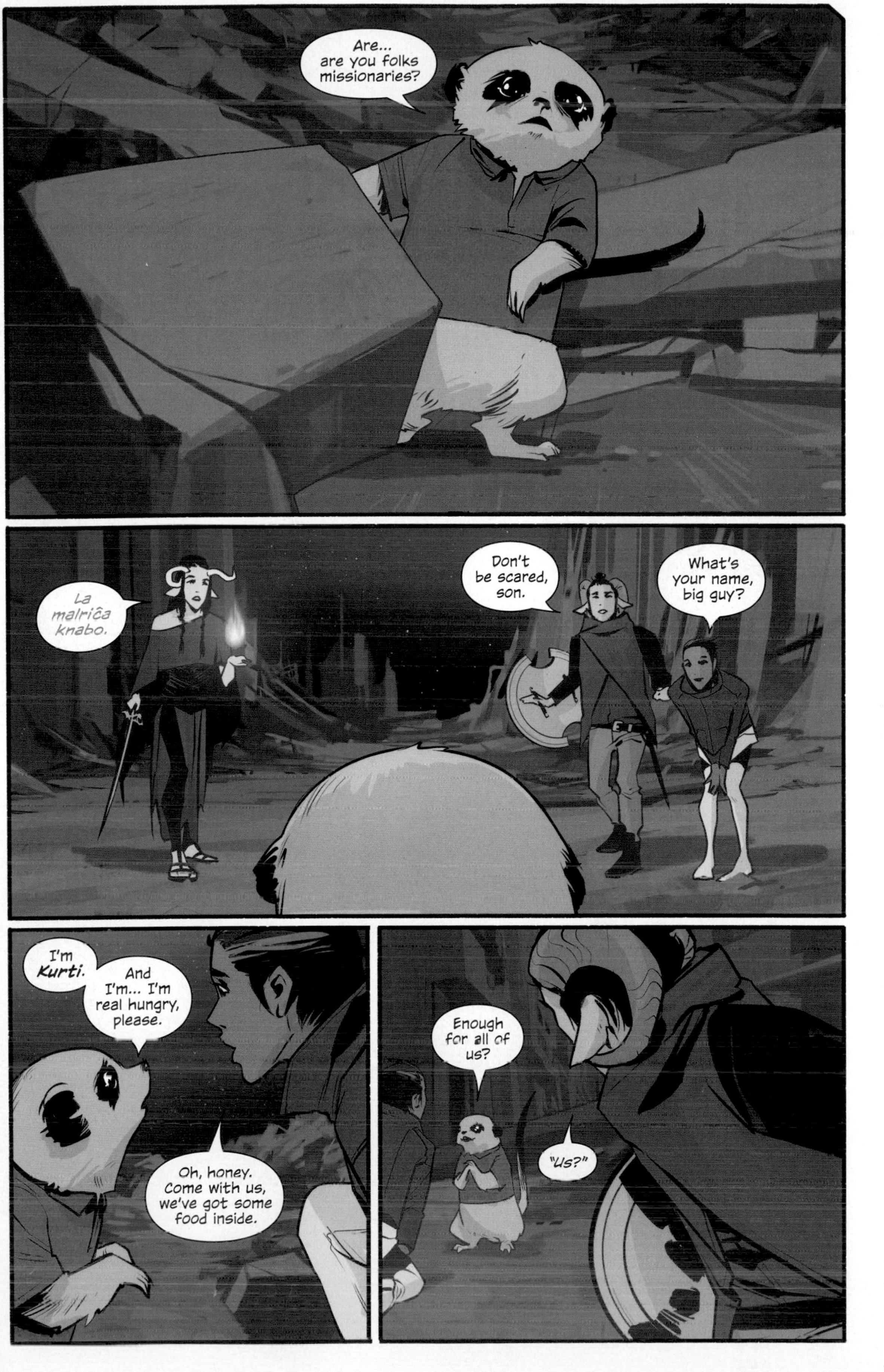
Are... are you folks missionaries?
La malriĉa knabo.
Don't be scared, son.
What's your name, big guy?
I'm Kurti.
And I'm... I'm real hungry, please.
Oh, honey. Come with us, we've got some food inside.
Enough for all of us?
"Us?"

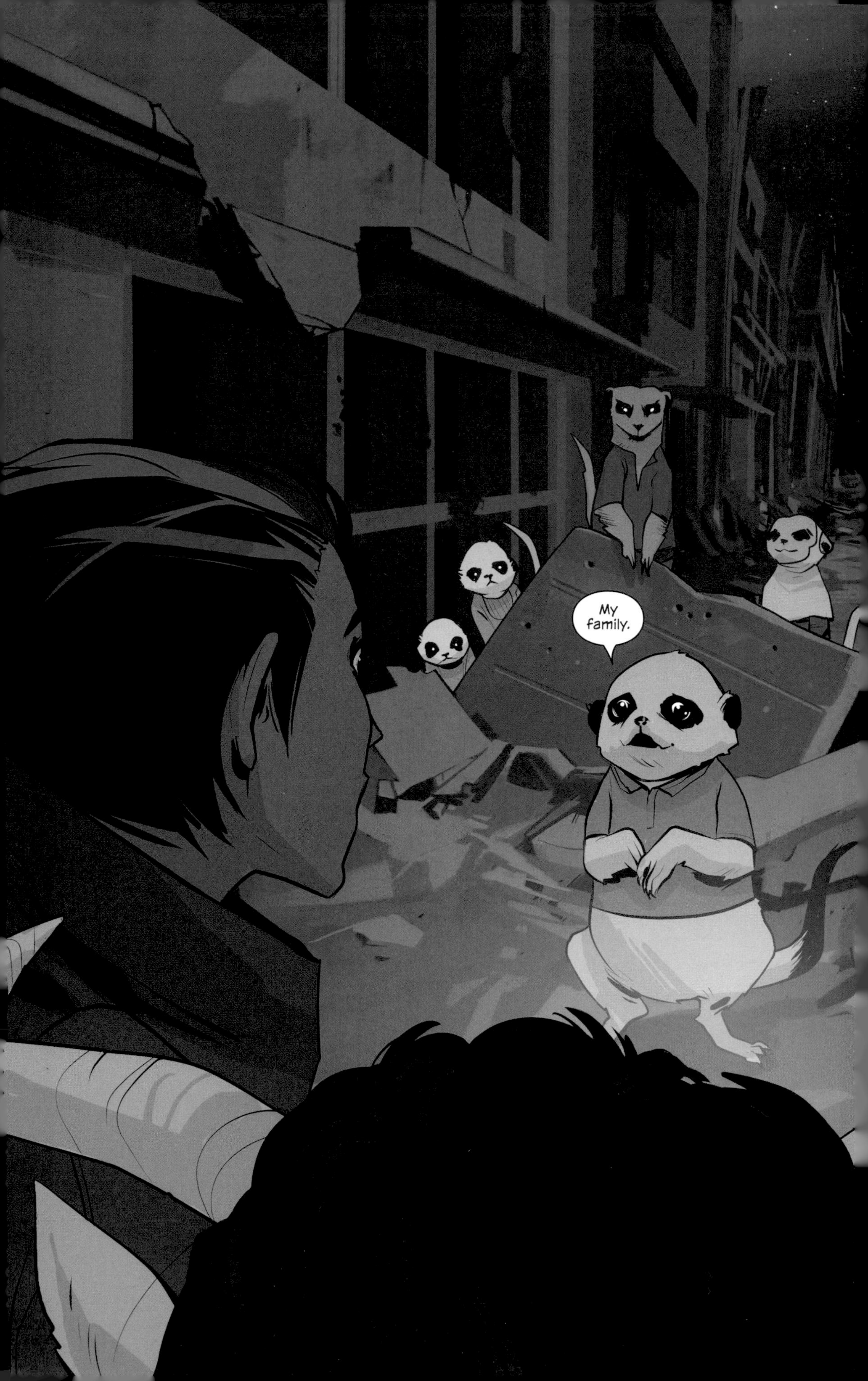
My family.

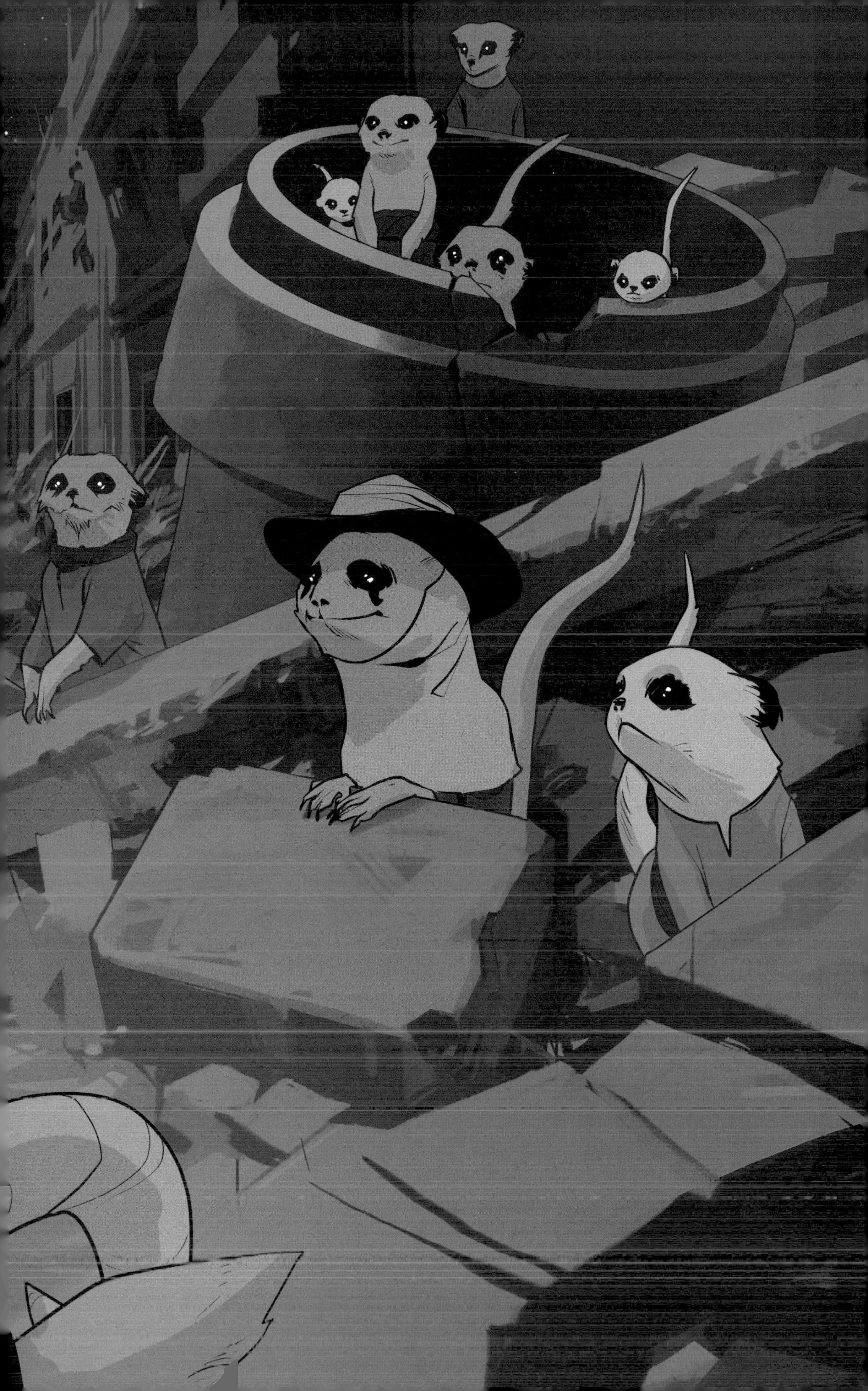

CHAPTER
THIRTY-EIGHT

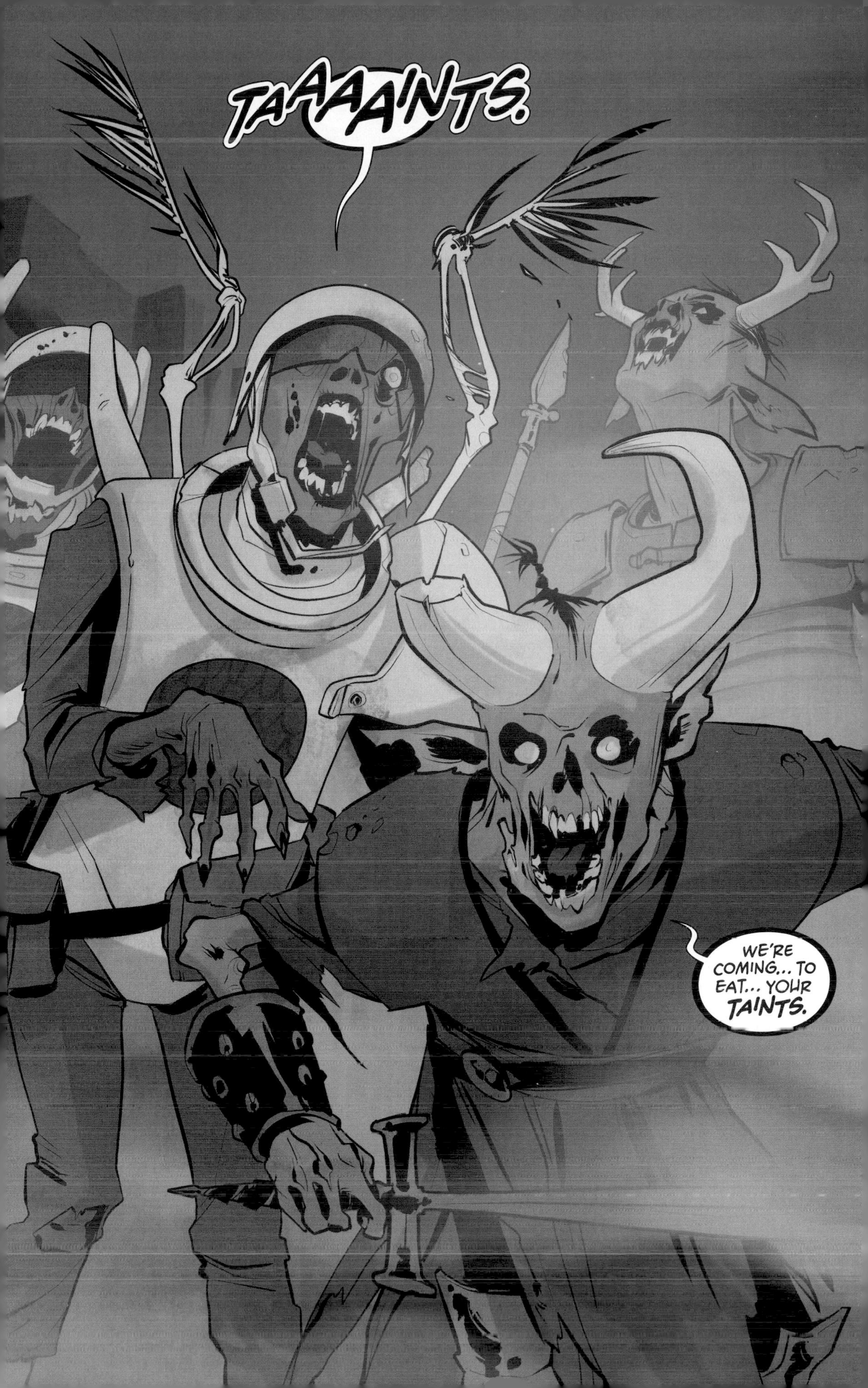
TAAAAINTS.
WE'RE COMING... TO EAT... YOUR TAINTS.

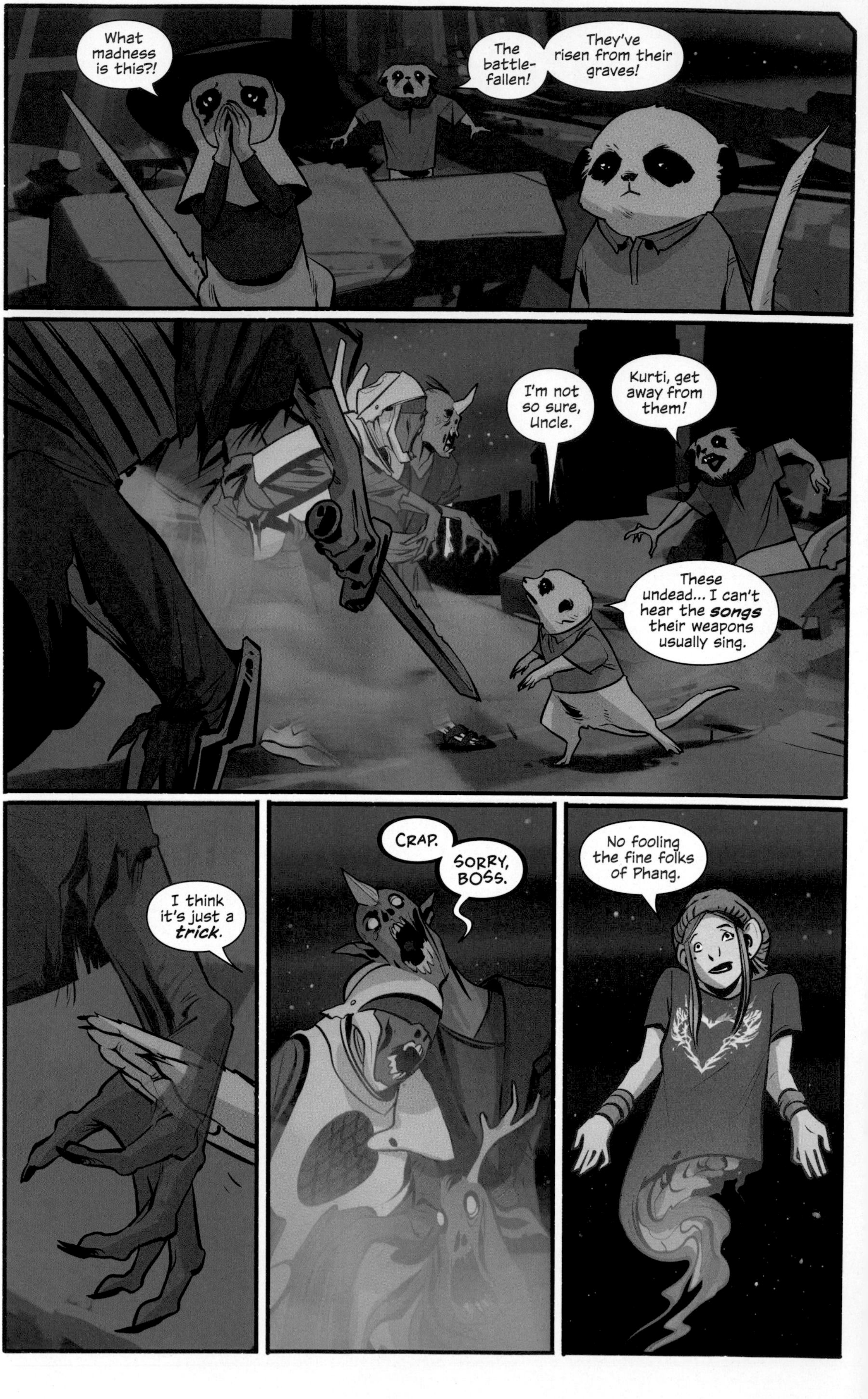
What madness is this?!
The battle-fallen!
They've risen from their graves!
I'm not so sure, Uncle.
Kurti, get away from them!
These undead... I can't hear the **songs** their weapons usually sing.
I think it's just a **trick**.
CRAP.
SORRY, BOSS.
No fooling the fine folks of Phang.

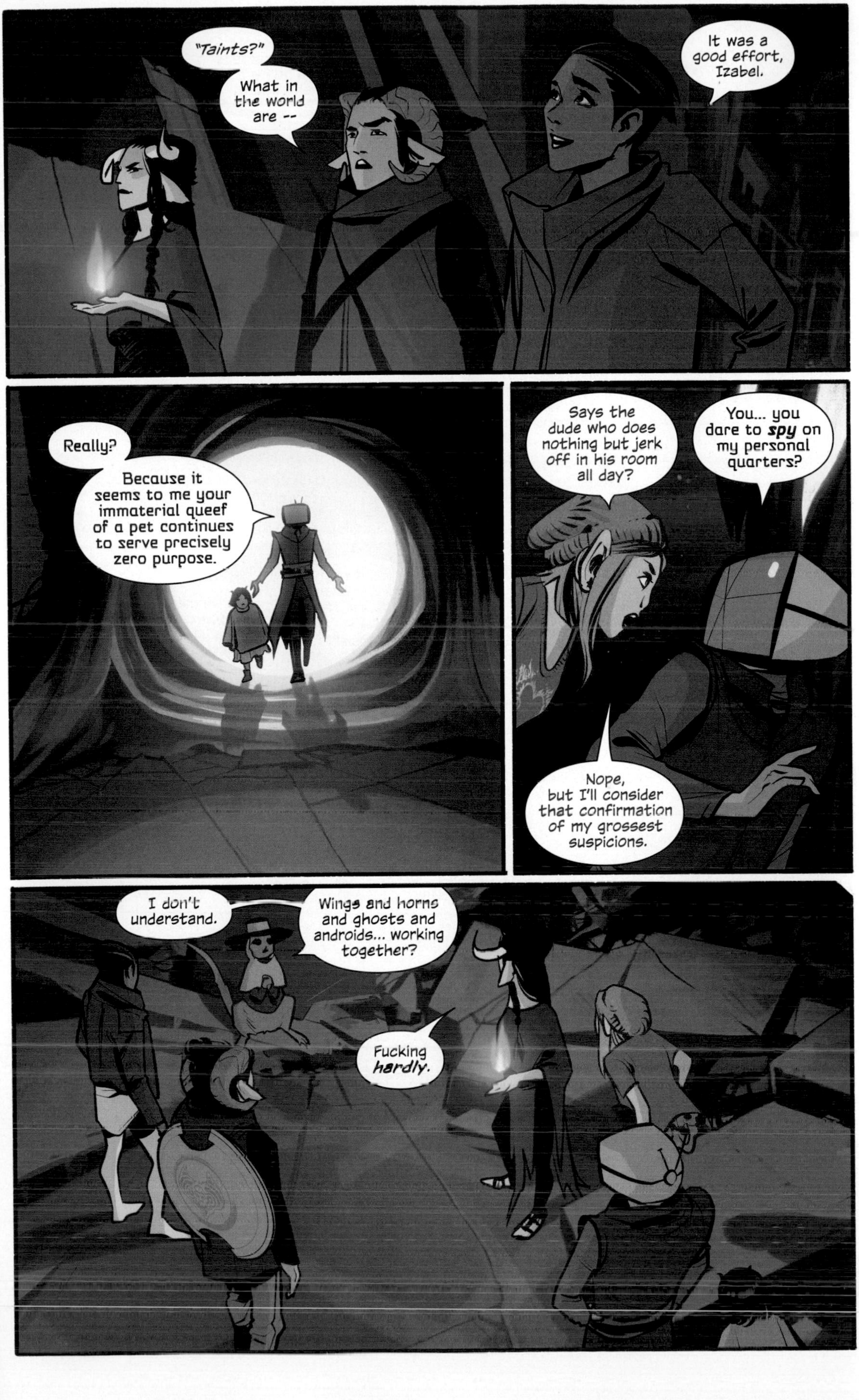
"Taints?"
What in the world are --
It was a good effort, Izabel.
Really?
Because it seems to me your immaterial queef of a pet continues to serve precisely zero purpose.
Says the dude who does nothing but jerk off in his room all day?
You... you dare to *spy* on my personal quarters?
Nope, but I'll consider that confirmation of my grossest suspicions.
I don't understand.
Wings and horns and ghosts and androids... working together?
Fucking *hardly*.

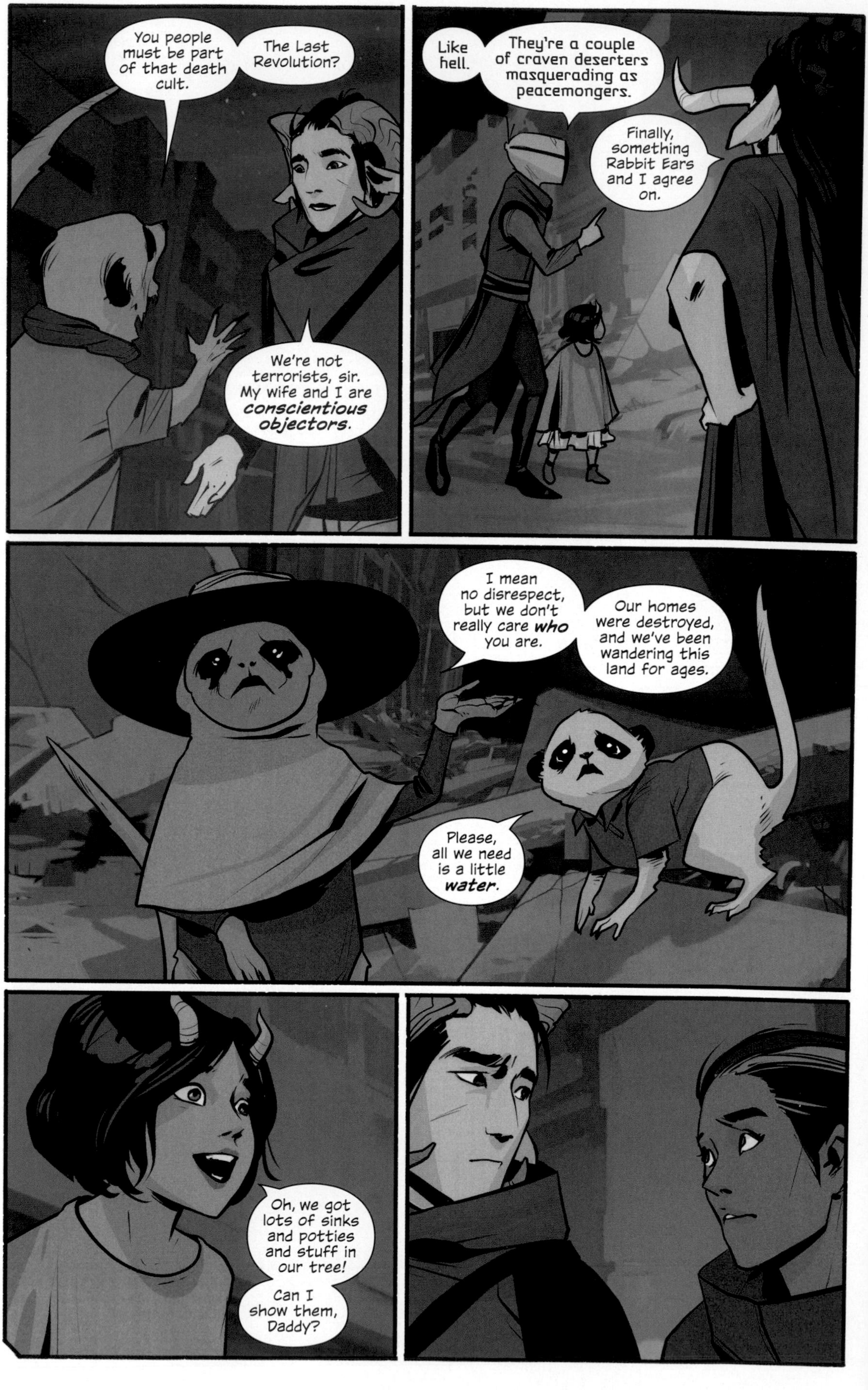
You people must be part of that death cult.
The Last Revolution?
We're not terrorists, sir. My wife and I are ***conscientious objectors***.
Like hell.
They're a couple of craven deserters masquerading as peacemongers.
Finally, something Rabbit Ears and I agree on.
I mean no disrespect, but we don't really care ***who*** you are.
Our homes were destroyed, and we've been wandering this land for ages.
Please, all we need is a little ***water***.
Oh, we got lots of sinks and potties and stuff in our tree!
Can I show them, Daddy?

Of course, my heart.

Marko--

These are innocent people displaced by an evil war. They're *us*.

You really want to turn them away in front of our daughter?

I really want Hazel to *survive*, which means getting out of this quagmire as soon as possible.

And we will.

But that doesn't mean we can't share what provisions we have while our rocket finishes refueling.

This comet's soil is rich with energy, so it shouldn't take long at all.

If there's one thing parents suck at, it's estimating how long any activity is going to take.

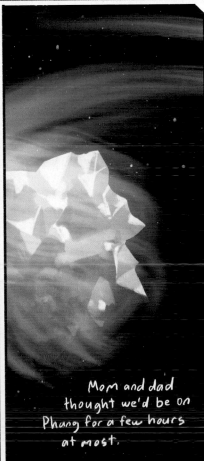

Mom and dad thought we'd be on Phang for a few hours at most.

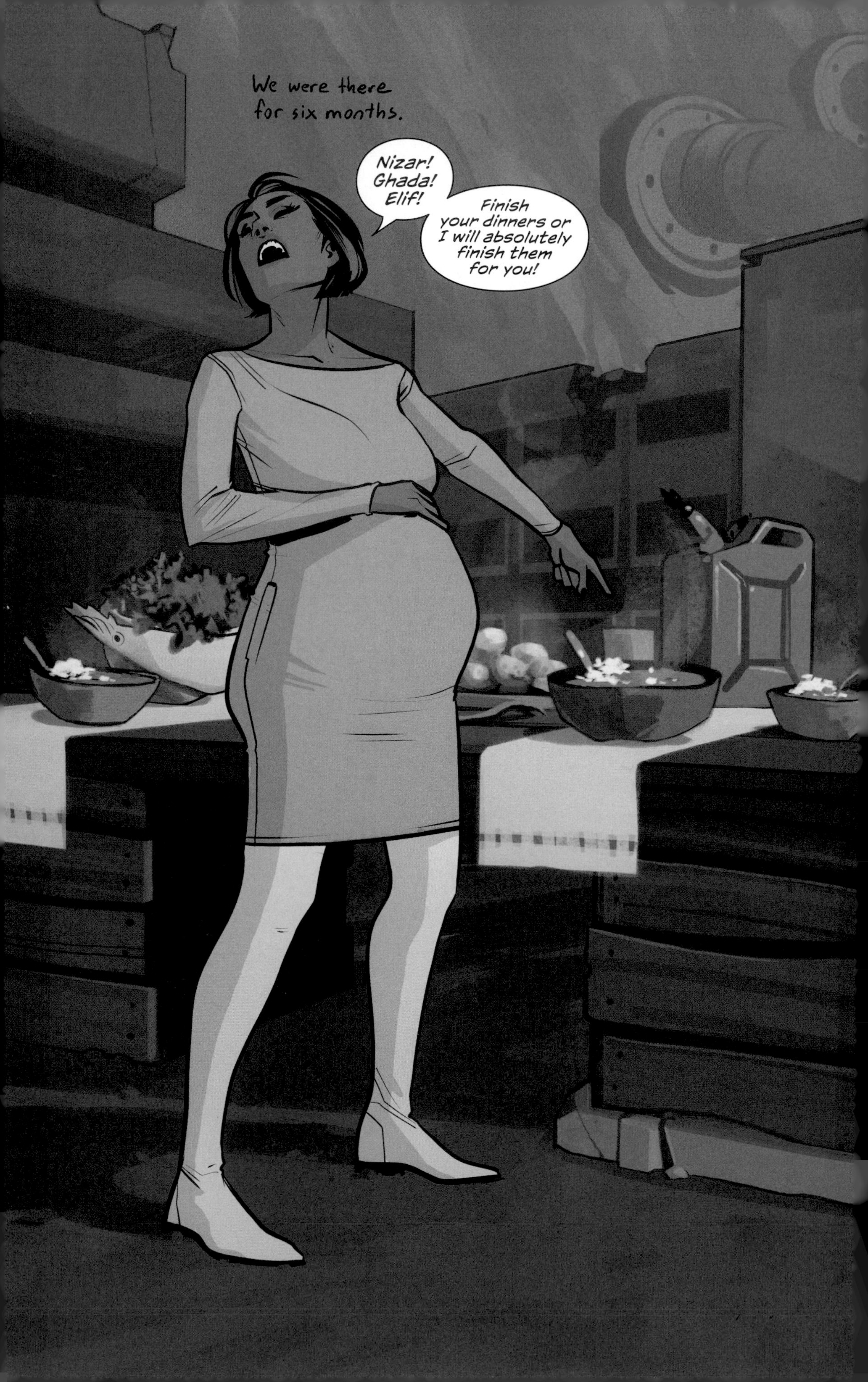
We were there for six months.
Nizar! Ghada! Elif!
Finish your dinners or I will absolutely finish them for you!

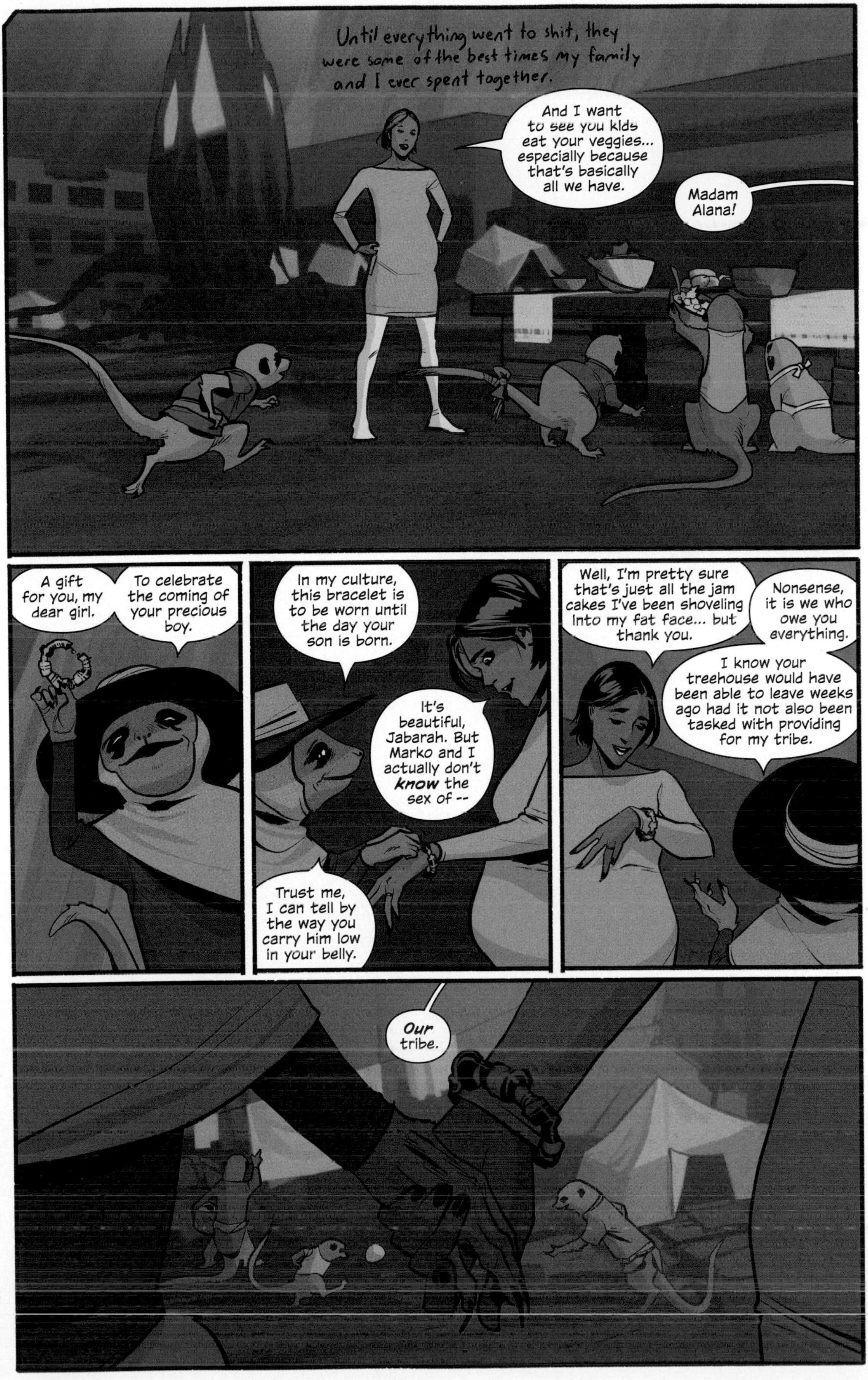

Until everything went to shit, they were some of the best times my family and I ever spent together.
And I want to see you kids eat your veggies... especially because that's basically all we have.
Madam Alana!
A gift for you, my dear girl.
To celebrate the coming of your precious boy.
In my culture, this bracelet is to be worn until the day your son is born.
It's beautiful, Jabarah. But Marko and I actually don't *know* the sex of --
Trust me, I can tell by the way you carry him low in your belly.
Well, I'm pretty sure that's just all the jam cakes I've been shoveling into my fat face... but thank you.
Nonsense, it is we who owe you everything.
I know your treehouse would have been able to leave weeks ago had it not also been tasked with providing for my tribe.
Our tribe.

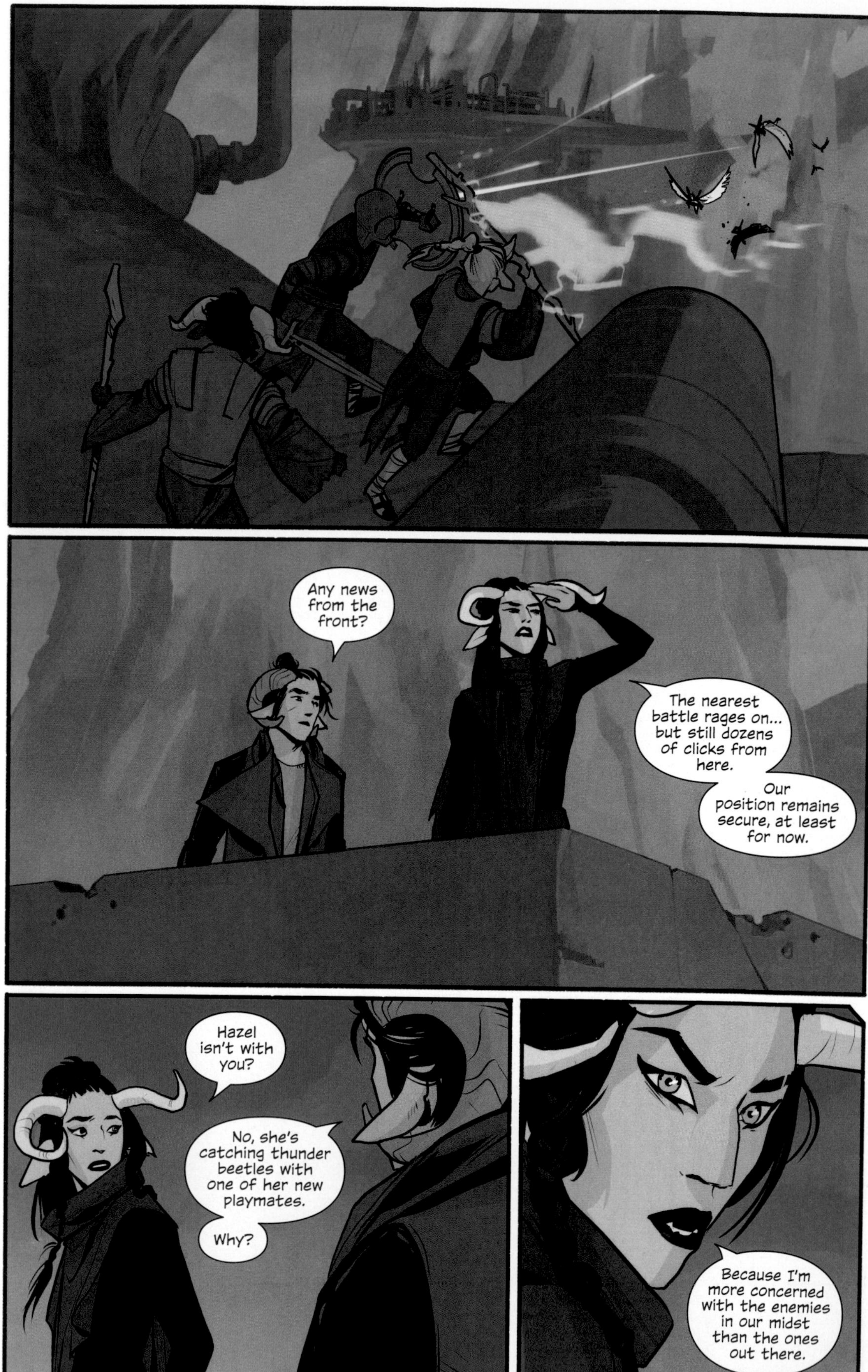
Any news from the front?
The nearest battle rages on... but still dozens of clicks from here.
Our position remains secure, at least for now.
Hazel isn't with you?
No, she's catching thunder beetles with one of her new playmates.
Why?
Because I'm more concerned with the enemies in our midst than the ones out there.

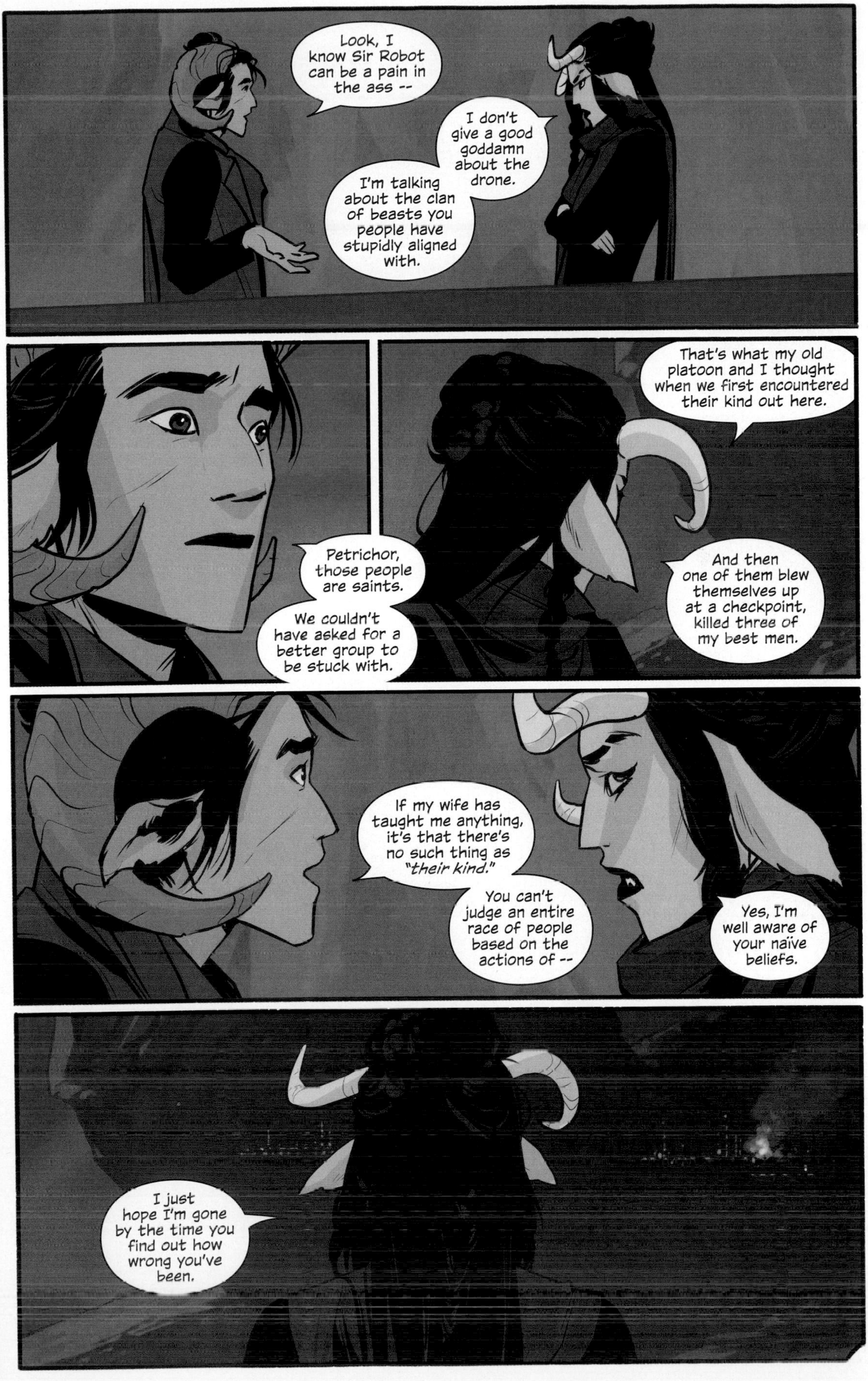
Look, I know Sir Robot can be a pain in the ass --
I don't give a good goddamn about the drone.
I'm talking about the clan of beasts you people have stupidly aligned with.
Petrichor, those people are saints.
We couldn't have asked for a better group to be stuck with.
That's what my old platoon and I thought when we first encountered their kind out here.
And then one of them blew themselves up at a checkpoint, killed three of my best men.
If my wife has taught me anything, it's that there's no such thing as *"their kind."*
You can't judge an entire race of people based on the actions of --
Yes, I'm well aware of your naïve beliefs.
I just hope I'm gone by the time you find out how wrong you've been.

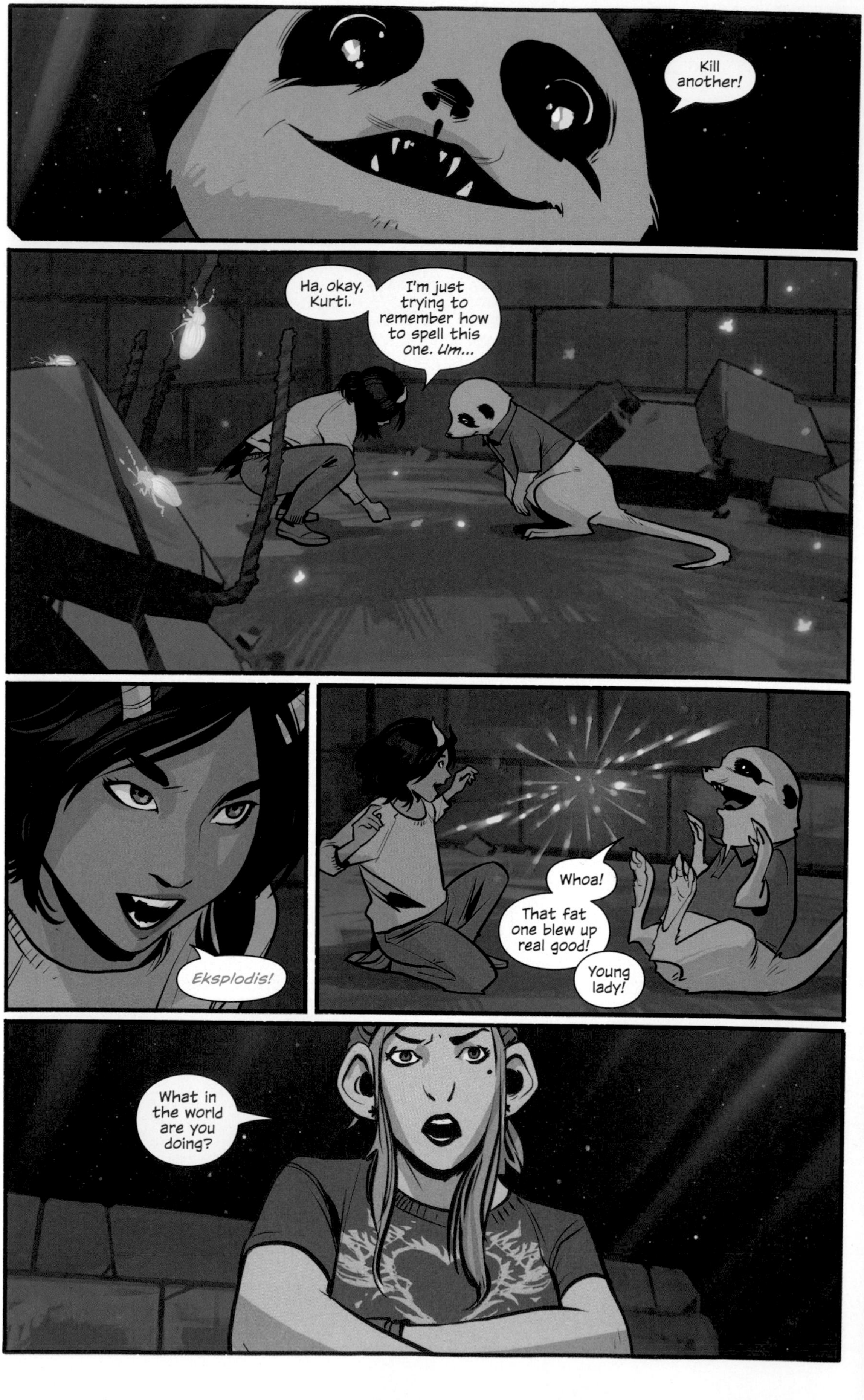
Kill another!
Ha, okay, Kurti.
I'm just trying to remember how to spell this one. *Um...*
Eksplodis!
Whoa!
That fat one blew up real good!
Young lady!
What in the world are you doing?

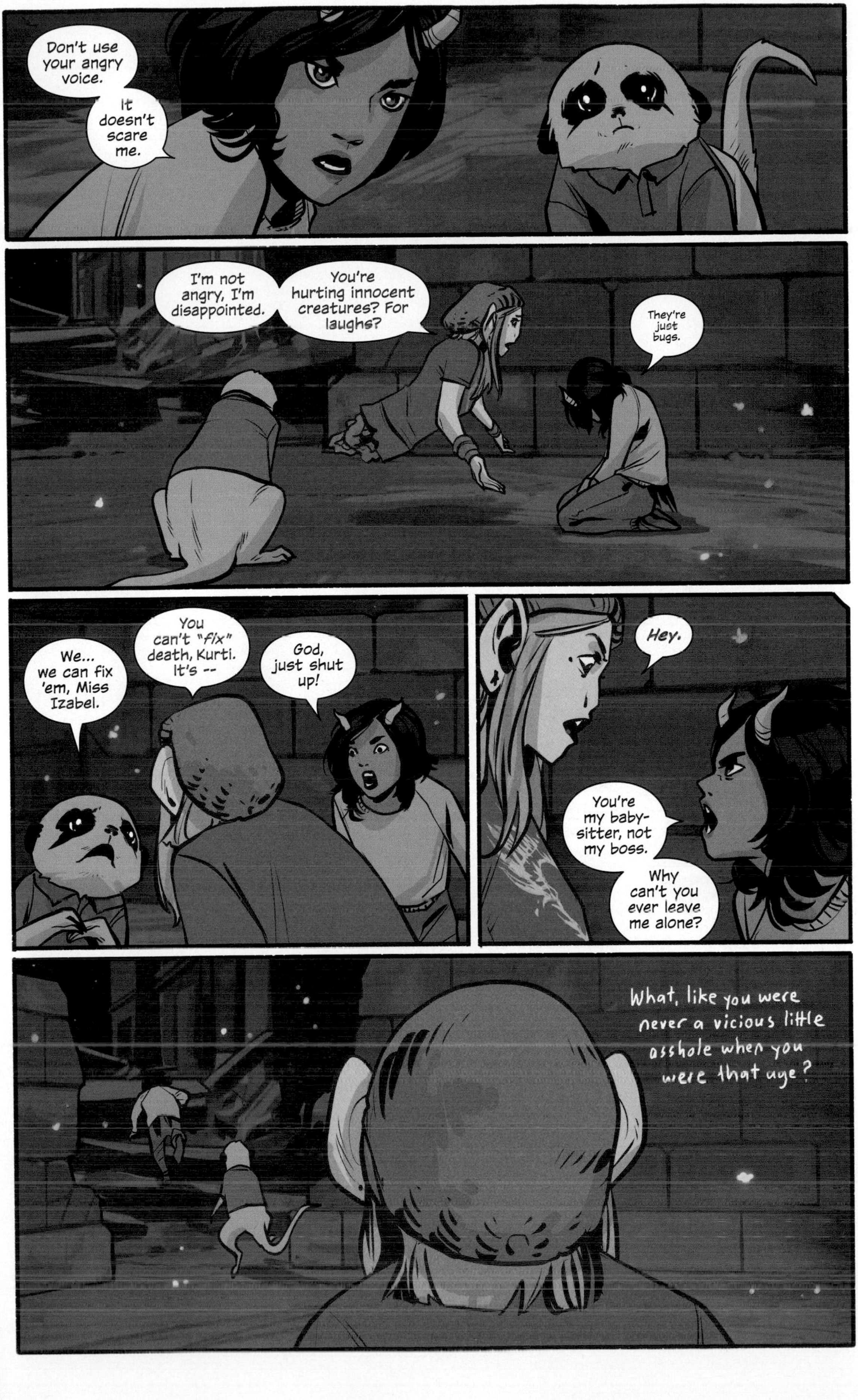
Don't use your angry voice.
It doesn't scare me.
I'm not angry, I'm disappointed.
You're hurting innocent creatures? For laughs?
They're just bugs.
We... we can fix 'em, Miss Izabel.
You can't "fix" death, Kurti. It's --
God, just shut up!
Hey.
You're my baby-sitter, not my boss.
Why can't you ever leave me alone?
What, like you were never a vicious little asshole when you were that age?

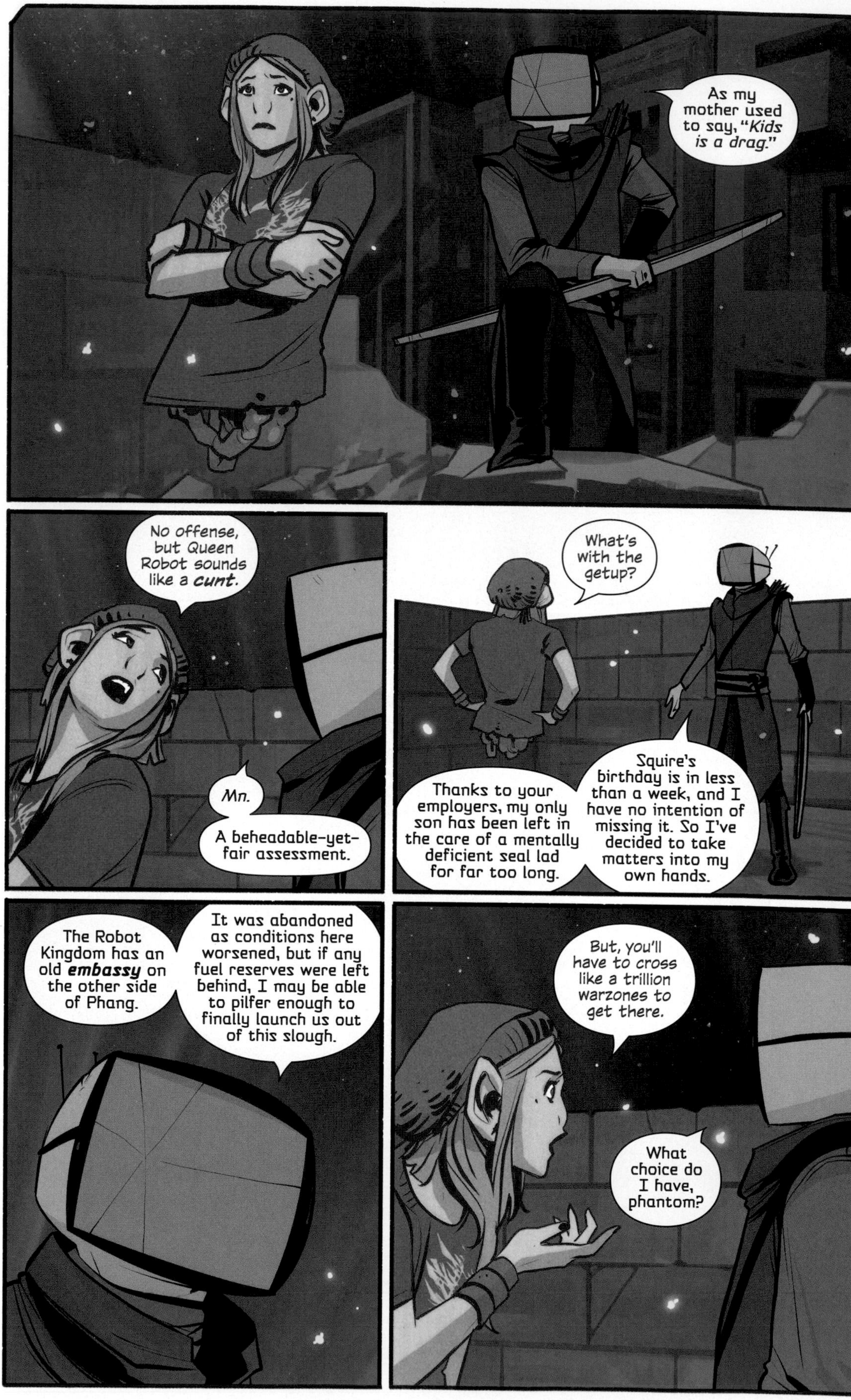
As my mother used to say, "*Kids is a drag.*"
No offense, but Queen Robot sounds like a ***cunt***.
Mn.
A beheadable-yet-fair assessment.
What's with the getup?
Thanks to your employers, my only son has been left in the care of a mentally deficient seal lad for far too long.
Squire's birthday is in less than a week, and I have no intention of missing it. So I've decided to take matters into my own hands.
The Robot Kingdom has an old ***embassy*** on the other side of Phang.
It was abandoned as conditions here worsened, but if any fuel reserves were left behind, I may be able to pilfer enough to finally launch us out of this slough.
But, you'll have to cross like a trillion warzones to get there.
What choice do I have, phantom?

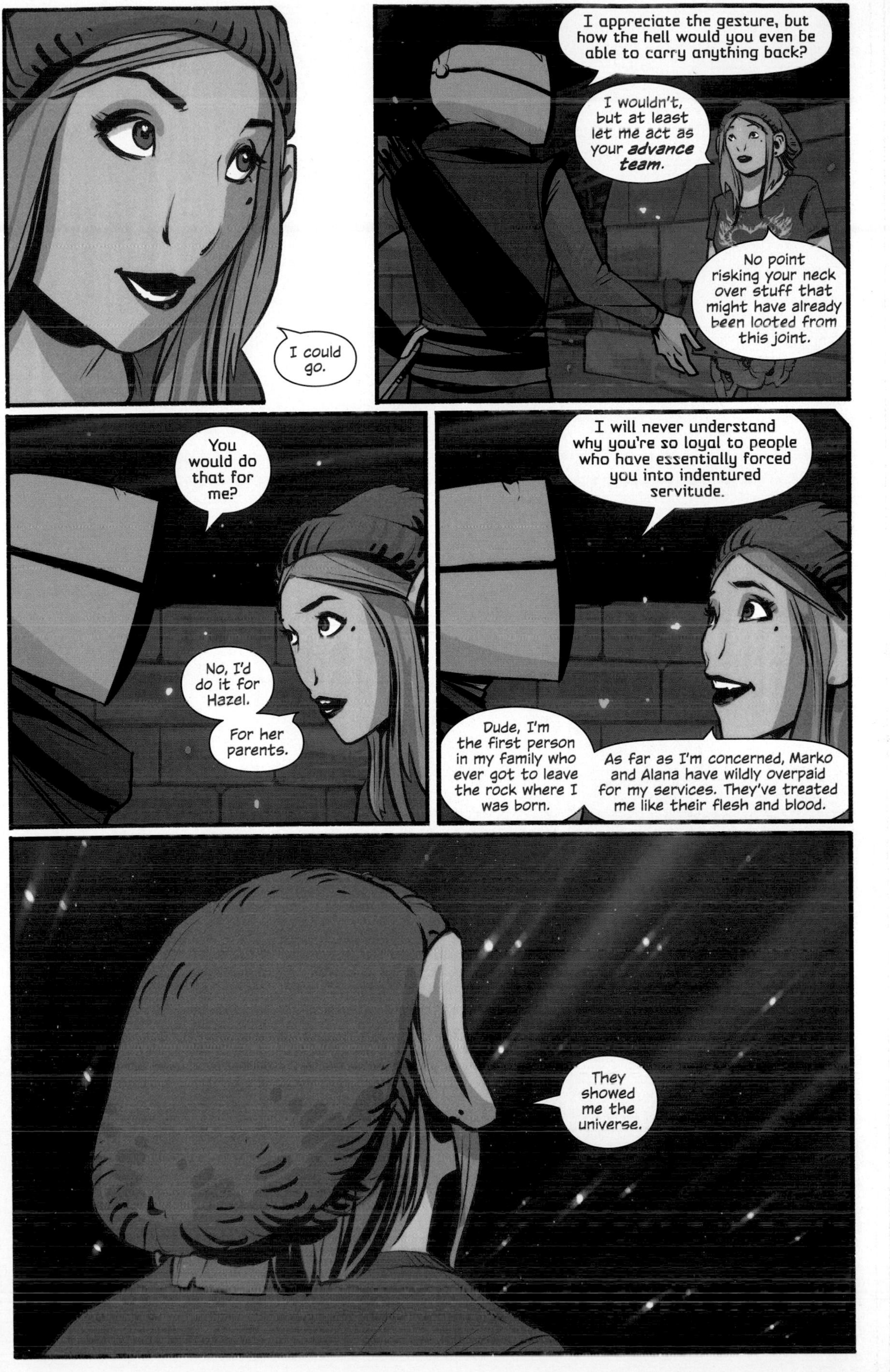
I could go.
I appreciate the gesture, but how the hell would you even be able to carry anything back?
I wouldn't, but at least let me act as your ***advance team***.
No point risking your neck over stuff that might have already been looted from this joint.
You would do that for me?
No, I'd do it for Hazel.
For her parents.
I will never understand why you're so loyal to people who have essentially forced you into indentured servitude.
Dude, I'm the first person in my family who ever got to leave the rock where I was born.
As far as I'm concerned, Marko and Alana have wildly overpaid for my services. They've treated me like their flesh and blood.
They showed me the universe.

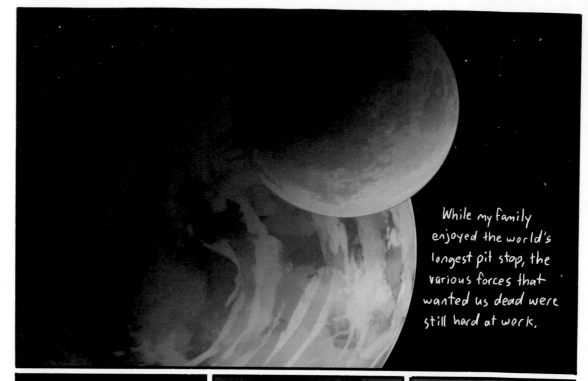

While my family enjoyed the world's longest pit stop, the various forces that wanted us dead were still hard at work.

Some harder than others.

BING BA DING

RRRRR

Knock it off, Sweet Boy.

I get she ain't your favorite cat, but --

Ĉu mi povas helpi vin?

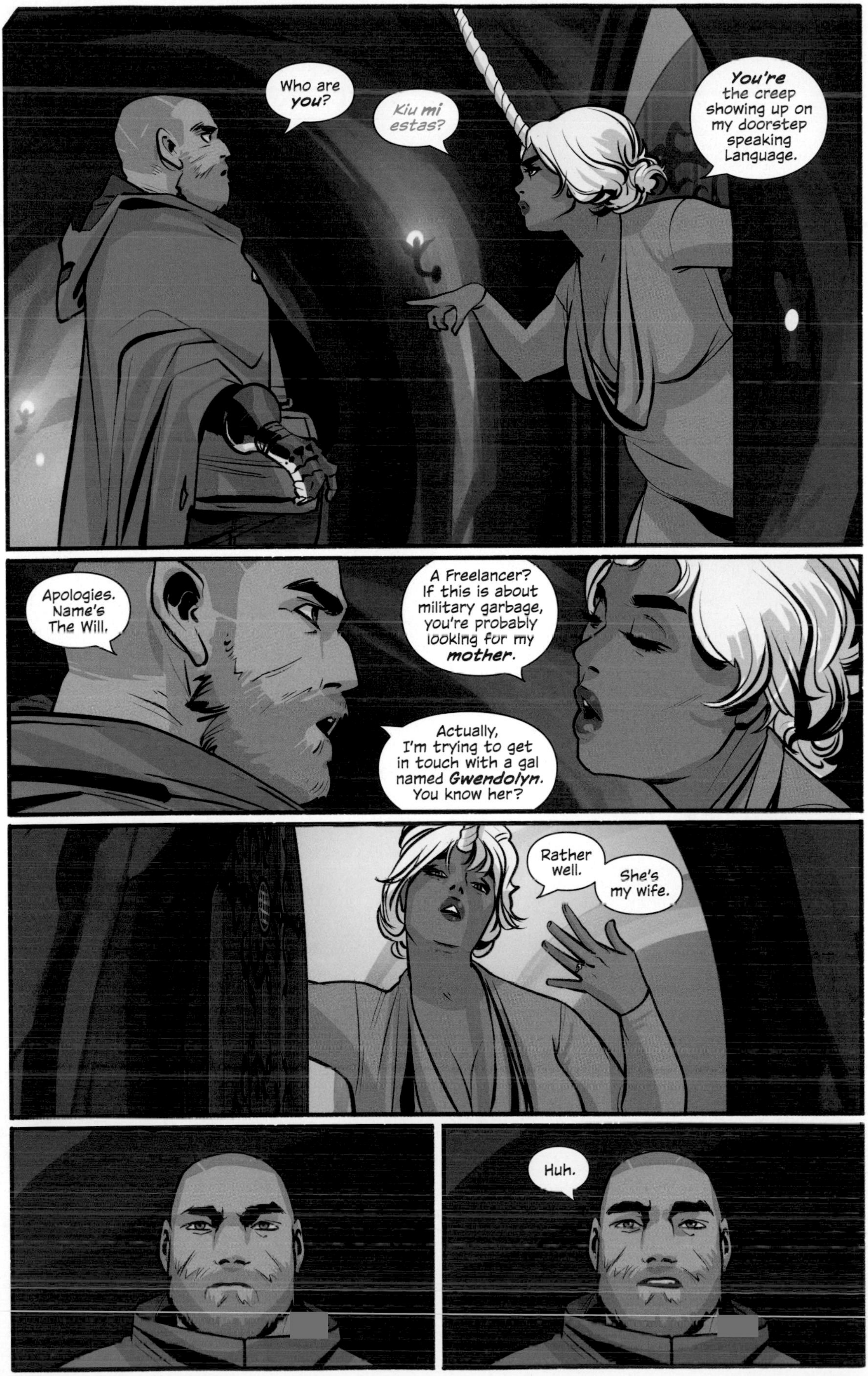

Who are you?
Kiu mi estas?
You're the creep showing up on my doorstep speaking Language.
Apologies. Name's The Will.
A Freelancer? If this is about military garbage, you're probably looking for my mother.
Actually, I'm trying to get in touch with a gal named Gwendolyn. You know her?
Rather well.
She's my wife.
Huh.

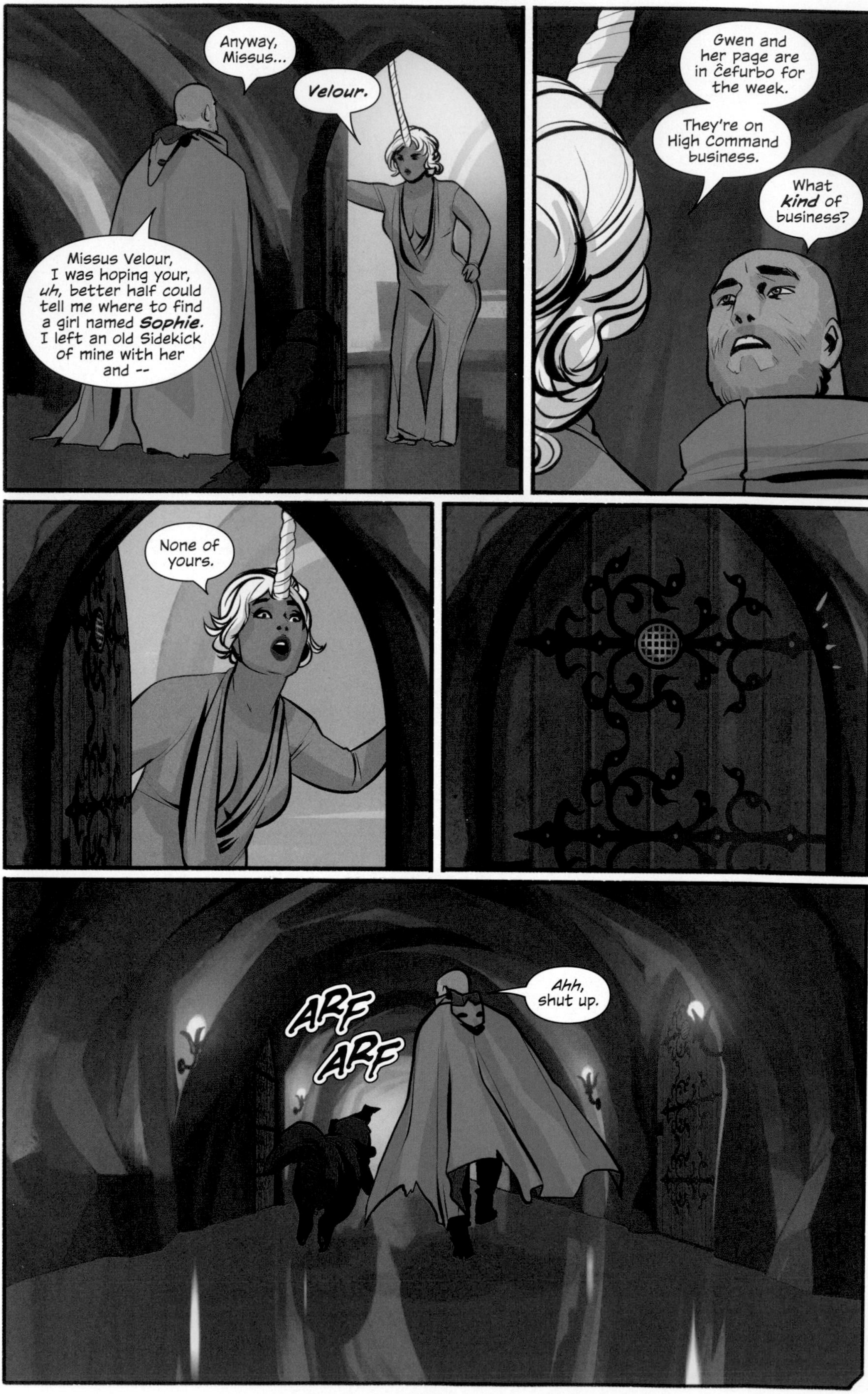

Anyway, Missus...
Velour.
Missus Velour, I was hoping your, uh, better half could tell me where to find a girl named Sophie. I left an old Sidekick of mine with her and --
Gwen and her page are in Ĉefurbo for the week.
They're on High Command business.
What kind of business?
None of yours.
ARF
ARF
Ahh, shut up.

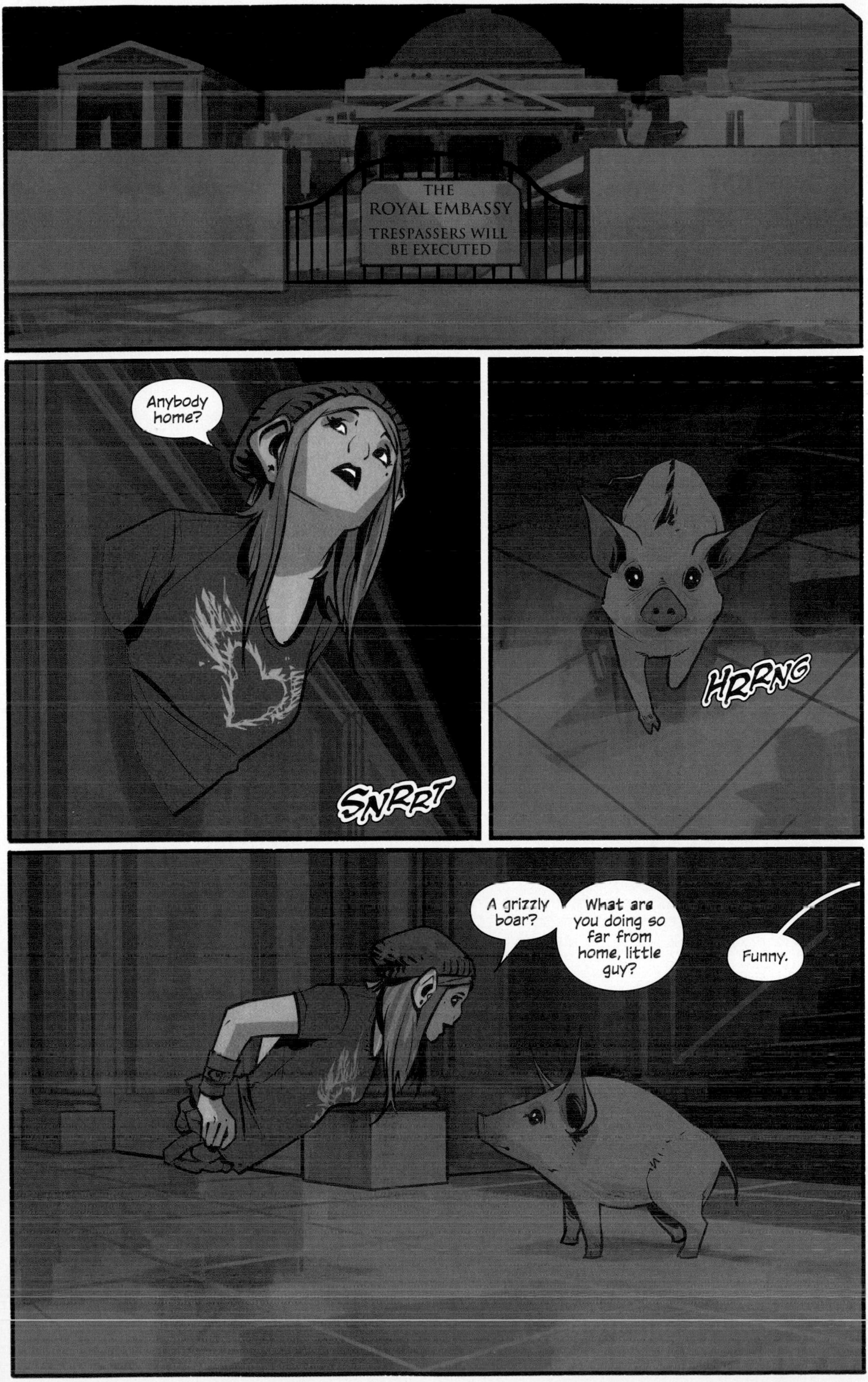
THE
ROYAL EMBASSY
TRESPASSERS WILL
BE EXECUTED
Anybody home?
SNRRT
HRRNG
A grizzly boar?
What are you doing so far from home, little guy?
Funny.

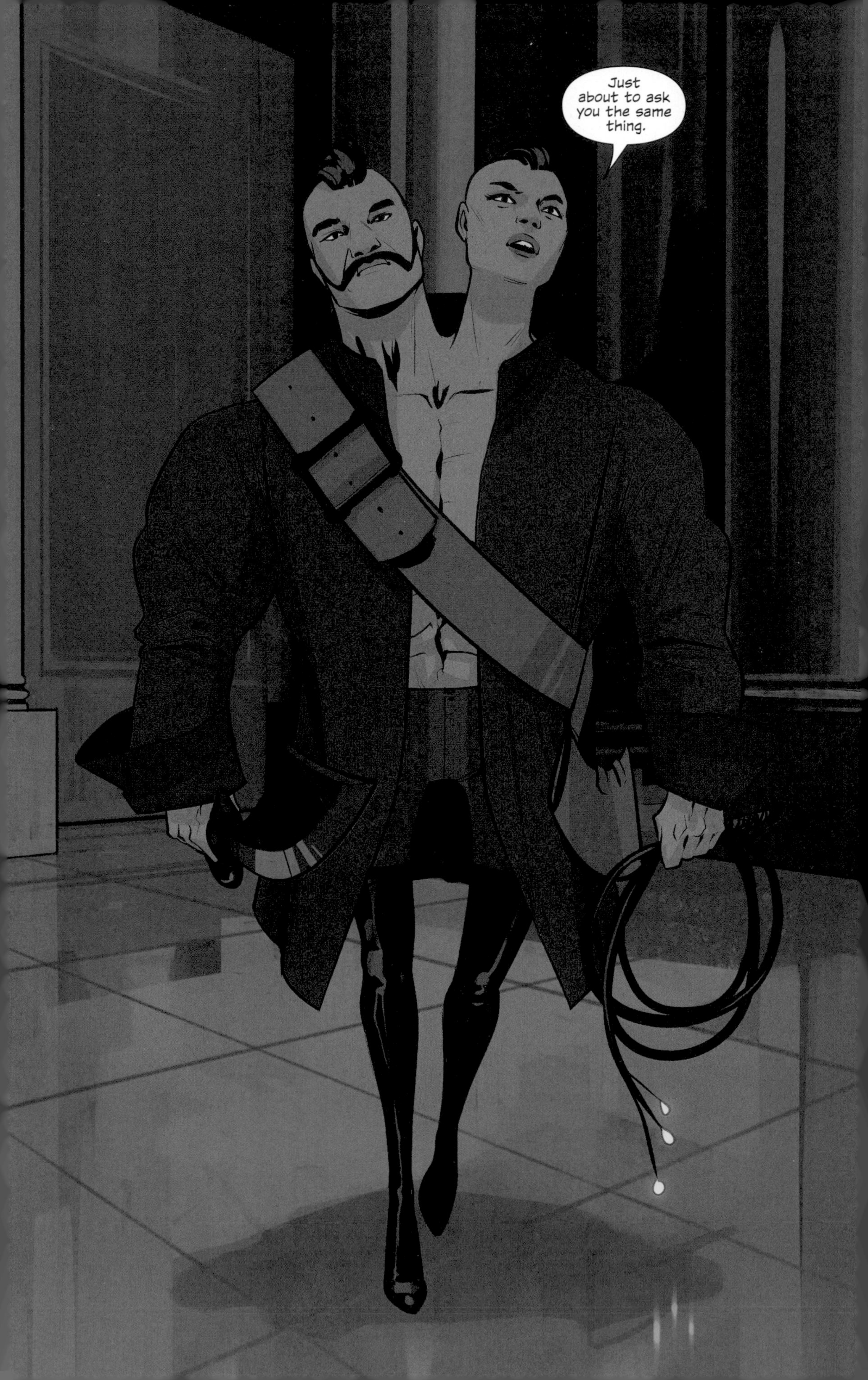
Just about to ask you the same thing.

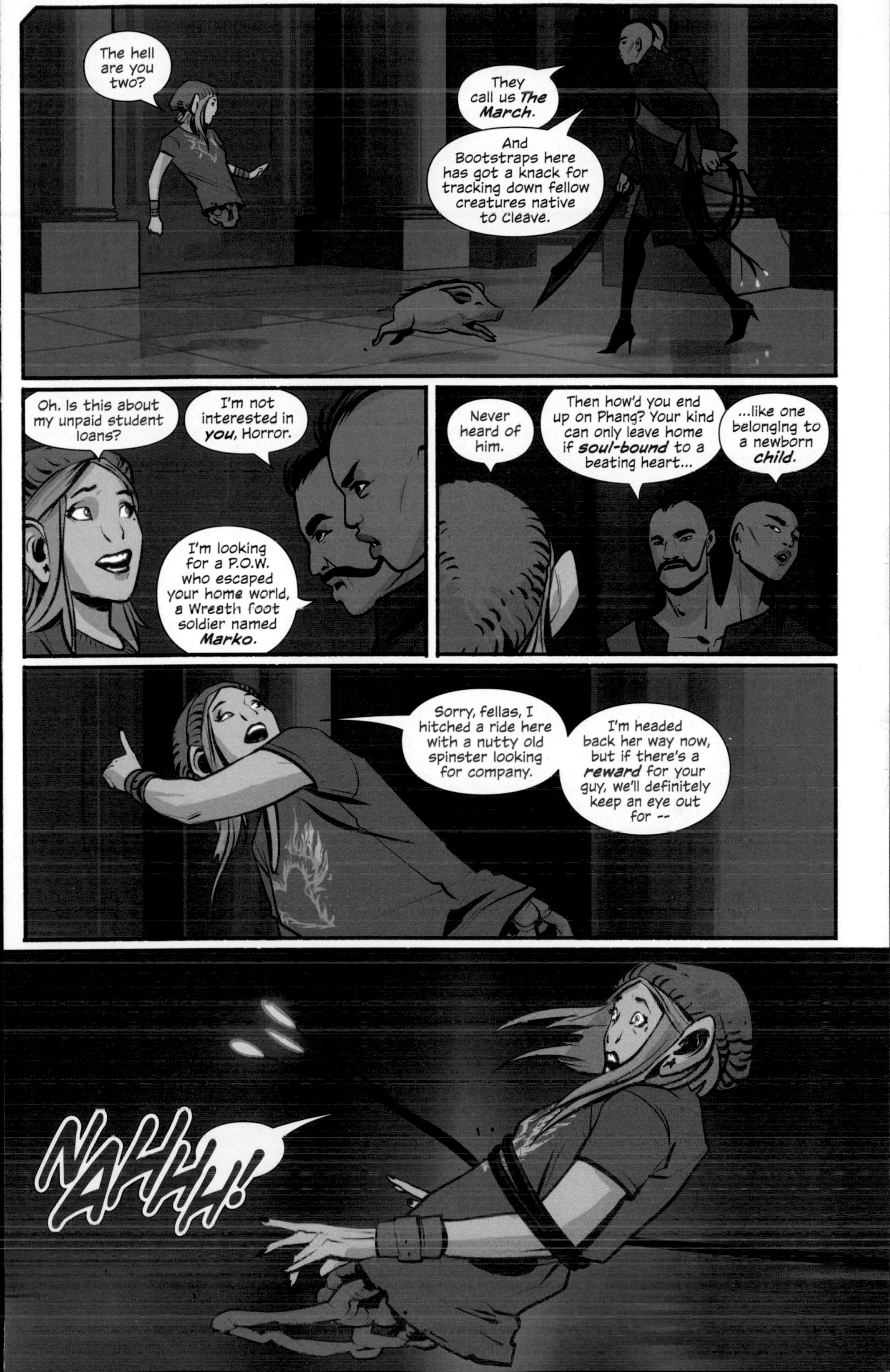
The hell are you two?
They call us *The March*.
And Bootstraps here has got a knack for tracking down fellow creatures native to Cleave.
Oh. Is this about my unpaid student loans?
I'm not interested in *you*, Horror.
I'm looking for a P.O.W. who escaped your home world, a Wreath foot soldier named *Marko*.
Never heard of him.
Then how'd you end up on Phang? Your kind can only leave home if *soul-bound* to a beating heart...
...like one belonging to a newborn *child*.
Sorry, fellas, I hitched a ride here with a nutty old spinster looking for company.
I'm headed back her way now, but if there's a *reward* for your guy, we'll definitely keep an eye out for --
NAHHH!

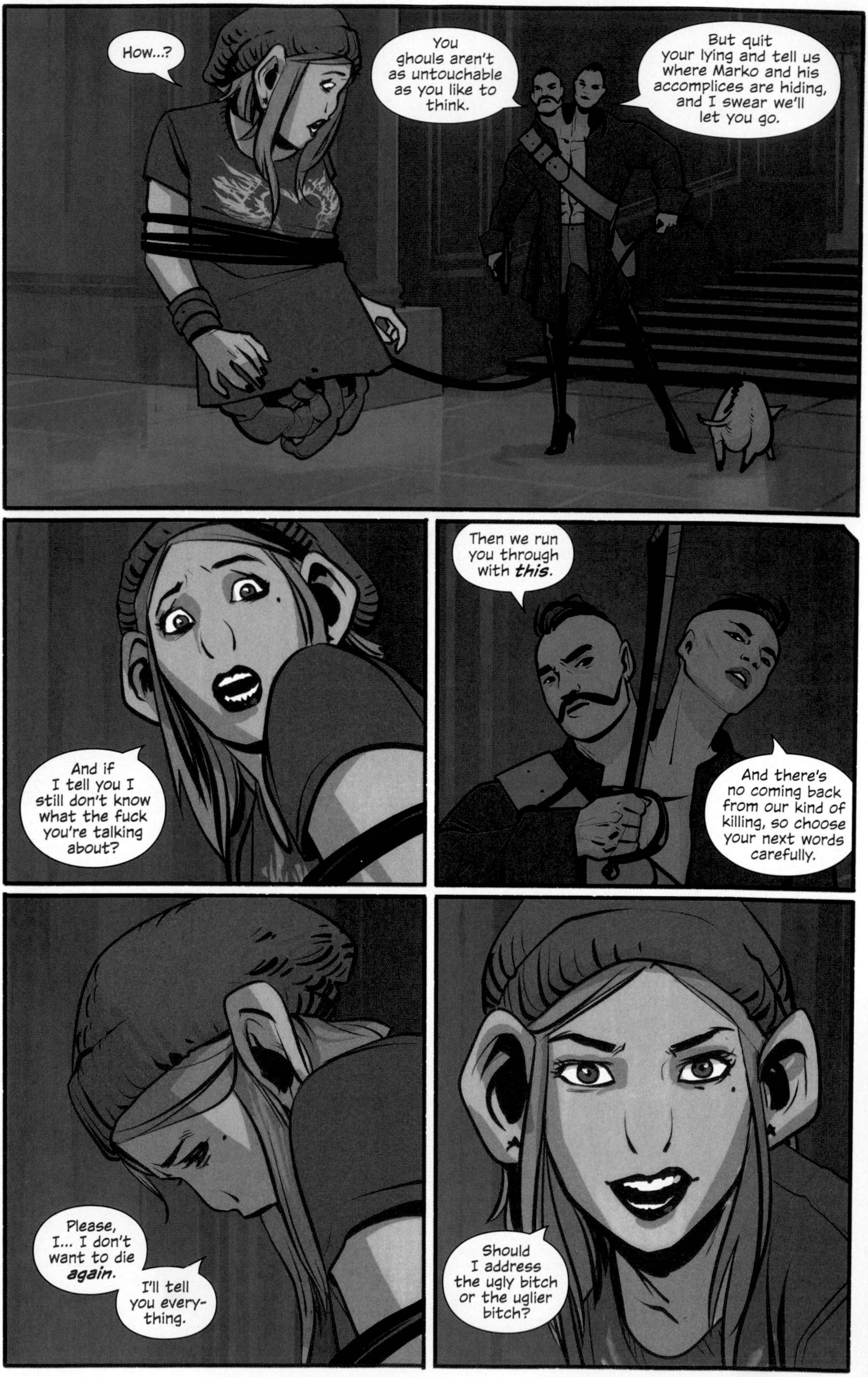
How...?
You ghouls aren't as untouchable as you like to think.
But quit your lying and tell us where Marko and his accomplices are hiding, and I swear we'll let you go.
And if I tell you I still don't know what the fuck you're talking about?
Then we run you through with *this*.
And there's no coming back from our kind of killing, so choose your next words carefully.
Please, I... I don't want to die *again*.
I'll tell you every-thing.
Should I address the ugly bitch or the uglier bitch?

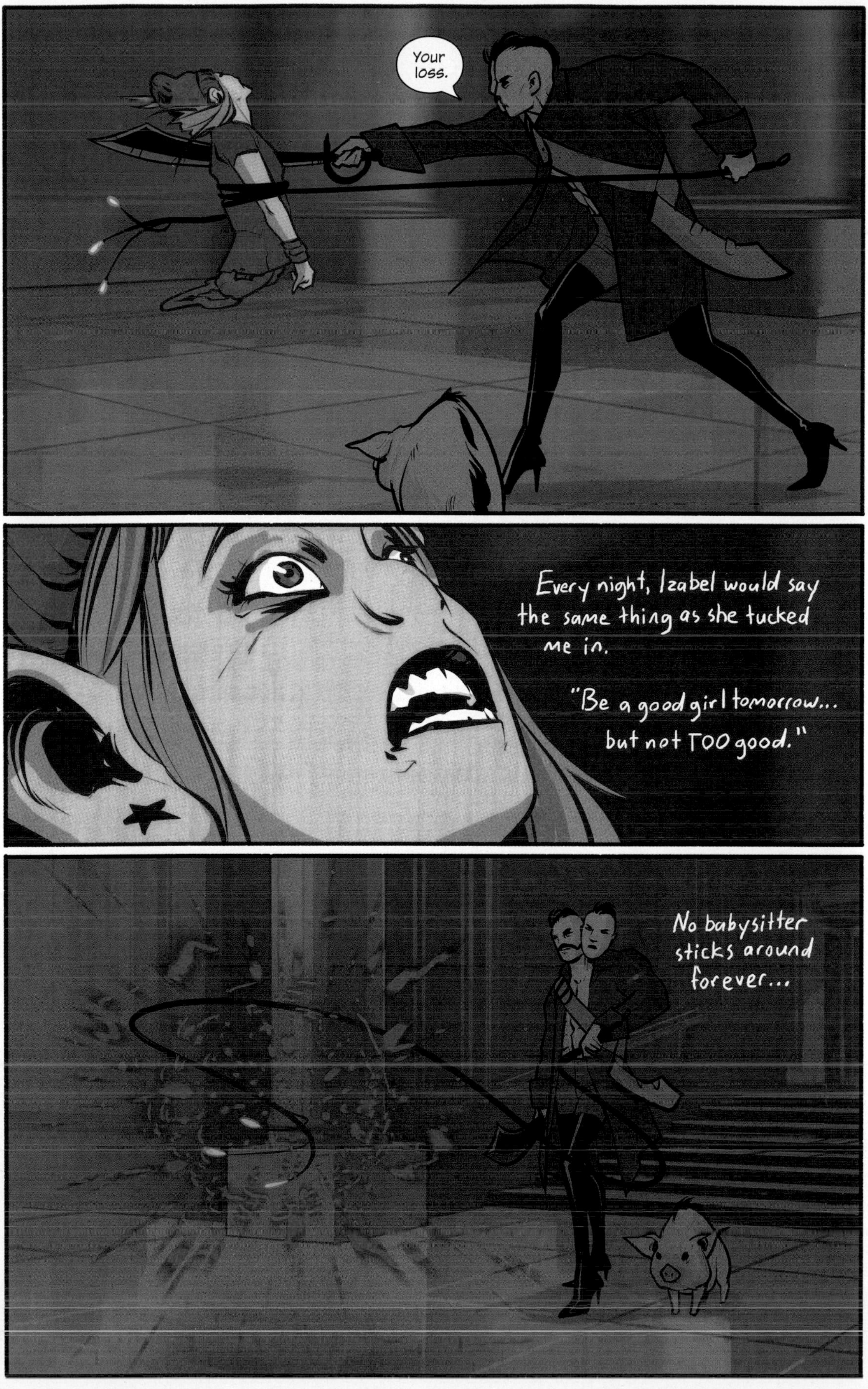
Your loss.
Every night, Izabel would say the same thing as she tucked me in.
"Be a good girl tomorrow... but not TOO good."
No babysitter sticks around forever...

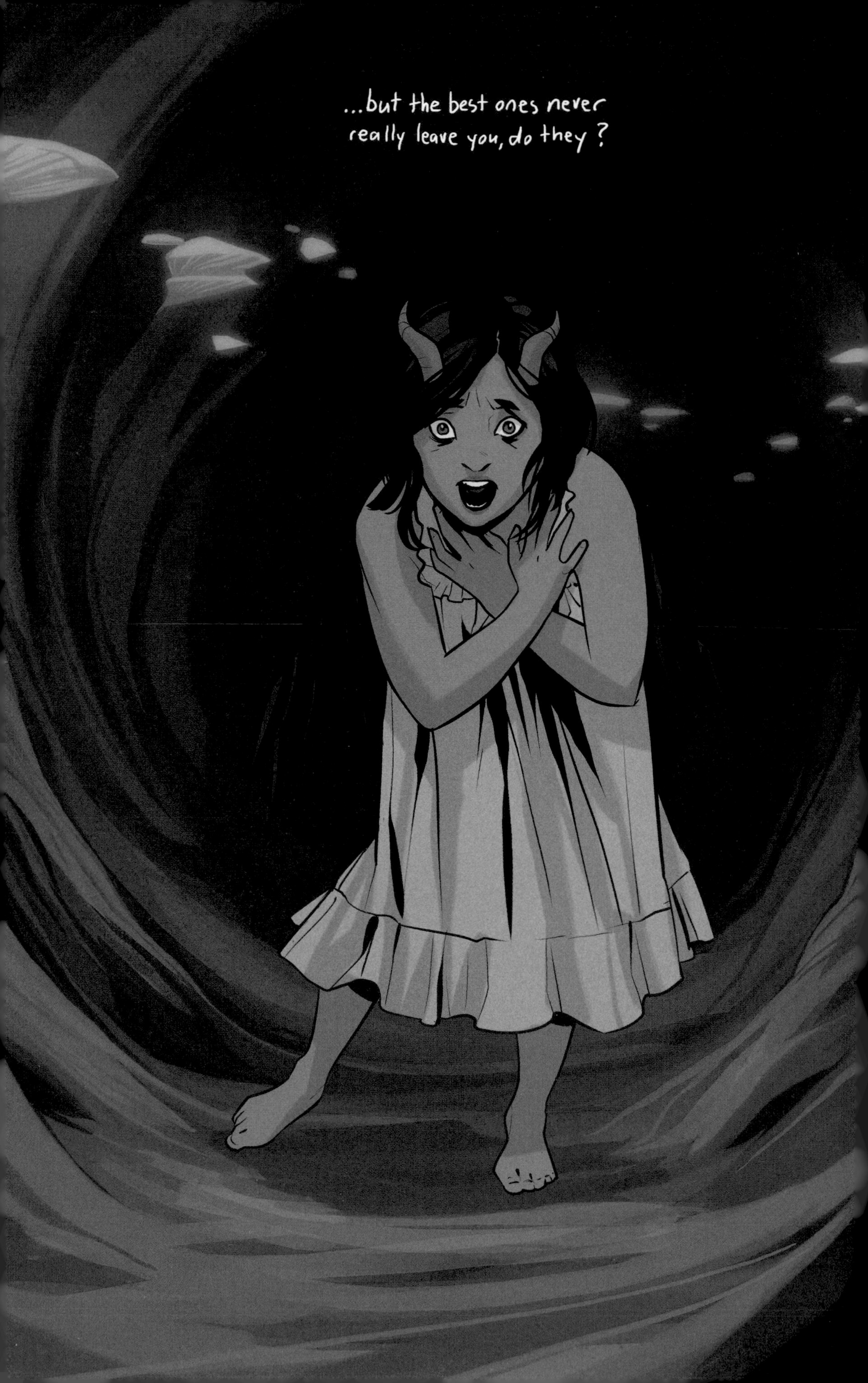
...but the best ones never really leave you, do they?

end chapter thirty-eight

CHAPTER

THIRTY-NINE

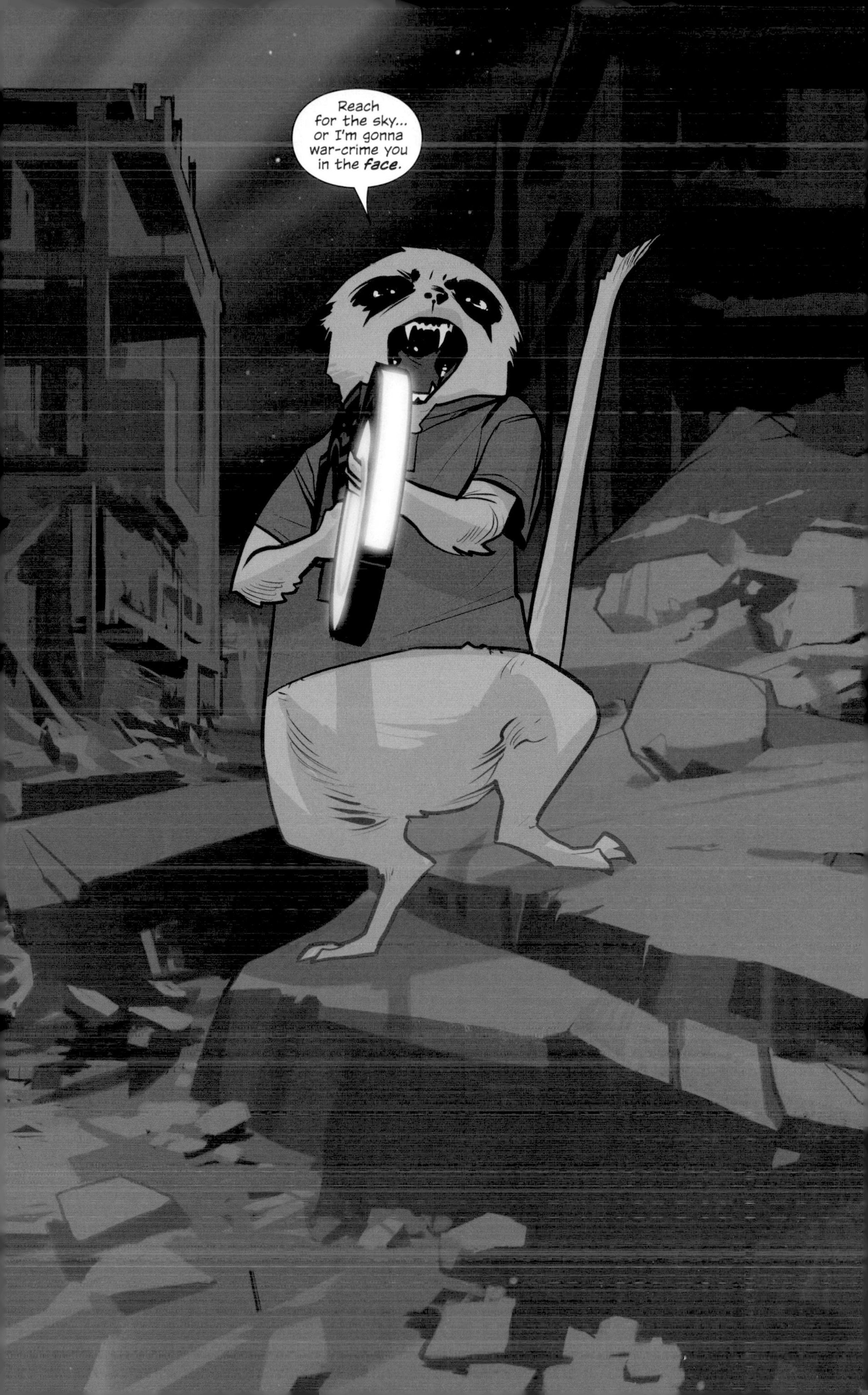
Reach for the sky... or I'm gonna war-crime you in the *face*.

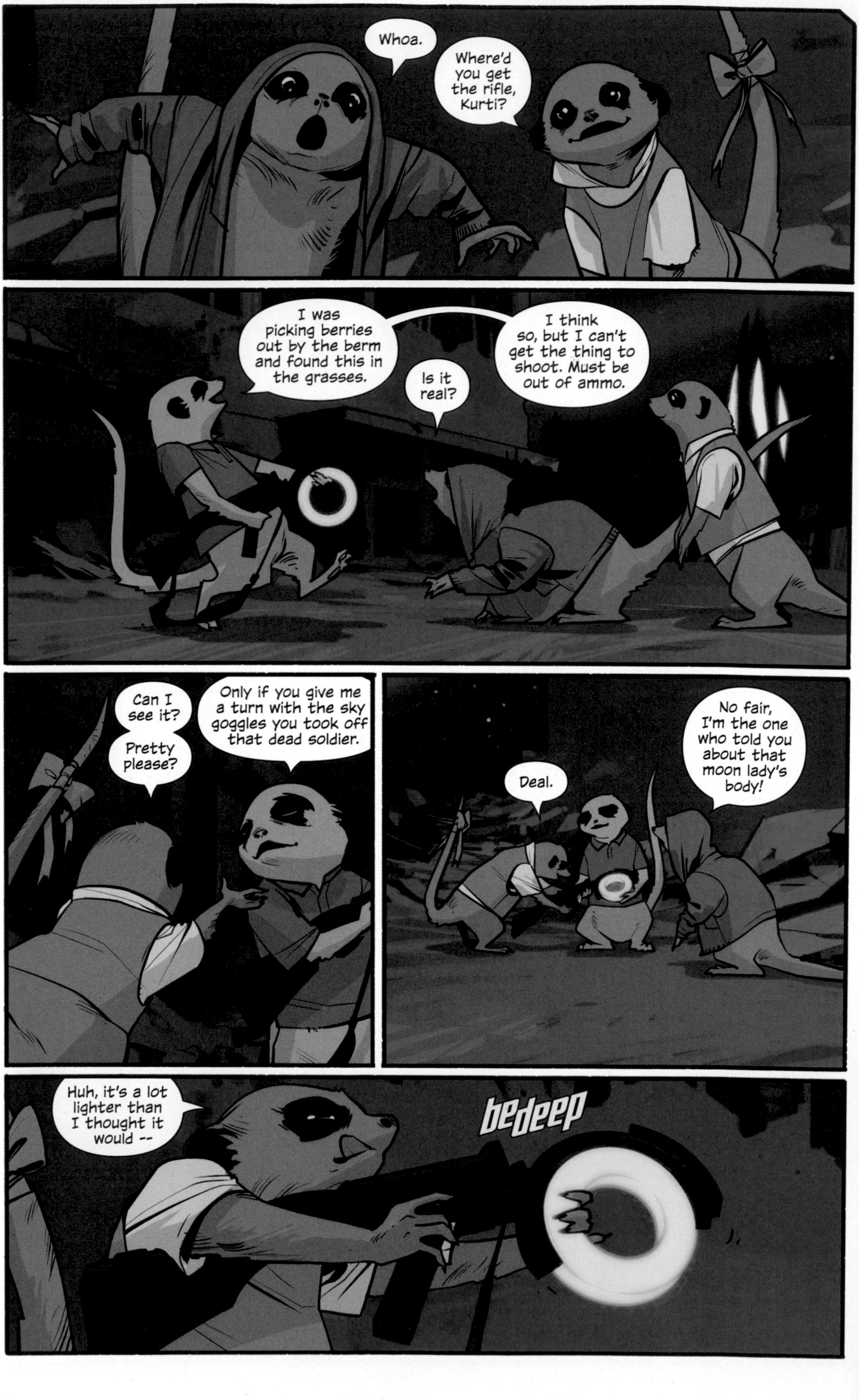
Whoa.
Where'd you get the rifle, Kurti?
I was picking berries out by the berm and found this in the grasses.
Is it real?
I think so, but I can't get the thing to shoot. Must be out of ammo.
Can I see it?
Pretty please?
Only if you give me a turn with the sky goggles you took off that dead soldier.
Deal.
No fair, I'm the one who told you about that moon lady's body!
Huh, it's a lot lighter than I thought it would --
bedeep

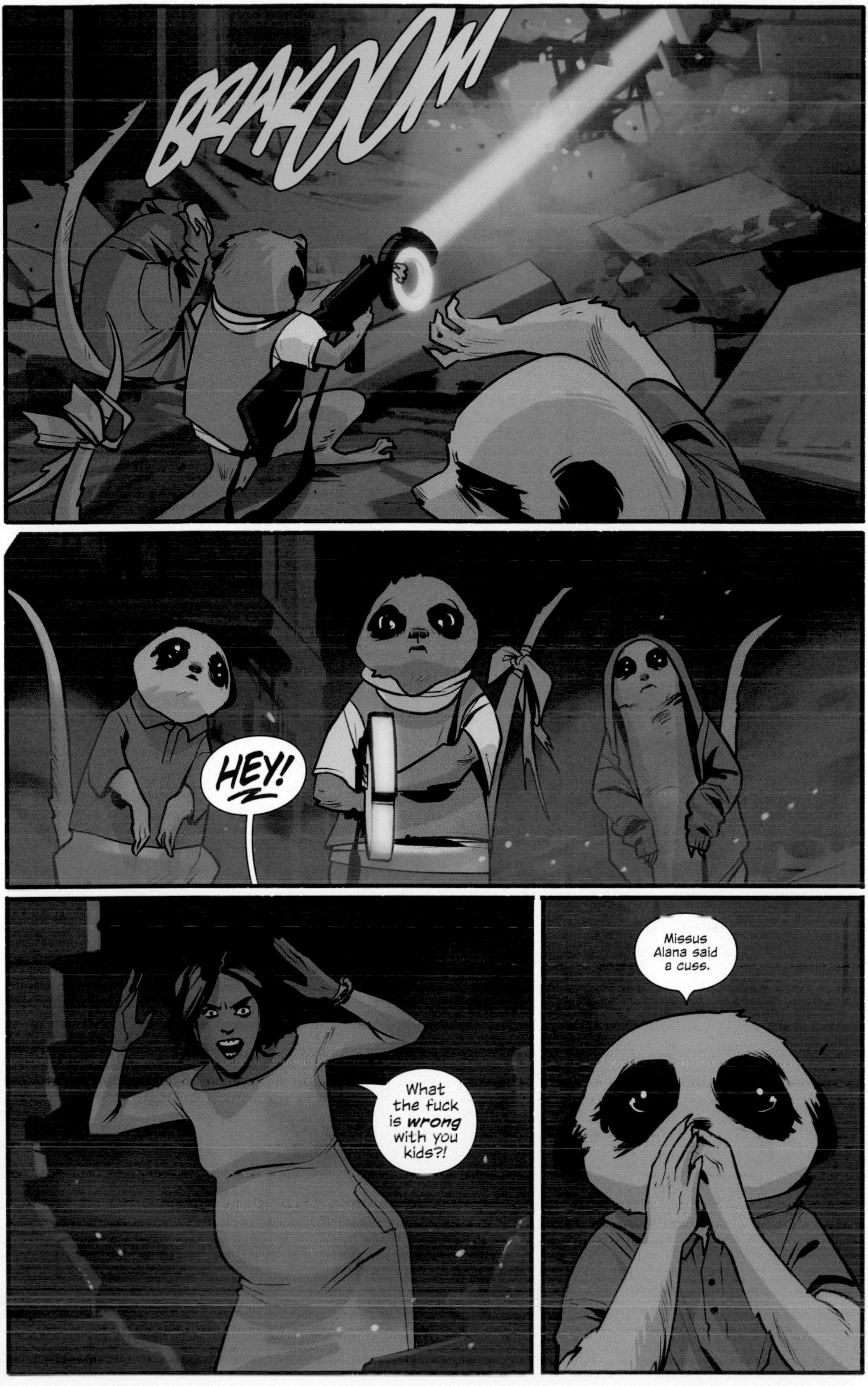
BRAKOOM
HEY!
What the fuck is **wrong** with you kids?!
Missus Alana said a cuss.

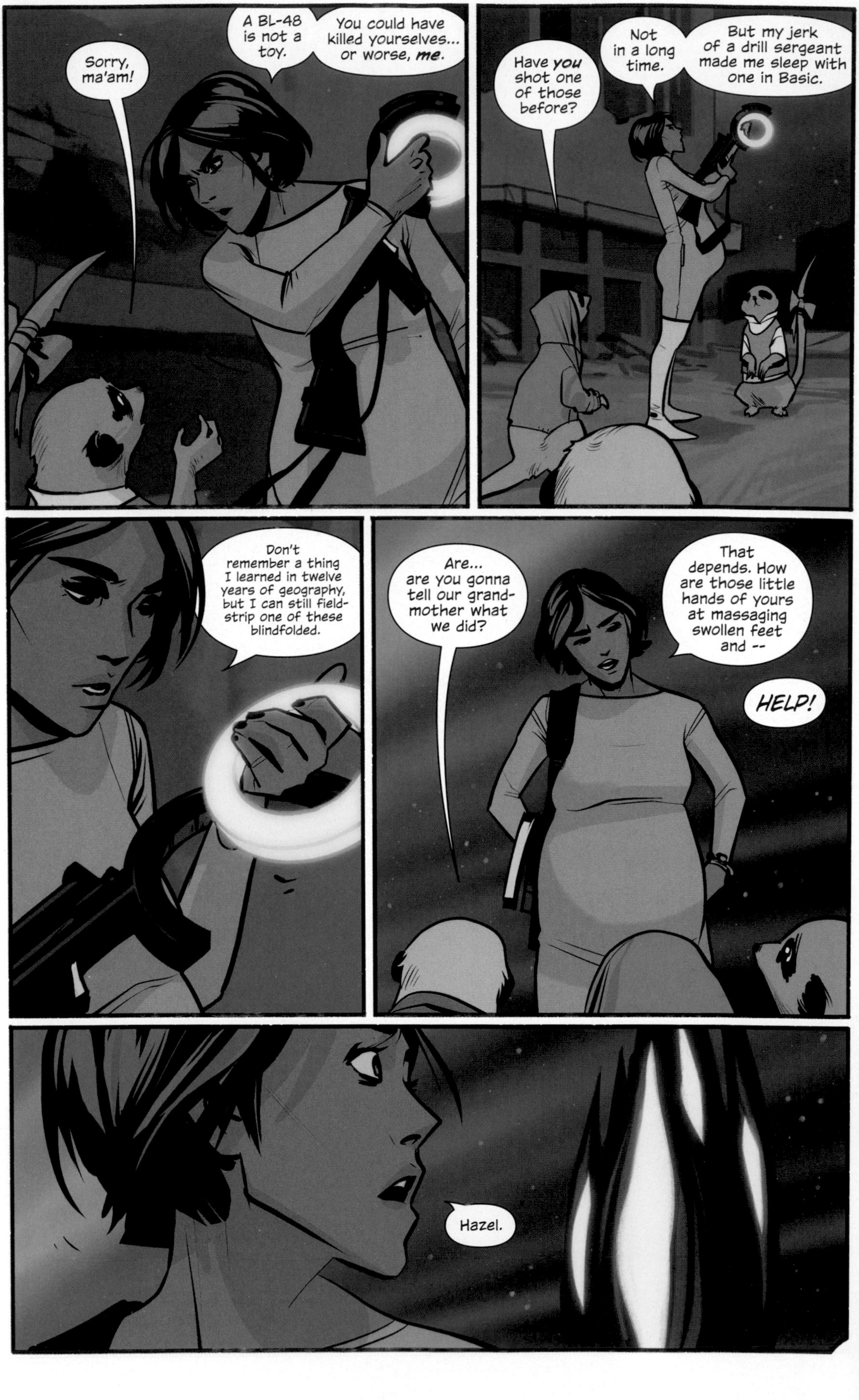
Sorry, ma'am!
A BL-48 is not a toy.
You could have killed yourselves... or worse, *me*.
Have *you* shot one of those before?
Not in a long time.
But my jerk of a drill sergeant made me sleep with one in Basic.
Don't remember a thing I learned in twelve years of geography, but I can still field-strip one of these blindfolded.
Are... are you gonna tell our grand-mother what we did?
That depends. How are those little hands of yours at massaging swollen feet and --
HELP!
Hazel.

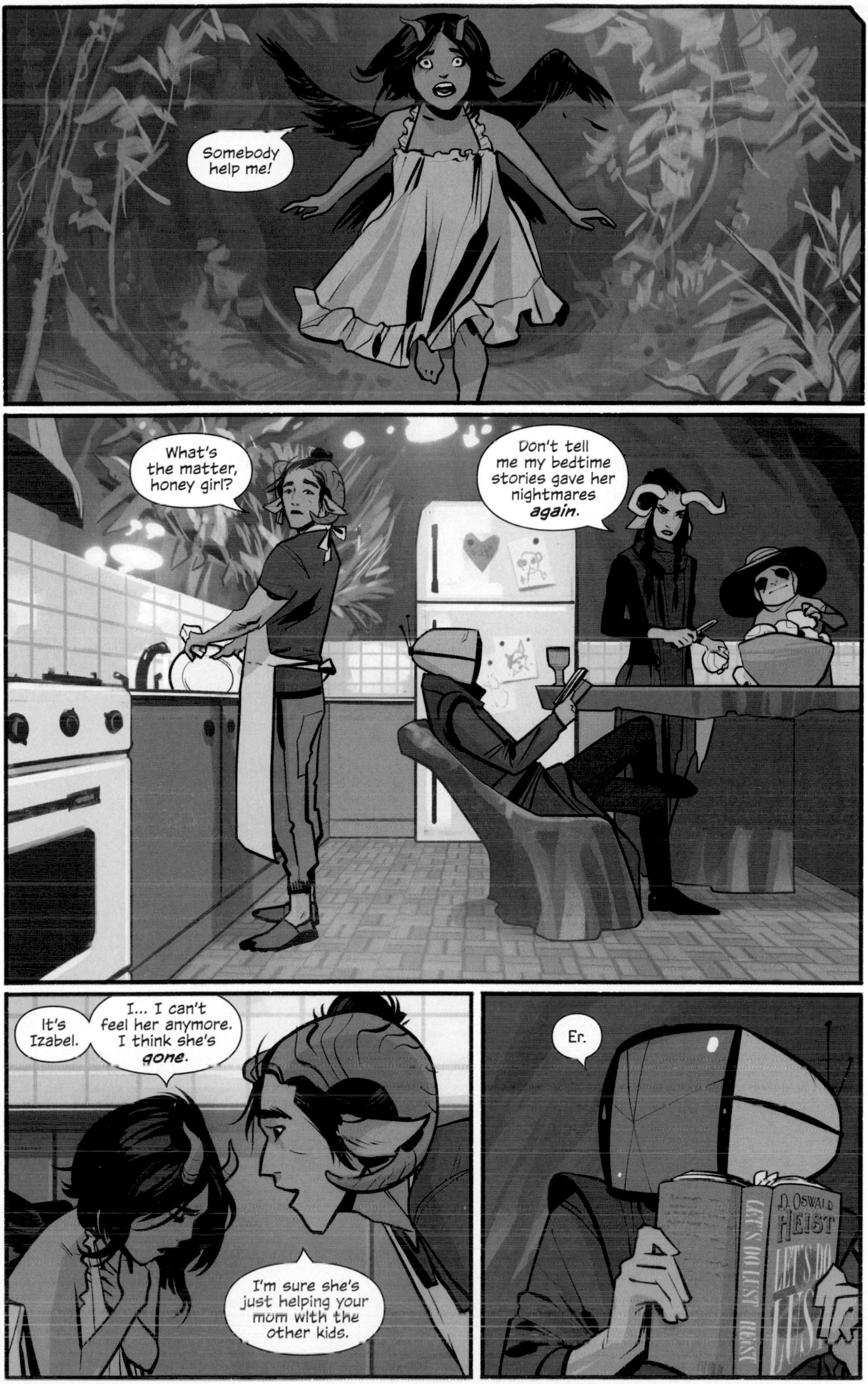
Somebody help me!
What's the matter, honey girl?
Don't tell me my bedtime stories gave her nightmares *again*.
It's Izabel.
I... I can't feel her anymore. I think she's *gone*.
I'm sure she's just helping your mom with the other kids.
Er.
D. OSWALD HEIST
LET'S DO LUST

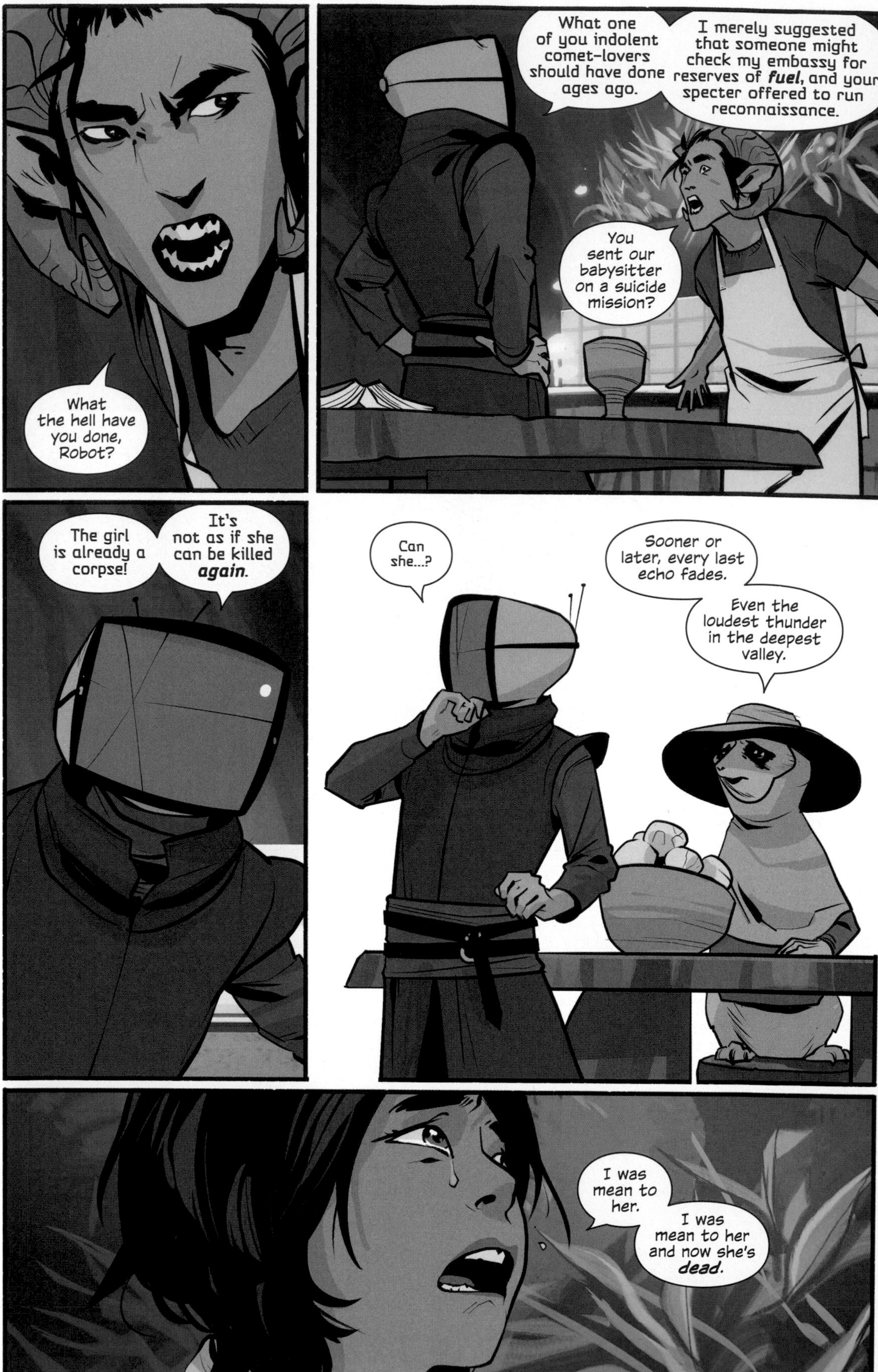
What the hell have you done, Robot?
What one of you indolent comet-lovers should have done ages ago.
I merely suggested that someone might check my embassy for reserves of *fuel*, and your specter offered to run reconnaissance.
You sent our babysitter on a suicide mission?
The girl is already a corpse!
It's not as if she can be killed *again*.
Can she...?
Sooner or later, every last echo fades.
Even the loudest thunder in the deepest valley.
I was mean to her.
I was mean to her and now she's *dead*.

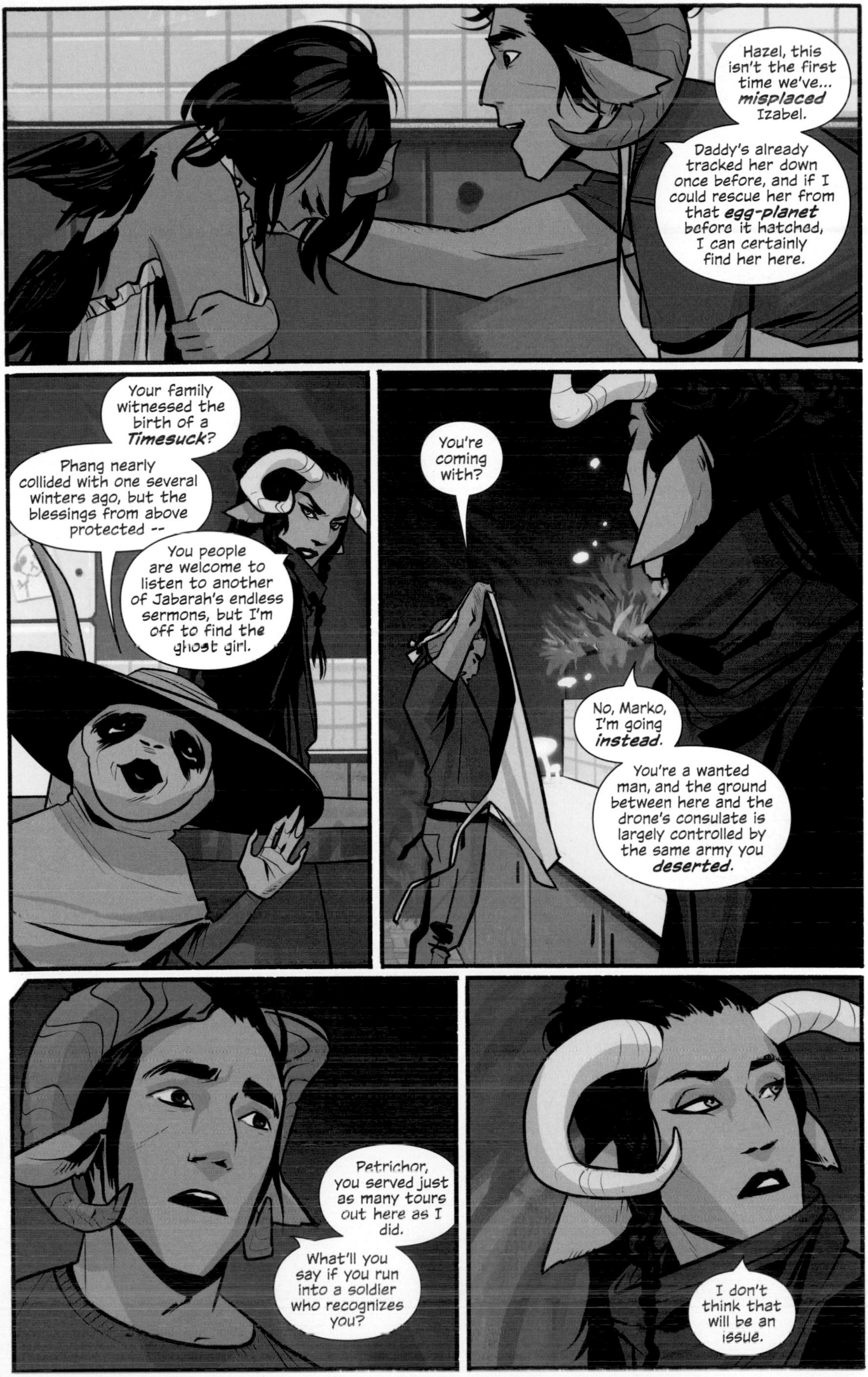
Hazel, this isn't the first time we've... *misplaced* Izabel.
Daddy's already tracked her down once before, and if I could rescue her from that *egg-planet* before it hatched, I can certainly find her here.
Your family witnessed the birth of a *Timesuck*?
Phang nearly collided with one several winters ago, but the blessings from above protected --
You people are welcome to listen to another of Jabarah's endless sermons, but I'm off to find the ghost girl.
You're coming with?
No, Marko, I'm going *instead*.
You're a wanted man, and the ground between here and the drone's consulate is largely controlled by the same army you *deserted*.
Petrichor, you served just as many tours out here as I did.
What'll you say if you run into a soldier who recognizes you?
I don't think that will be an issue.

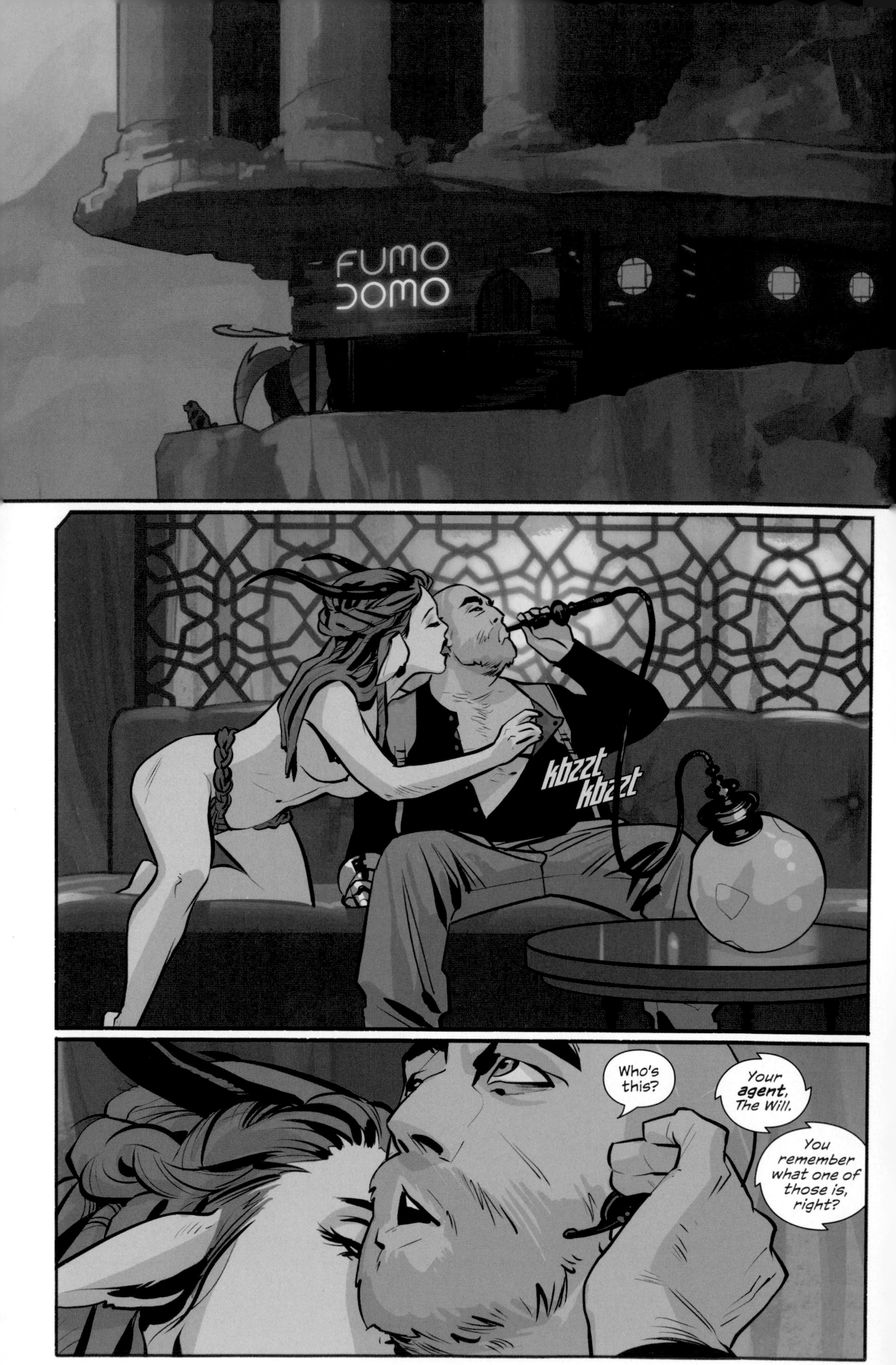
FUMO DOMO
kbzzt kbzzt
Who's this?
Your agent, The Will.
You remember what one of those is, right?

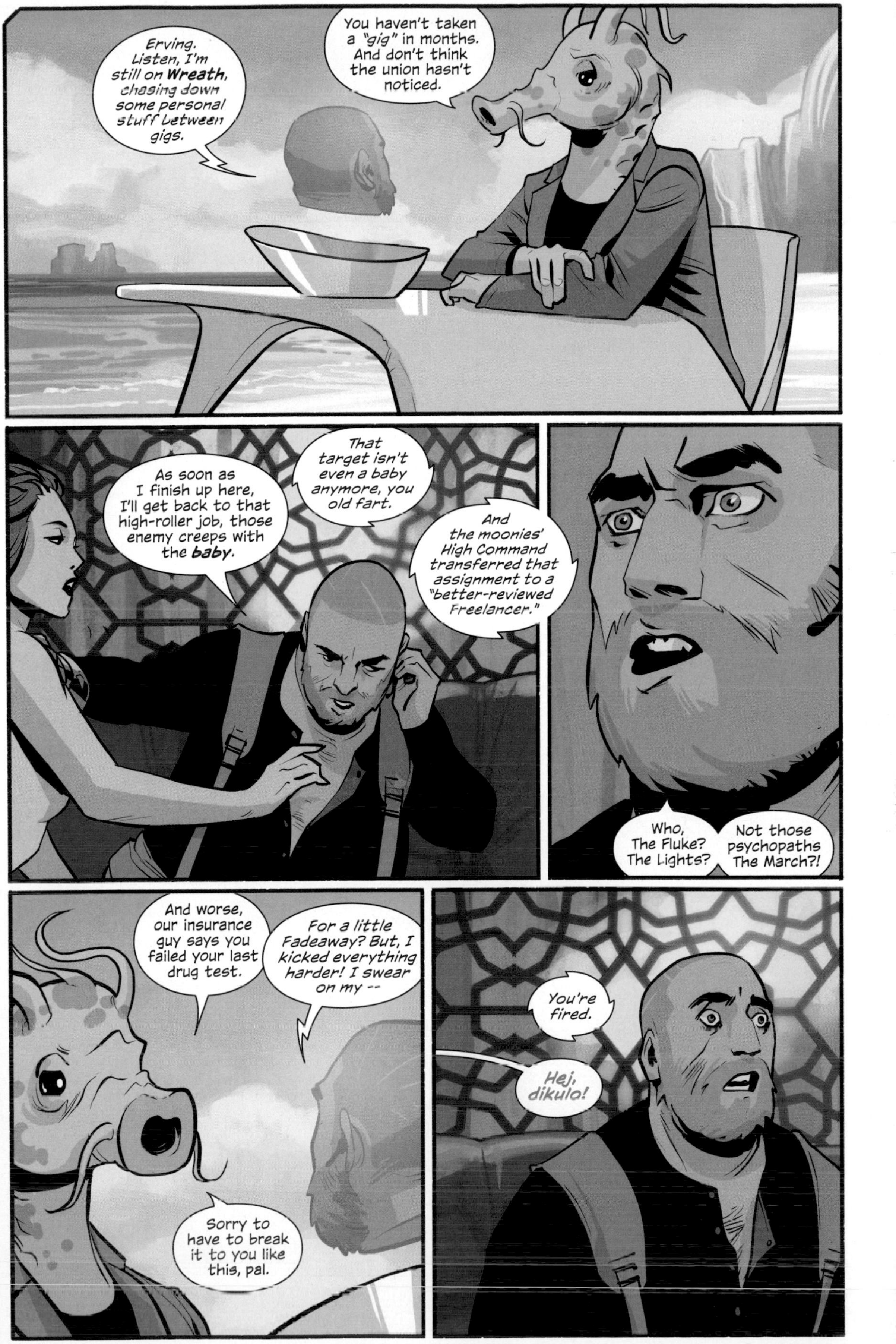

Erving. Listen, I'm still on **Wreath**, chasing down some personal stuff between gigs.
You haven't taken a *"gig"* in months. And don't think the union hasn't noticed.
As soon as I finish up here, I'll get back to that high-roller job, those enemy creeps with the ***baby***.
That target isn't even a baby anymore, you old fart.
And the moonies' High Command transferred that assignment to a "better-reviewed Freelancer."
Who, The Fluke? The Lights?
Not those psychopaths The March?!
And worse, our insurance guy says you failed your last drug test.
For a little Fadeaway? But, I kicked everything harder! I swear on my --
Sorry to have to break it to you like this, pal.
You're fired.
Hej, dikulo!

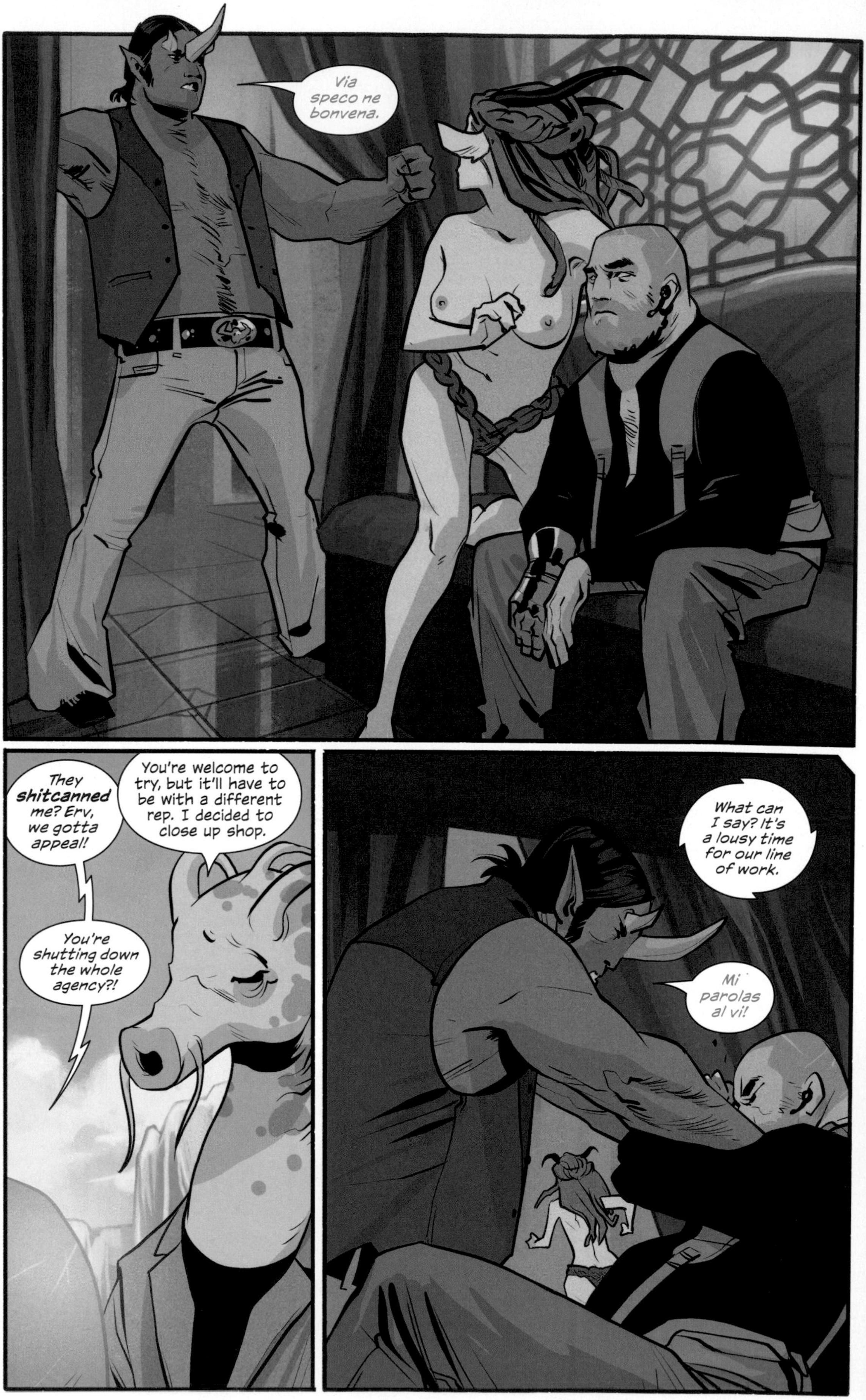
Via speco ne bonvena.
They **shitcanned** me? Erv, we gotta appeal!
You're welcome to try, but it'll have to be with a different rep. I decided to close up shop.
You're shutting down the whole agency?!
What can I say? It's a lousy time for our line of work.
Mi parolas al vi!

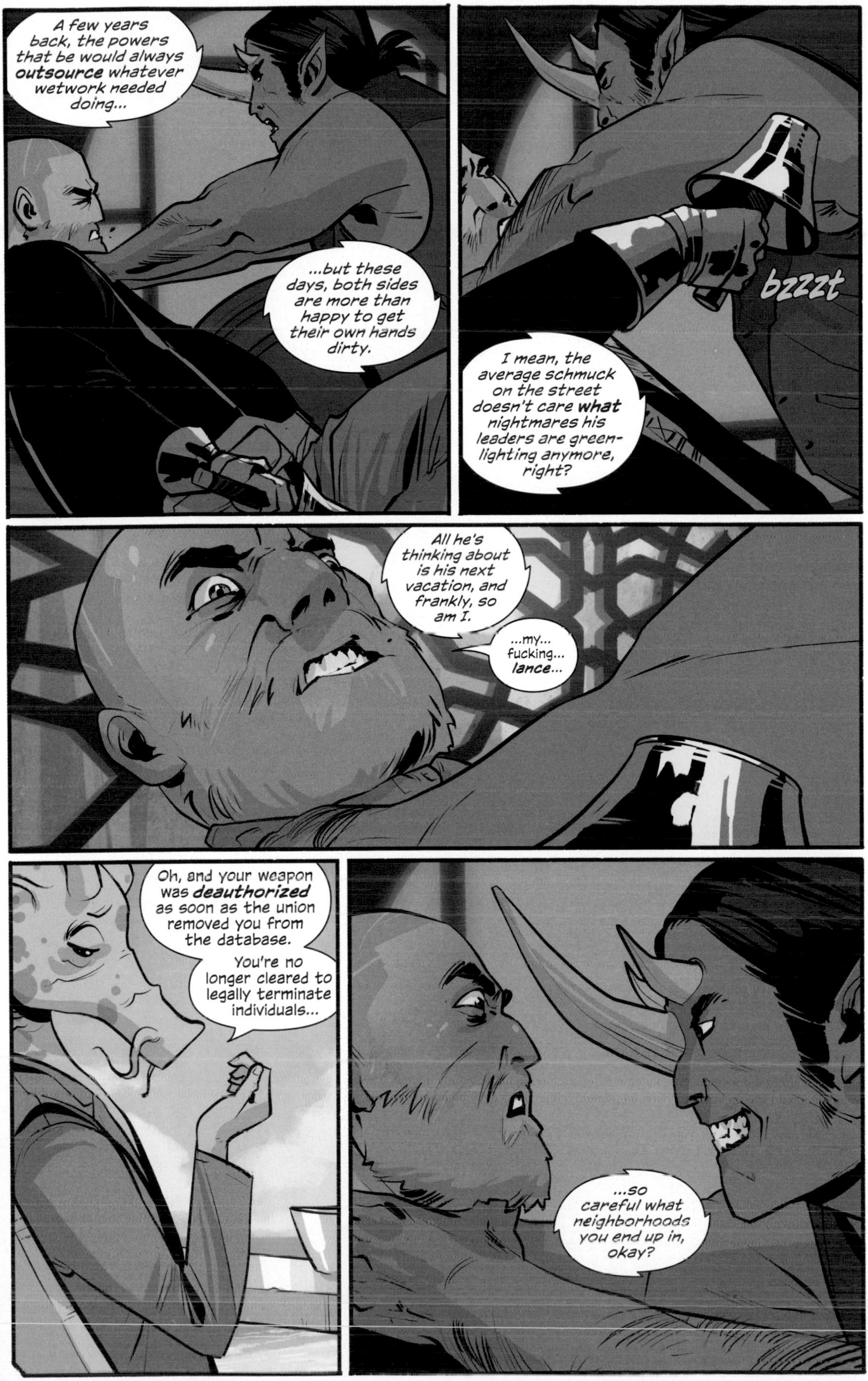
A few years back, the powers that be would always **outsource** whatever wetwork needed doing...
...but these days, both sides are more than happy to get their own hands dirty.
bzzzt
I mean, the average schmuck on the street doesn't care **what** nightmares his leaders are green-lighting anymore, right?
All he's thinking about is his next vacation, and frankly, so am I.
...my... fucking... **lance**...
Oh, and your weapon was **deauthorized** as soon as the union removed you from the database.
You're no longer cleared to legally terminate individuals...
...so careful what neighborhoods you end up in, okay?

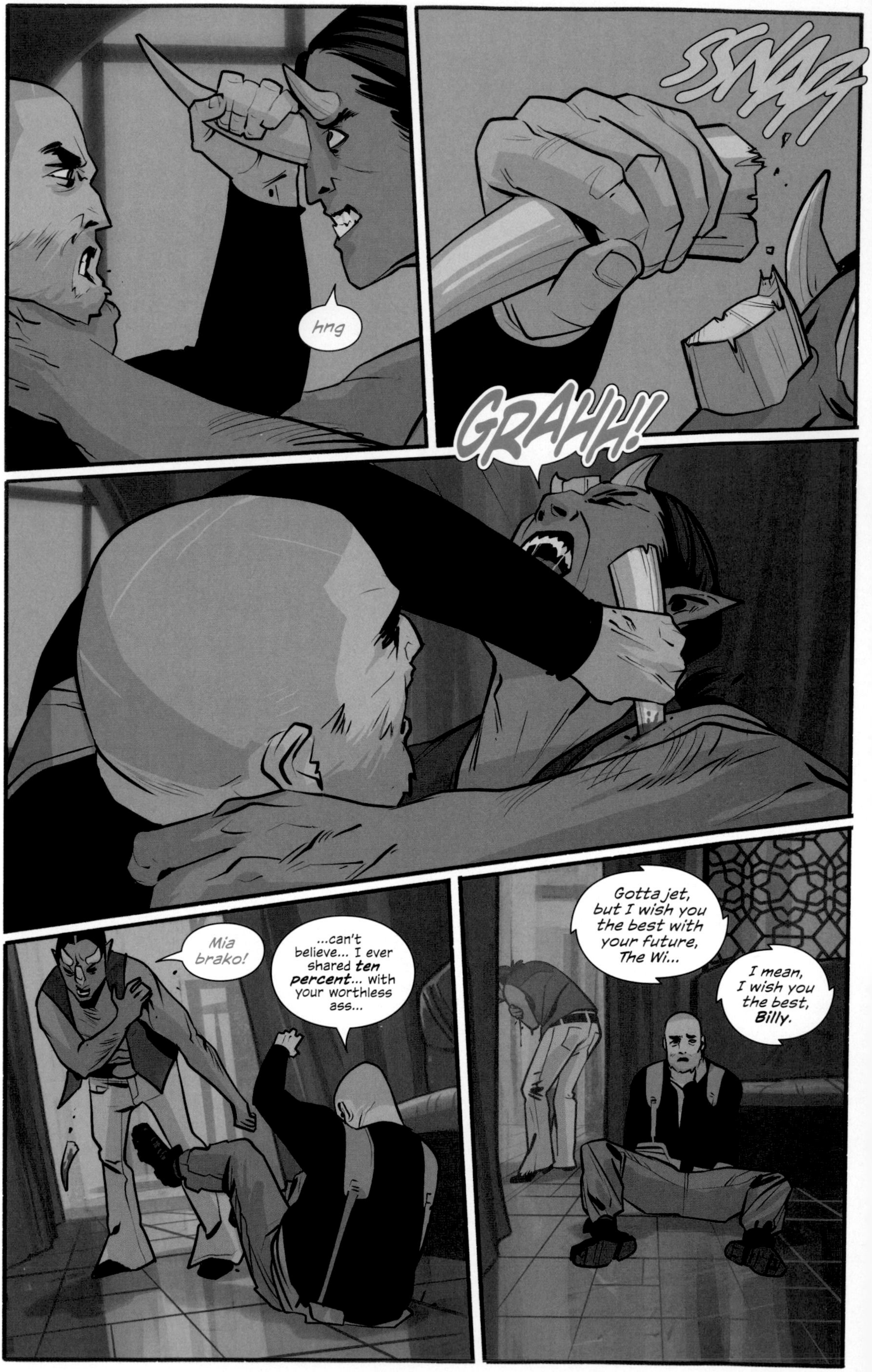
hng
SSNAP!
GRAHH!
Mia brako!
...can't believe... I ever shared **ten percent**... with your worthless ass...
Gotta jet, but I wish you the best with your future, The Wi...
I mean, I wish you the best, **Billy**.

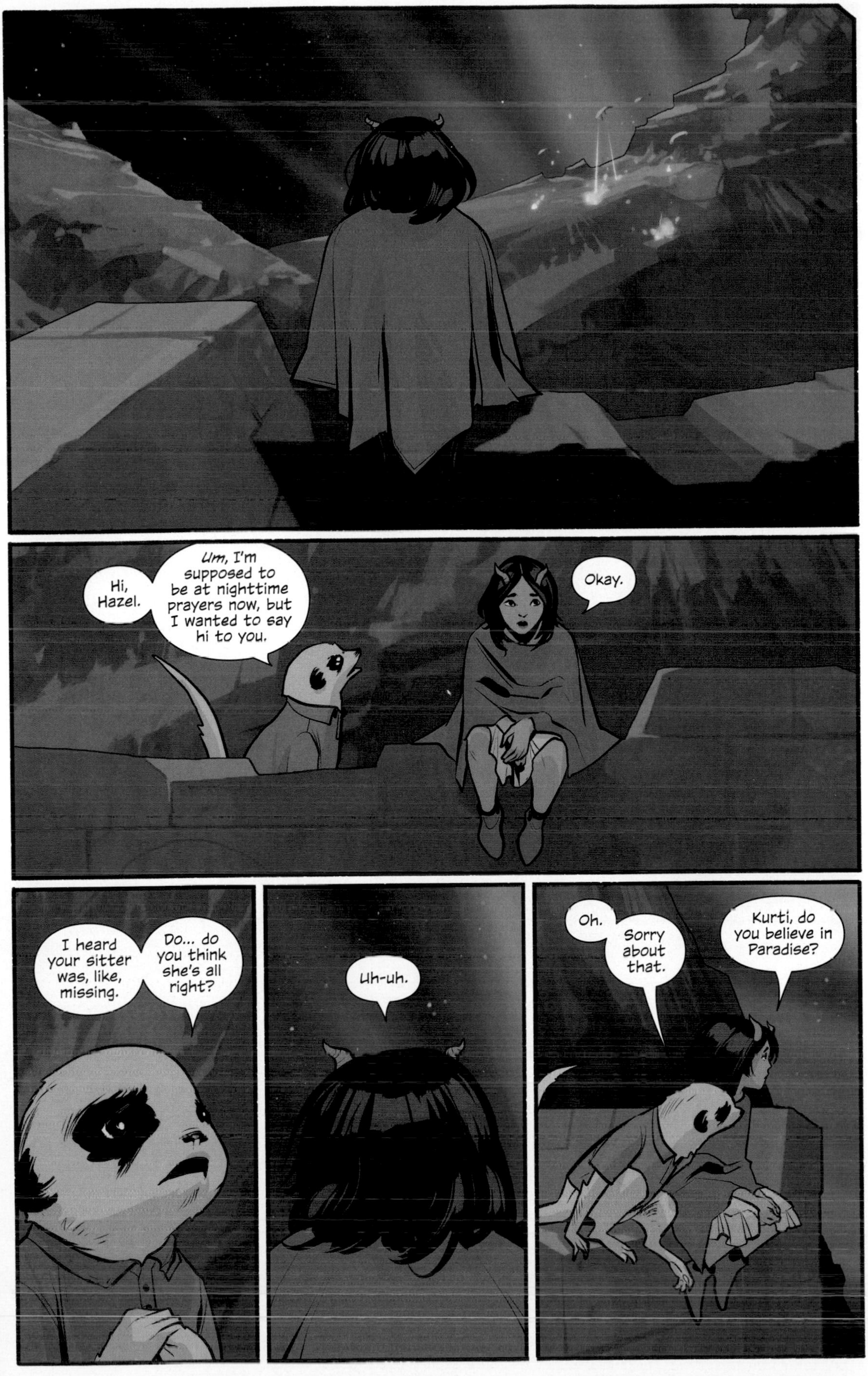
Hi, Hazel.
Um, I'm supposed to be at nighttime prayers now, but I wanted to say hi to you.
Okay.
I heard your sitter was, like, missing.
Do... do you think she's all right?
Uh-uh.
Oh.
Sorry about that.
Kurti, do you believe in Paradise?

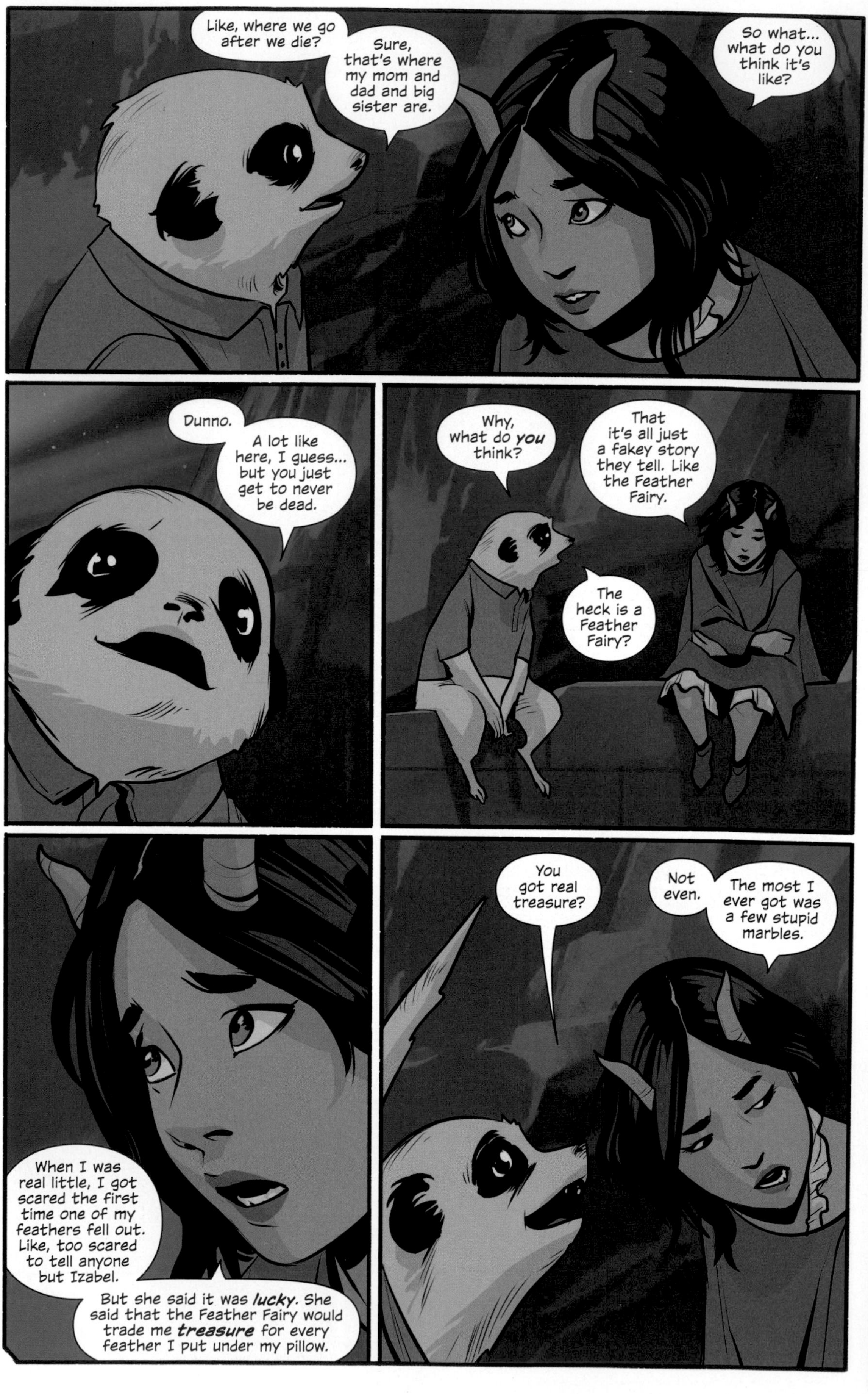
Like, where we go after we die?
Sure, that's where my mom and dad and big sister are.
So what... what do you think it's like?
Dunno.
A lot like here, I guess... but you just get to never be dead.
Why, what do you think?
That it's all just a fakey story they tell. Like the Feather Fairy.
The heck is a Feather Fairy?
When I was real little, I got scared the first time one of my feathers fell out. Like, too scared to tell anyone but Izabel.
But she said it was lucky. She said that the Feather Fairy would trade me treasure for every feather I put under my pillow.
You got real treasure?
Not even.
The most I ever got was a few stupid marbles.

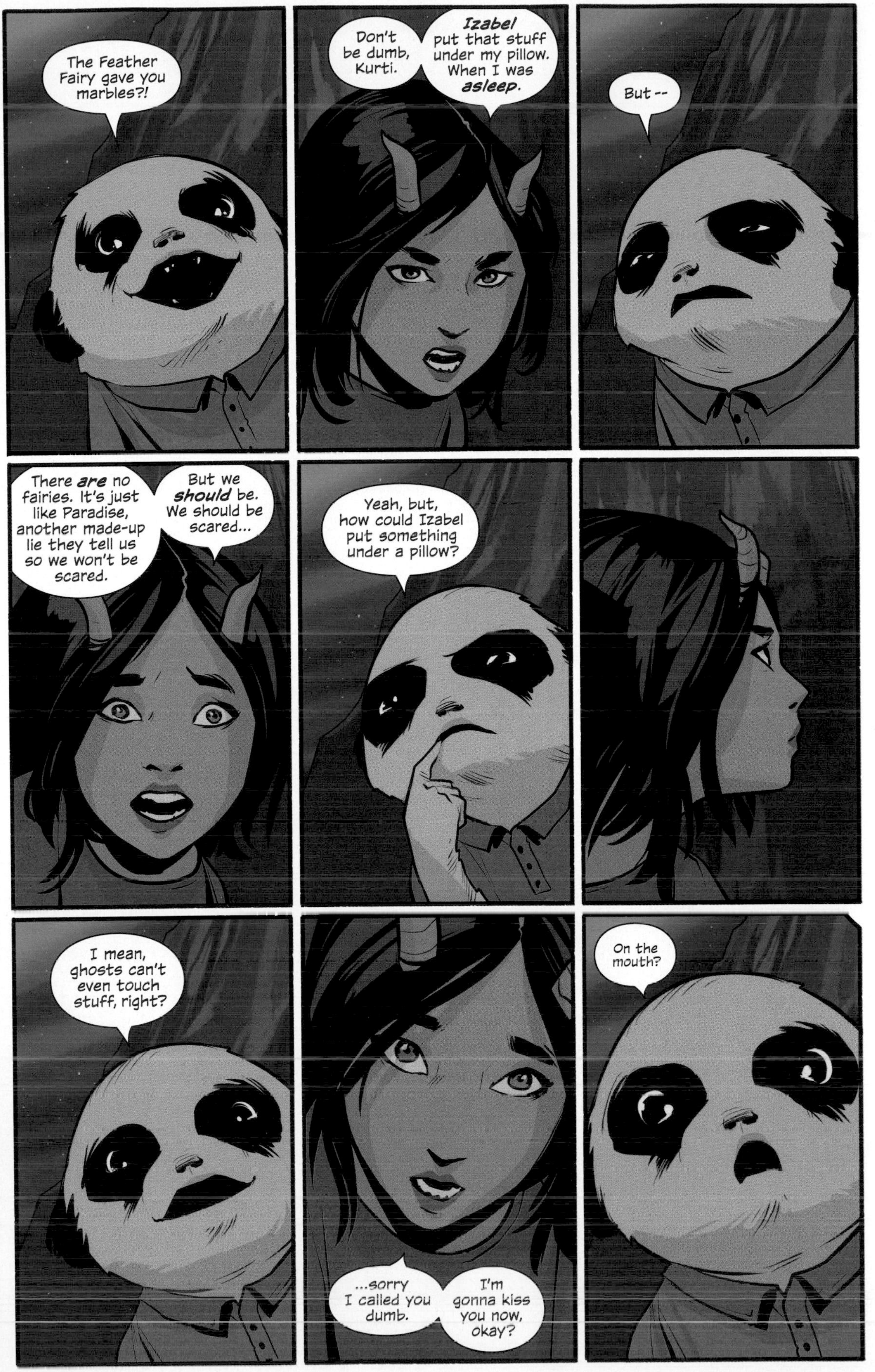

The Feather Fairy gave you marbles?!
Don't be dumb, Kurti.
Izabel put that stuff under my pillow. When I was *asleep*.
But --
There *are* no fairies. It's just like Paradise, another made-up lie they tell us so we won't be scared.
But we *should* be. We should be scared...
Yeah, but, how could Izabel put something under a pillow?
I mean, ghosts can't even touch stuff, right?
...sorry I called you dumb.
I'm gonna kiss you now, okay?
On the mouth?

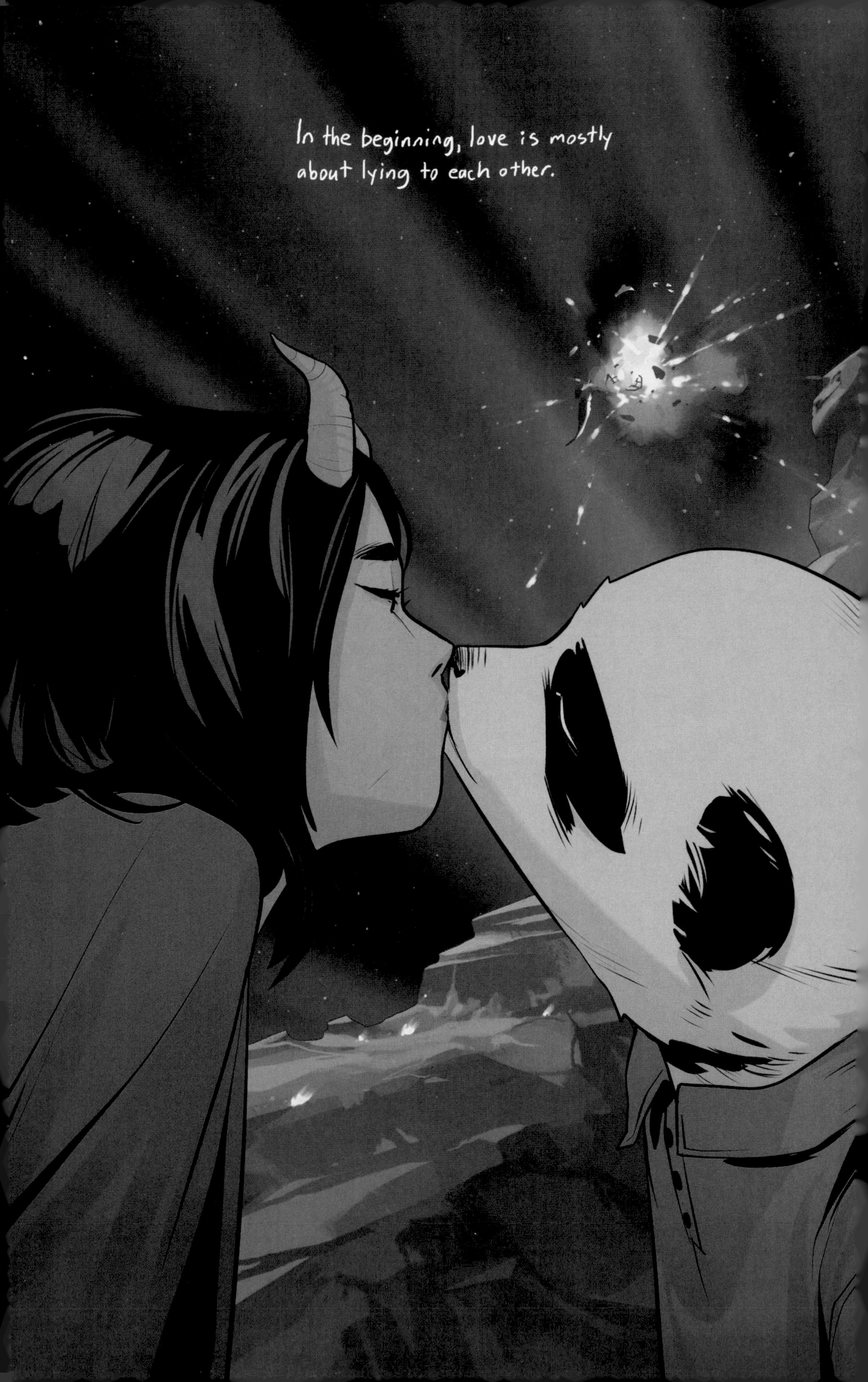
In the beginning, love is mostly about lying to each other.

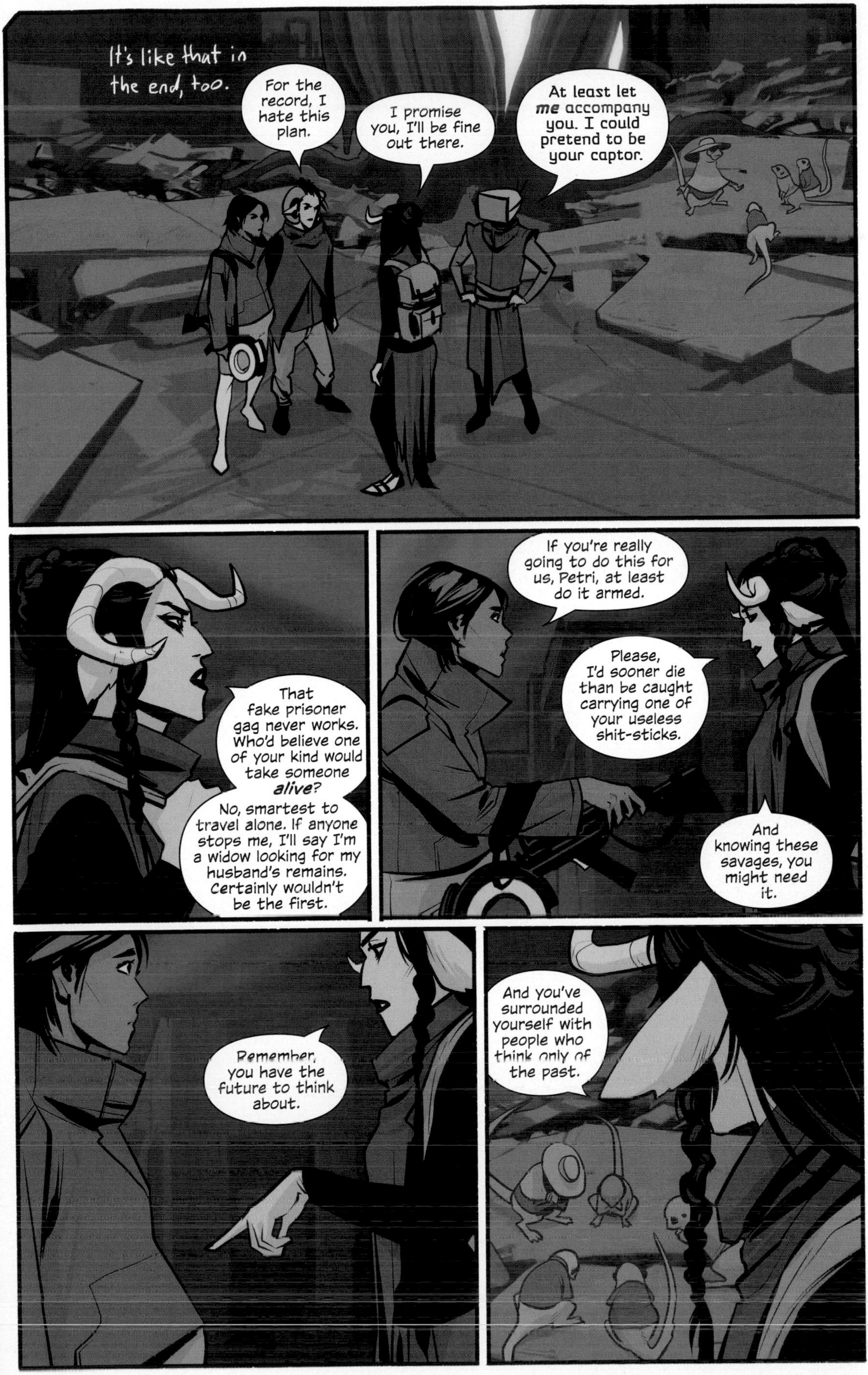
It's like that in the end, too.
For the record, I hate this plan.
I promise you, I'll be fine out there.
At least let *me* accompany you. I could pretend to be your captor.
That fake prisoner gag never works. Who'd believe one of your kind would take someone *alive*?
No, smartest to travel alone. If anyone stops me, I'll say I'm a widow looking for my husband's remains. Certainly wouldn't be the first.
If you're really going to do this for us, Petri, at least do it armed.
Please, I'd sooner die than be caught carrying one of your useless shit-sticks.
And knowing these savages, you might need it.
Remember, you have the future to think about.
And you've surrounded yourself with people who think only of the past.

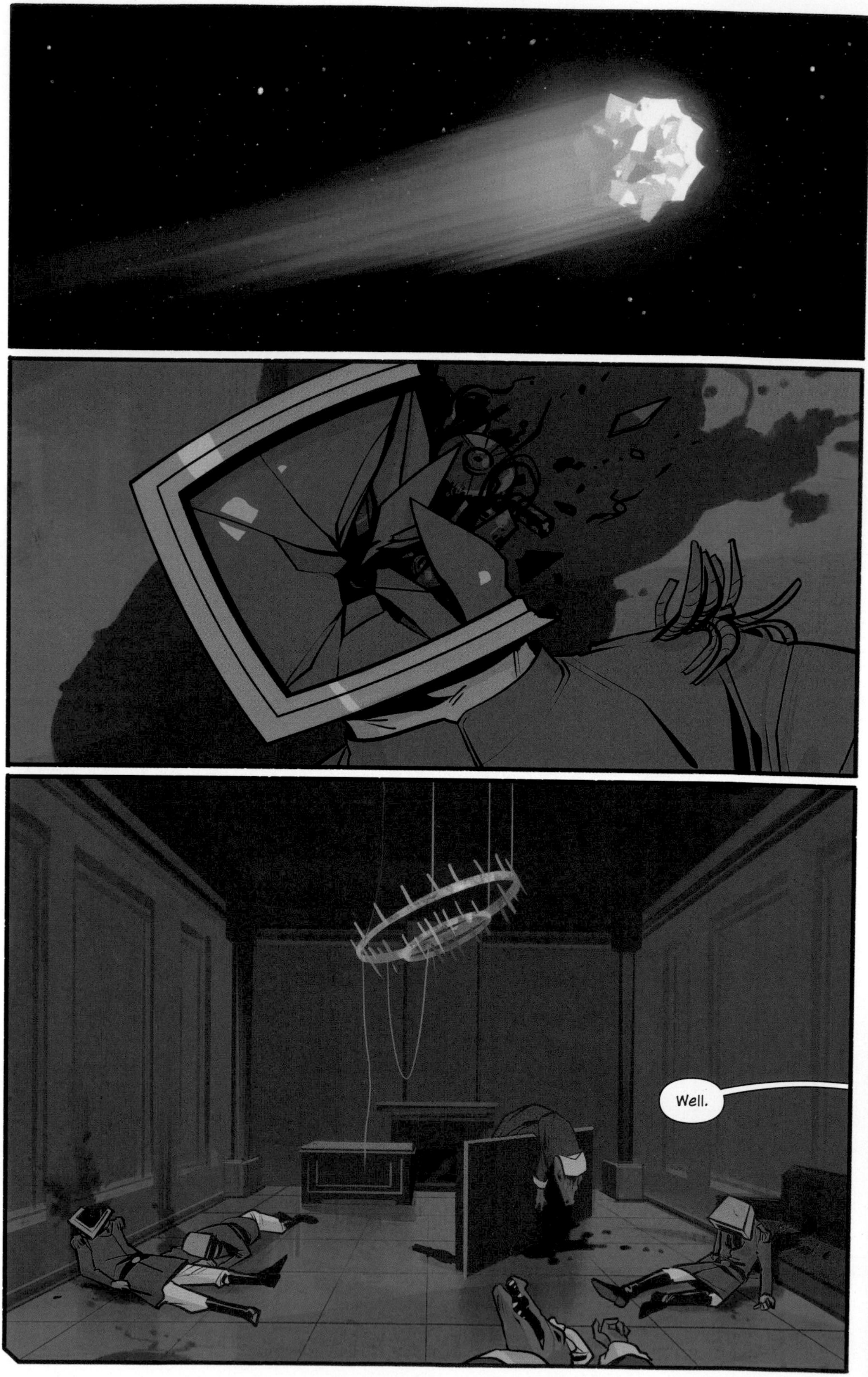
Well.

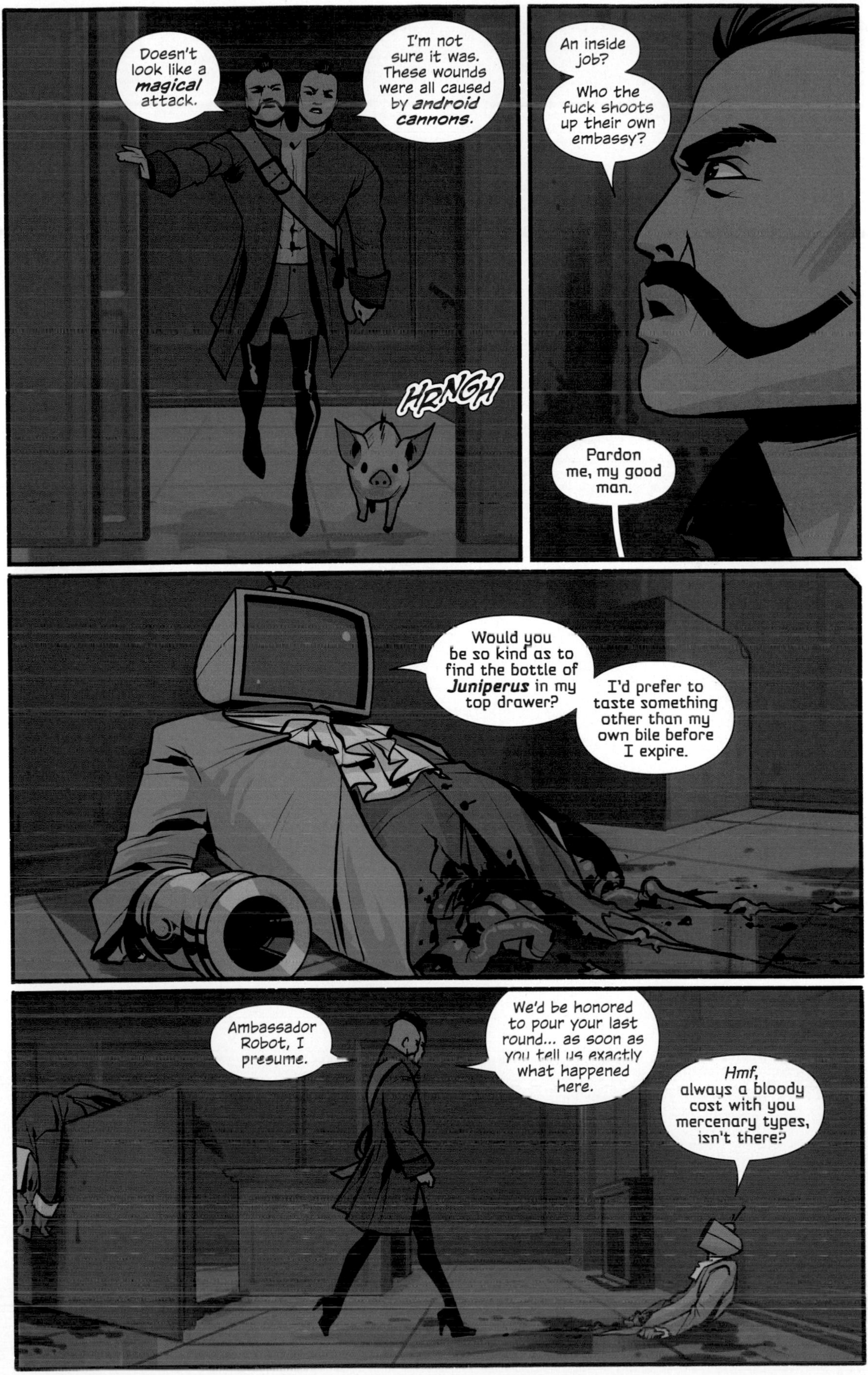
Doesn't look like a ***magical*** attack.
I'm not sure it was. These wounds were all caused by ***android cannons***.
HRNGH
An inside job?
Who the fuck shoots up their own embassy?
Pardon me, my good man.
Would you be so kind as to find the bottle of ***Juniperus*** in my top drawer?
I'd prefer to taste something other than my own bile before I expire.
Ambassador Robot, I presume.
We'd be honored to pour your last round... as soon as you tell us exactly what happened here.
Hmf, always a bloody cost with you mercenary types, isn't there?

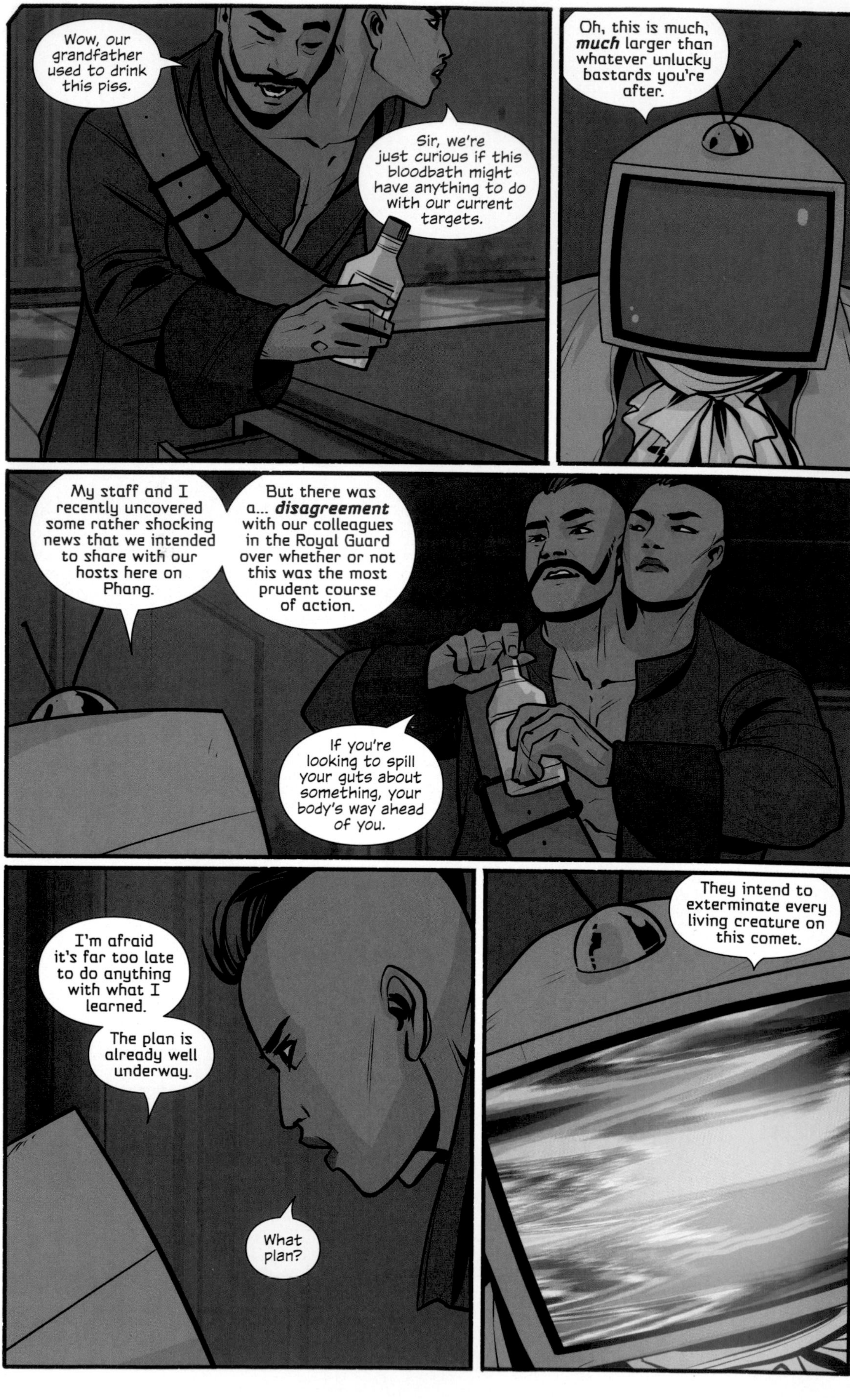
Wow, our grandfather used to drink this piss.
Sir, we're just curious if this bloodbath might have anything to do with our current targets.
Oh, this is much, ***much*** larger than whatever unlucky bastards you're after.
My staff and I recently uncovered some rather shocking news that we intended to share with our hosts here on Phang.
But there was a... ***disagreement*** with our colleagues in the Royal Guard over whether or not this was the most prudent course of action.
If you're looking to spill your guts about something, your body's way ahead of you.
I'm afraid it's far too late to do anything with what I learned.
The plan is already well underway.
What plan?
They intend to exterminate every living creature on this comet.

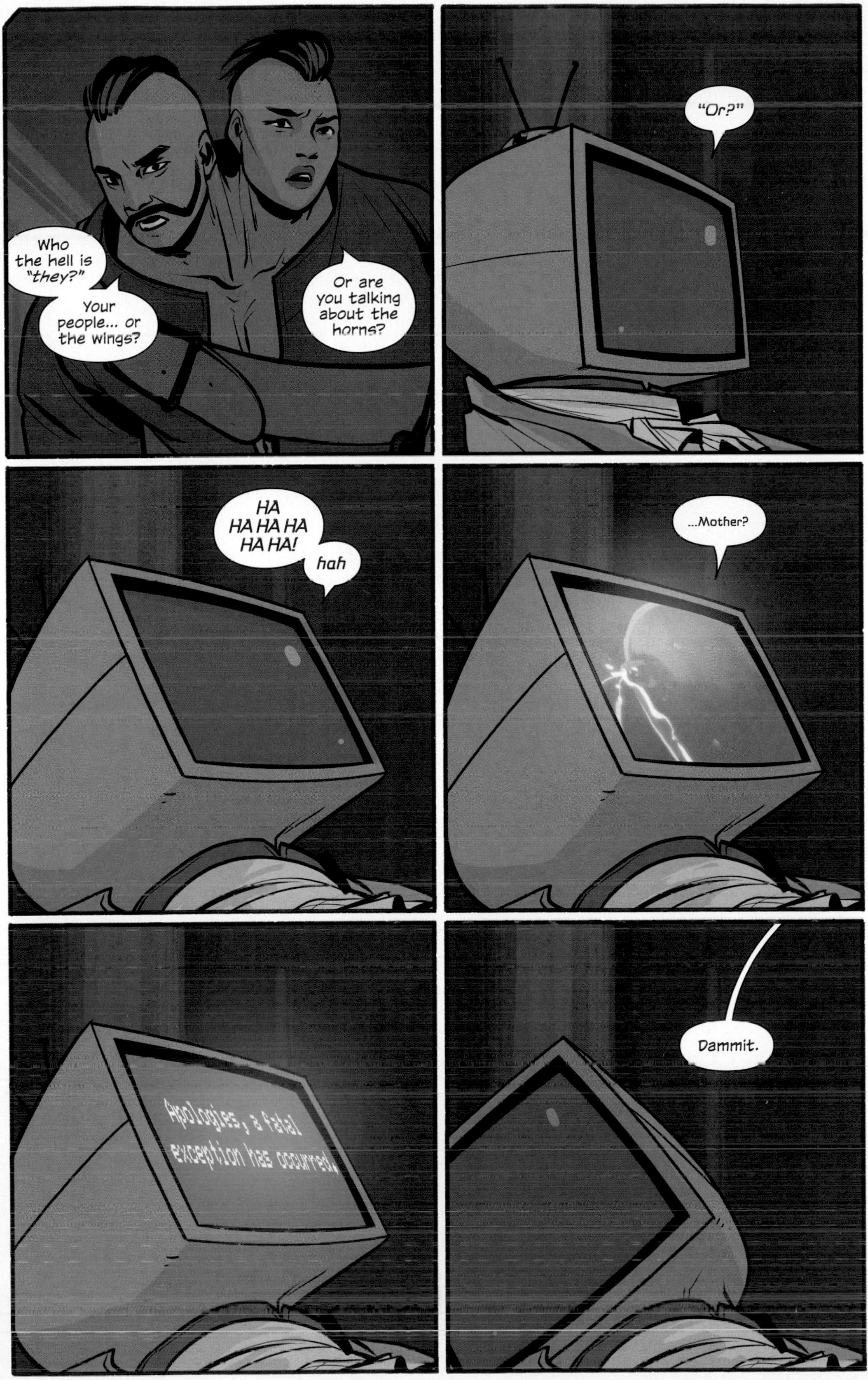
Who the hell is "they?"
Your people... or the wings?
Or are you talking about the horns?
"Or?"
HA HA HA HA HA HA!
hah
...Mother?
Apologies, a fatal exception has occurred.
Dammit.

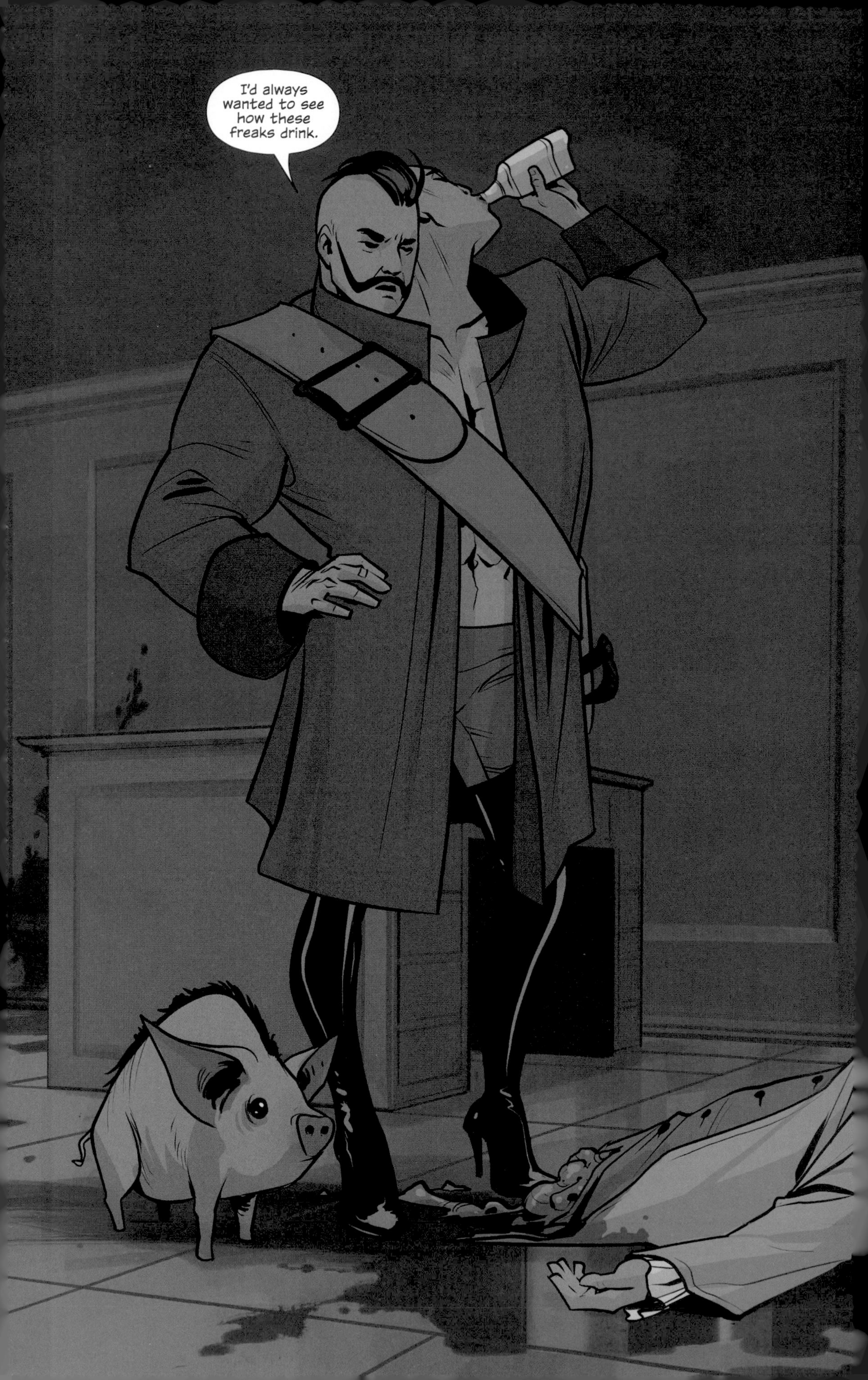
I'd always wanted to see how these freaks drink.

end chapter thirty-nine

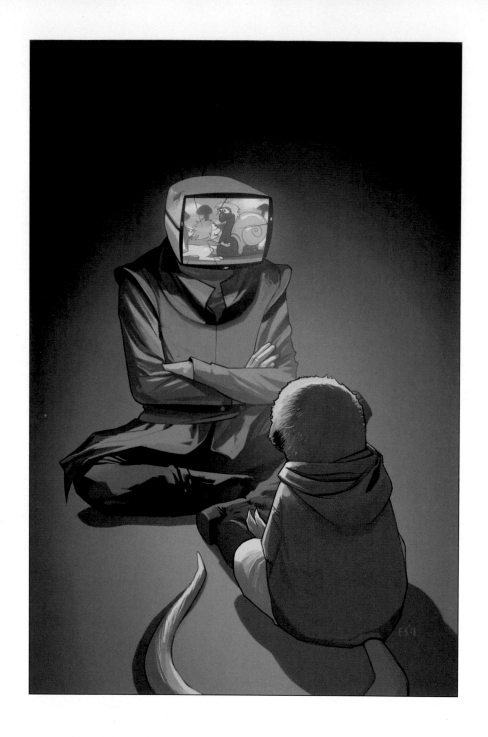

CHAPTER

FORTY

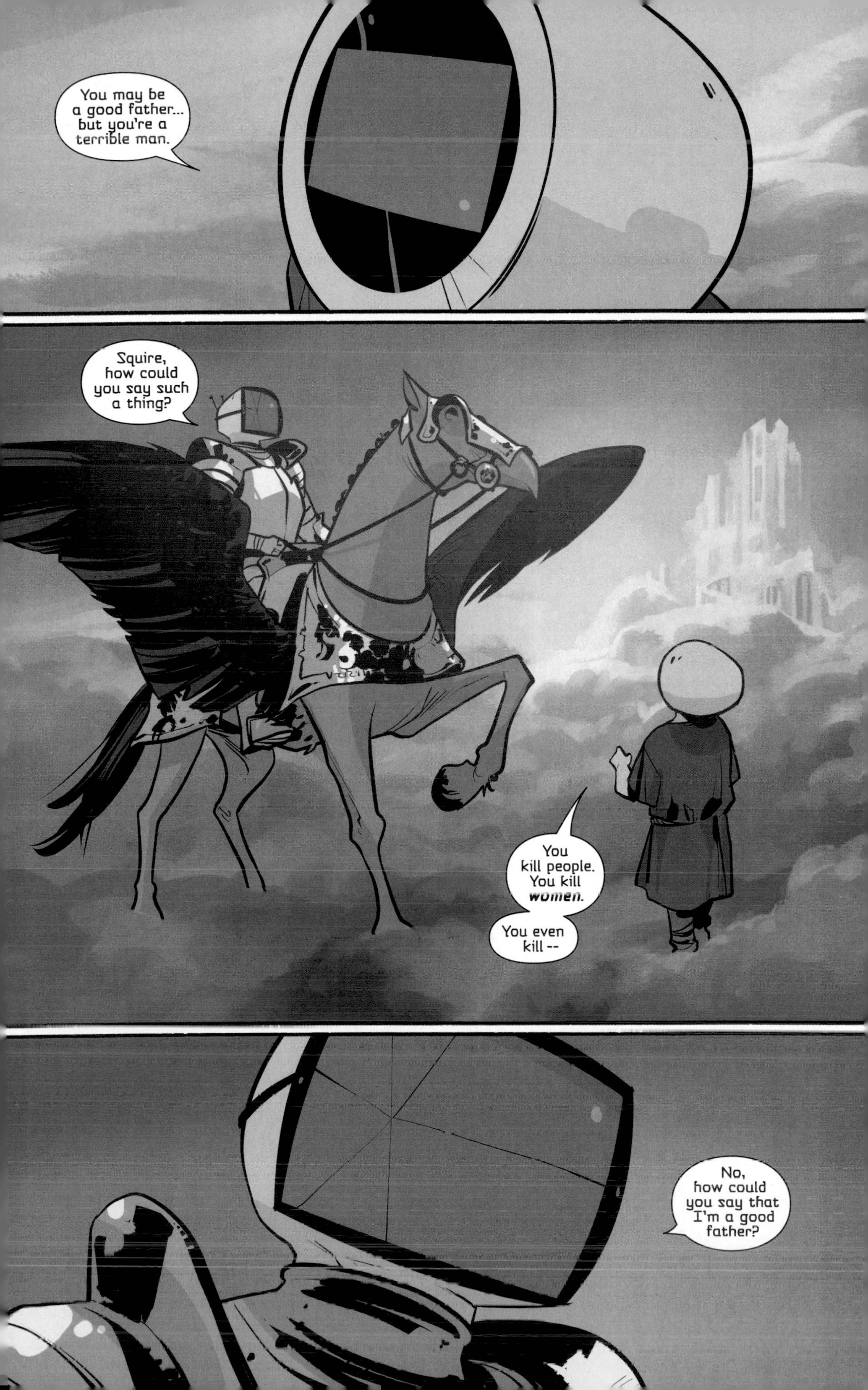
You may be a good father... but you're a terrible man.
Squire, how could you say such a thing?
You kill people. You kill *women*.
You even kill --
No, how could you say that I'm a good father?

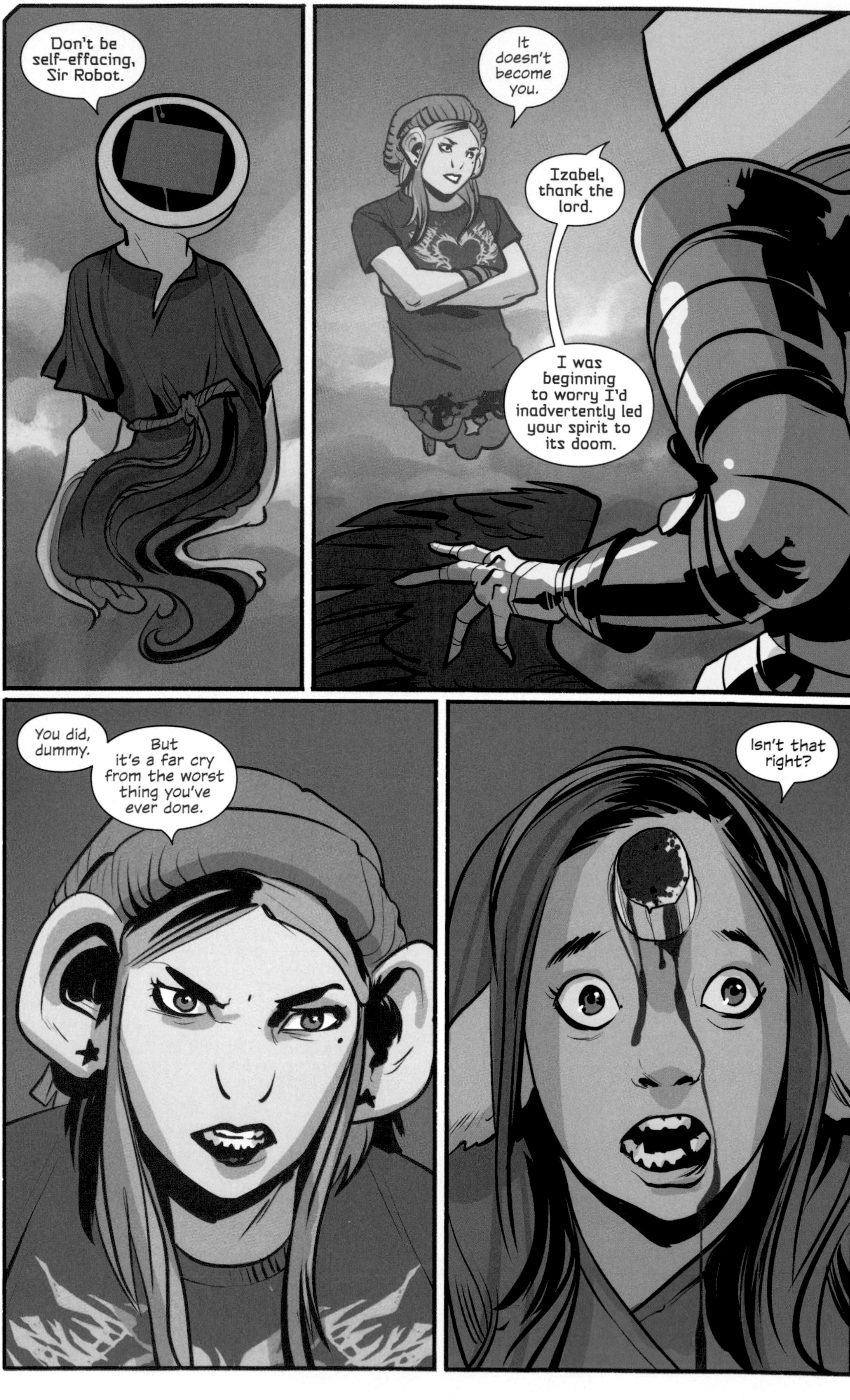
Don't be self-effacing, Sir Robot.
It doesn't become you.
Izabel, thank the lord.
I was beginning to worry I'd inadvertently led your spirit to its doom.
You did, dummy.
But it's a far cry from the worst thing you've ever done.
Isn't that right?

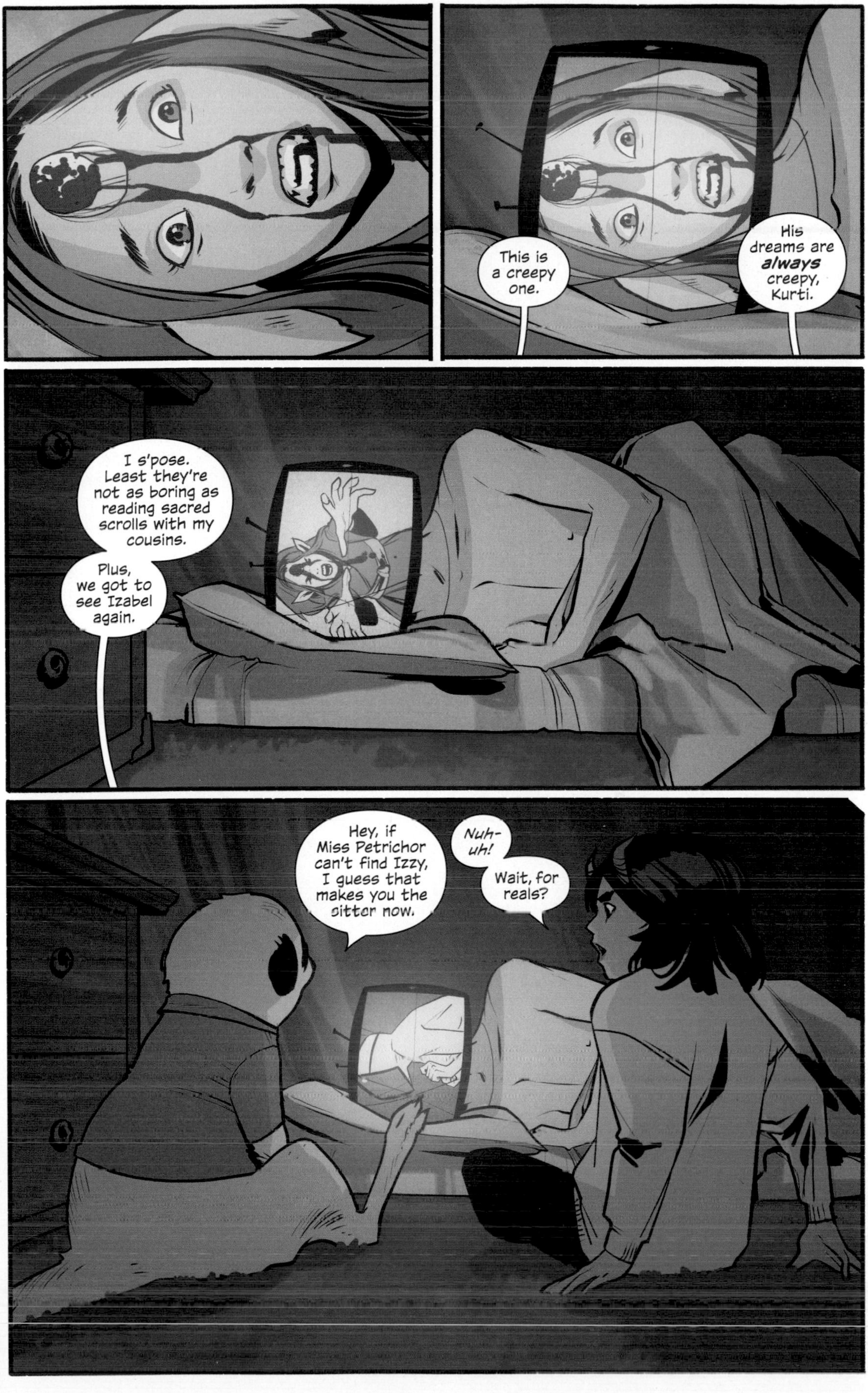
This is a creepy one.
His dreams are *always* creepy, Kurti.
I s'pose. Least they're not as boring as reading sacred scrolls with my cousins.
Plus, we got to see Izabel again.
Hey, if Miss Petrichor can't find Izzy, I guess that makes you the sitter now.
Nuh-uh!
Wait, for reals?

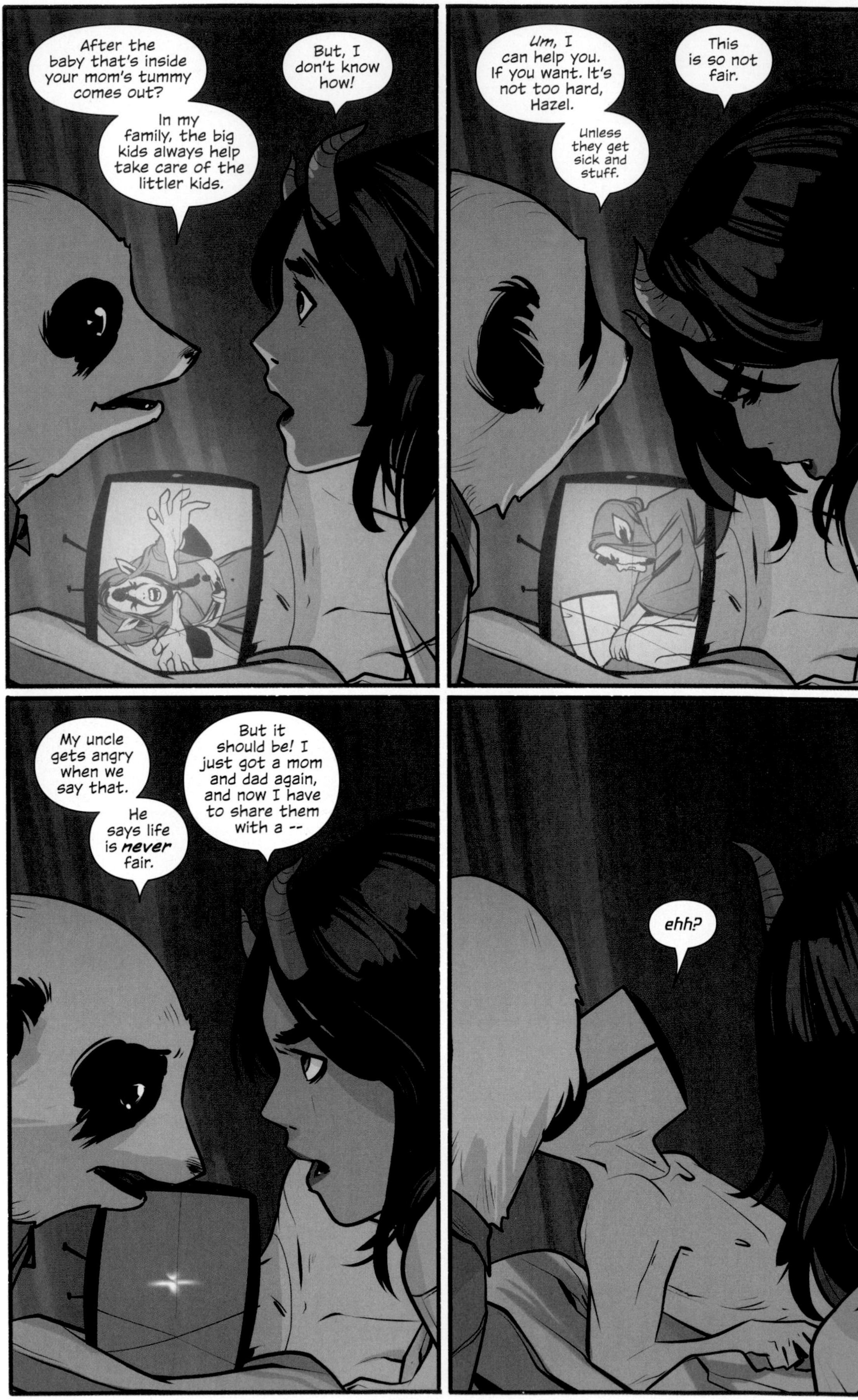
After the baby that's inside your mom's tummy comes out?
In my family, the big kids always help take care of the littler kids.
But, I don't know how!
Um, I can help you. If you want. It's not too hard, Hazel.
Unless they get sick and stuff.
This is so not fair.
My uncle gets angry when we say that.
He says life is never fair.
But it should be! I just got a mom and dad again, and now I have to share them with a --
ehh?

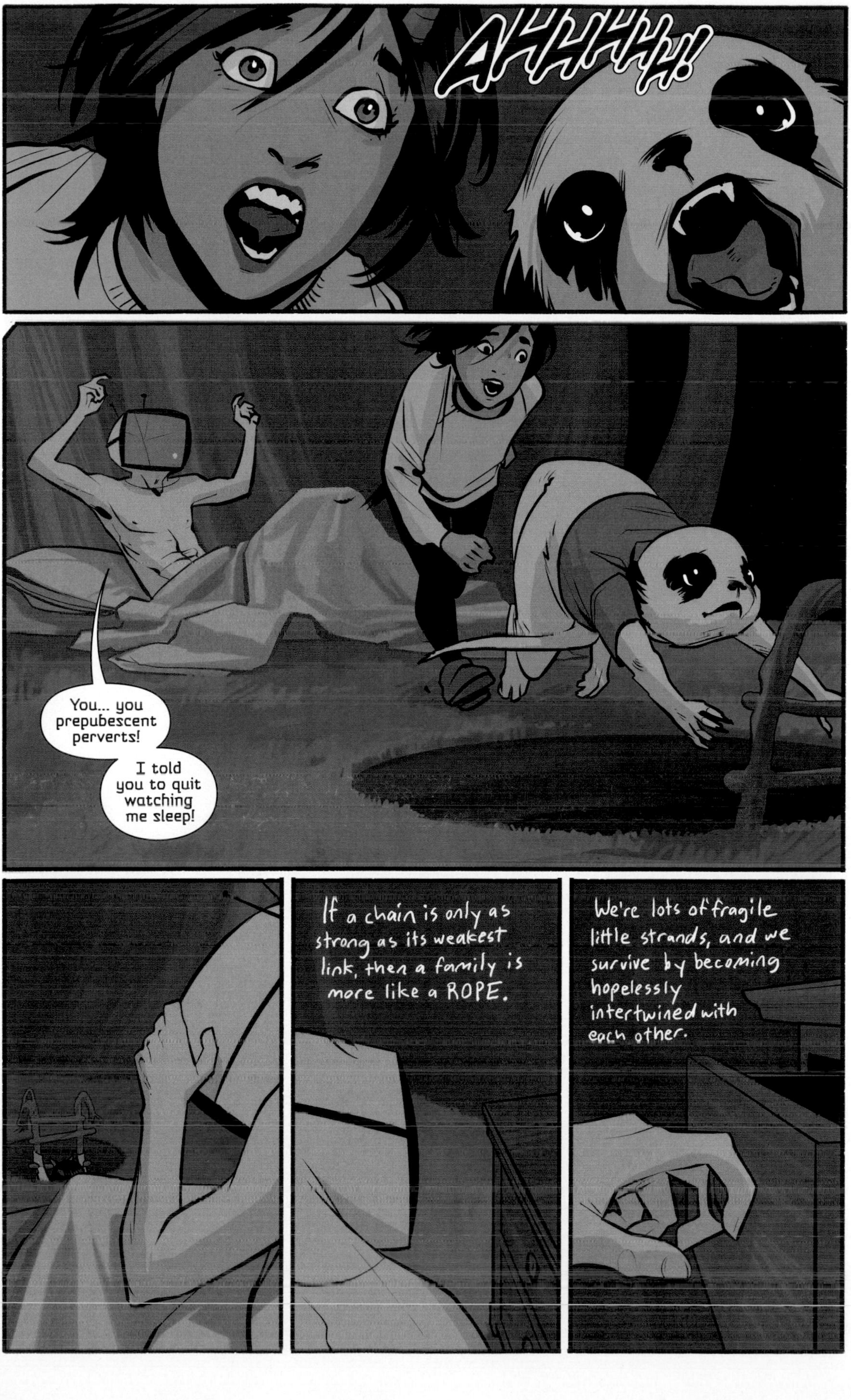
AHHHHH!
You... you prepubescent perverts!
I told you to quit watching me sleep!
If a chain is only as strong as its weakest link, then a family is more like a ROPE.
We're lots of fragile little strands, and we survive by becoming hopelessly intertwined with each other.

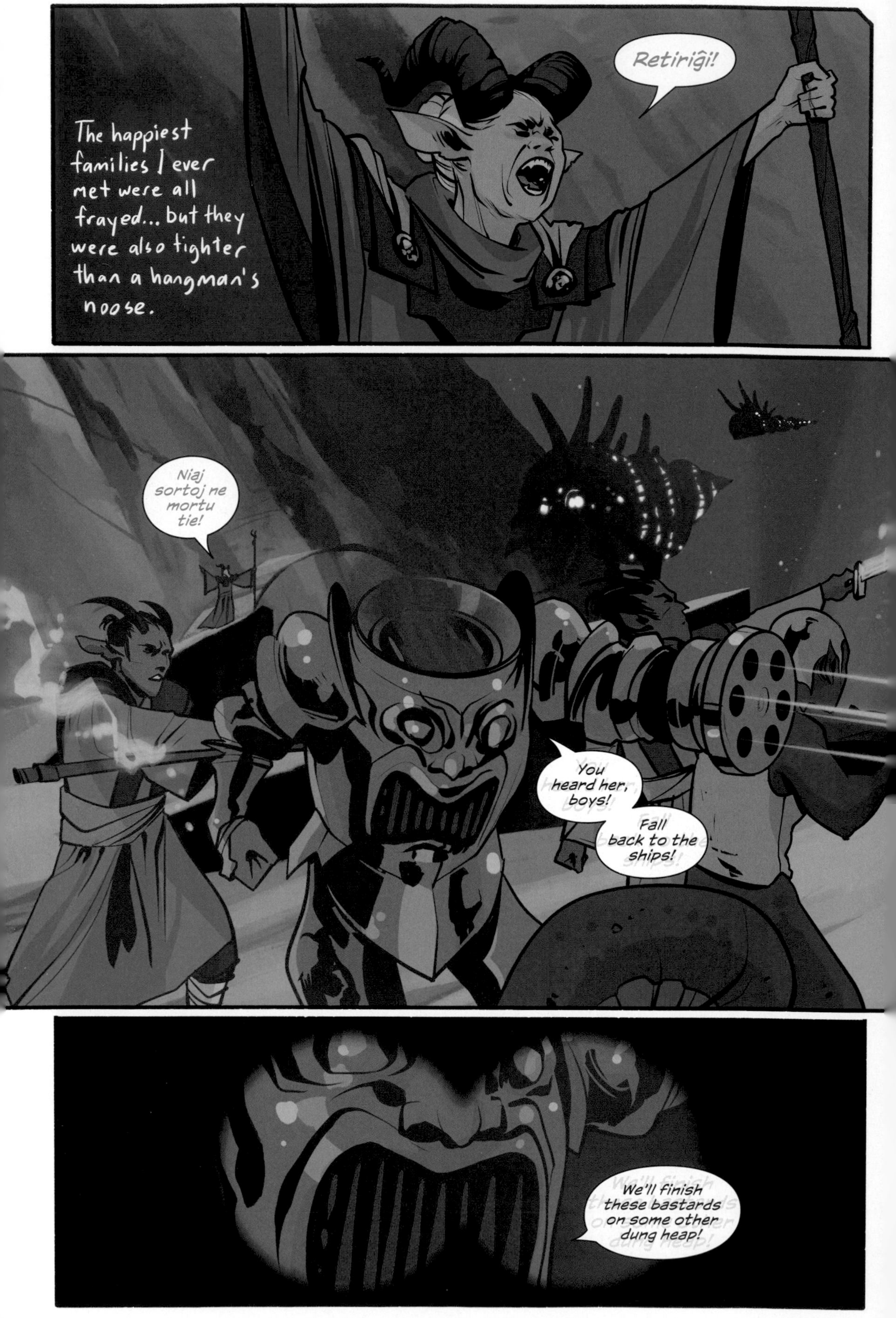
Retiriĝi!
The happiest families I ever met were all frayed... but they were also tighter than a hangman's noose.
Niaj sortoj ne mortu tie!
You heard her, boys!
Fall back to the ships!
We'll finish these bastards on some other dung heap!

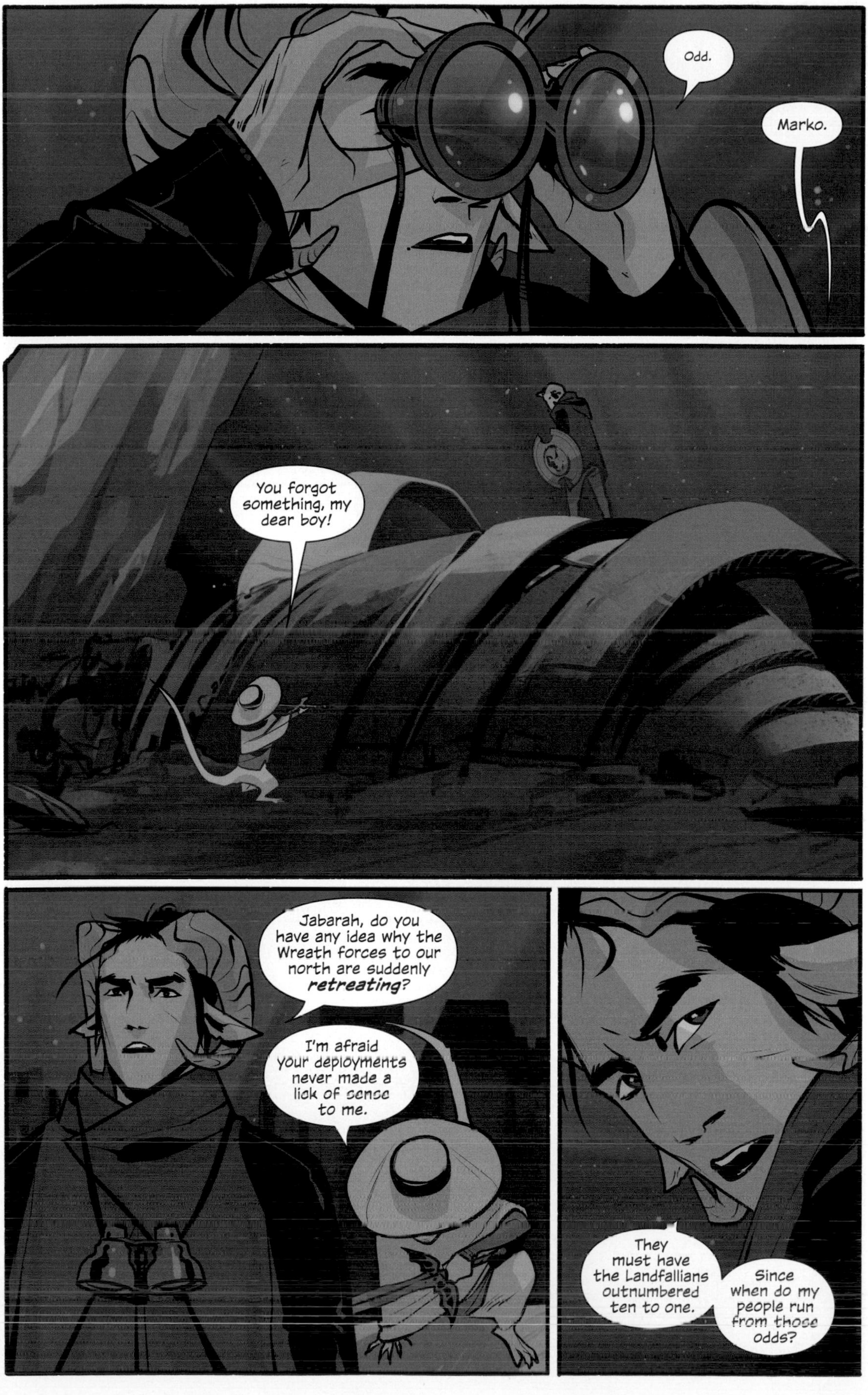
Odd.
Marko.
You forgot something, my dear boy!
Jabarah, do you have any idea why the Wreath forces to our north are suddenly ***retreating***?
I'm afraid your deployments never made a lick of sense to me.
They must have the Landfallians outnumbered ten to one.
Since when do my people run from those odds?

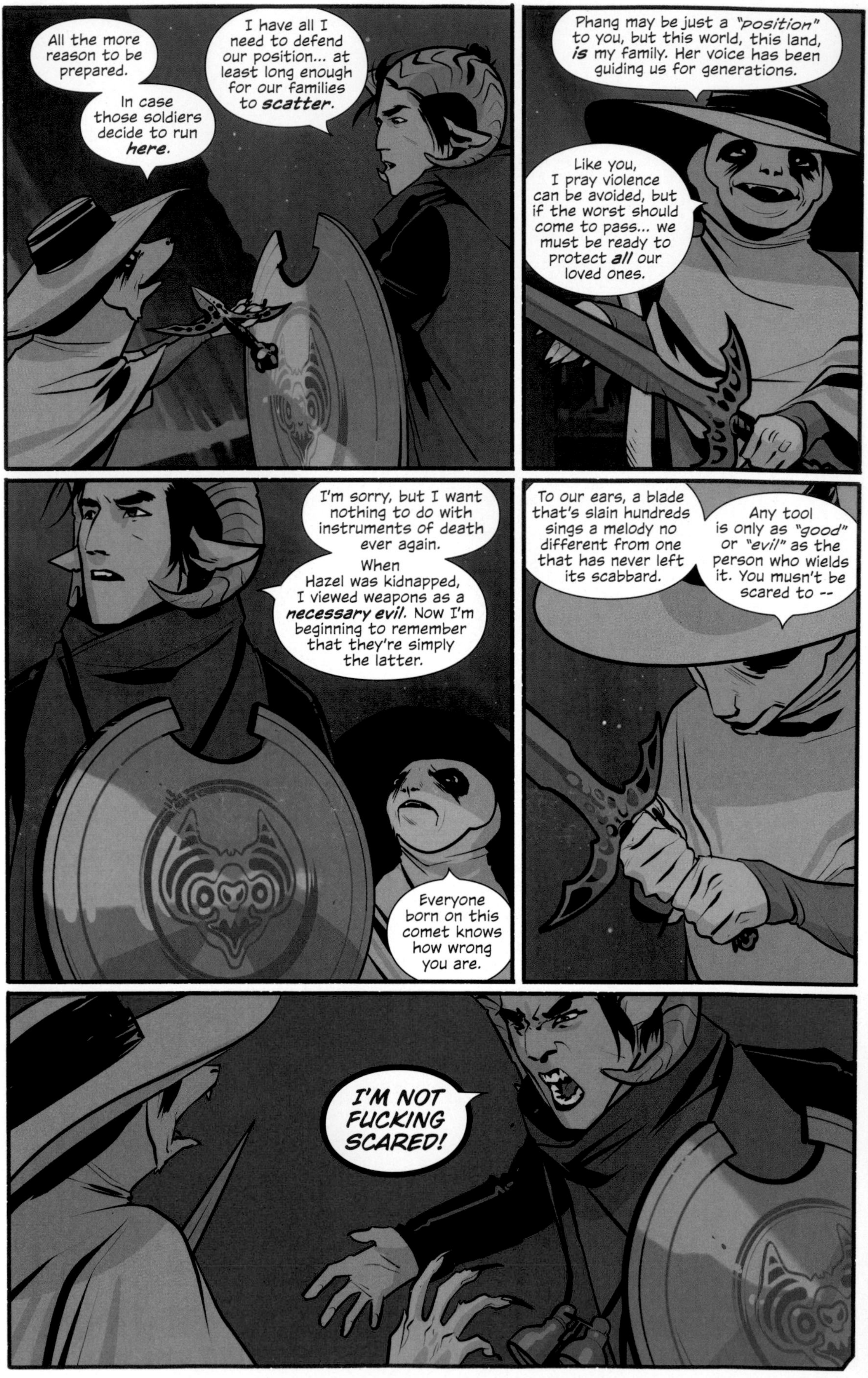

All the more reason to be prepared.
In case those soldiers decide to run *here*.
I have all I need to defend our position... at least long enough for our families to *scatter*.
Phang may be just a *"position"* to you, but this world, this land, *is* my family. Her voice has been guiding us for generations.
Like you, I pray violence can be avoided, but if the worst should come to pass... we must be ready to protect *all* our loved ones.
I'm sorry, but I want nothing to do with instruments of death ever again.
When Hazel was kidnapped, I viewed weapons as a *necessary evil*. Now I'm beginning to remember that they're simply the latter.
Everyone born on this comet knows how wrong you are.
To our ears, a blade that's slain hundreds sings a melody no different from one that has never left its scabbard.
Any tool is only as *"good"* or *"evil"* as the person who wields it. You musn't be scared to --
I'M NOT FUCKING SCARED!

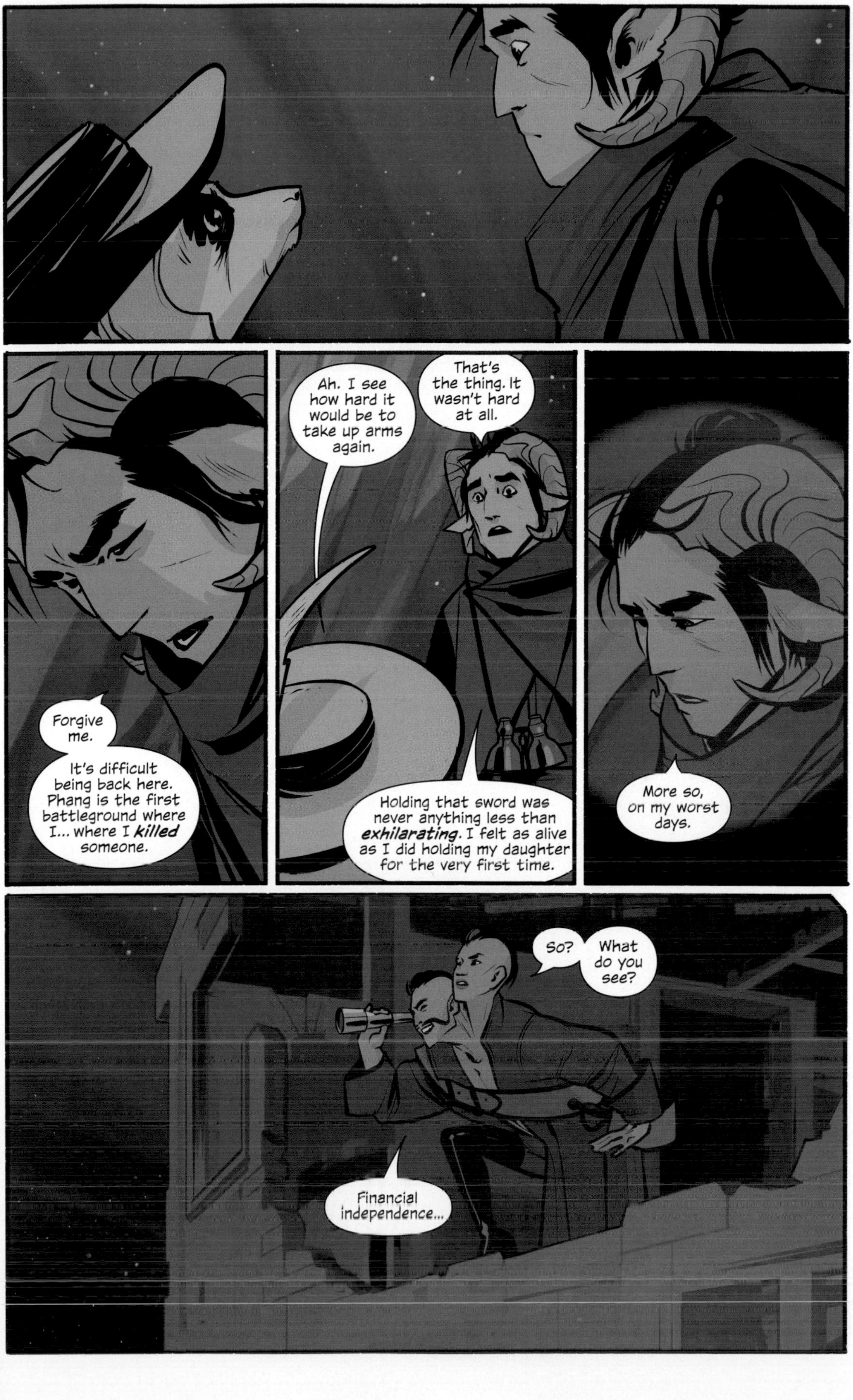
Forgive me.
It's difficult being back here. Phang is the first battleground where I... where I ***killed*** someone.
Ah. I see how hard it would be to take up arms again.
That's the thing. It wasn't hard at all.
Holding that sword was never anything less than ***exhilarating***. I felt as alive as I did holding my daughter for the very first time.
More so, on my worst days.
So?
What do you see?
Financial independence...

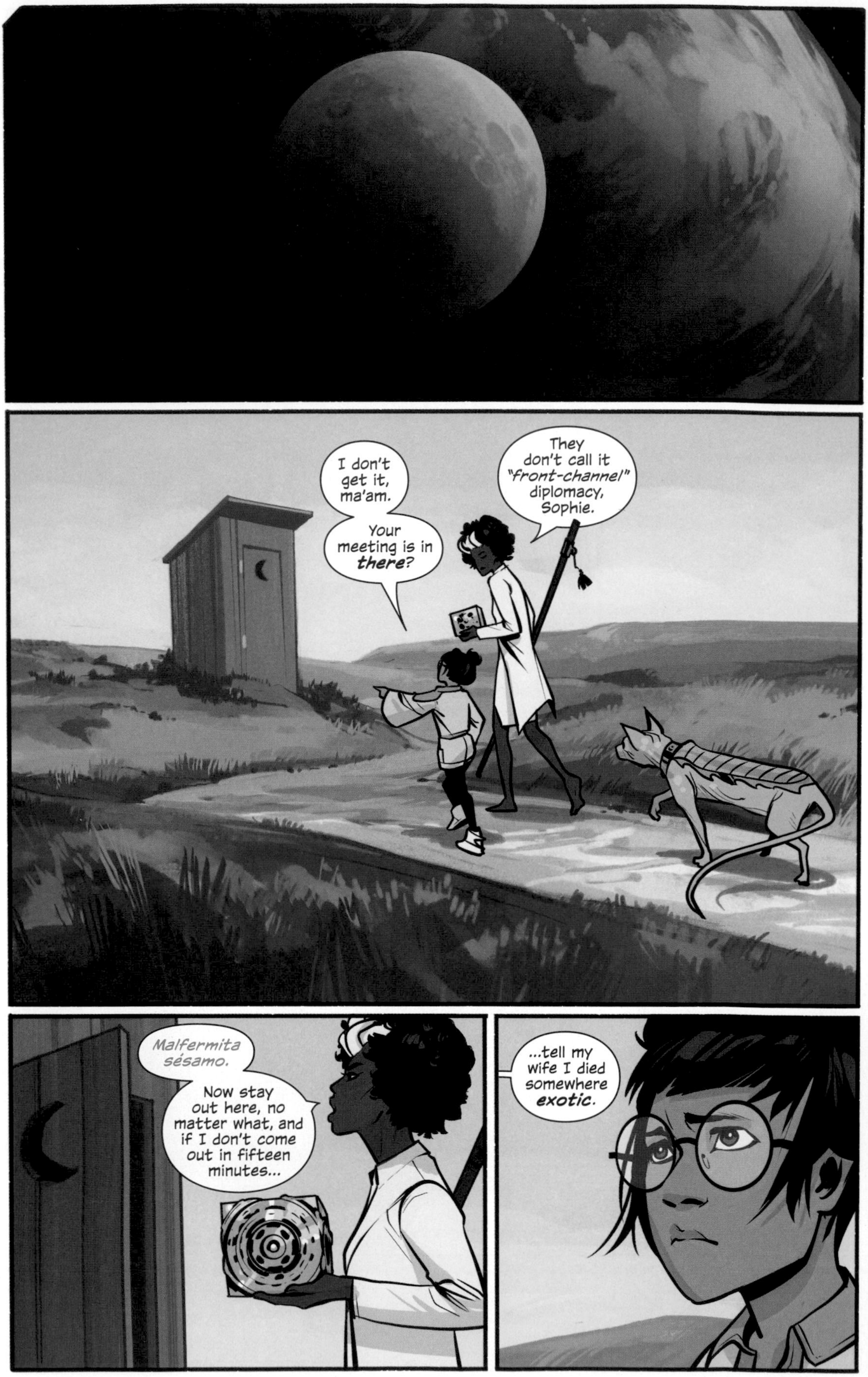

I don't get it, ma'am.
Your meeting is in ***there***?
They don't call it *"front-channel"* diplomacy, Sophie.
Malfermita sésamo.
Now stay out here, no matter what, and if I don't come out in fifteen minutes...
...tell my wife I died somewhere ***exotic***.

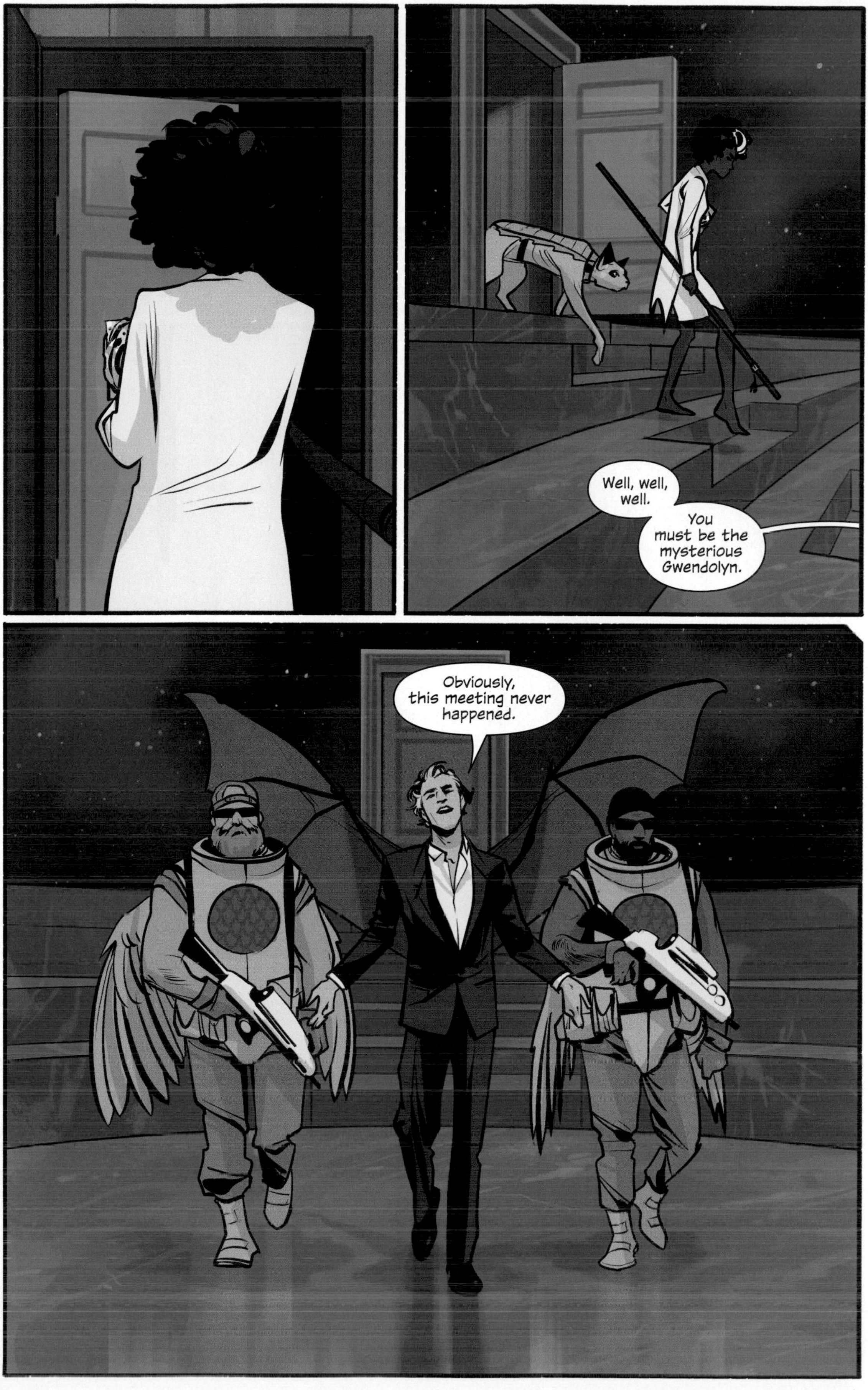
Well, well, well.
You must be the mysterious Gwendolyn.
Obviously, this meeting never happened.

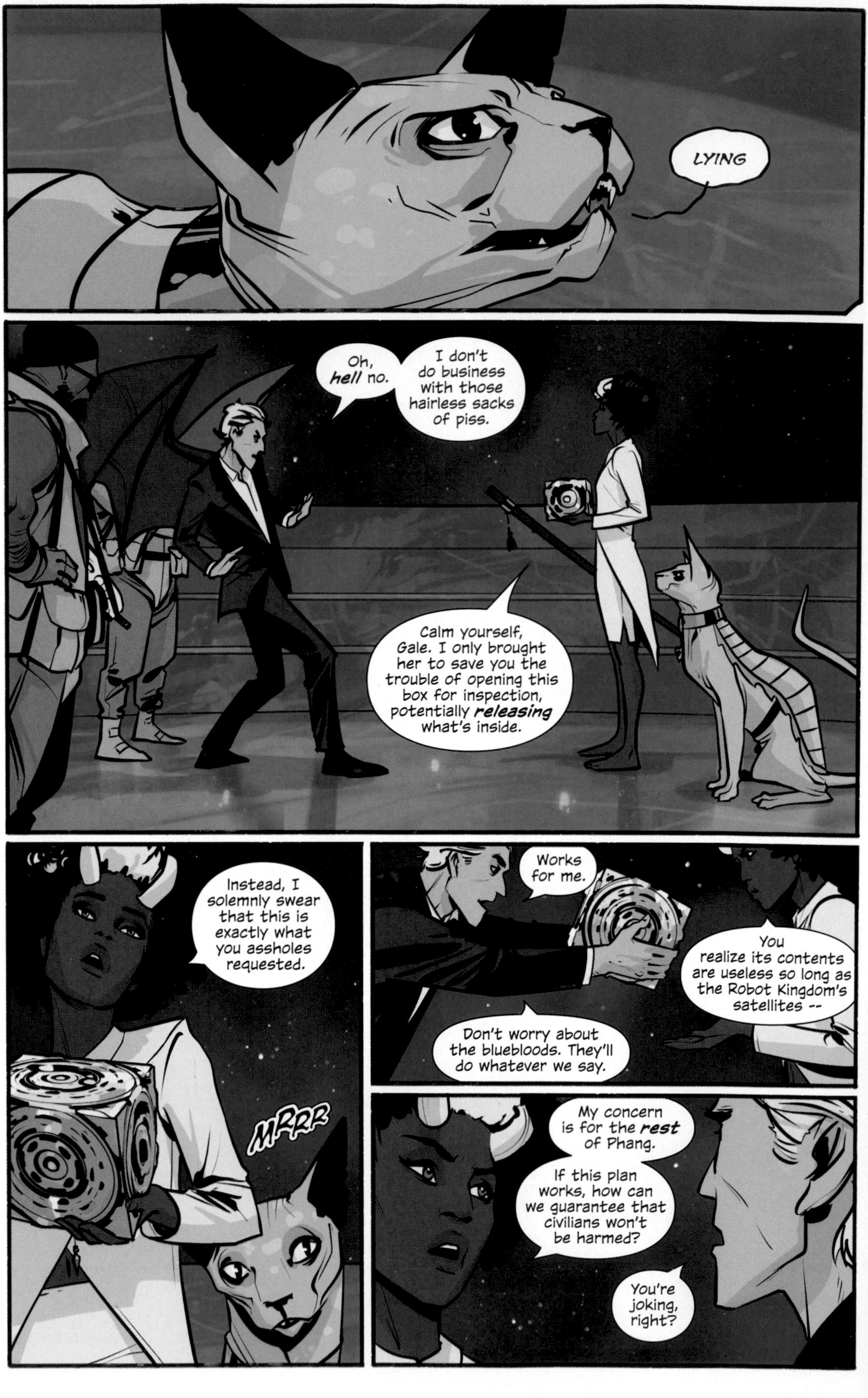
LYING
Oh, hell no.
I don't do business with those hairless sacks of piss.
Calm yourself, Gale. I only brought her to save you the trouble of opening this box for inspection, potentially releasing what's inside.
Instead, I solemnly swear that this is exactly what you assholes requested.
MRRR
Works for me.
You realize its contents are useless so long as the Robot Kingdom's satellites --
Don't worry about the bluebloods. They'll do whatever we say.
My concern is for the rest of Phang.
If this plan works, how can we guarantee that civilians won't be harmed?
You're joking, right?

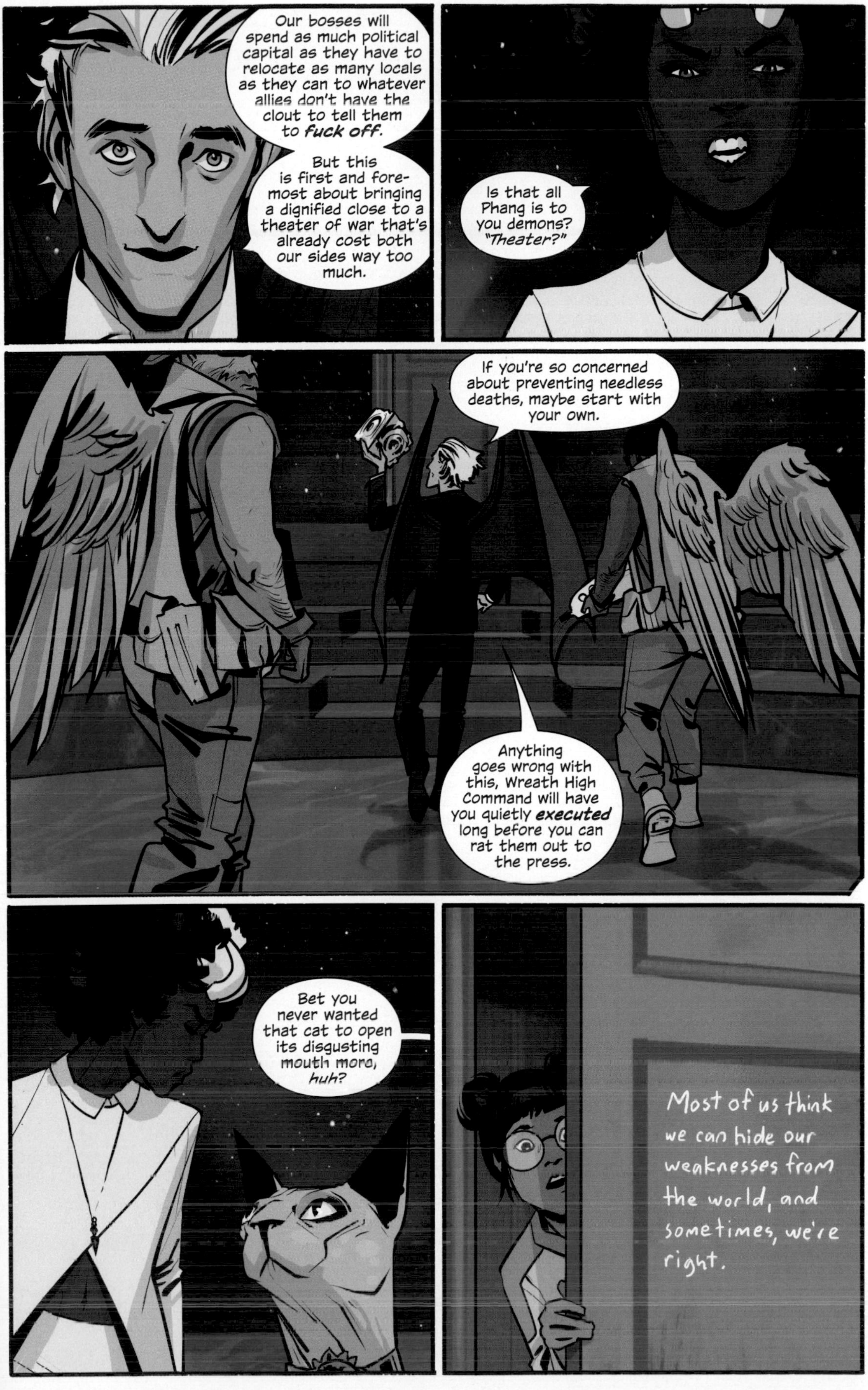
Our bosses will spend as much political capital as they have to relocate as many locals as they can to whatever allies don't have the clout to tell them to *fuck off*.
But this is first and foremost about bringing a dignified close to a theater of war that's already cost both our sides way too much.
Is that all Phang is to you demons? "*Theater?*"
If you're so concerned about preventing needless deaths, maybe start with your own.
Anything goes wrong with this, Wreath High Command will have you quietly ***executed*** long before you can rat them out to the press.
Bet you never wanted that cat to open its disgusting mouth more, *huh?*
Most of us think we can hide our weaknesses from the world, and sometimes, we're right.

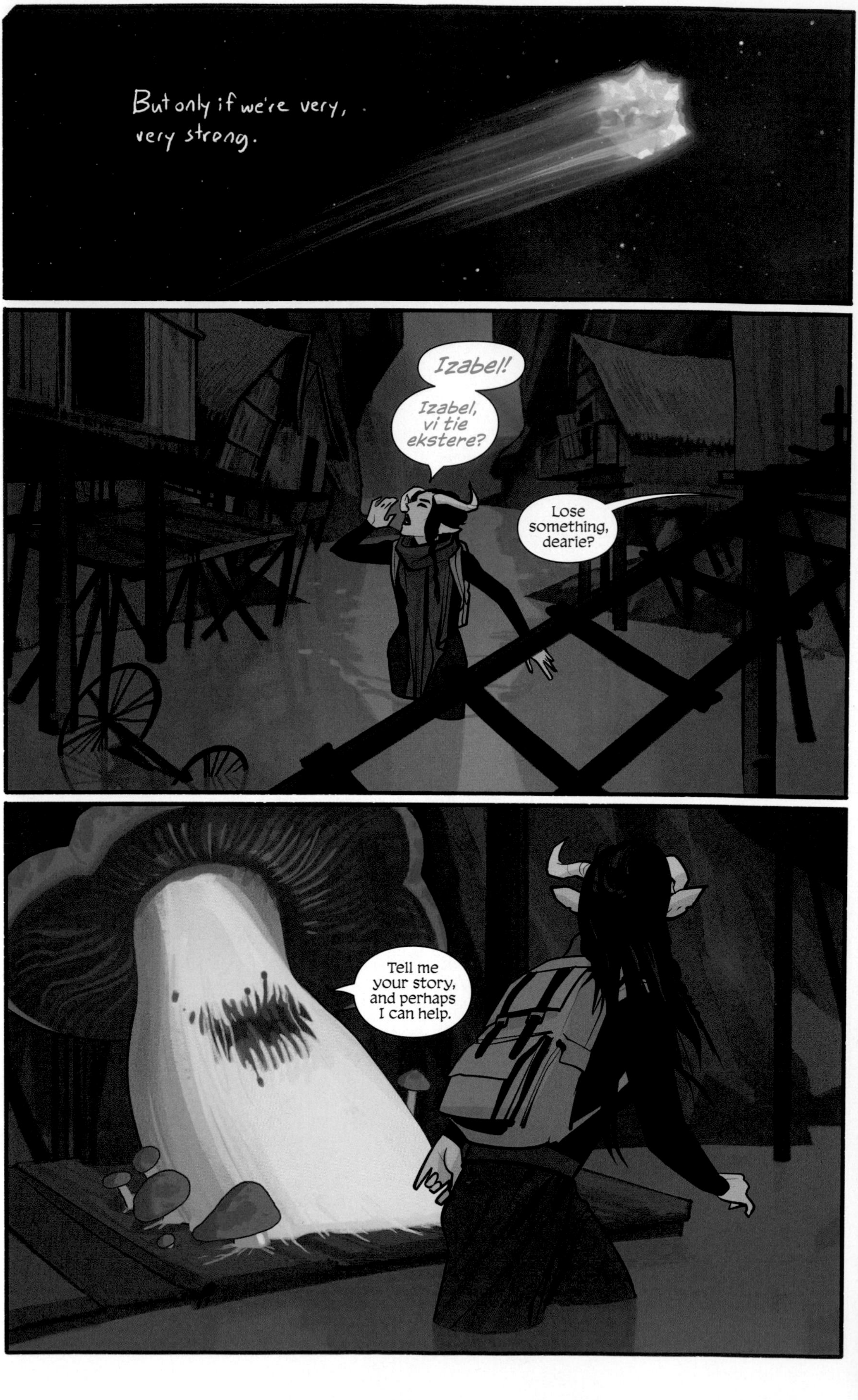
But only if we're very, very strong.
Izabel!
Izabel, vi tie ekstere?
Lose something, dearie?
Tell me your story, and perhaps I can help.

What be you?

Merely an impartial observer.

We bluecaps are planted in places of conflict, to remember tales of battle for future --

I looking for friend.

You see *spirit* pass this way?

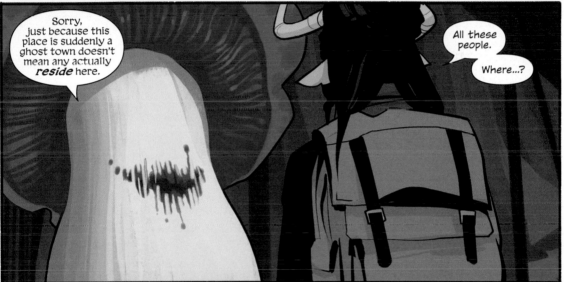

Sorry, just because this place is suddenly a ghost town doesn't mean any actually *reside* here.

All these people.

Where...?

Evacuated from Phang. Some of their own free will, most at gunpoint.

Why?

What is coming?

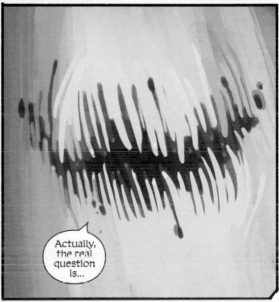

Actually, the real question is...

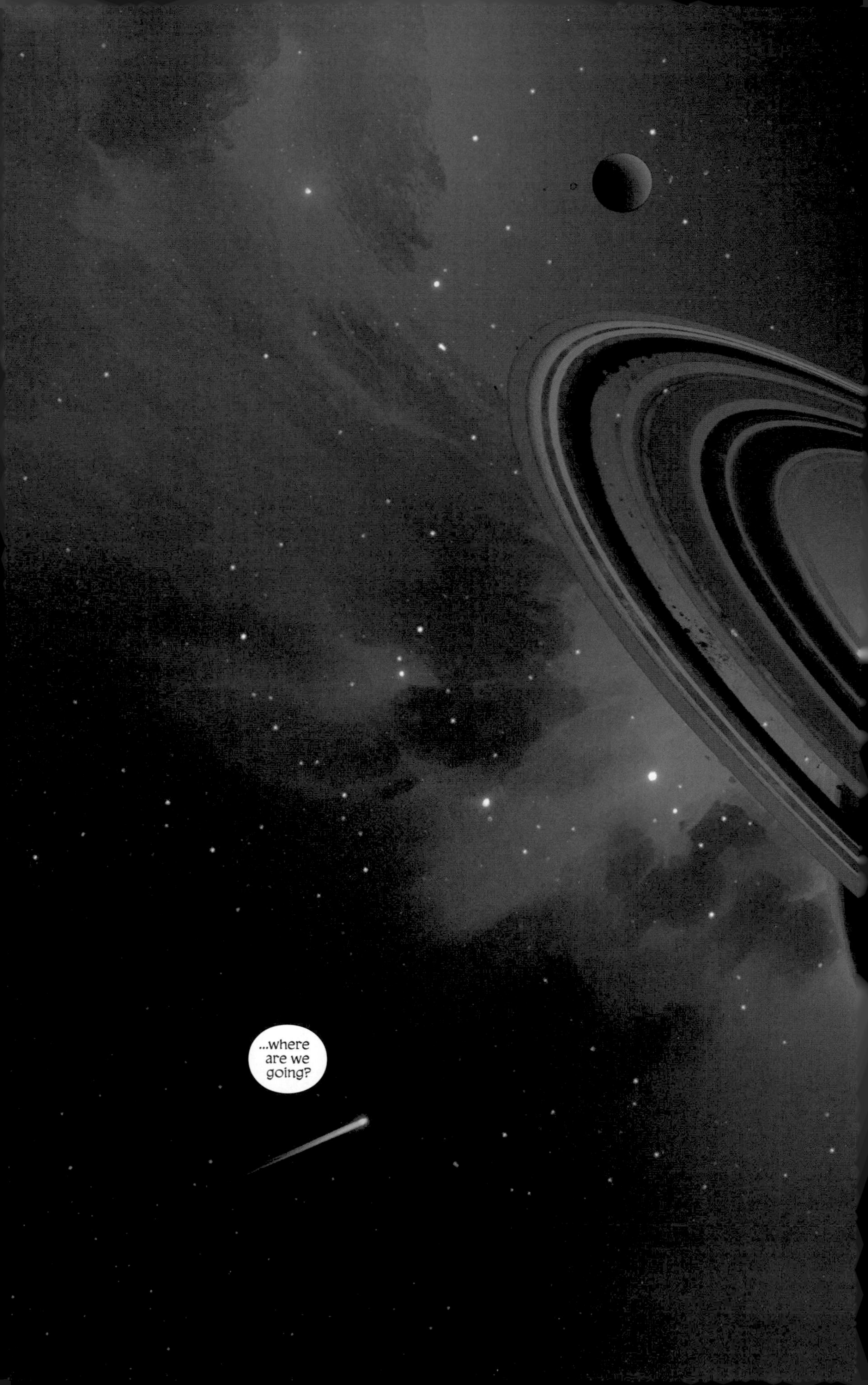
...where are we going?

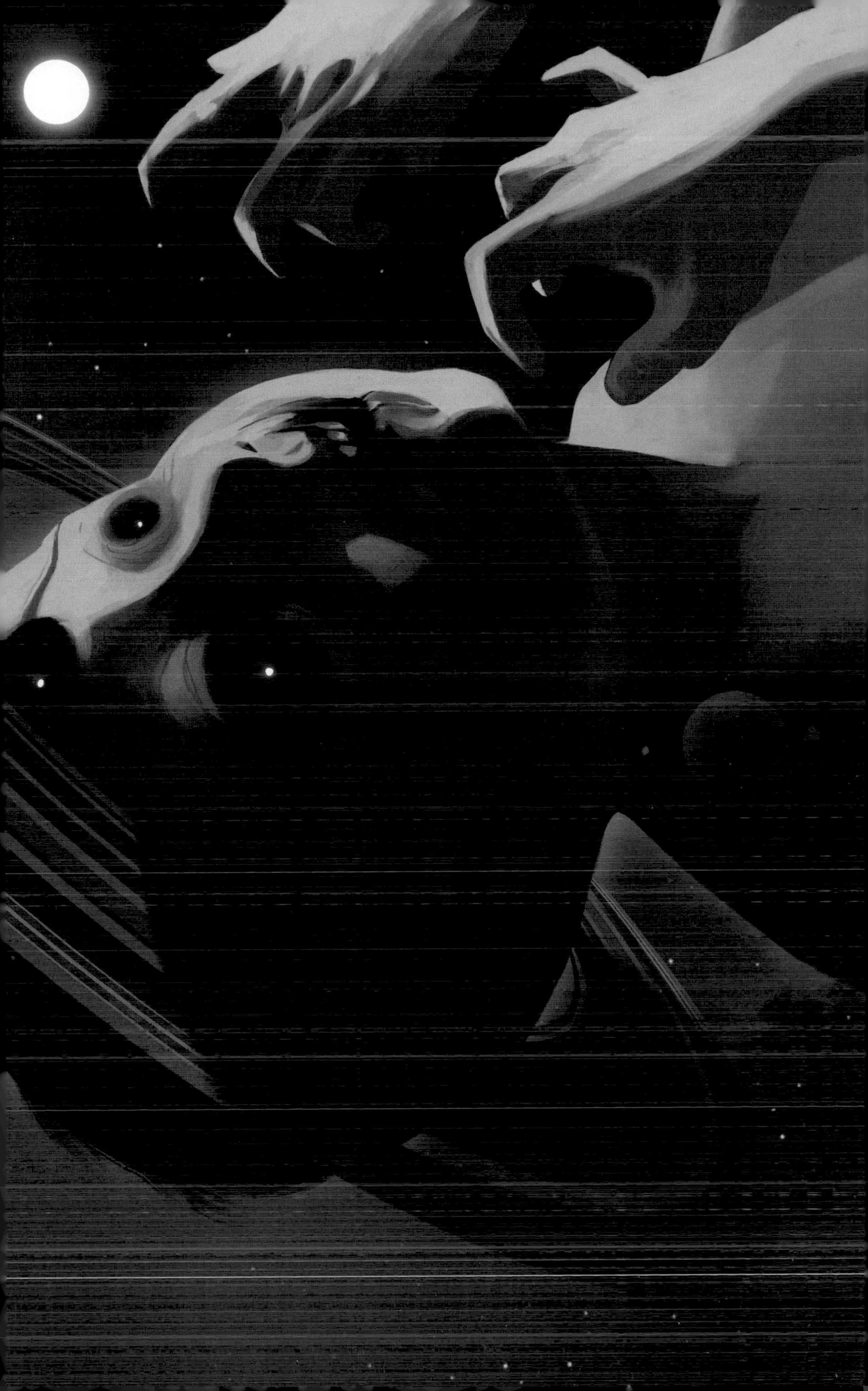

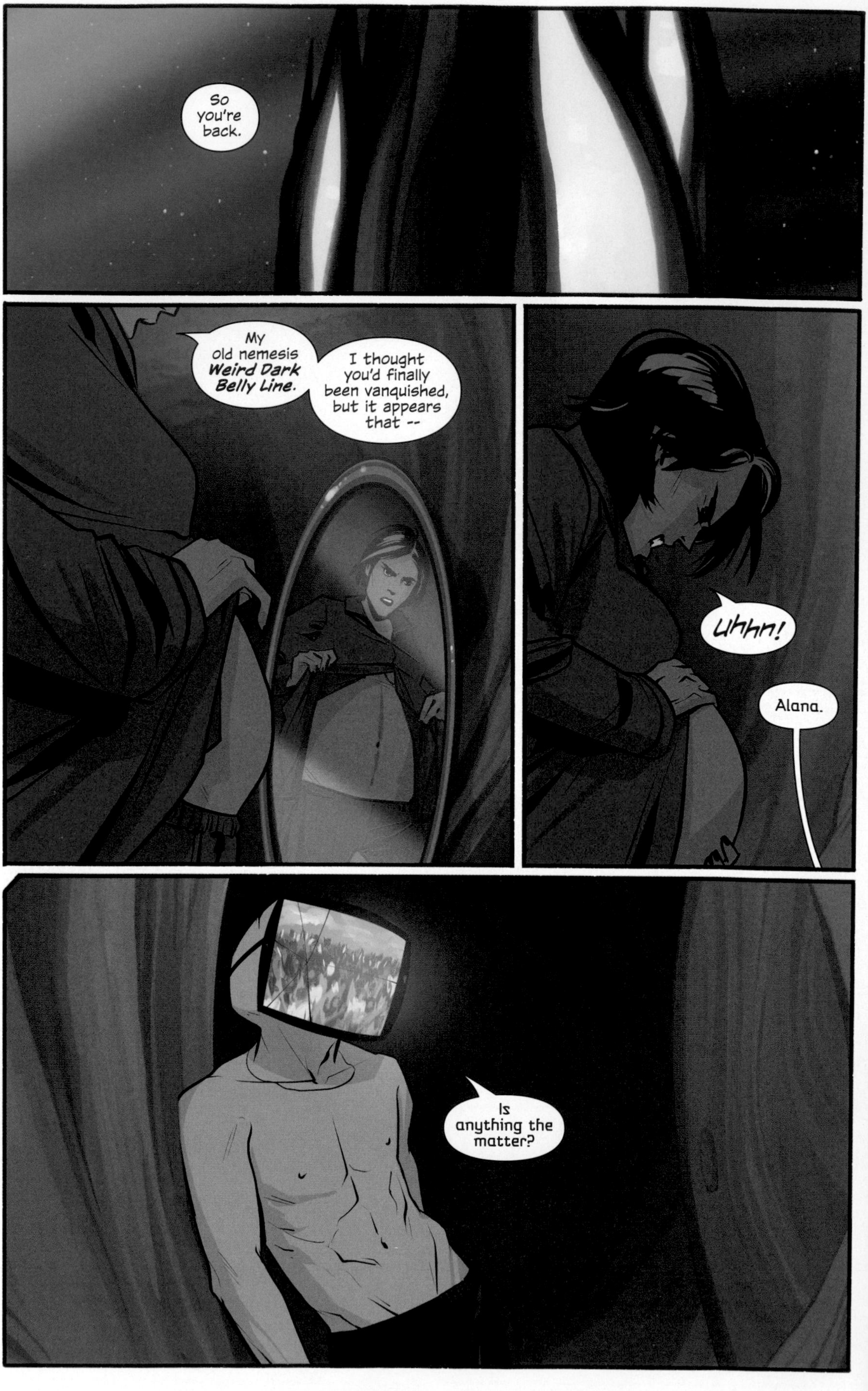

So you're back.
My old nemesis **Weird Dark Belly Line.**
I thought you'd finally been vanquished, but it appears that --
Uhhn!
Alana.
Is anything the matter?

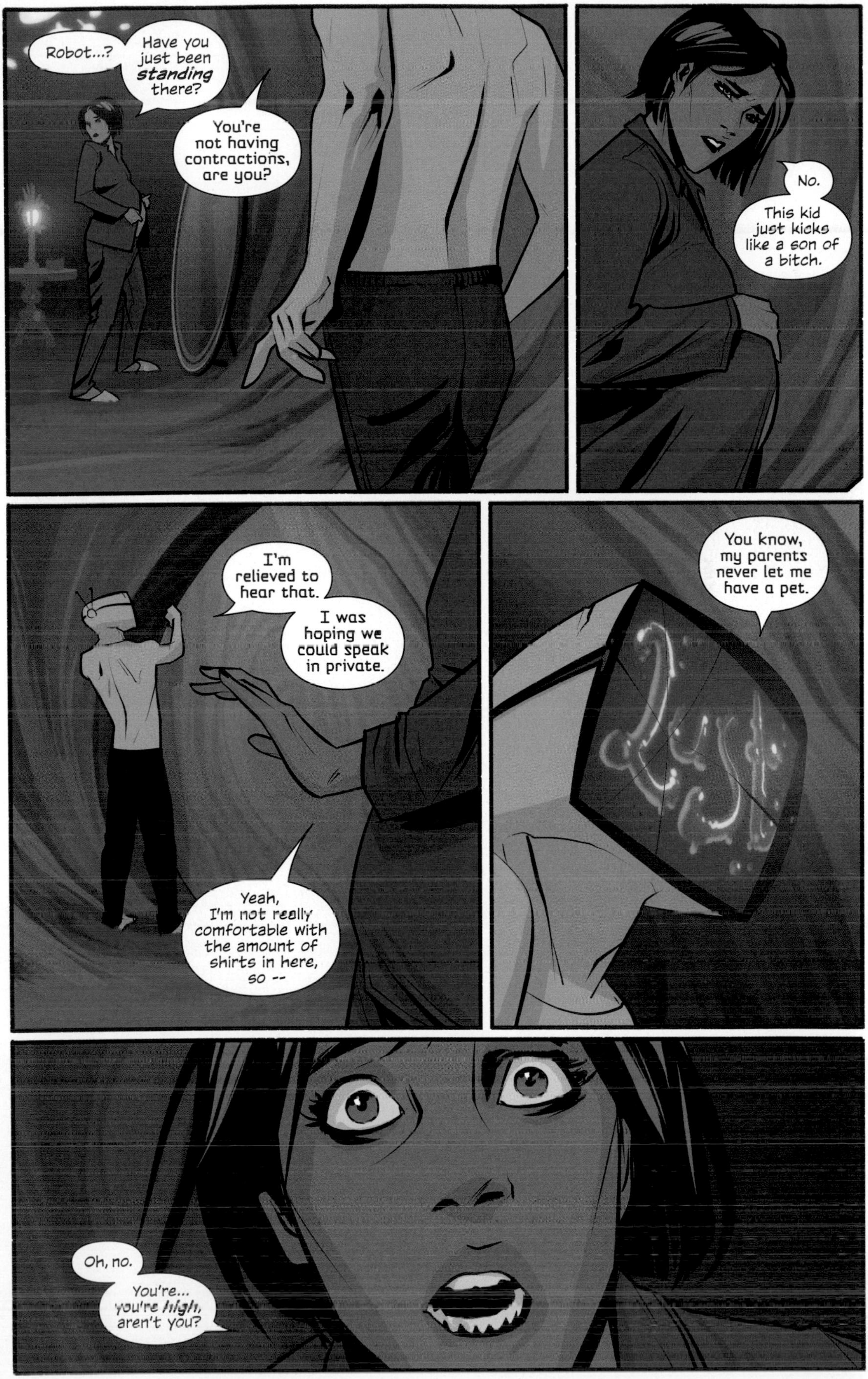
Robot...?
Have you just been *standing* there?
You're not having contractions, are you?
No.
This kid just kicks like a son of a bitch.
I'm relieved to hear that.
I was hoping we could speak in private.
Yeah, I'm not really comfortable with the amount of shirts in here, so --
You know, my parents never let me have a pet.
Oh, no.
You're... you're *high*, aren't you?

The opposite of war may be fucking, but that doesn't mean *peace* is a fiction.

As a matter of fact, I've just realized a surefire way to achieve it.

Where the hell did you get *Fadeaway*?!

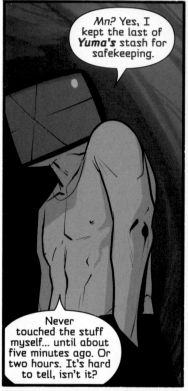

Mn? Yes, I kept the last of *Yuma's* stash for safekeeping.

Never touched the stuff myself... until about five minutes ago. Or two hours. It's hard to tell, isn't it?

I still have another square if you'd care to --

Listen to me.

I don't know what that crap does to brains like yours, but I promise that you're not thinking straight right now.

You're wrong, Alana.

For the first time, I can see myself as I really am, with all my countless sins in highest definition.

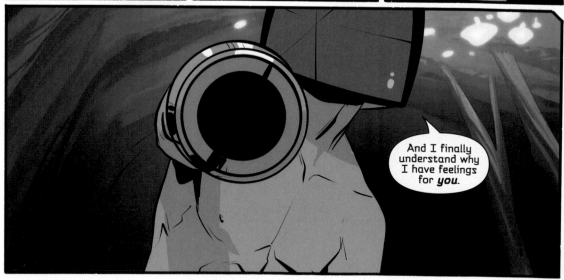

And I finally understand why I have feelings for *you*.

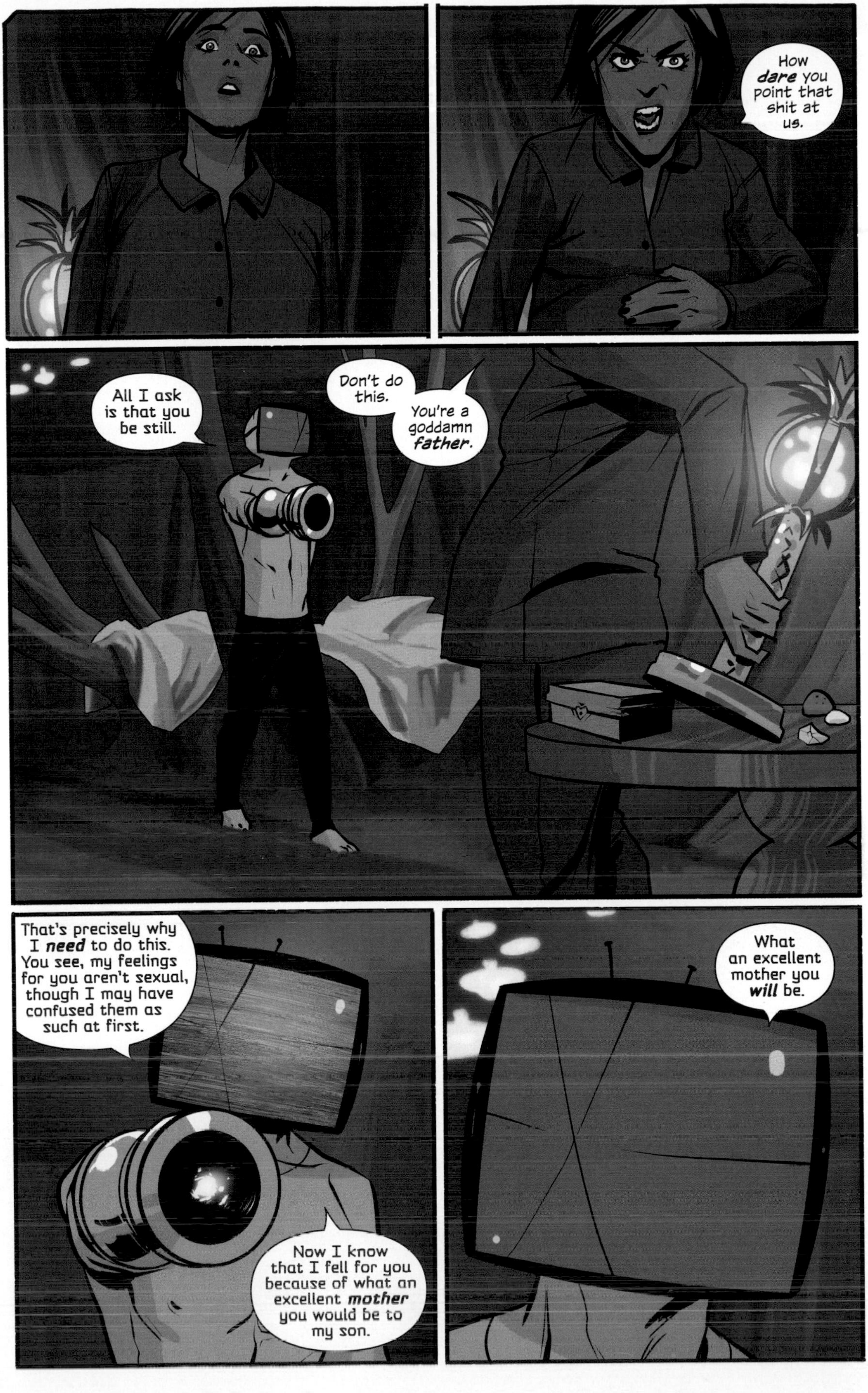
How *dare* you point that shit at us.
All I ask is that you be still.
Don't do this.
You're a goddamn *father*.
That's precisely why I *need* to do this. You see, my feelings for you aren't sexual, though I may have confused them as such at first.
Now I know that I fell for you because of what an excellent *mother* you would be to my son.
What an excellent mother you *will* be.

CHAPTER

FORTY-ONE

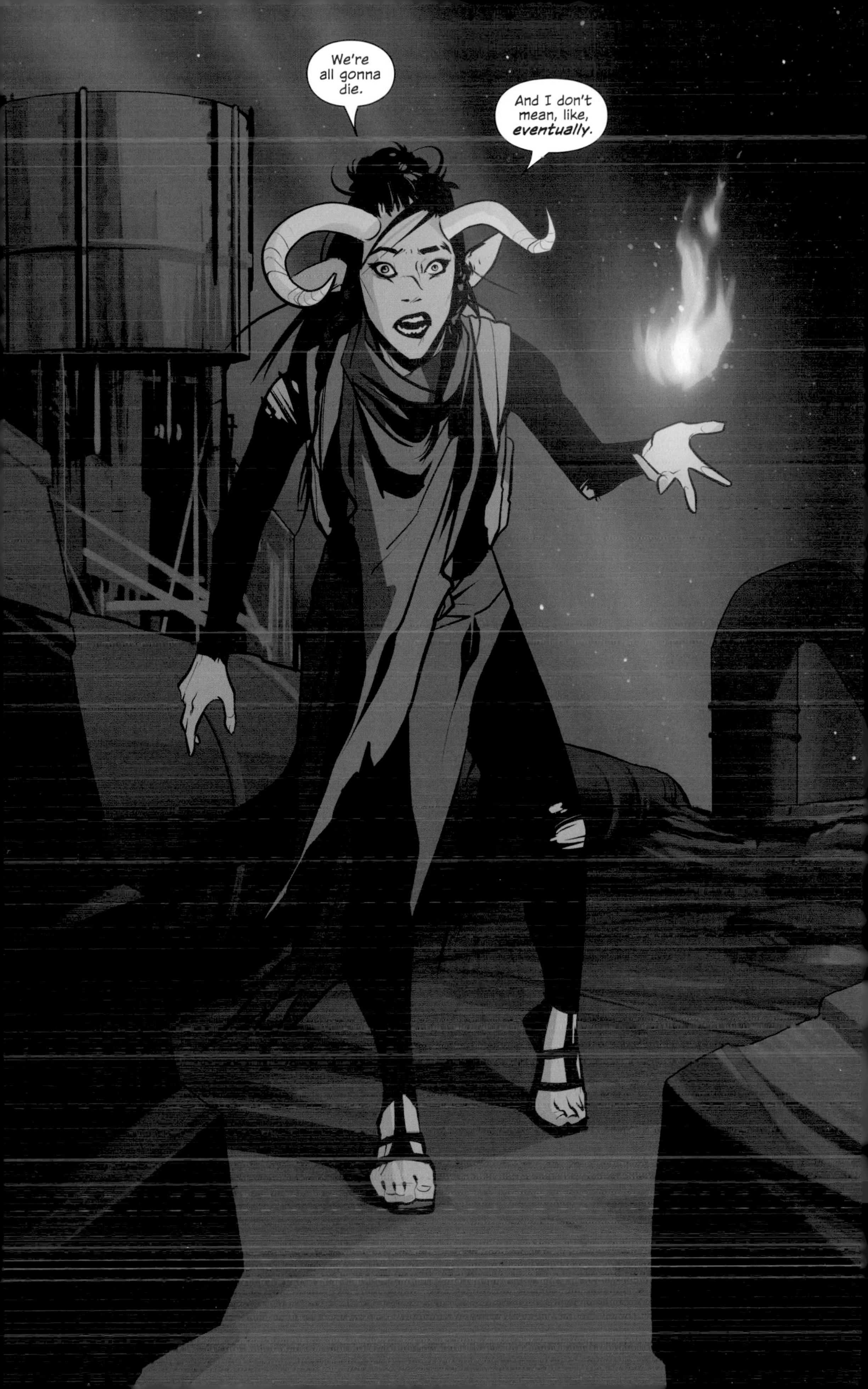
We're all gonna die.
And I don't mean, like, *eventually*.

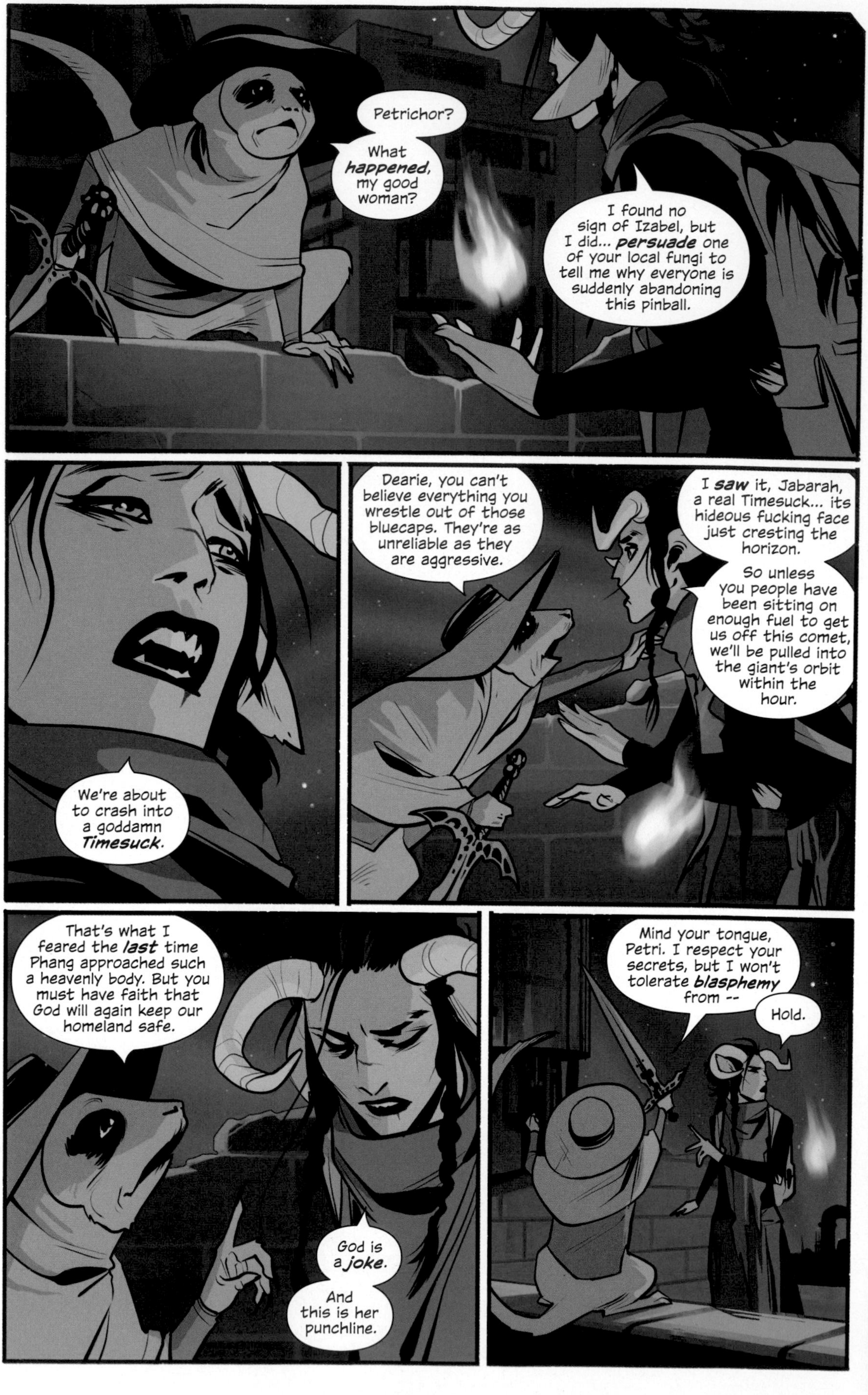
Petrichor?
What *happened*, my good woman?
I found no sign of Izabel, but I did... *persuade* one of your local fungi to tell me why everyone is suddenly abandoning this pinball.
We're about to crash into a goddamn *Timesuck*.
Dearie, you can't believe everything you wrestle out of those bluecaps. They're as unreliable as they are aggressive.
I *saw* it, Jabarah, a real Timesuck... its hideous fucking face just cresting the horizon.
So unless you people have been sitting on enough fuel to get us off this comet, we'll be pulled into the giant's orbit within the hour.
That's what I feared the *last* time Phang approached such a heavenly body. But you must have faith that God will again keep our homeland safe.
God is a *joke*.
And this is her punchline.
Mind your tongue, Petri. I respect your secrets, but I won't tolerate *blasphemy* from --
Hold.

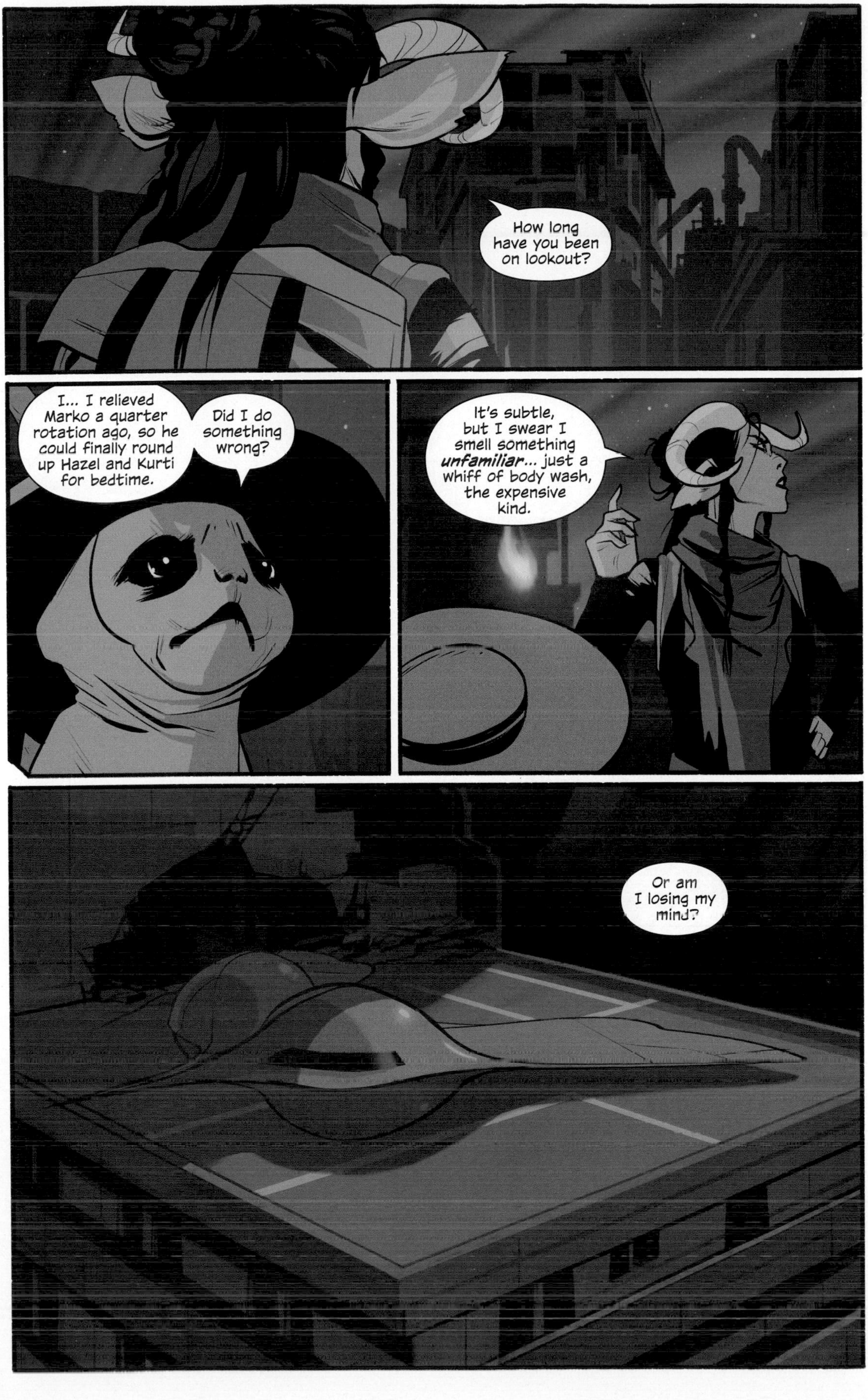
How long have you been on lookout?
I... I relieved Marko a quarter rotation ago, so he could finally round up Hazel and Kurti for bedtime.
Did I do something wrong?
It's subtle, but I swear I smell something *unfamiliar*... just a whiff of body wash, the expensive kind.
Or am I losing my mind?

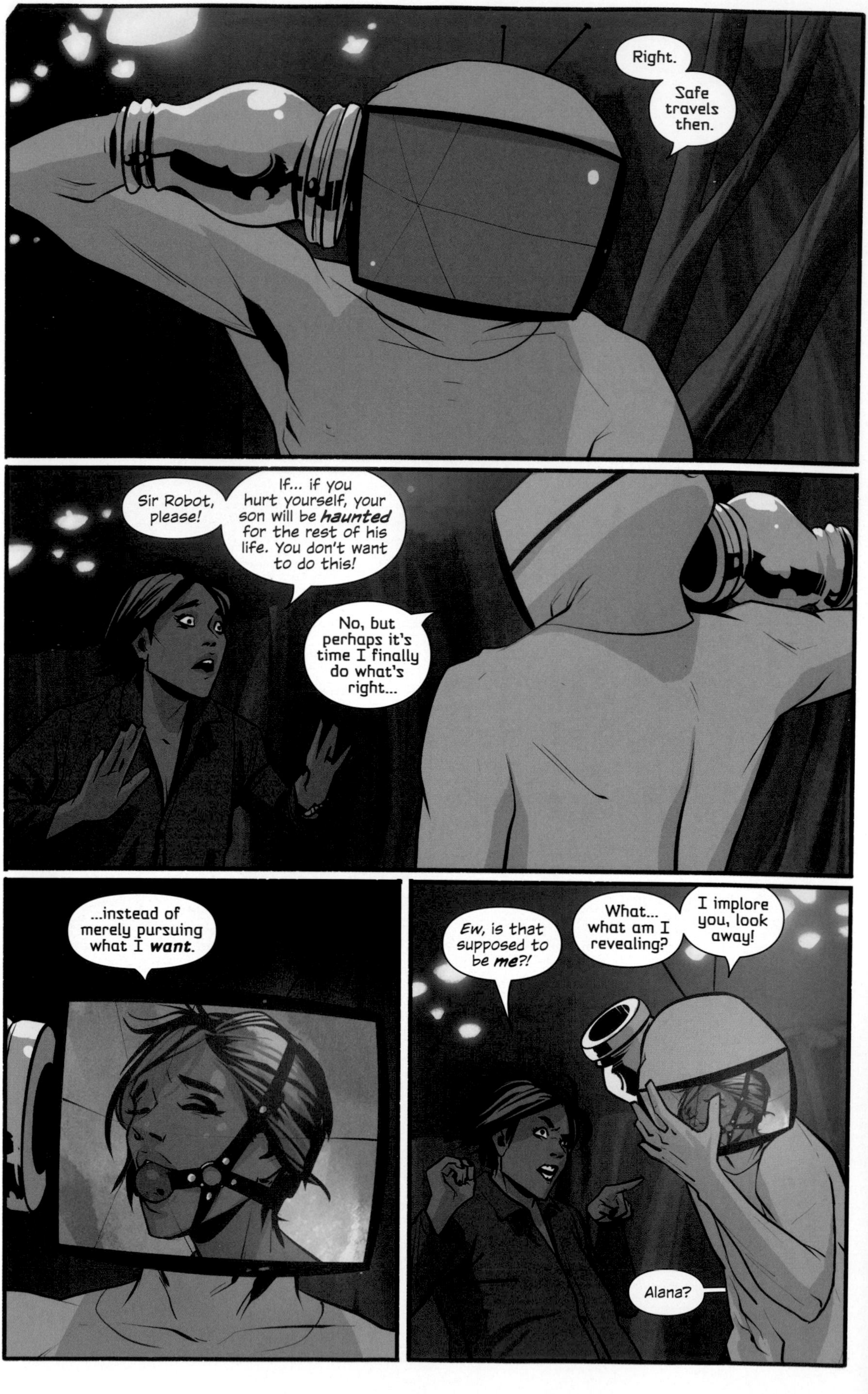
Right.
Safe travels then.
Sir Robot, please!
If... if you hurt yourself, your son will be ***haunted*** for the rest of his life. You don't want to do this!
No, but perhaps it's time I finally do what's right...
...instead of merely pursuing what I ***want***.
Ew, is that supposed to be ***me***?!
What... what am I revealing?
I implore you, look away!
Alana?

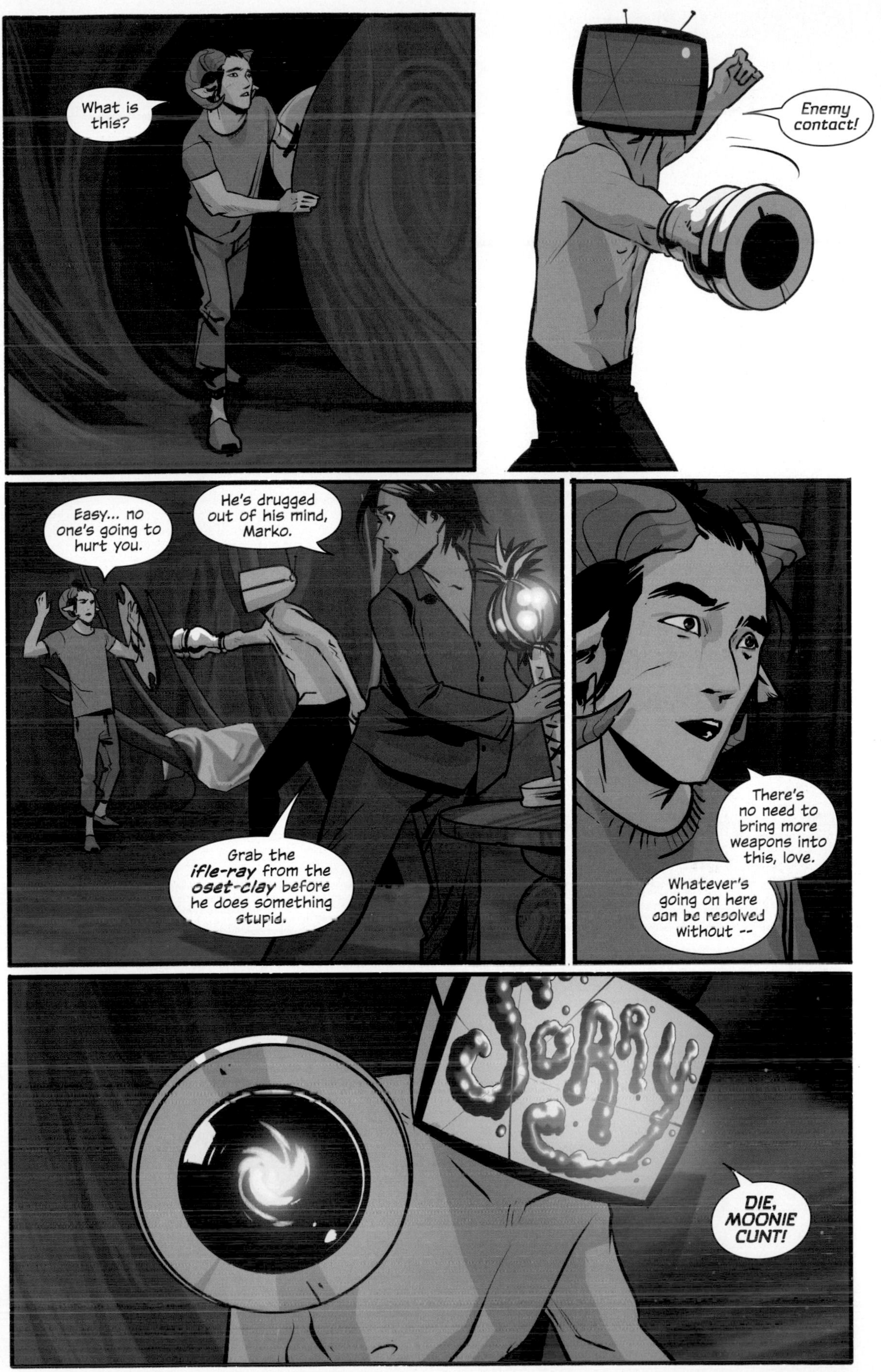
What is this?
Enemy contact!
Easy... no one's going to hurt you.
He's drugged out of his mind, Marko.
Grab the *ifle-ray* from the *oset-clay* before he does something stupid.
There's no need to bring more weapons into this, love.
Whatever's going on here can be resolved without --
SORRY
DIE, MOONIE CUNT!

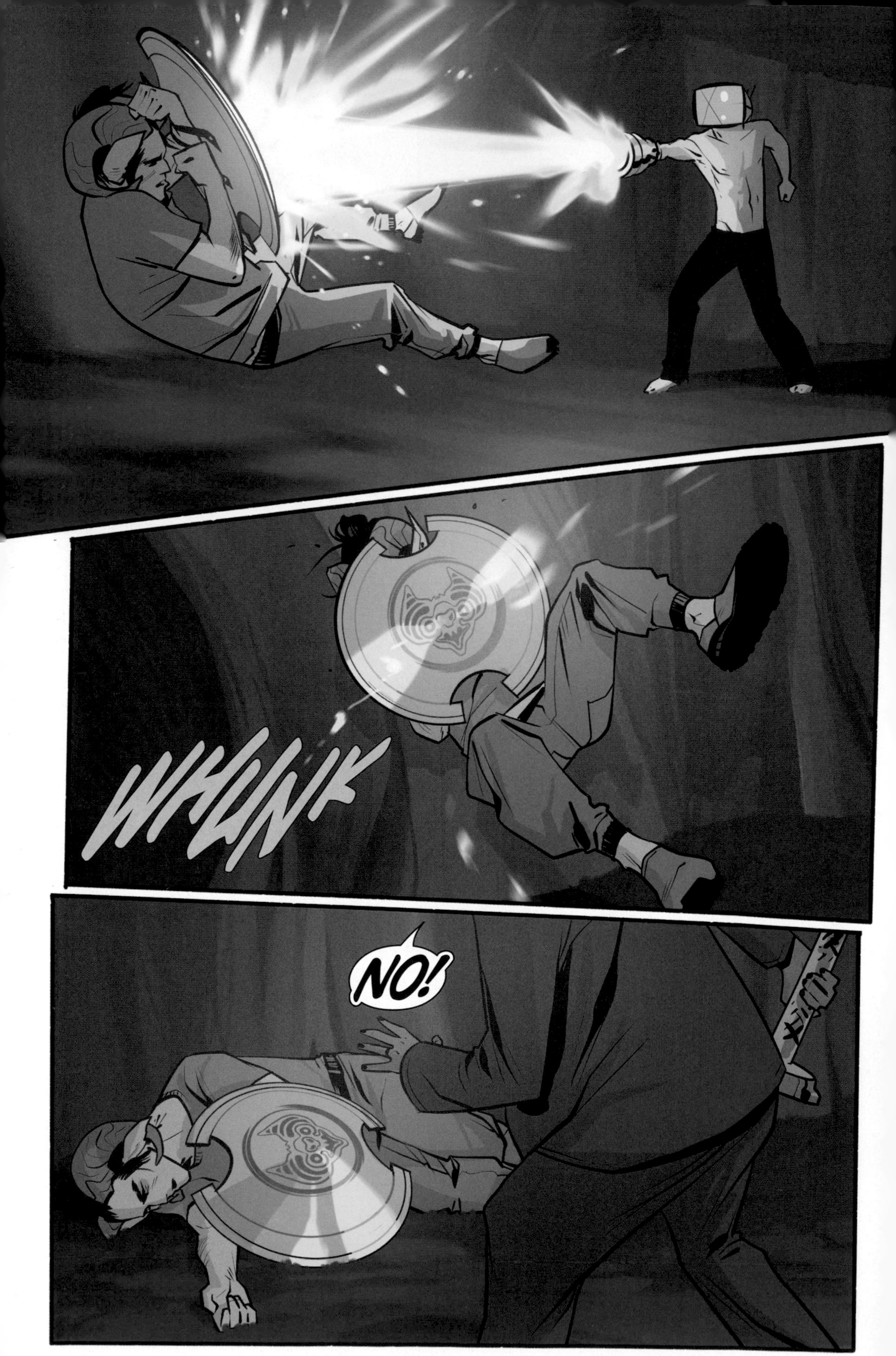
WHUNK
NO!

Oh, God.

What have I --

KALANK

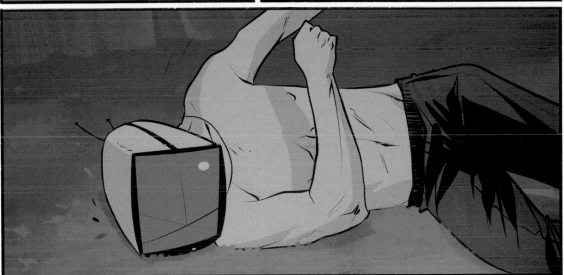

By the time they're out of preschool, most children have already seen thousands of acts of violence.

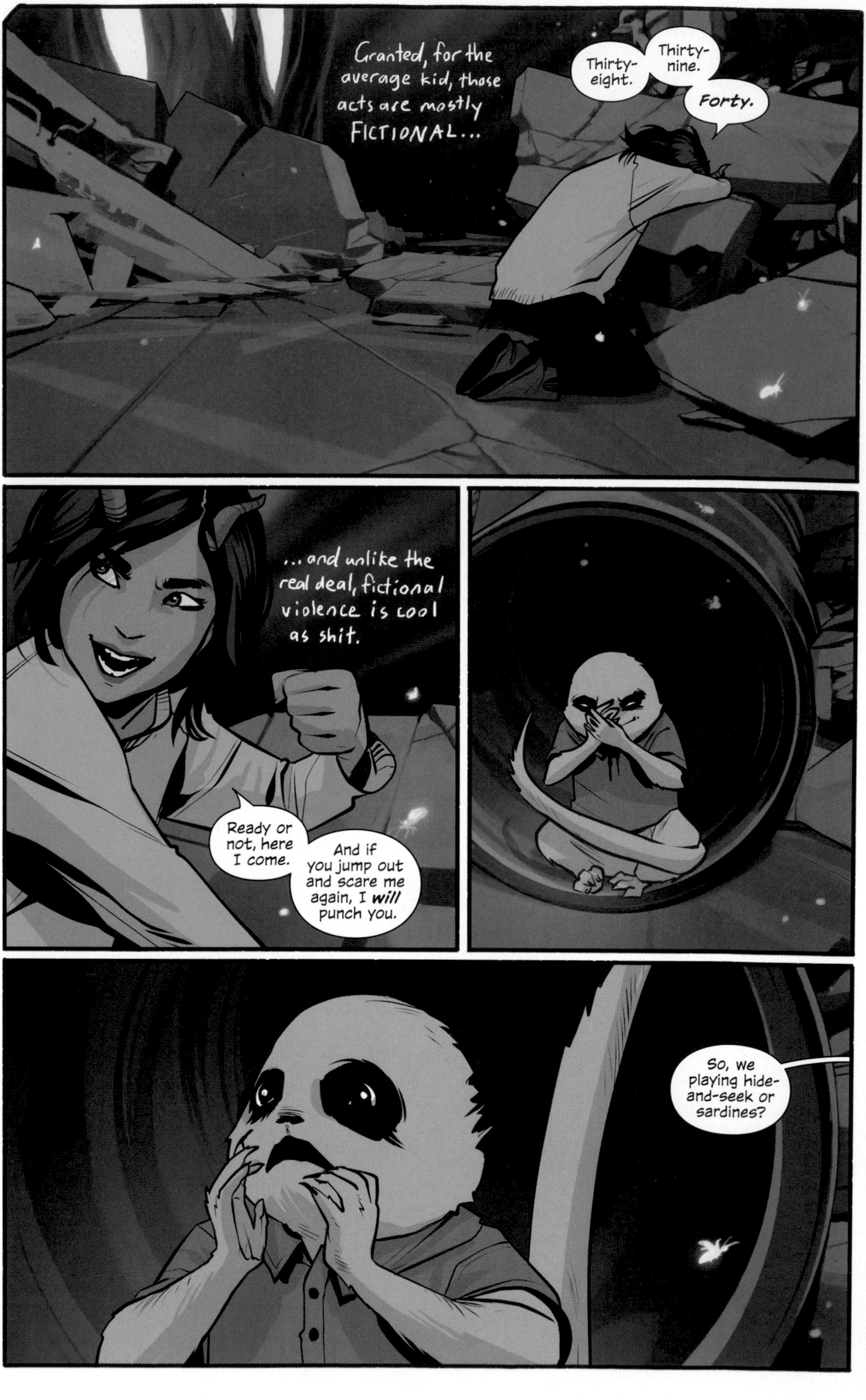
Granted, for the average kid, those acts are mostly FICTIONAL...
Thirty-eight.
Thirty-nine.
Forty.
...and unlike the real deal, fictional violence is cool as shit.
Ready or not, here I come.
And if you jump out and scare me again, I will punch you.
So, we playing hide-and-seek or sardines?

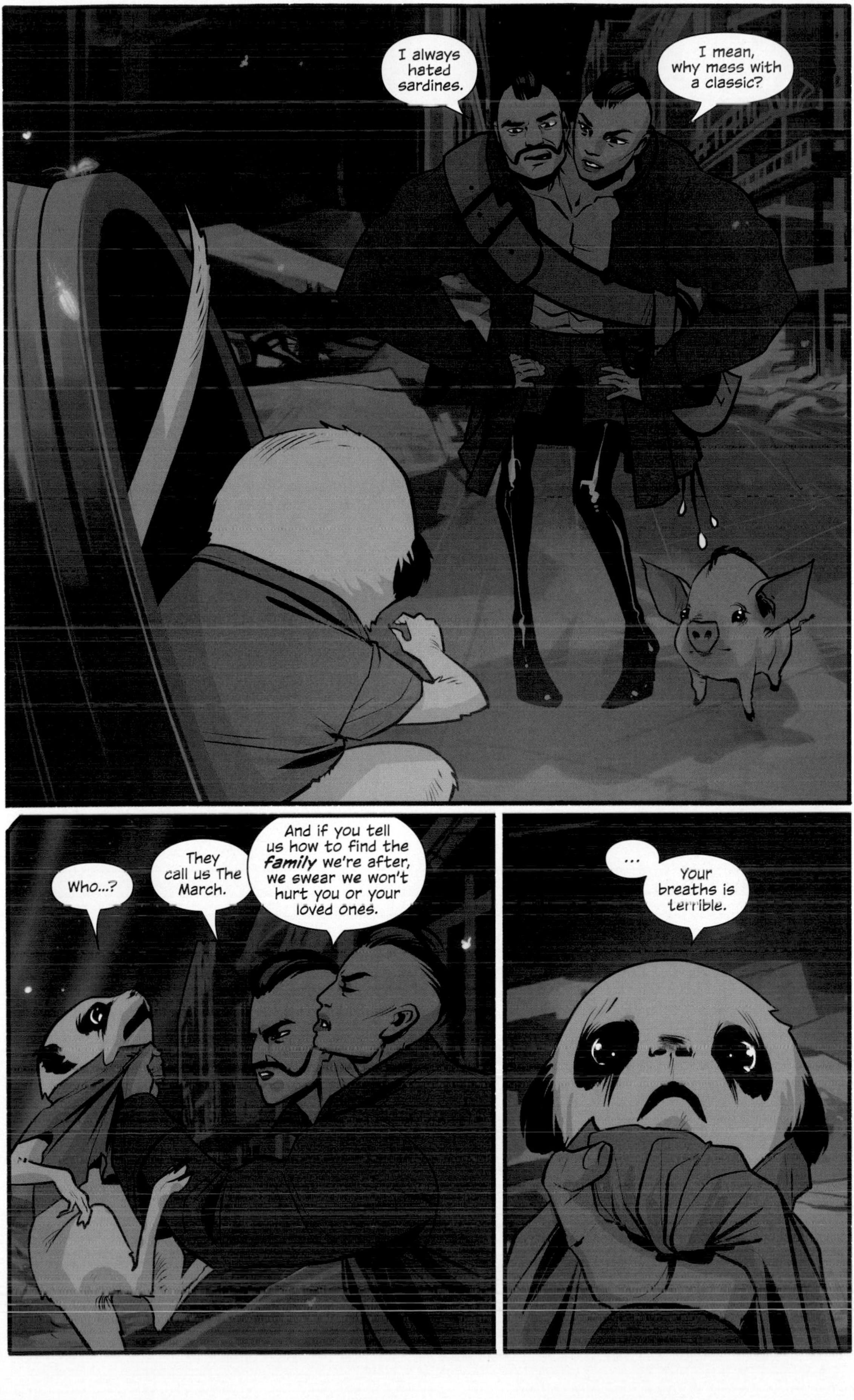
I always hated sardines.
I mean, why mess with a classic?
Who...?
They call us The March.
And if you tell us how to find the *family* we're after, we swear we won't hurt you or your loved ones.
...
Your breaths is terrible.

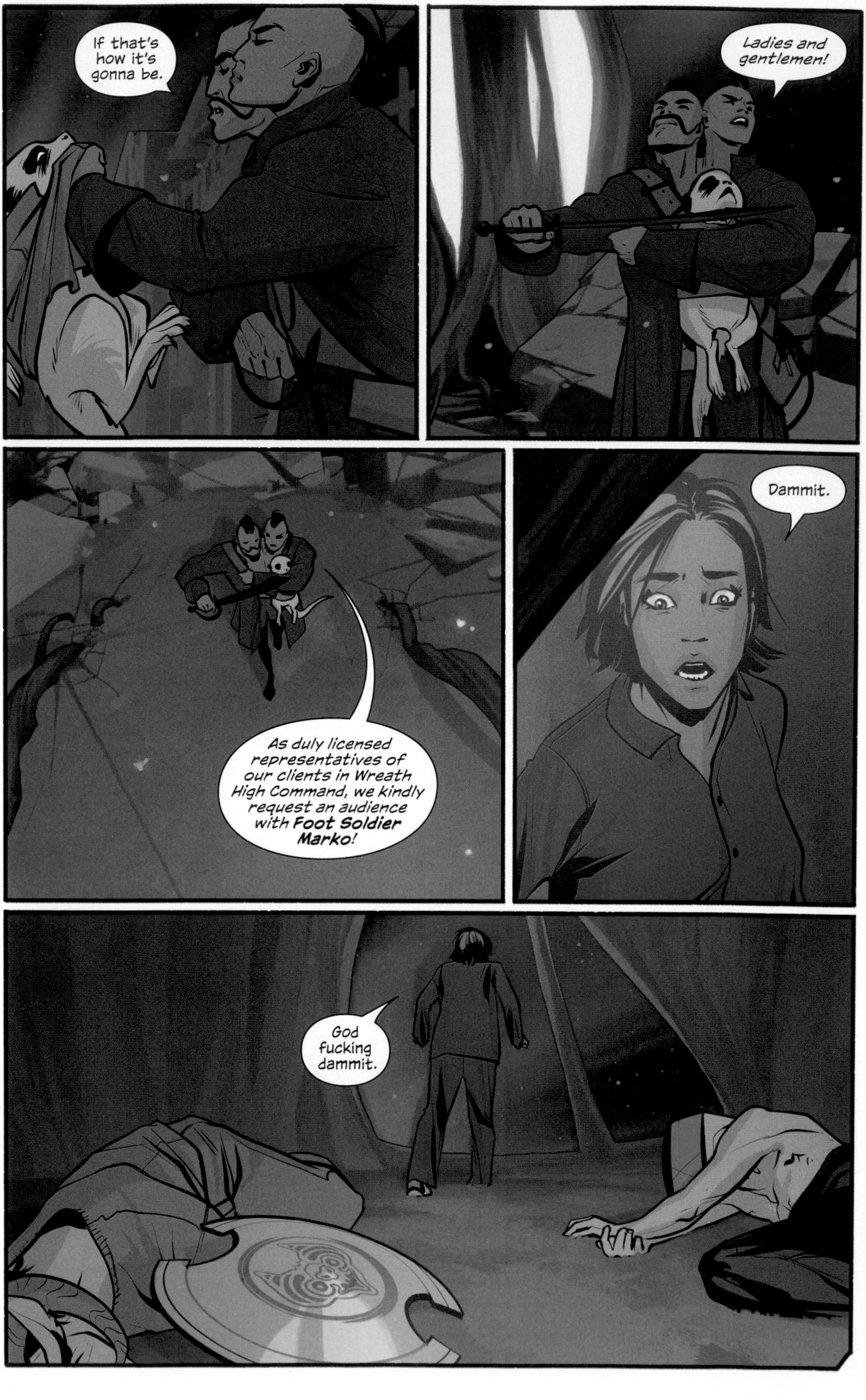
If that's how it's gonna be.
Ladies and gentlemen!
As duly licensed representatives of our clients in Wreath High Command, we kindly request an audience with Foot Soldier Marko!
Dammit.
God fucking dammit.

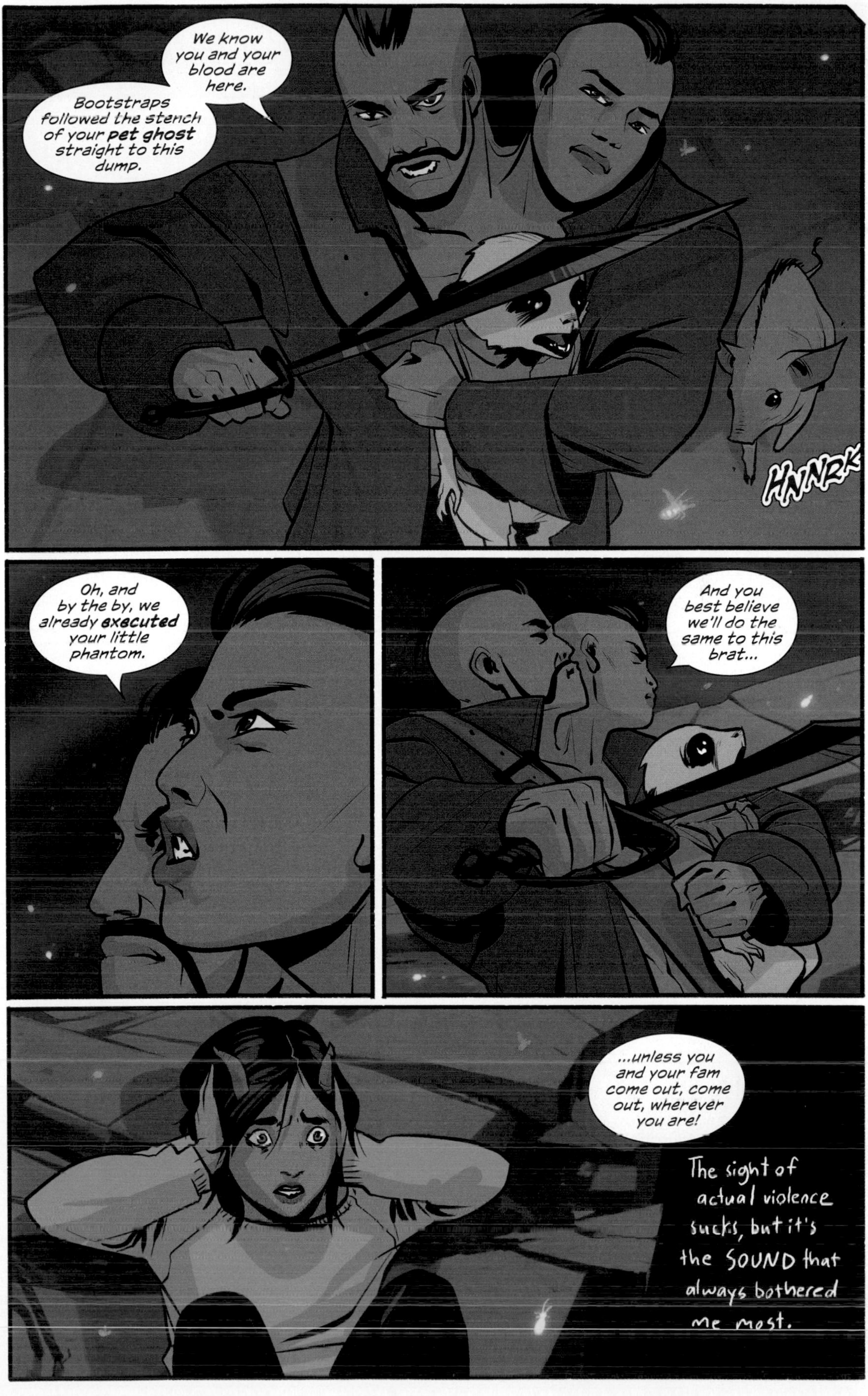

We know you and your blood are here.
Bootstraps followed the stench of your **pet ghost** straight to this dump.
HNNRK
Oh, and by the by, we already **executed** your little phantom.
And you best believe we'll do the same to this brat...
...unless you and your fam come out, come out, wherever you are!
The sight of actual violence sucks, but it's the SOUND that always bothered me most.

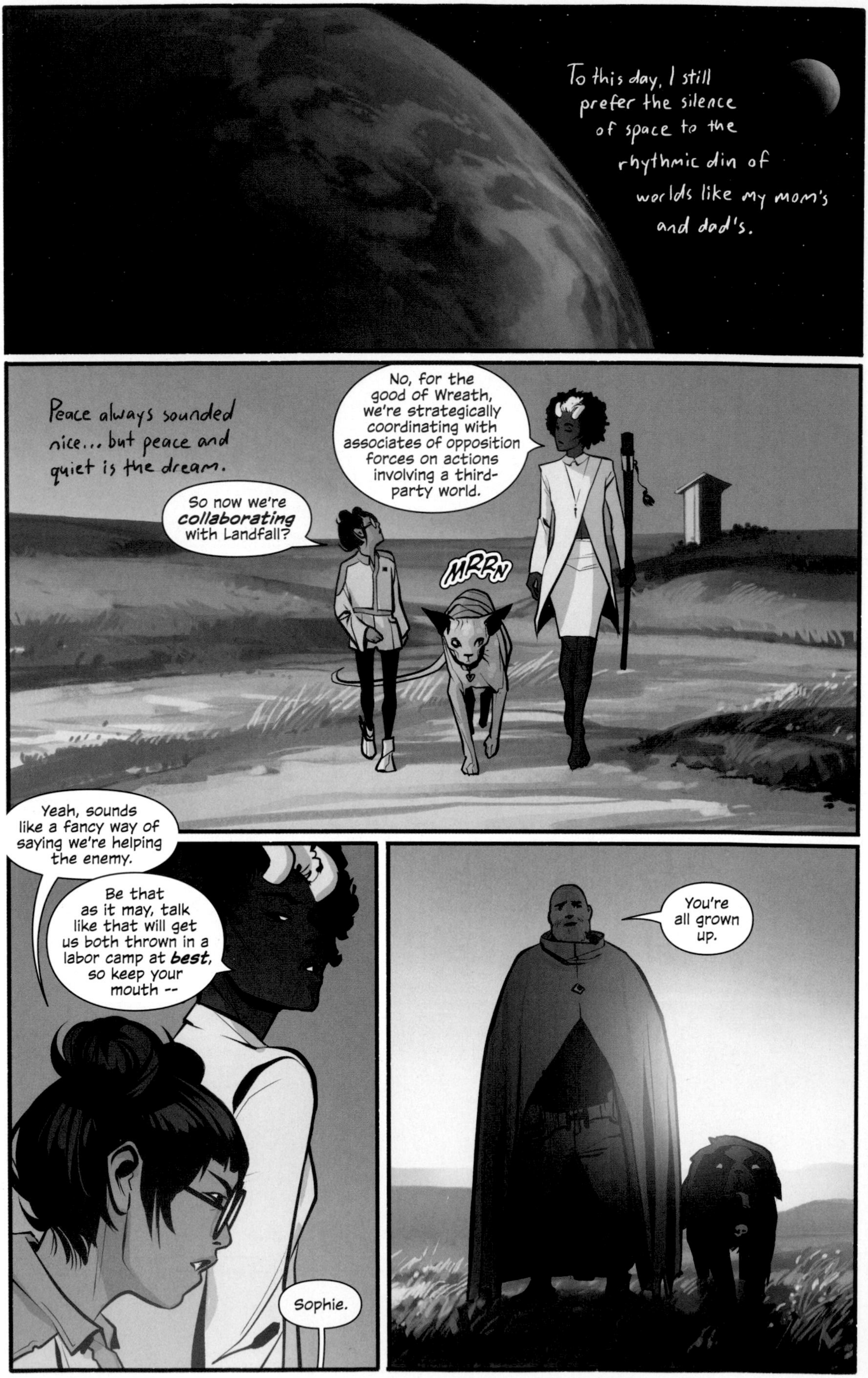
To this day, I still prefer the silence of space to the rhythmic din of worlds like my mom's and dad's.
Peace always sounded nice... but peace and quiet is the dream.
So now we're ***collaborating*** with Landfall?
No, for the good of Wreath, we're strategically coordinating with associates of opposition forces on actions involving a third-party world.
MRRN
Yeah, sounds like a fancy way of saying we're helping the enemy.
Be that as it may, talk like that will get us both thrown in a labor camp at ***best***, so keep your mouth --
Sophie.
You're all grown up.

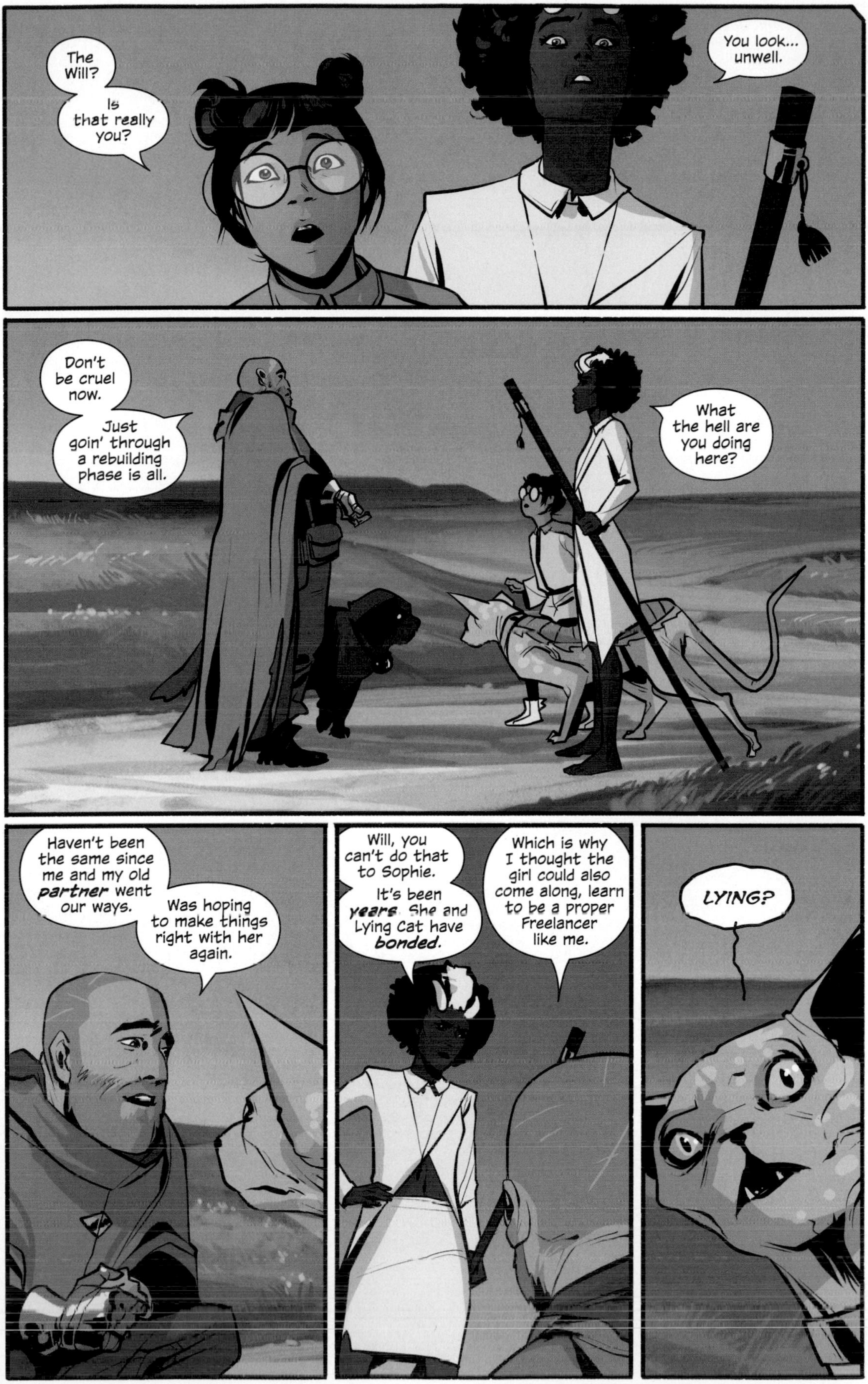
The Will?
Is that really you?
You look... unwell.
Don't be cruel now.
Just goin' through a rebuilding phase is all.
What the hell are you doing here?
Haven't been the same since me and my old **partner** went our ways.
Was hoping to make things right with her again.
Will, you can't do that to Sophie.
It's been **years**. She and Lying Cat have **bonded**.
Which is why I thought the girl could also come along, learn to be a proper Freelancer like me.
LYING?

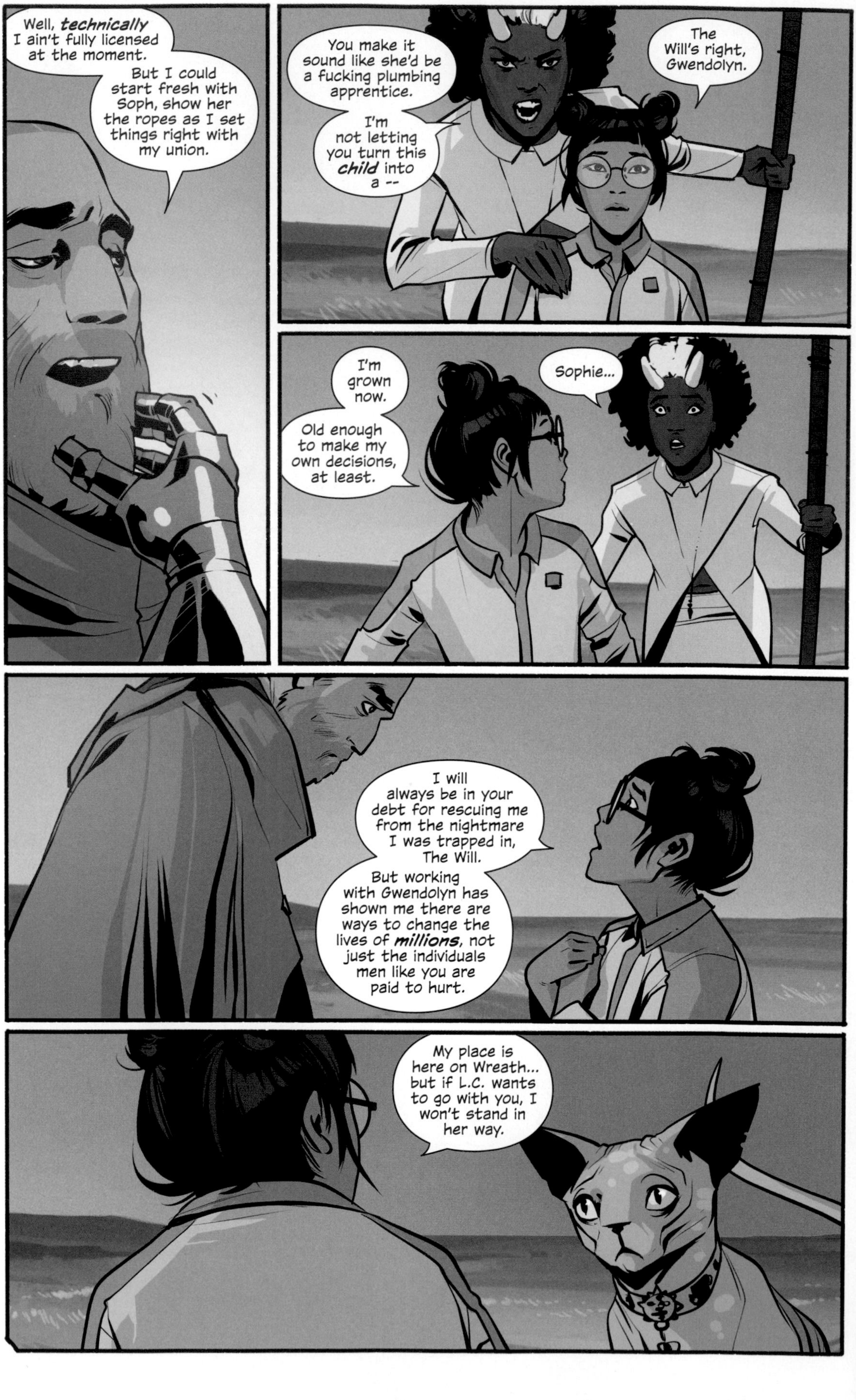
Well, technically I ain't fully licensed at the moment.
But I could start fresh with Soph, show her the ropes as I set things right with my union.
You make it sound like she'd be a fucking plumbing apprentice.
I'm not letting you turn this child into a --
The Will's right, Gwendolyn.
I'm grown now.
Old enough to make my own decisions, at least.
Sophie...
I will always be in your debt for rescuing me from the nightmare I was trapped in, The Will.
But working with Gwendolyn has shown me there are ways to change the lives of millions, not just the individuals men like you are paid to hurt.
My place is here on Wreath... but if L.C. wants to go with you, I won't stand in her way.

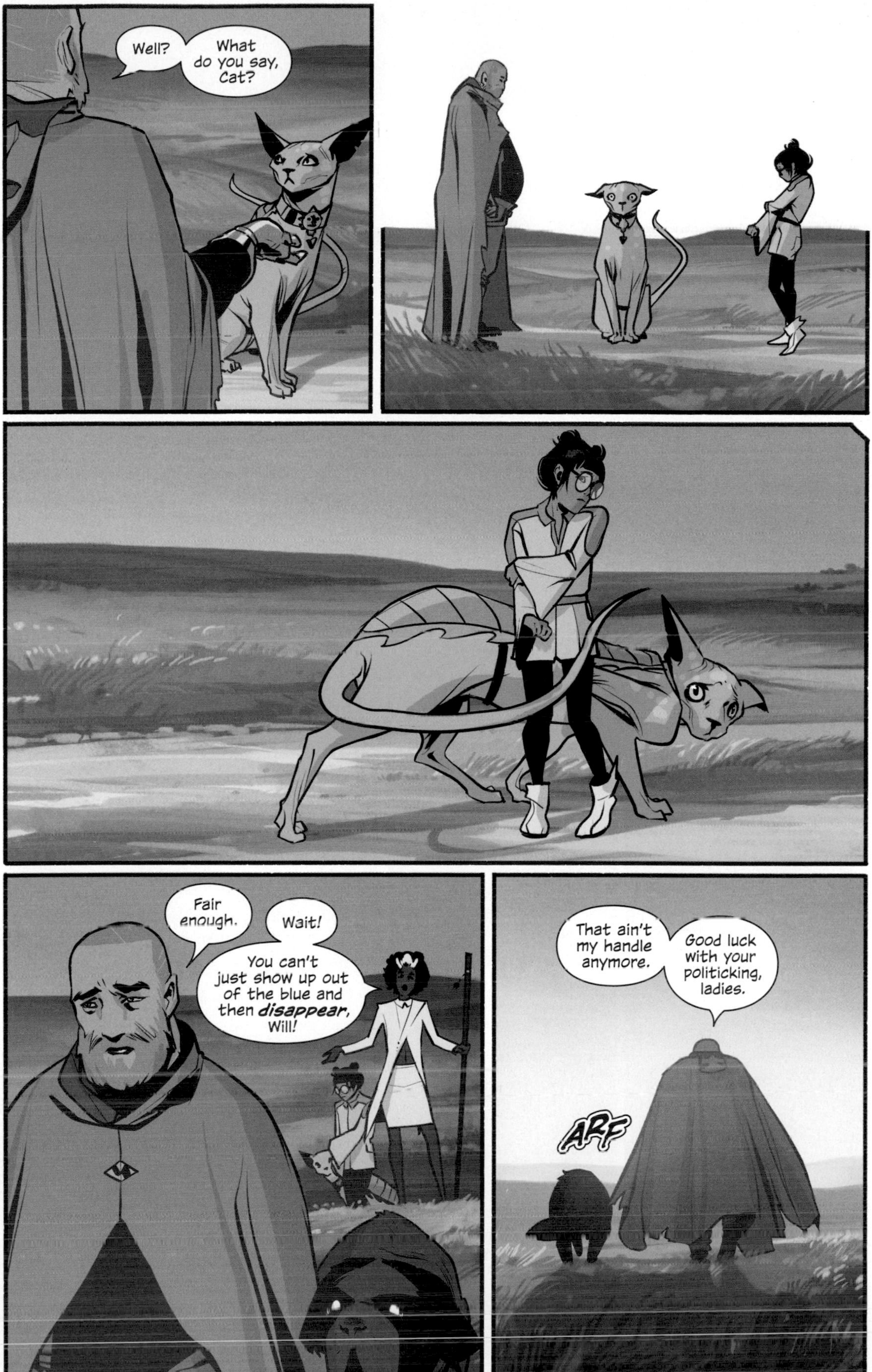
Well?
What do you say, Cat?
Fair enough.
Wait!
You can't just show up out of the blue and then *disappear*, Will!
That ain't my handle anymore.
Good luck with your politicking, ladies.
ARF

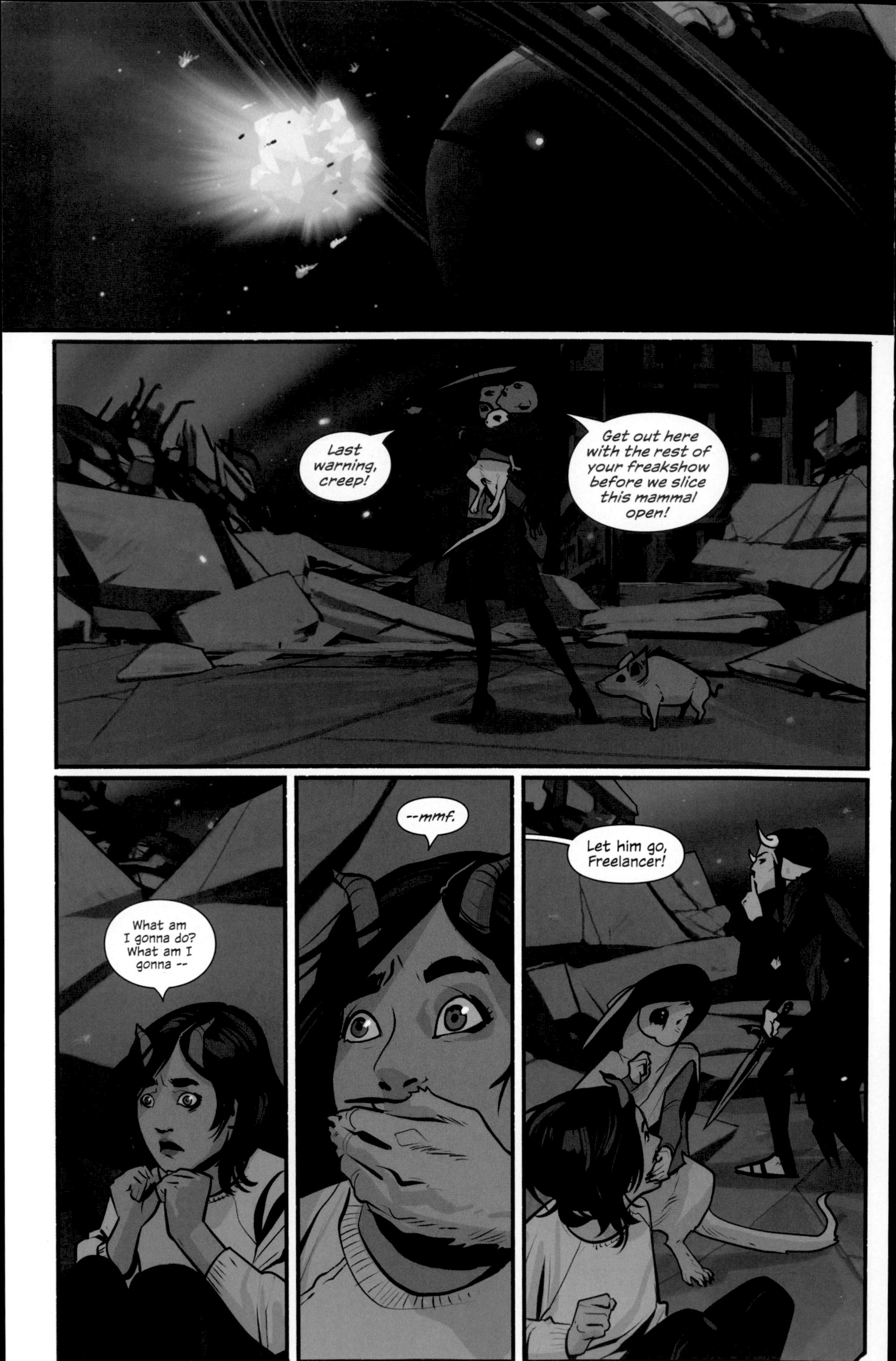
Last warning, creep!
Get out here with the rest of your freakshow before we slice this mammal open!
What am I gonna do? What am I gonna --
--mmf.
Let him go, Freelancer!

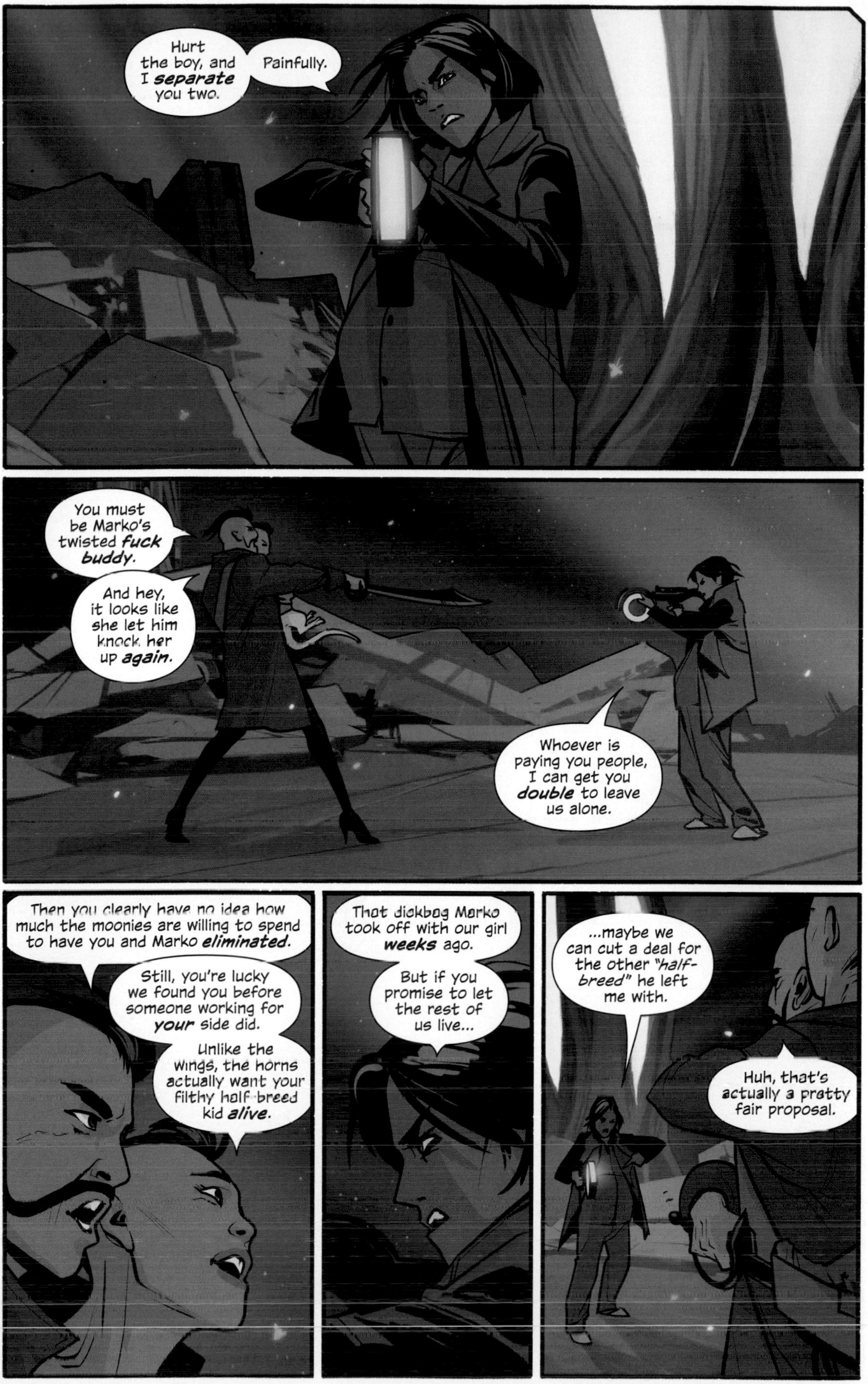
Hurt the boy, and I **separate** you two.
Painfully.
You must be Marko's twisted **fuck buddy**.
And hey, it looks like she let him knock her up **again**.
Whoever is paying you people, I can get you **double** to leave us alone.
Then you clearly have no idea how much the moonies are willing to spend to have you and Marko **eliminated**.
Still, you're lucky we found you before someone working for **your** side did.
Unlike the wings, the horns actually want your filthy half-breed kid **alive**.
That dickbag Marko took off with our girl **weeks** ago.
But if you promise to let the rest of us live...
...maybe we can cut a deal for the other *"half-breed"* he left me with.
Huh, that's actually a pretty fair proposal.

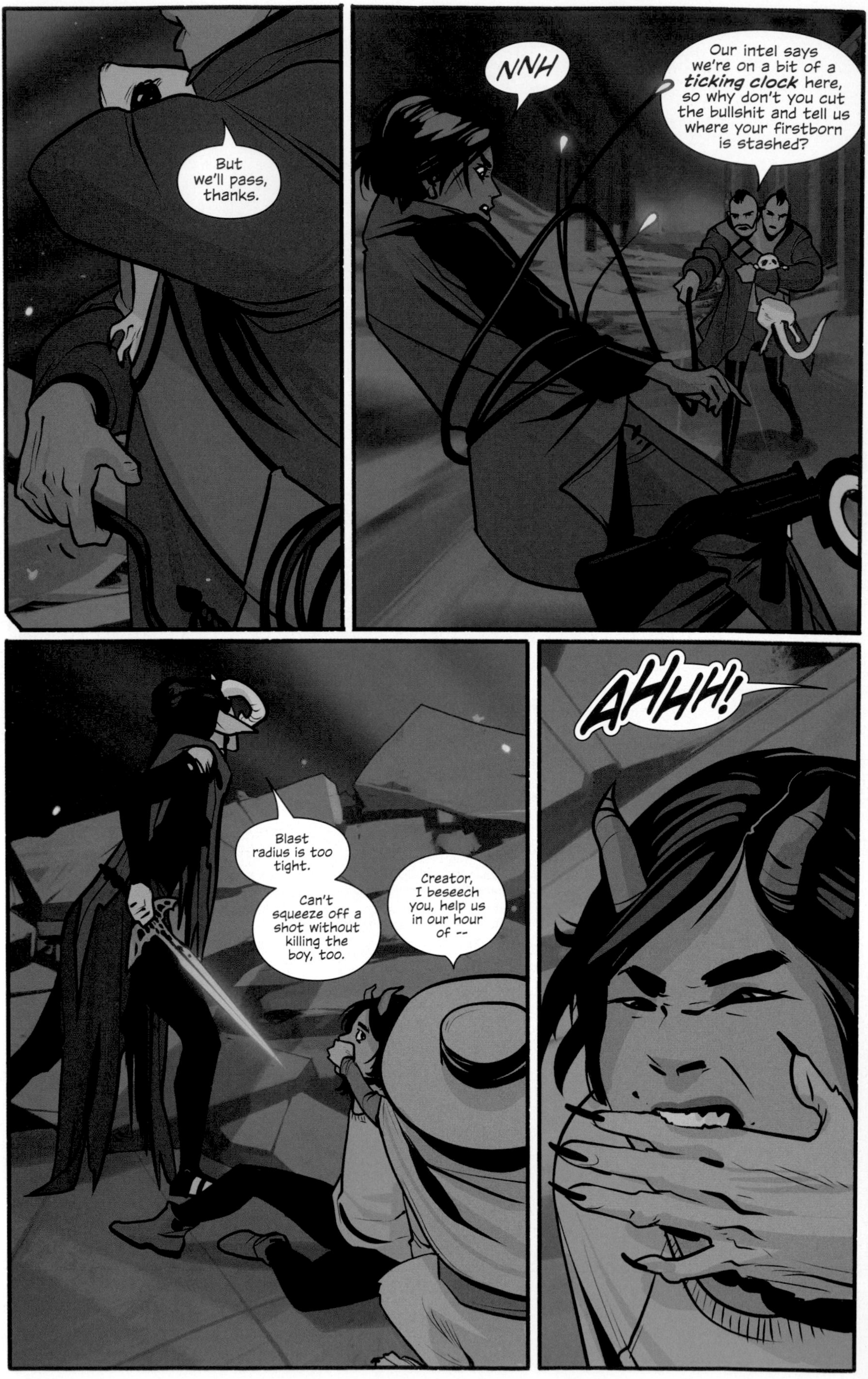
But we'll pass, thanks.
NNH
Our intel says we're on a bit of a ***ticking clock*** here, so why don't you cut the bullshit and tell us where your firstborn is stashed?
Blast radius is too tight.
Can't squeeze off a shot without killing the boy, too.
Creator, I beseech you, help us in our hour of --
AHHH!

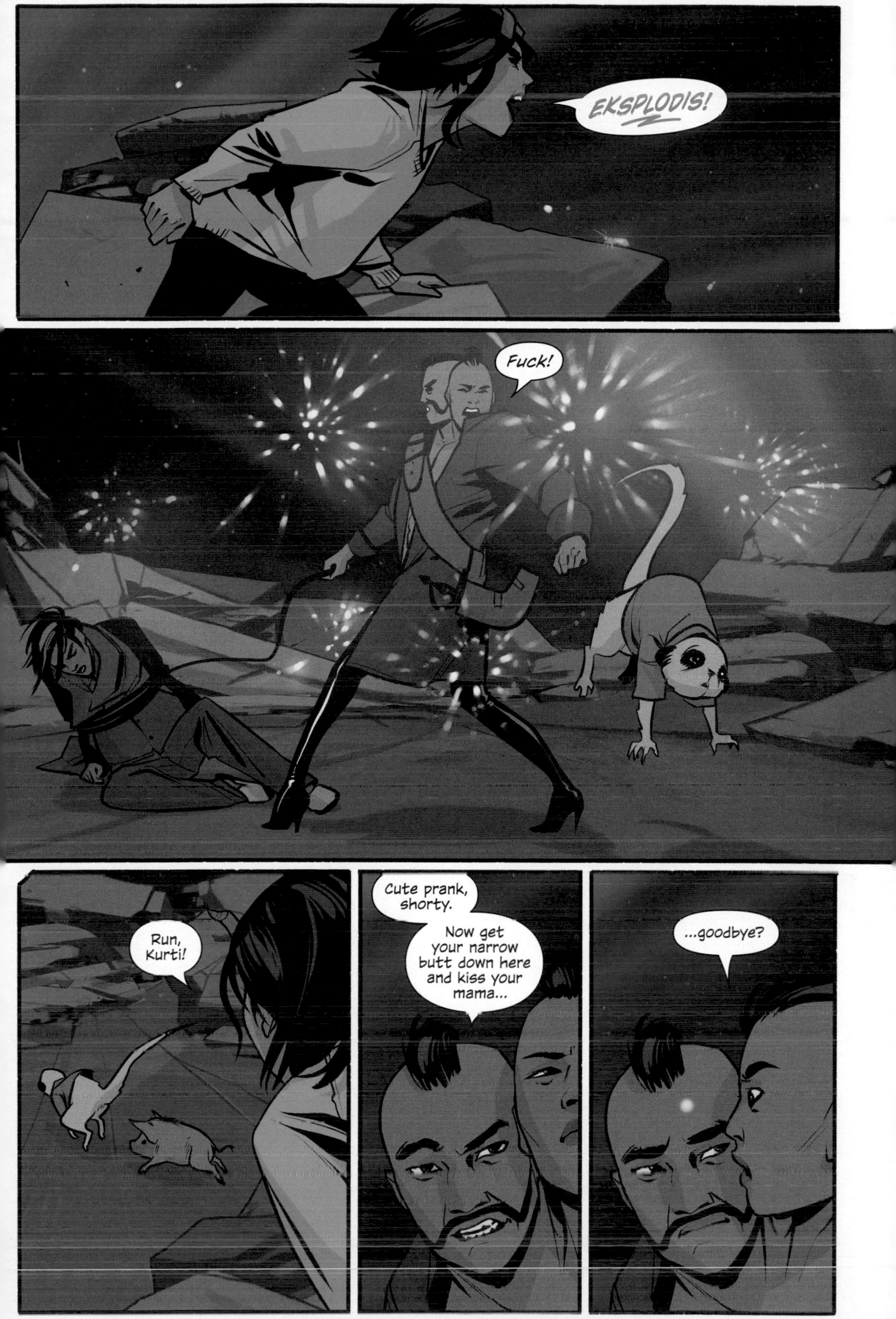
EKSPLODIS!
Fuck!
Run, Kurti!
Cute prank, shorty.
Now get your narrow butt down here and kiss your mama...
...goodbye?

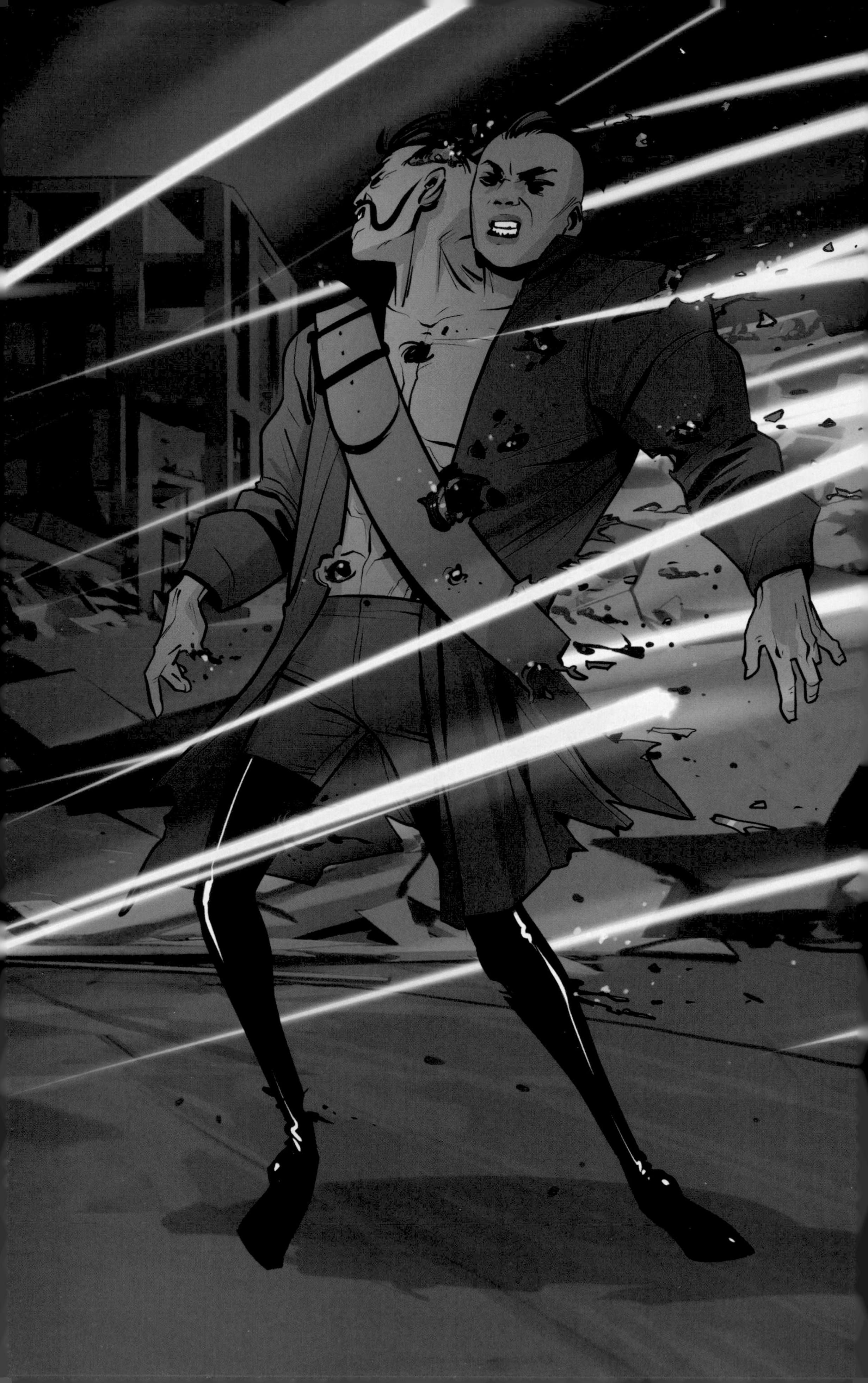

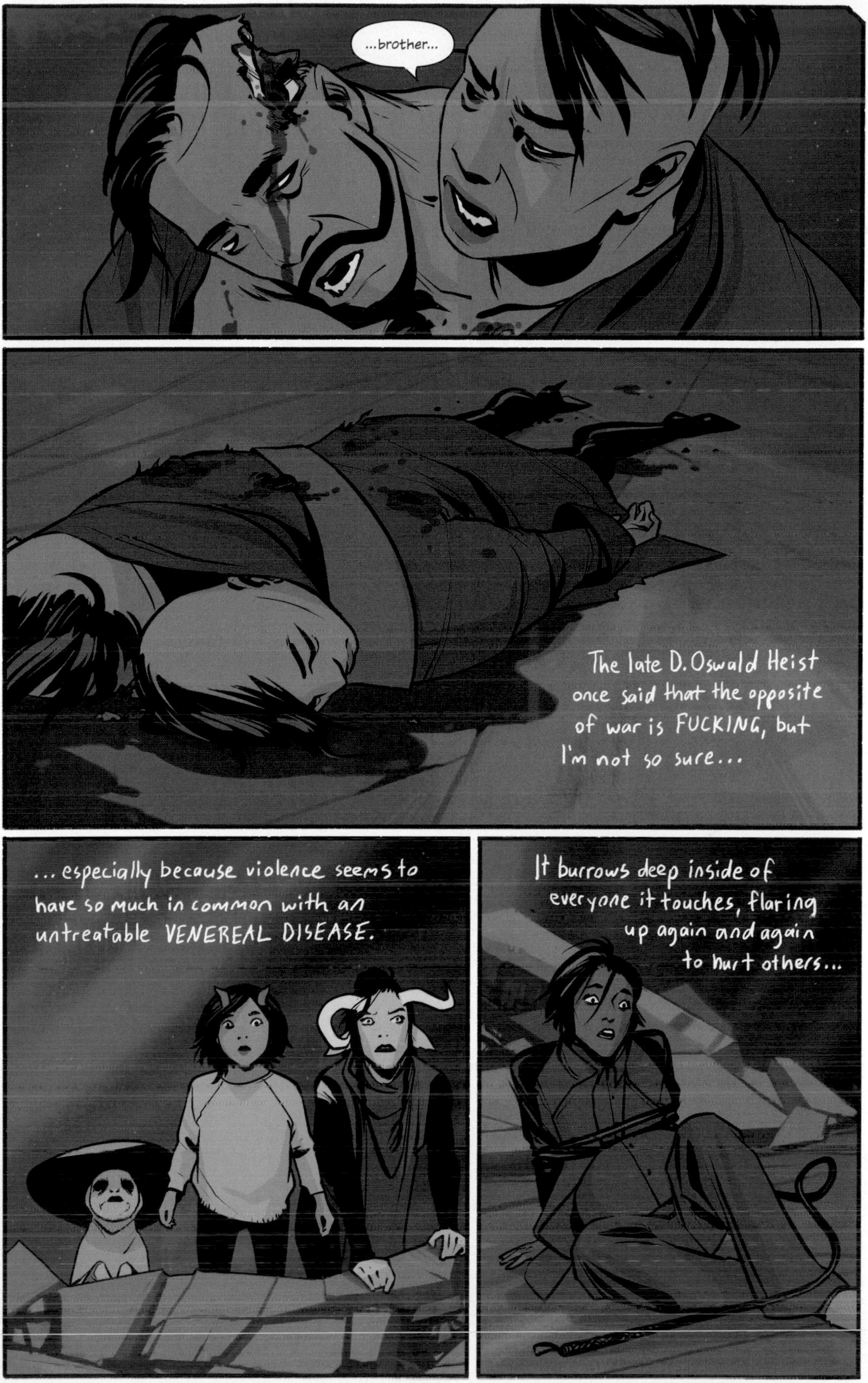
...brother...
The late D. Oswald Heist once said that the opposite of war is FUCKING, but I'm not so sure...
...especially because violence seems to have so much in common with an untreatable VENEREAL DISEASE.
It burrows deep inside of everyone it touches, flaring up again and again to hurt others...

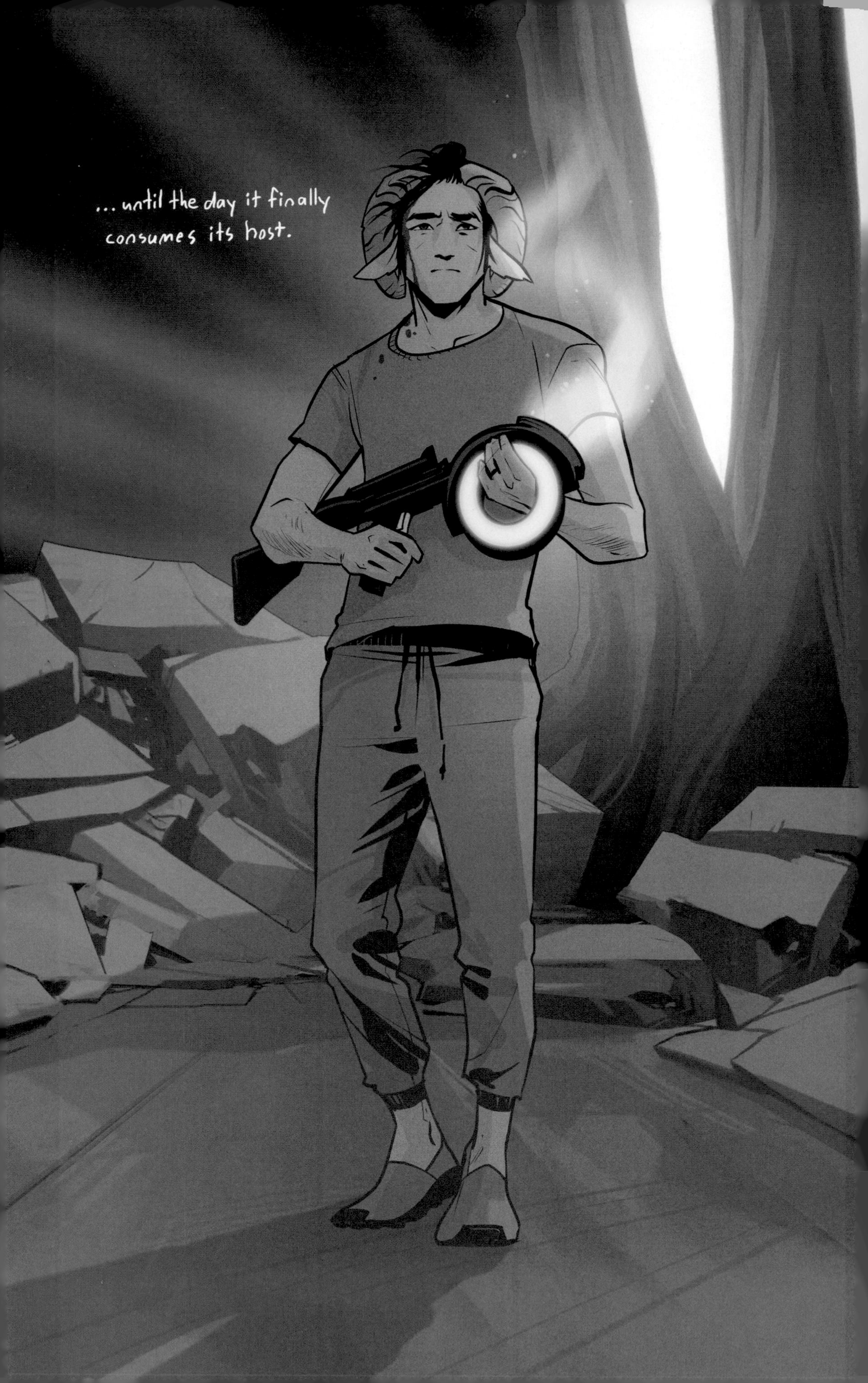
...until the day it finally consumes its host.

end chapter forty-one

CHAPTER
FORTY-TWO

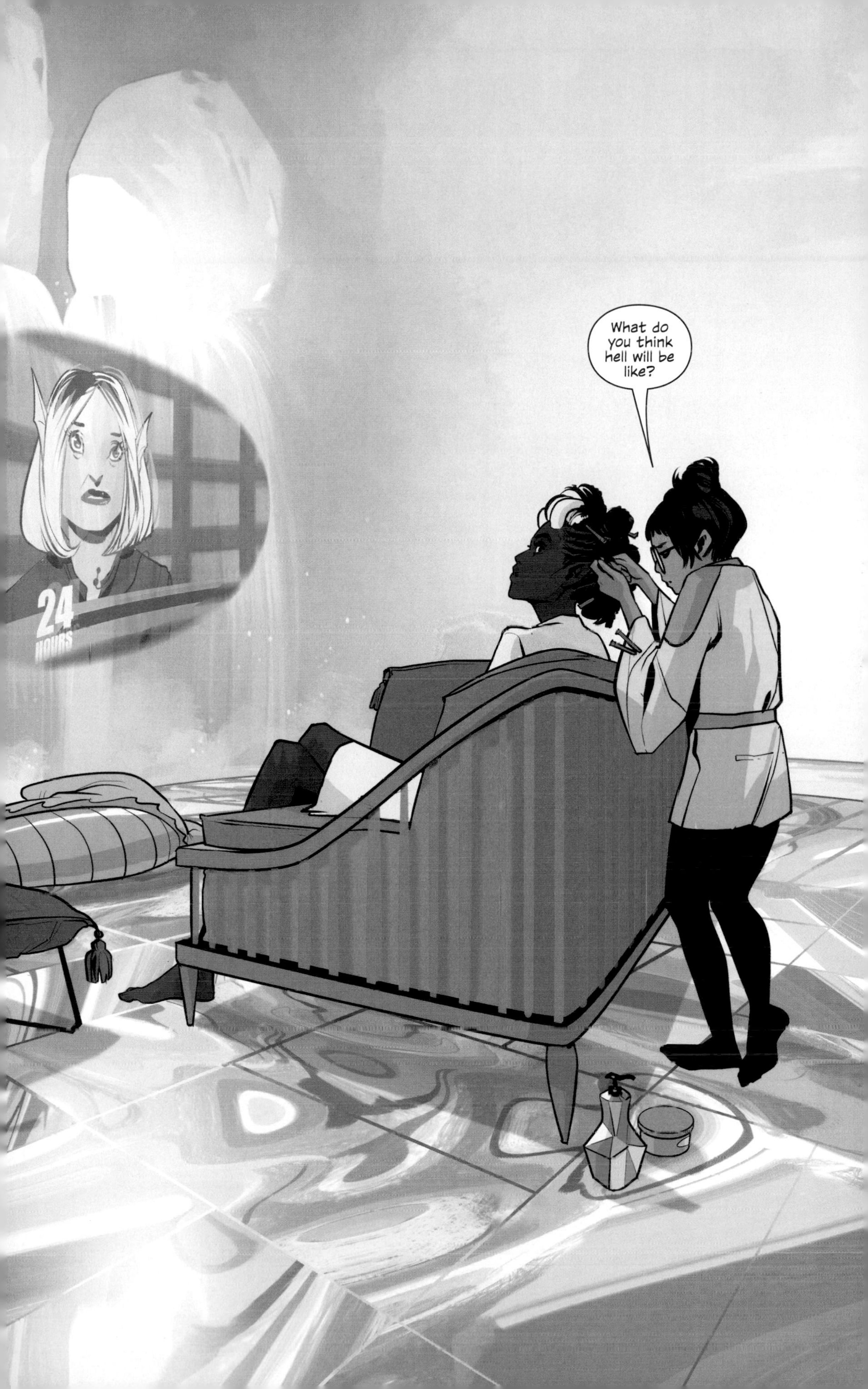
What do you think hell will be like?
24 HOURS

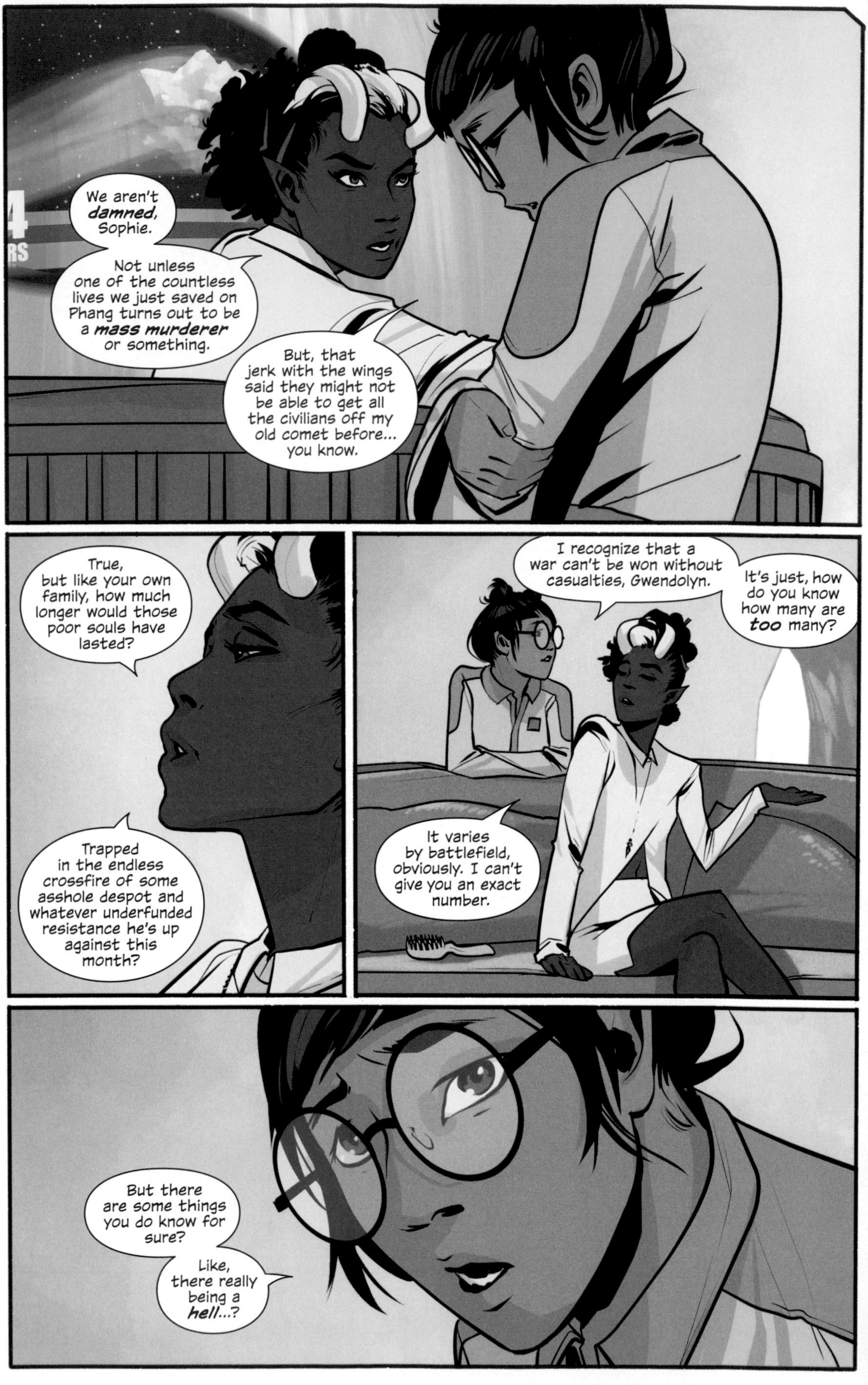
We aren't ***damned***, Sophie.
Not unless one of the countless lives we just saved on Phang turns out to be a ***mass murderer*** or something.
But, that jerk with the wings said they might not be able to get all the civilians off my old comet before... you know.
True, but like your own family, how much longer would those poor souls have lasted?
Trapped in the endless crossfire of some asshole despot and whatever underfunded resistance he's up against this month?
I recognize that a war can't be won without casualties, Gwendolyn.
It's just, how do you know how many are ***too*** many?
It varies by battlefield, obviously. I can't give you an exact number.
But there are some things you do know for sure?
Like, there really being a ***hell***...?

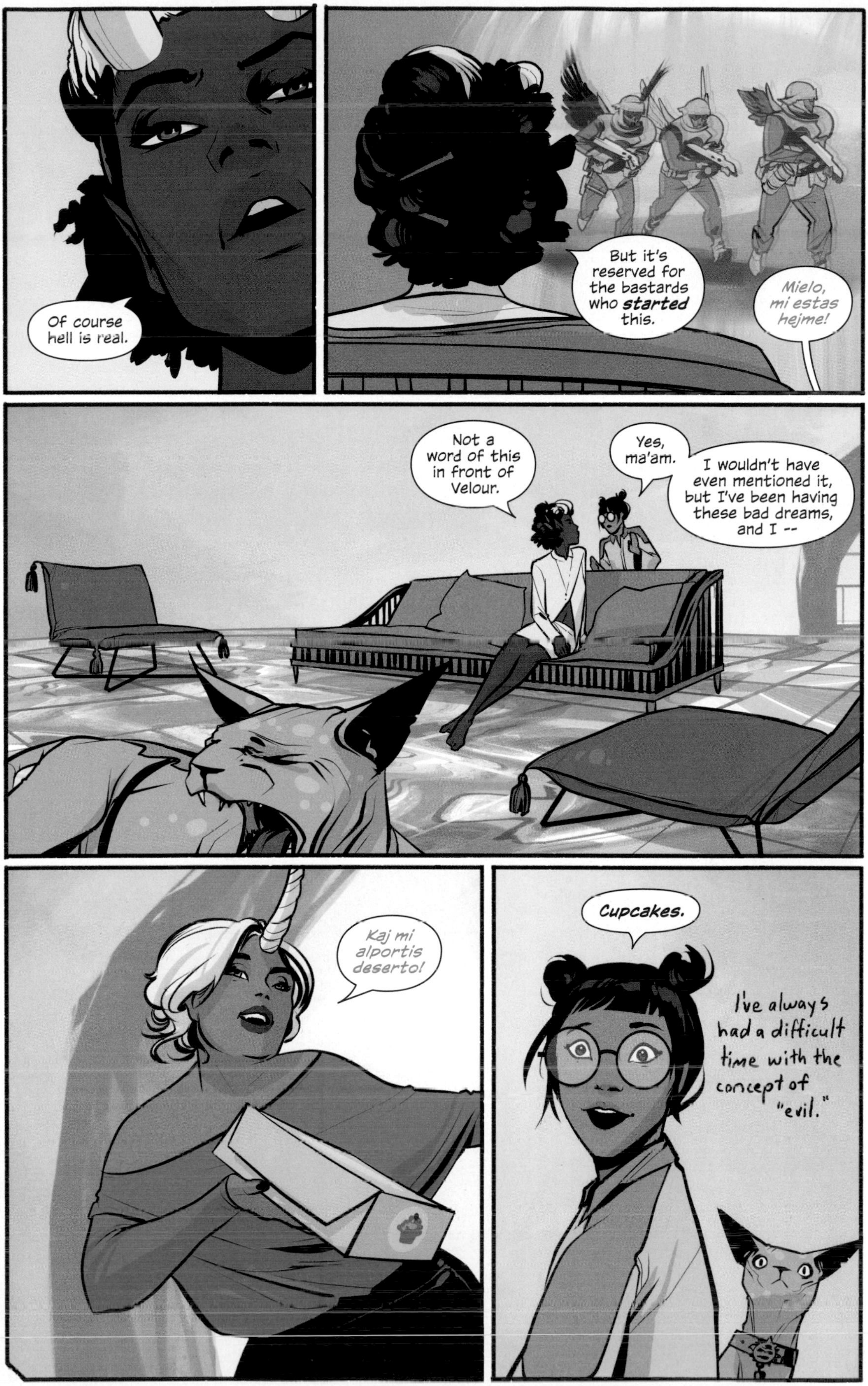
Of course hell is real.
But it's reserved for the bastards who *started* this.
Mielo, mi estas hejme!
Not a word of this in front of Velour.
Yes, ma'am.
I wouldn't have even mentioned it, but I've been having these bad dreams, and I --
Kaj mi alportis deserto!
Cupcakes.
I've always had a difficult time with the concept of "evil."

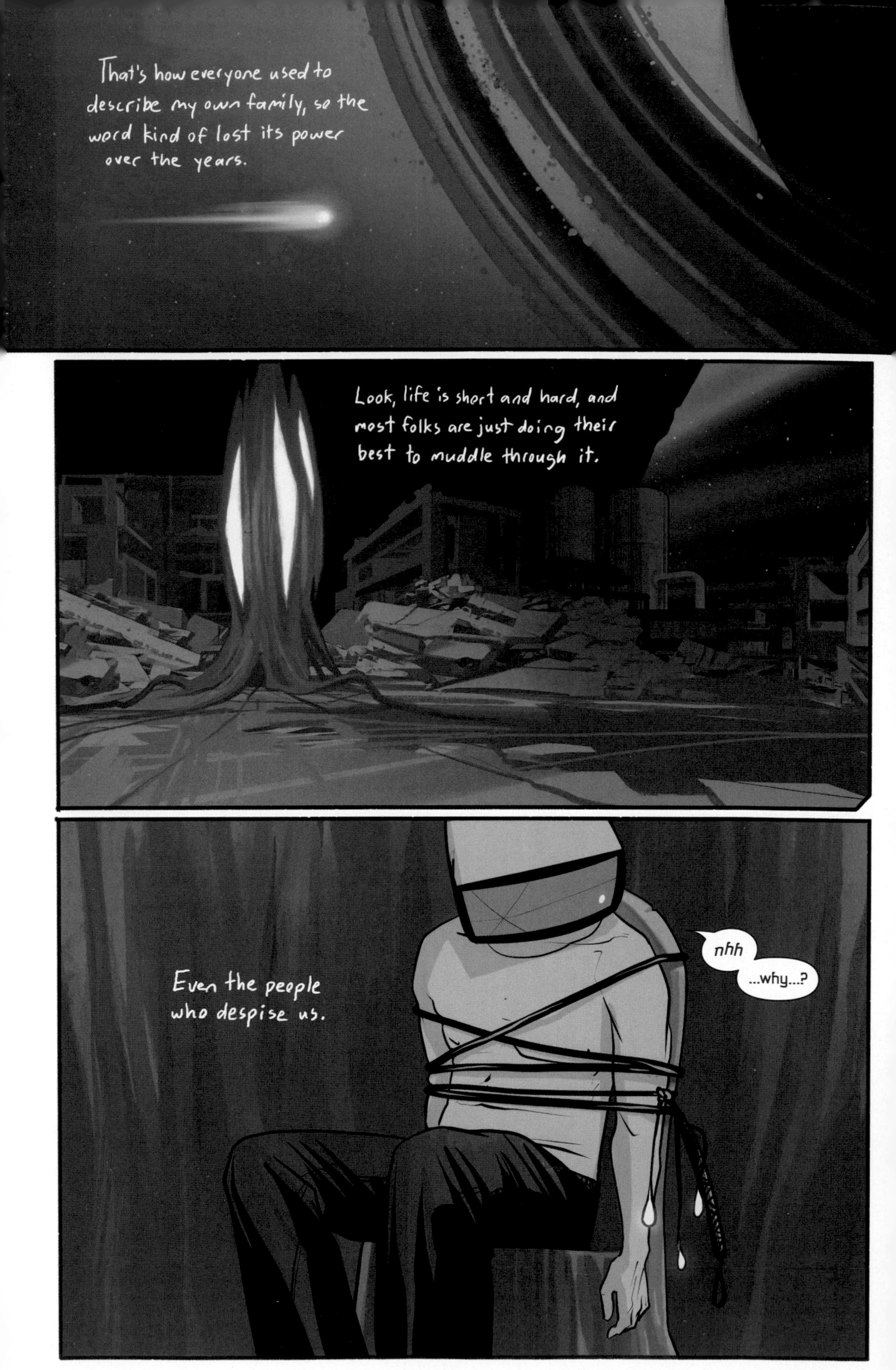
That's how everyone used to describe my own family, so the word kind of lost its power over the years.
Look, life is short and hard, and most folks are just doing their best to muddle through it.
Even the people who despise us.
nhh
...why...?

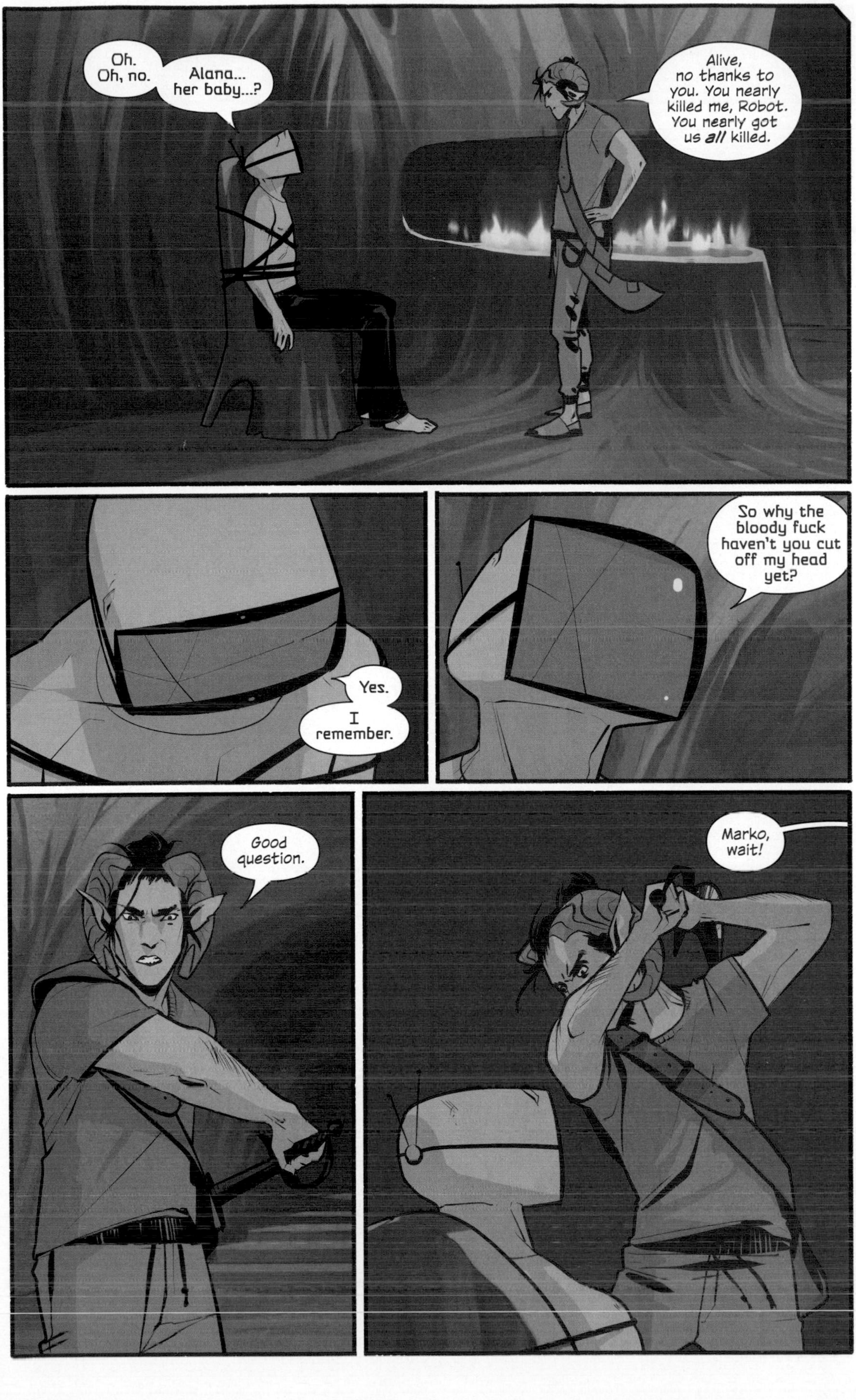
Oh.
Oh, no.
Alana...
her baby...?
Alive, no thanks to you. You nearly killed me, Robot. You nearly got us all killed.
Yes.
I remember.
So why the bloody fuck haven't you cut off my head yet?
Good question.
Marko, wait!

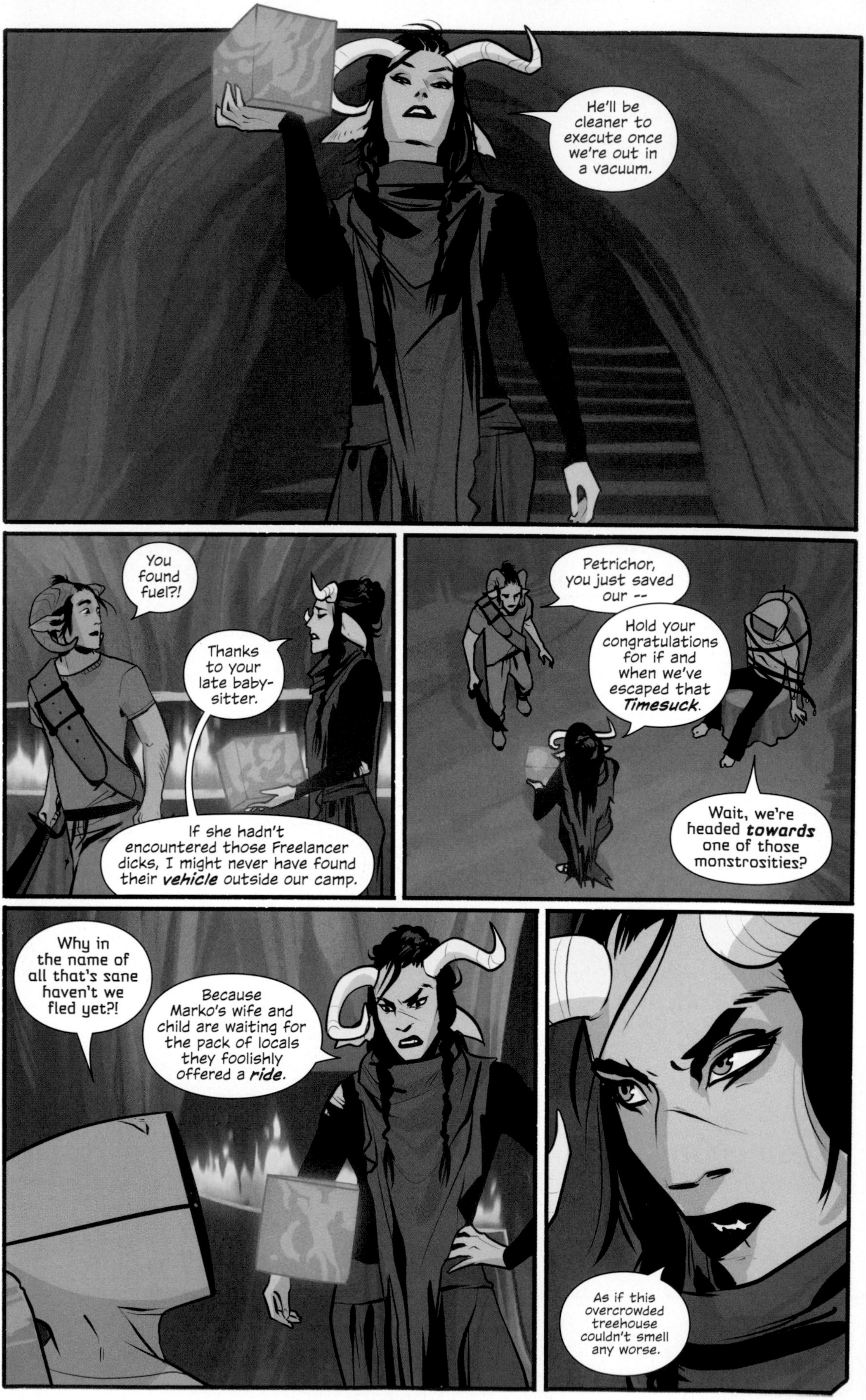
He'll be cleaner to execute once we're out in a vacuum.
You found fuel?!
Thanks to your late baby-sitter.
If she hadn't encountered those Freelancer dicks, I might never have found their *vehicle* outside our camp.
Petrichor, you just saved our --
Hold your congratulations for if and when we've escaped that *Timesuck*.
Wait, we're headed *towards* one of those monstrosities?
Why in the name of all that's sane haven't we fled yet?!
Because Marko's wife and child are waiting for the pack of locals they foolishly offered a *ride*.
As if this overcrowded treehouse couldn't smell any worse.

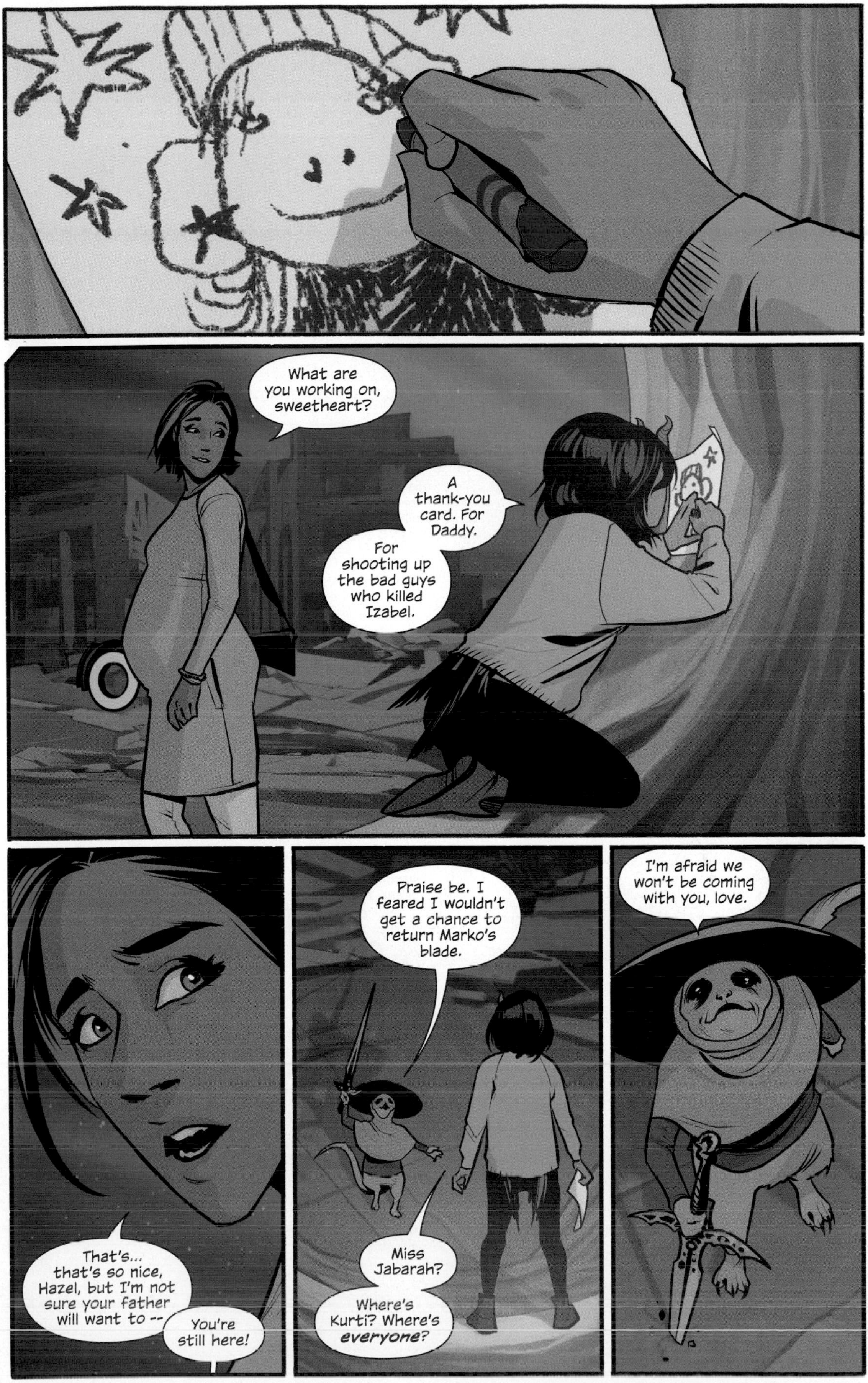
What are you working on, sweetheart?
A thank-you card. For Daddy.
For shooting up the bad guys who killed Izabel.
That's... that's so nice, Hazel, but I'm not sure your father will want to --
You're still here!
Praise be. I feared I wouldn't get a chance to return Marko's blade.
Miss Jabarah?
Where's Kurti? Where's *everyone*?
I'm afraid we won't be coming with you, love.

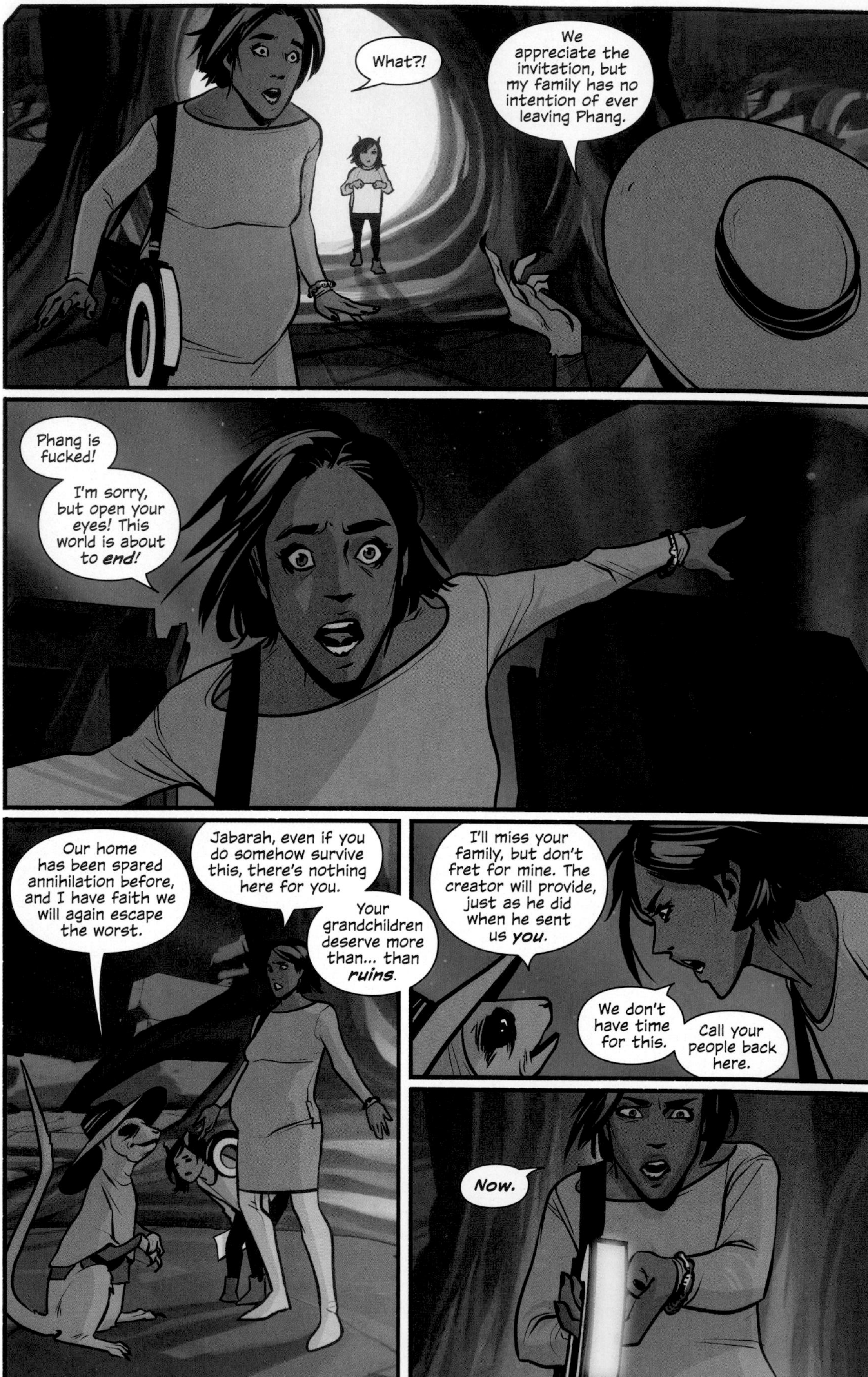
What?!
We appreciate the invitation, but my family has no intention of ever leaving Phang.
Phang is fucked!
I'm sorry, but open your eyes! This world is about to *end!*
Our home has been spared annihilation before, and I have faith we will again escape the worst.
Jabarah, even if you do somehow survive this, there's nothing here for you.
Your grandchildren deserve more than... than *ruins*.
I'll miss your family, but don't fret for mine. The creator will provide, just as he did when he sent us *you*.
We don't have time for this.
Call your people back here.
Now.

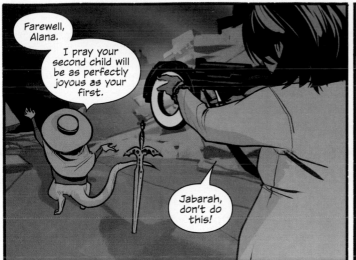

Farewell, Alana.

I pray your second child will be as perfectly joyous as your first.

Jabarah, don't do this!

If you're still looking for a name, might I suggest *Kurti?*

In our tongue, it means *"sunshine!"*

Mommy?

Where... where is she going?

I didn't even say goodbye to my friend!

JABARAH!

I didn't get to say goodbye!

The more you care about someone, the more likely it is that your eventual parting of ways will be as sudden as it is baffling.

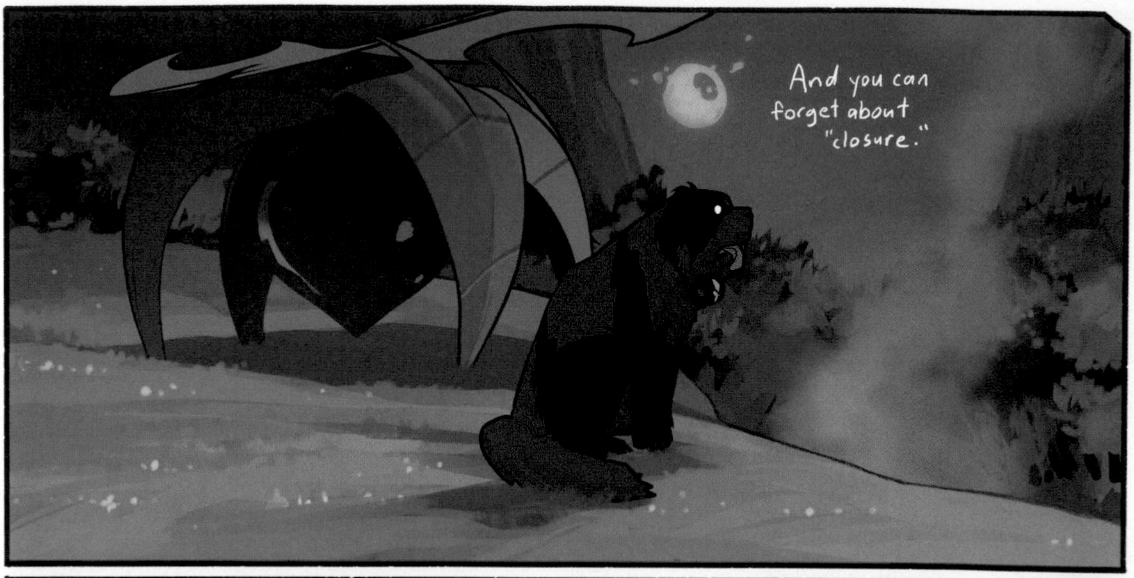
And you can forget about "closure."

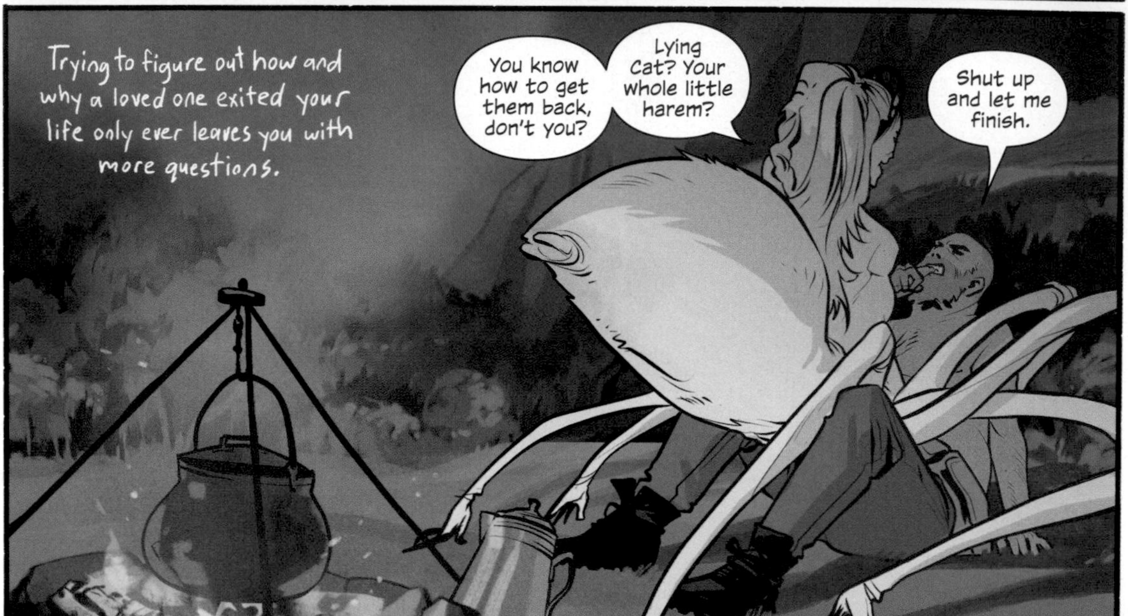
Trying to figure out how and why a loved one exited your life only ever leaves you with more questions.
You know how to get them back, don't you?
Lying Cat? Your whole little harem?
Shut up and let me finish.

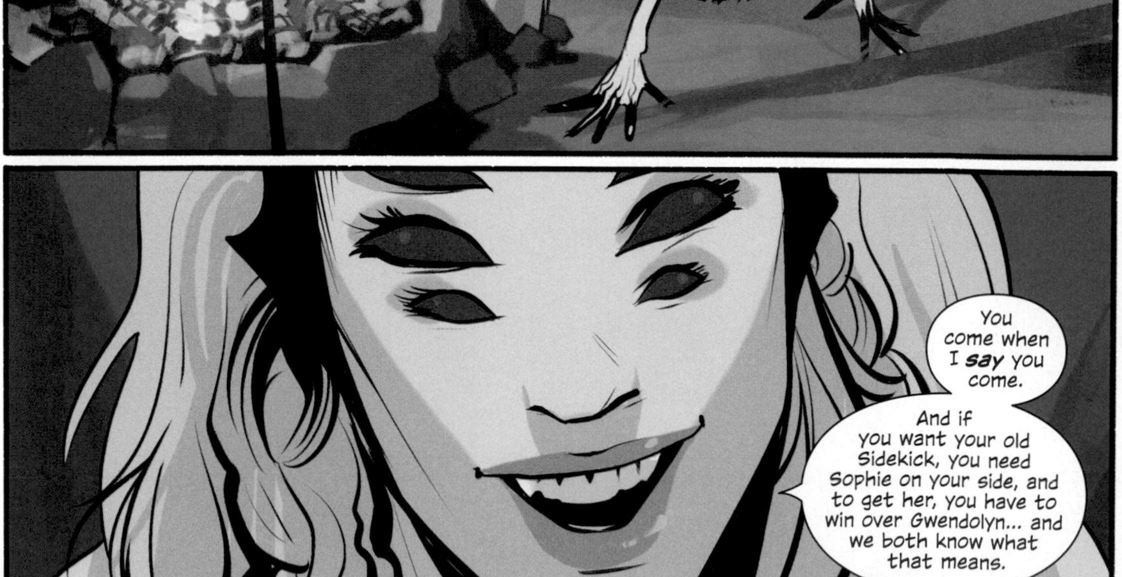
You come when I ***say*** you come.
And if you want your old Sidekick, you need Sophie on your side, and to get her, you have to win over Gwendolyn... and we both know what that means.

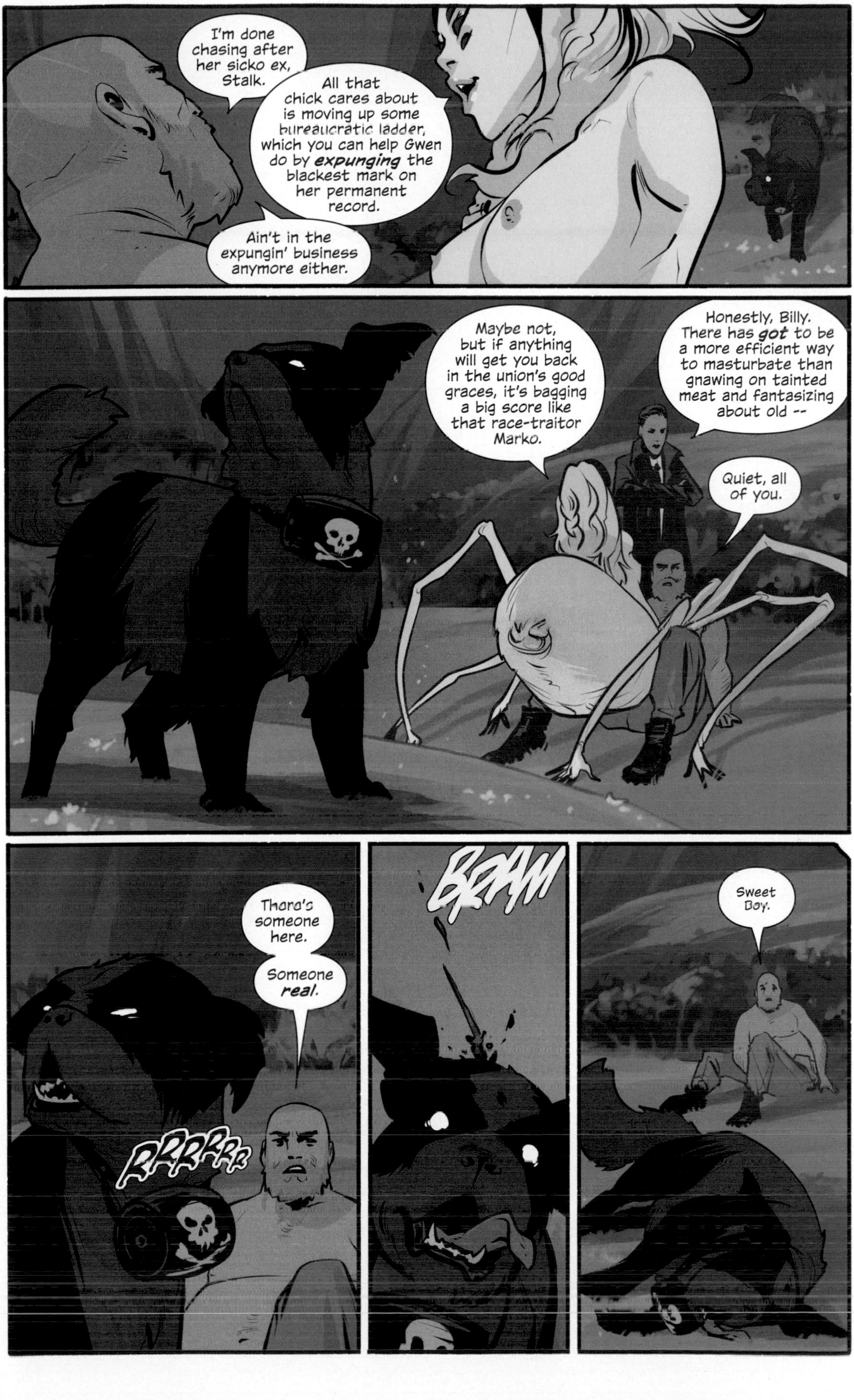
I'm done chasing after her sicko ex, Stalk.
All that chick cares about is moving up some bureaucratic ladder, which you can help Gwen do by *expunging* the blackest mark on her permanent record.
Ain't in the expungin' business anymore either.
Maybe not, but if anything will get you back in the union's good graces, it's bagging a big score like that race-traitor Marko.
Honestly, Billy. There has *got* to be a more efficient way to masturbate than gnawing on tainted meat and fantasizing about old --
Quiet, all of you.
There's someone here.
Someone *real*.
RRRRRR
BLAM
Sweet Boy.

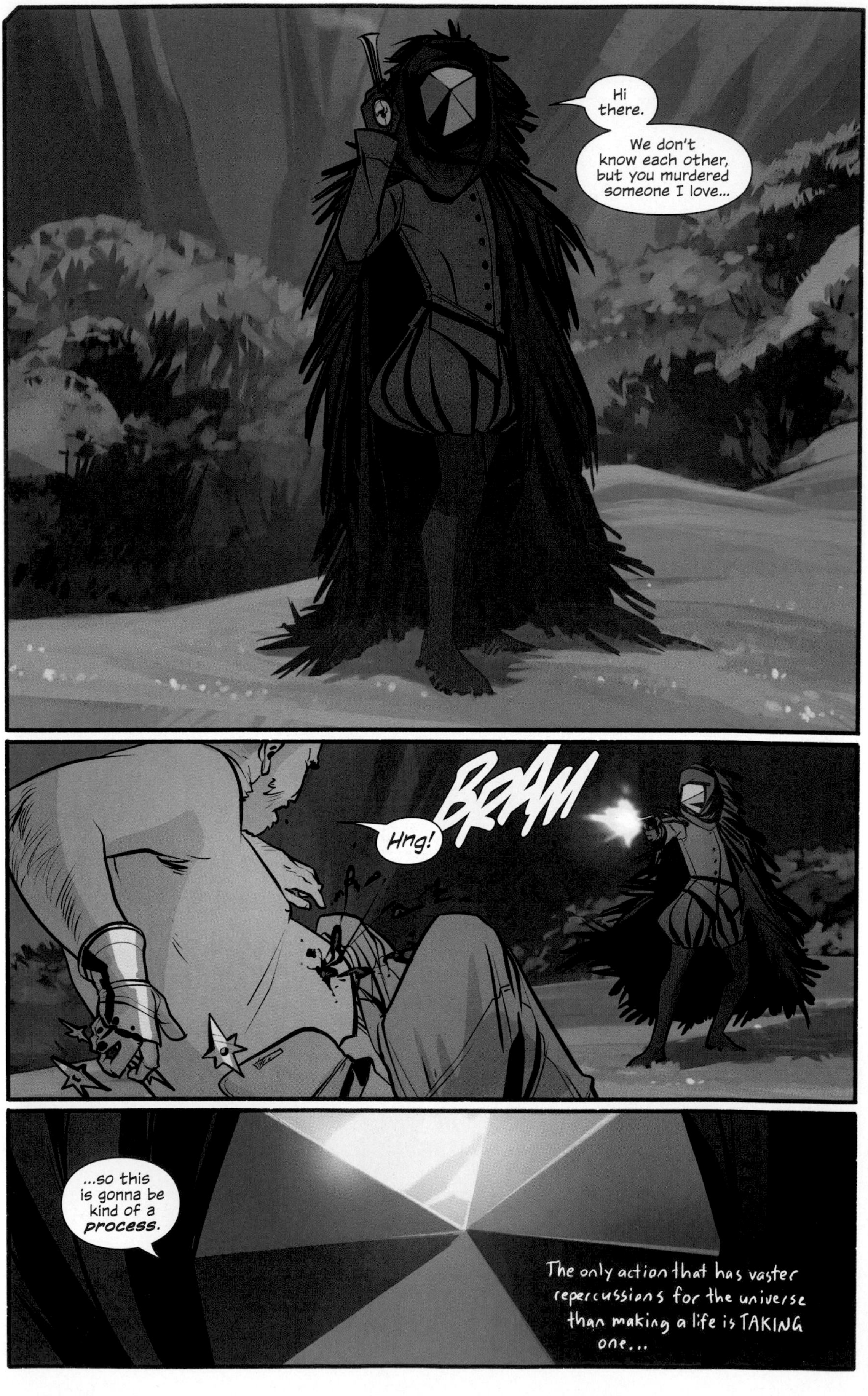

Hi there.
We don't know each other, but you murdered someone I love...
BRAM
Hng!
...so this is gonna be kind of a *process*.
The only action that has vaster repercussions for the universe than making a life is TAKING one...

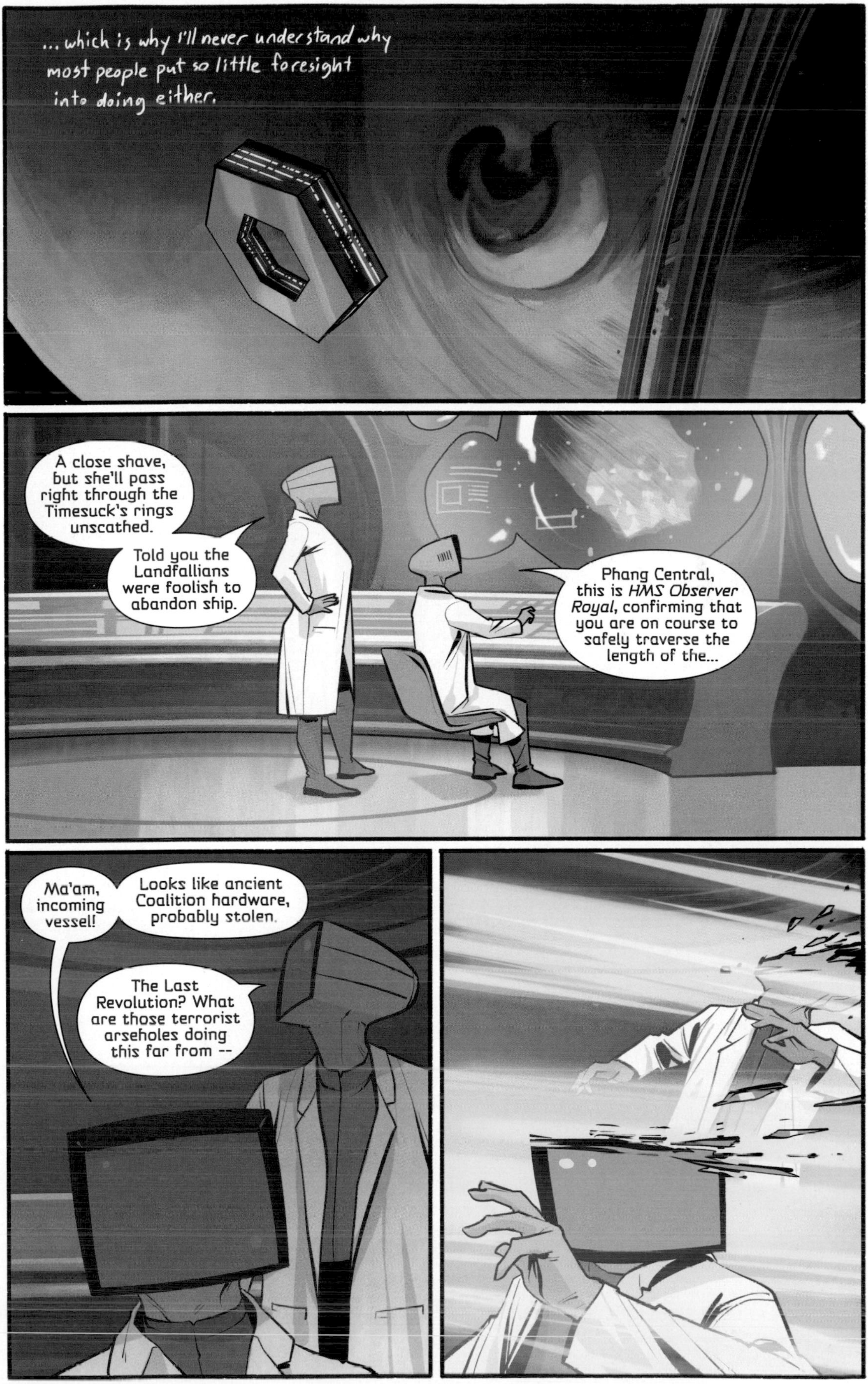
...which is why I'll never understand why most people put so little foresight into doing either.
A close shave, but she'll pass right through the Timesuck's rings unscathed.
Told you the Landfallians were foolish to abandon ship.
Phang Central, this is *HMS Observer Royal*, confirming that you are on course to safely traverse the length of the...
Ma'am, incoming vessel!
Looks like ancient Coalition hardware, probably stolen.
The Last Revolution? What are those terrorist arseholes doing this far from --

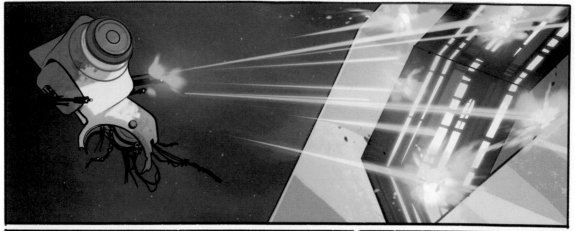

We... we just executed a *friendly*.

We executed *orders*, Gibson.

And you know they probably had to run this *false-flag* shit all the way up to the commander in chief.

So what? I didn't vote for that fucktard.

It's not about him, dude.

We're releasing this payload for Aftel and Chordo and McDirk. For motherfucking Hippo Company!

This is for all the guys Phang took from us.

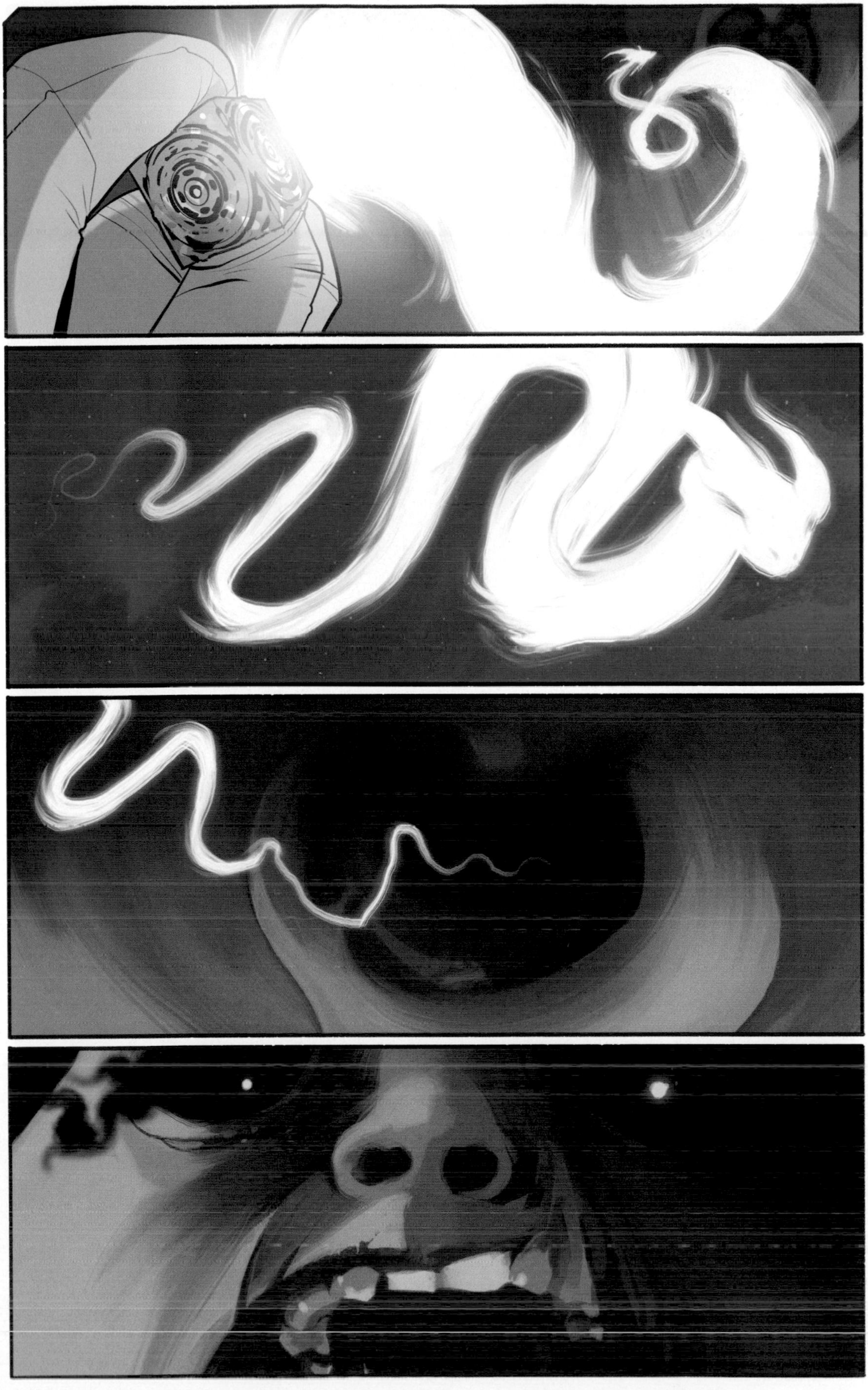

Trust in the lord!

He will never forsake your homeland!

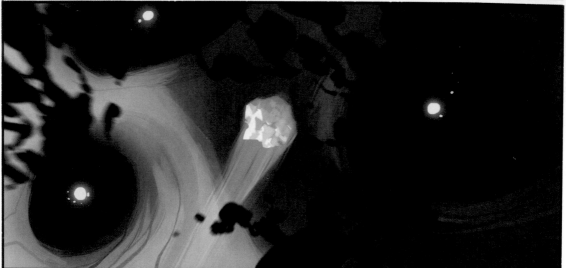

Holy...

PETRI, GO FOR LAUNCH!

Fucking finally.

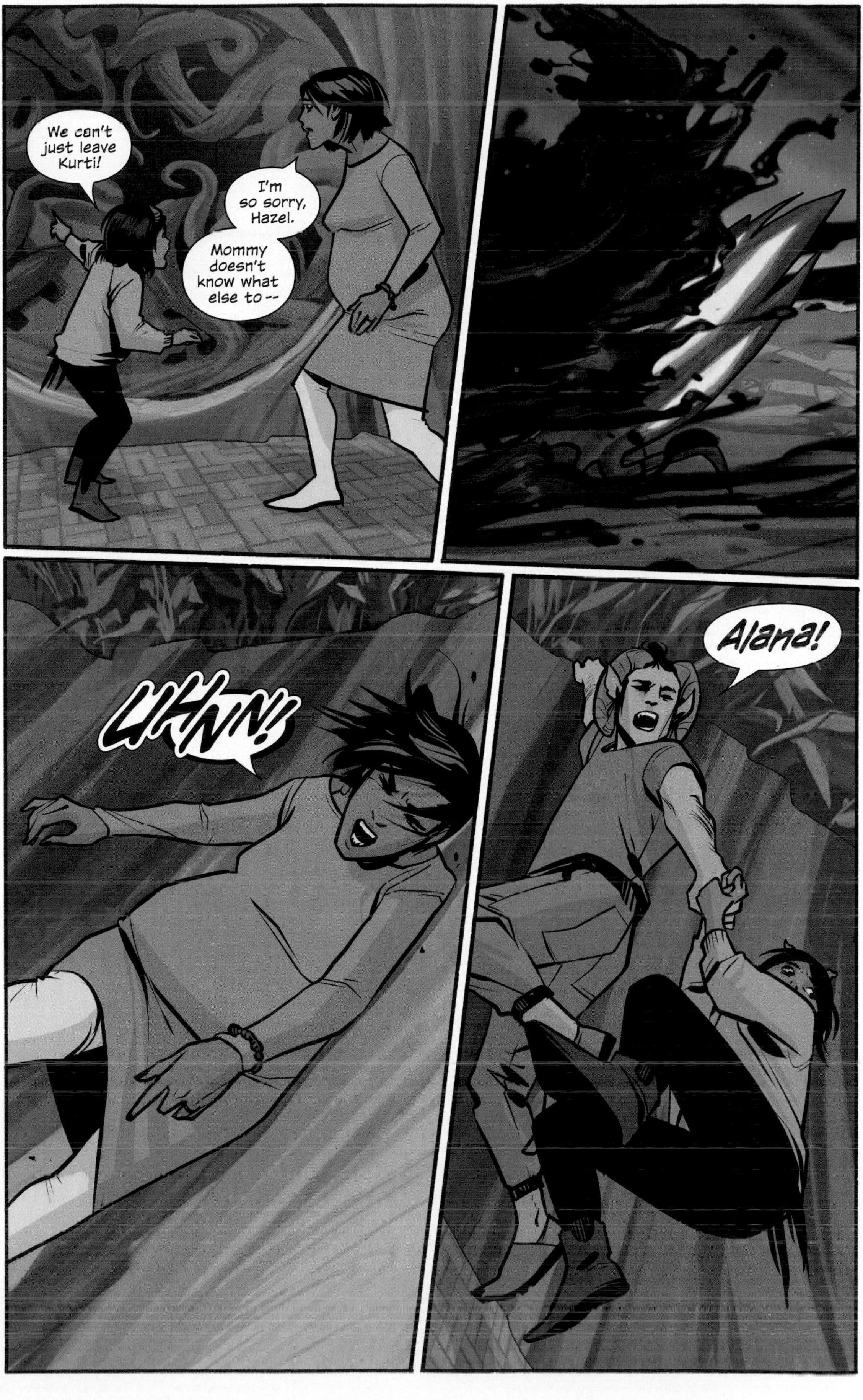
We can't just leave Kurti!
I'm so sorry, Hazel.
Mommy doesn't know what else to --
UHNN!
Alana!

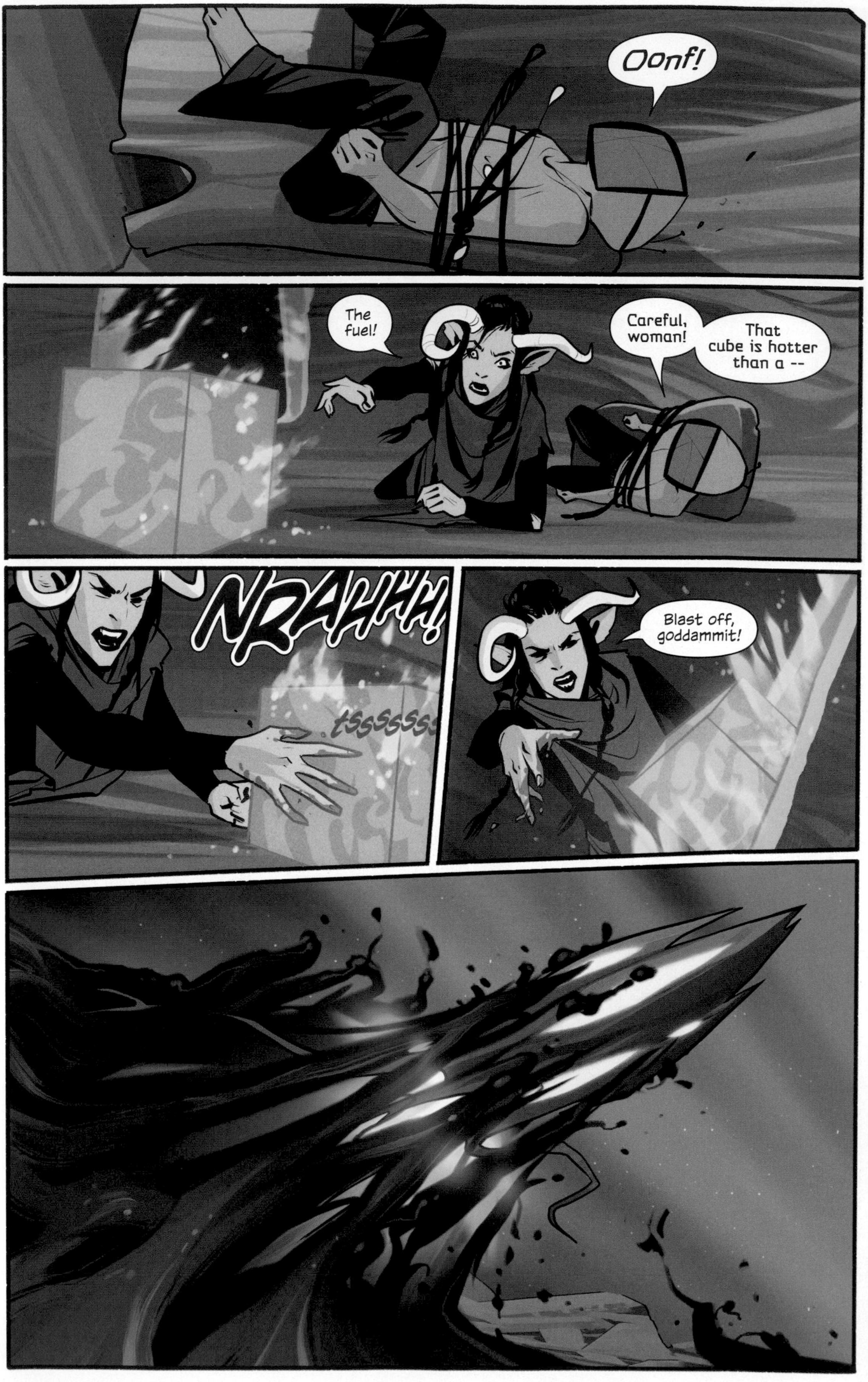
Oonf!
The fuel!
Careful, woman!
That cube is hotter than a --
NRAHHH!
tssssss
Blast off, goddammit!

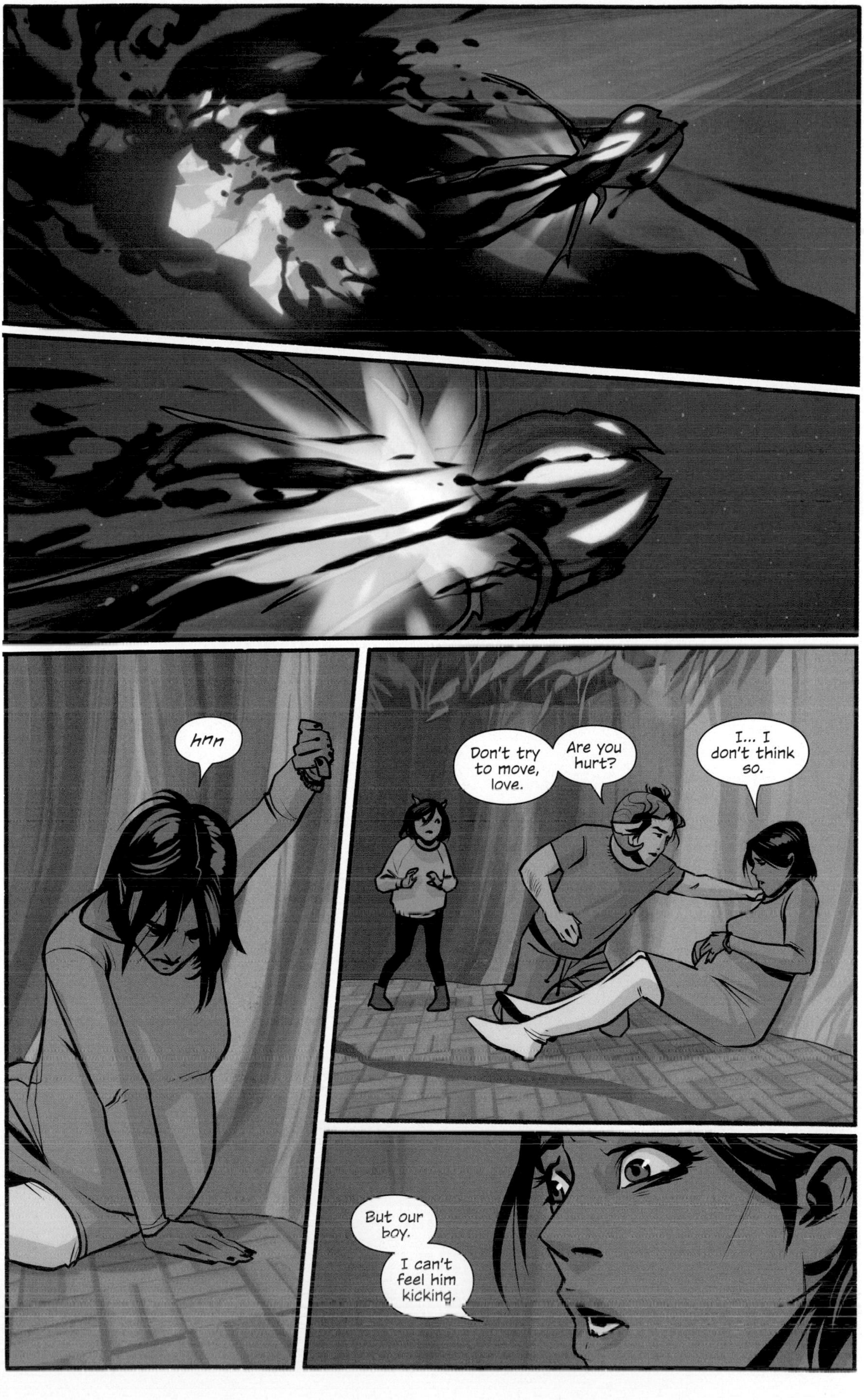
hnn
Don't try to move, love.
Are you hurt?
I... I don't think so.
But our boy.
I can't feel him kicking.

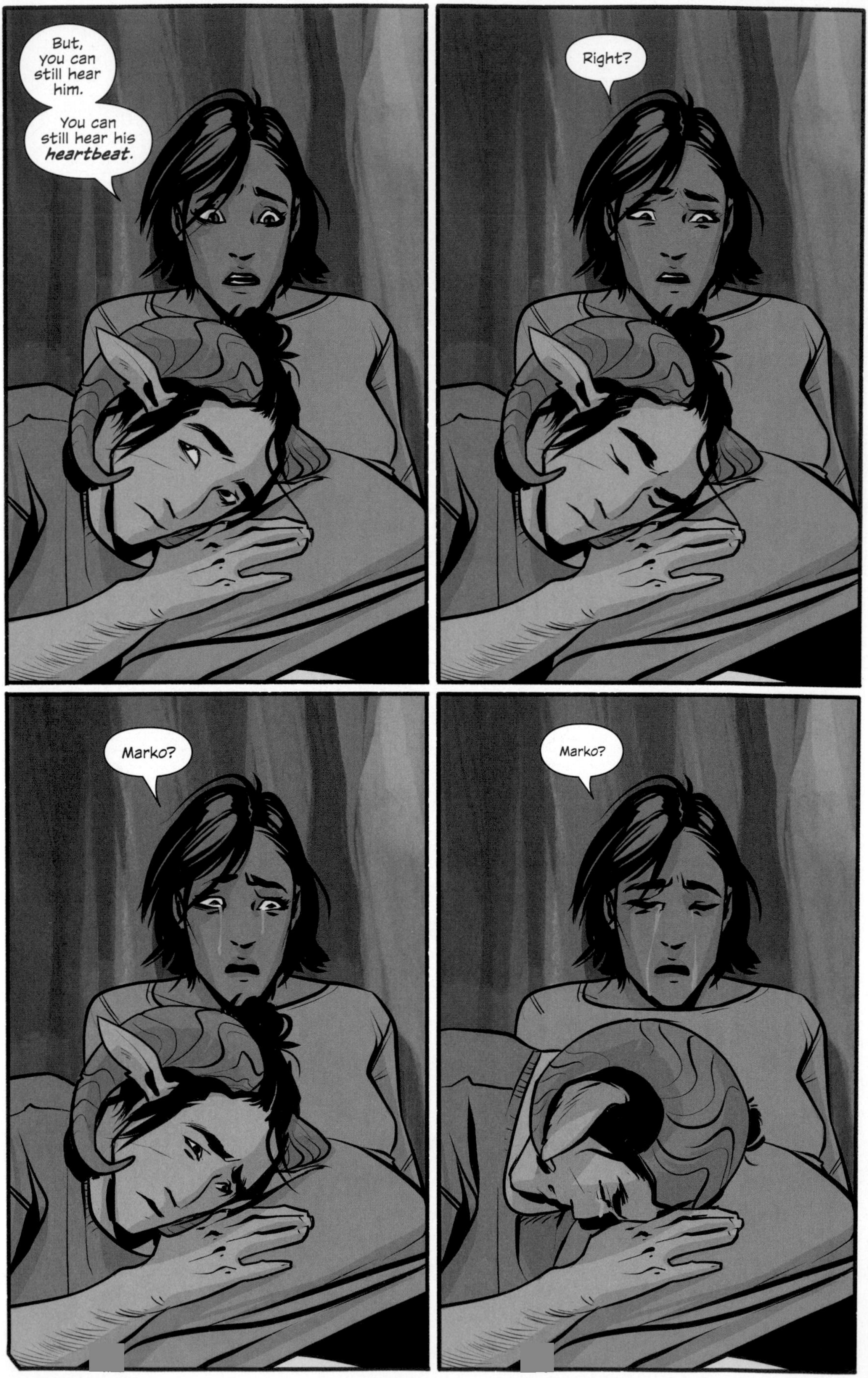
But, you can still hear him.
You can still hear his ***heartbeat***.
Right?
Marko?
Marko?

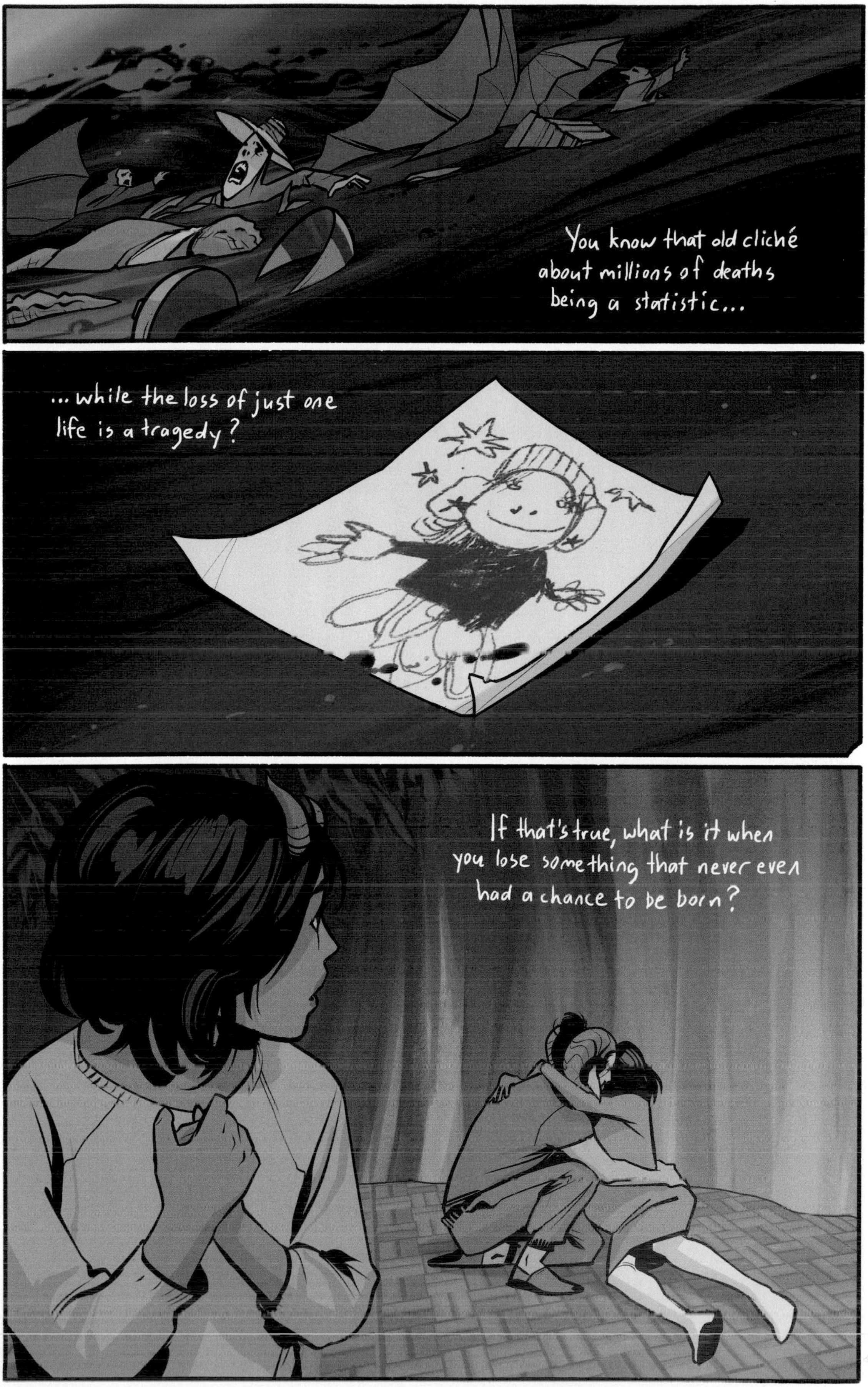
You know that old cliché about millions of deaths being a statistic...
... while the loss of just one life is a tragedy?
If that's true, what is it when you lose something that never even had a chance to be born?

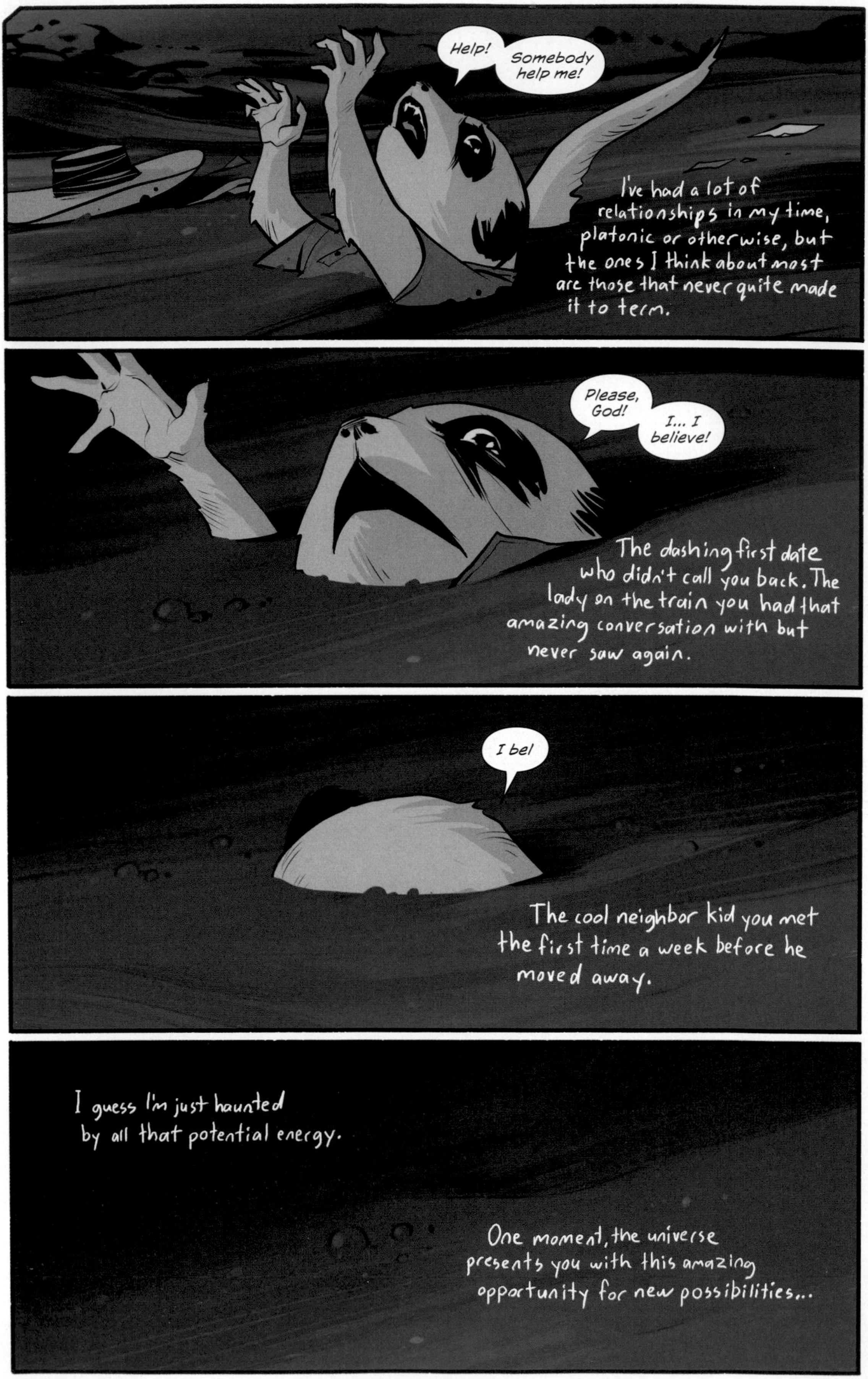
Help!
Somebody help me!
I've had a lot of relationships in my time, platonic or otherwise, but the ones I think about most are those that never quite made it to term.
Please, God!
I... I believe!
The dashing first date who didn't call you back. The lady on the train you had that amazing conversation with but never saw again.
I bel
The cool neighbor kid you met the first time a week before he moved away.
I guess I'm just haunted by all that potential energy.
One moment, the universe presents you with this amazing opportunity for new possibilities...

...and then...